ABSOLUTION

ABSOLUTION

SIR WOLFDOGG MOSES-FRENCH

TATE PUBLISHING
AND ENTERPRISES, LLC

Published by Tate Publishing & Enterprises, LLC
127 E. Trade Center Terrace | Mustang, Oklahoma 73064 USA
1.888.361.9473 | www.tatepublishing.com

Tate Publishing is committed to excellence in the publishing industry. The company reflects the philosophy established by the founders, based on Psalm 68:11,
"The Lord gave the word and great was the company of those who published it."

Published in the United States of America

ISBN: 978-1-62563-587-7
1. Fiction / Mystery & Detective / Private Investigators
2. True Crime / Murder / General
14.11.04

Absolution is Part One of a marvelous trilogy!
Sir Wolfdogg Moses-French

"Thanks for Joining My Literary Crew!"

INTRODUCTION

The more things changed in the 1970's the more they remained the same. Sircus Junction is an old money town atop Virginia's Shenandoah Mountains. Horse breeding, wine vineyards, and infidelity preserved over 200 years of social culture.

Bold investors pounced on Sircus Junction's real estate as the generations died. Urban change captured an already scandalous countryside.

Bishop Calloway is a big-city detective in a very small town. A philosopher at heart... he struggles with all crimes against mankind, long-term loves, and religious persecutions from any historical era.

Literary mindsets should overlook Bishop's sexist and sarcastic humor throughout this arduous journey. However, if absolution has key meaning to your delicate character... Bishop Calloway is your kind of guy!

CHAPTER 1

It was the long hot summer of '71. I stood outside a battered front door. I needed fresh air before witnessing the devil's workshop.

Captain Franks arrived with an attitude. He grabbed a fistful of my coat. He pushed me inside. I adopted a facial smirk not receptive to his small talk. "Not tonight, Captain!" I thought while challenging his ungrateful stare. He cared less for my antics. He forced a fired-up cigar between my lips. "Get on with this case," he ordered. Our stares at each other examined respect for authority. They also questioned the motives for several decaying bodies. I guess the Captain and I were finally on the same page.

There existed an immediate need for answers. Dead bodies had been lying about for days. The odor was tolerable thanks to the Captain's cheap cigar. The smoke was doing its job tonight! I'll thank him later… maybe.

I heard about the deadly attacks over the police radio. Some idiot put the call out as a sarcastic joke. I didn't hear the total broadcast. A city bus passed by that very second.

I put on a pair of latex gloves and prepared for the worst. It was time to walk the crime scene. It was time I did what I do best.

The presence of cocaine was the prime piece of evidence. White powder had been razor-bladed into smooth rows on a cracked glass coffee table. A half-filled bottle of Johnny Walker

Red sat on the far corner. It sat inches higher than the bound wrists of a rather good lookin' dead man. The man was Black... in his 40's... with "Why me?" frowns frozen across his face. Life, as he knew it, ended with several shots to the back of his head. This fella' seemingly violated a drug dealer's trust. Everyone knows, when it's time to pay the drug dealer, pay it you must or become a "Late-breakin' news story!"

"Nothin' but wasted lives," I've always said.

The victim was wearing an expensive light blue suit. His bloody silk shirt had been ripped off leaving him bare-chested. The shirt was twisted rope-like to tie his hands behind his back. A black sandal comforted his left foot. The other sandal was connected strap-only to a broken right ankle. The dead man's clothing was common to fashions in the Midwest. Ironically, America's best drug smuggling route was by way of Canada's St. Lawrence Seaway. It offered easy access to Cleveland, Chicago, and other Midwest cities. I'd bet a 7-Eleven donut this man had ties to one of those jurisdictions.

My expertise for solving murders depended on my ability to not overlook minor details. "Everything means something" the old saying goes. That's why I'm Sircus Junction's best investigator.

A dead brunette was fifteen feet away on the hardwood floor. She was Caucasian... in her mid-30s. It's difficult to predict ages of women over 25 and fewer than 40. Her obvious facial alterations placed that age in my head. It wouldn't surprise me if I were off a year or two.

The woman's blue polyester dress had been pulled up just below her shoulders. Soiled cotton panties dangled by a thread from her right hip.

Her narrow forehead rested in a pool of thickened blood 'bout three days old. Dried cracks in her mascara implied a level of innocence. Her final body position, unfortunately, suggested the assassins had their way with her before pulling the trigger.

She probably stared into their eyes. That's a definite no-no! Drug assassins never leave eyewitnesses. Never!

She was a high-priced hooker earning her pay at the wrong time and place. She accepted the hazards of her business. I'm pretty sure she felt nothing deadly would ever happen to her. Prostitutes tend to feel that way. Drug-related murders occur once a week in Sircus Junction. They don't bother me anymore. It's like I said earlier, "Nothing but a bunch of wasted lives!"

The snuffed-out victims weren't lovers. They were strictly business associates. I could tell based on the victims' materialistic personalities. The male wore expensive clothing. The female did not. He wore the best leather sandals I'd ever seen on a dead man. Her flats were purchased at Dollar John's. His pockets overflowed with fifty-dollar bills. She had a $5 phone card and several bus tokens. Thus, no true motive could be attached to the dead lady. The true motive would come from the dead man's past.

No shots were heard. Plastic 2-litre Pepsi bottles were found on the kitchen floor. Gunshots blew holes clean through the end of each. Plastic bottles are known as a poor man's silencer. Another thought came to mind. This was probably the work of two rookie executioners.

Exact times of death were unknown. The cute brunette took the first hit to force the man to pay up. He was killed a short minute later when he didn't. These fellas' didn't waste much time. There's actually no bargaining for your life... no buy-out clause. Once assassins are hired, the only thing important is maintaining their reputations as quick and efficient killers. Sorry, but no refunds accepted. All gunshots were final!

Burn marks covered the victims' hands and feet. A blunt instrument did unthinkable damage while they begged to live. Illegal pills, cash money, and the hooker's number were recovered and tagged. These knowledge discoveries enhanced my theory about the deaths. A random burglar would never leave cash and drugs like this behind. Hired assassins, on the other hand, don't touch the spoils to remind others they can't be bought. It sends a loud and clear message, "Pay on time or you're already dead!"

Expensive beige carpet absorbed much of the bodies' odorous moisture. The raw scent traveled down the floor's ventilation system. It delivered a rotten wake-up call to the occupant below.

Death has its own special aroma. There's nothing like it. It changes minute by minute. When a body succumbs to trauma, environmental factors directly affect the cycle of human decay. Based on this week's humidity, the foul moisture's gravitational journey took only a few days. Understanding this process plays a valuable role in solving murders.

This double homicide was officially mine. I was first to walk the crime scene… and stupid for being the first response to the radio call. I haven't solved two homicides from a short month ago. I could holla' at the Captain about being over-worked. I won't. Nobody wants to have that conversation. The Morning Star will crucify the Police Chief in tomorrow's paper. I'd better find some answers or I'll be walking a foot-beat on the darker side of town.

I'll waste few precious minutes interviewing the first witness. Ms. Barbara Woodson is her name, I think. She resides in the apartment directly below the heating vents. I'll thank her for reporting the strange odor… for being a good citizen! Who knows? Maybe she saw more than she's tellin'?

I decided to kill two birds with one stone. The Department wanted us veterans to shed unwanted pounds. I had fifteen pounds to lose. No better time than the present. When inquisitive cop eyes weren't looking, I energetically jogged down 17 stairs. It took 10 short seconds. I averaged more than a step per second. Wow! That must be an Olympic record or somethin', I figured.

I smiled. My jogging performance was a good one. Then again, I'm too old for this stuff. Getting into better shape is gonna' kill me. I'll slow it down a tad next time. I'll do some preliminary stretchin' so I won't hurt myself.

It was close to midnight. I gave a quick thought about interviewing a witness at this late hour... but "What the heck?" Barbara Woodson might be up watching David Letterman or some other news show.

I knocked on her door. I waited several minutes. I knocked harder several more times. I continued to knock 'til I heard tiny footsteps approaching.

"Who's knocking on my door at this late hour?" a woman's voice yelled.

"Sircus Junction Police!" I returned... while wondering "Who else would be kicking on her door this time of night?"

The resident tried to push her inquisitive eye through the peephole. I held my badge closer. A second later the door opened with the security chain still attached. I moved closer to the door's four-inch opening. I wanted a good look at the voice on the other side. My curiosity found a set of gorgeous hazel eyes. They belonged to Ms. Woodson. She was wearing a flimsy peach-colored nightgown. I waited another second or two while she twisted a short golden wig into place.

"You wanna' talk about that funky smell from upstairs don'tcha', darling?" she probed.

"Yes ma'am if you don't mind," I responded. "I know it's late. This is very, very important police business."

The next several minutes were filled with cop-related questions. Ms. Woodson finally removed the door's chain. She allowed me to enter. Her fingers pointed down a hallway of framed pictures of trees and mountains and stuff.

I followed her with my eyes wide open. I'd already noticed her dainty nightgown... an intentional teaser if I ever saw one.

"Remember why you're here!" I kept telling myself.

Ms. Woodson came to an abrupt halt. She stood directly under a ceiling vent with a crooked smile on her face. The smile was one I questioned. Ms. Woodson widened her stance. She struck a pose similar to an unemployed stripper. The brightness from the next room's light bulb acted like a spotlight. It highlighted her shapely figure under that nightgown. This demeanor caught me off guard.

"What's this all about?" I wondered… but really didn't. Ms. Woodson took a long, gentle step forward. She pointed her tiny fingers to the questionable ceiling. A bloody air vent immediately became a valuable piece of the murder scene.

Something more physical was happening. Ms. Woodson twisted her hips while pointing upward. That action caused her flimsy nightgown to rise a good six inches higher. Yes! I knew… she knew… I had previously undressed her comin' down that pictured hallway. She grabbed her nightgown. She pulled it tightly around her waist. Her hazel eyes returned to meet mine. She asked, seductively… "Would you like to see more of my personal evidence, Mr. Detective man?"

I had no answer to her question. I knew neither what to say nor how to say it. Certain words were spoken. Her lips were the only ones moving up and down. That's all I remembered 'til my professional ethics took over. They made me honor my oath as a Sircus Junction law enforcement official. My ethics begged me to keep my doggish actions out of this questionable equation. I would not fall weak to unethical behaviors… Hers or mine! I twisted my lips into a knot. I shook my head in disgust.

"Some women have no shame!" I mumbled to myself. "I'm better than this."

I completed my crime scene investigatin'. I hustled to the front door. I never said another word. I never showcased any reciprocal body language. I would not agree to this fine lady's offer. I would stay loyal to this big small town. Besides, my retirement package was worth far more than her pleasures… A close call though!

I turned…

I turned… and reached for the doorknob. I would thank Ms. Woodson from an outside hallway distance. My left foot was firmly out the front door when Ms. Woodson softly purred… "There's another funky ceiling vent in my bedroom. Come take a closer peek… at the ceiling vent… that is!"

I froze in my tracks. I was twelve inches from psychological freedom. Twelve inches challenged my oath to "Protect and Serve" the residents of the biggest little small town in Virginia. The dog in me barked louder than ever. The manliness within me was responding to her sensitivity. The taller part of me had more sense. I would only seek enough evidence to solve a ghastly crime. Receiving unethical favors from this lady could be considered nothing more than following a good lead. I could legally get closer to solving these capital crimes on the behalf of our beloved citizens.

Who knows? Maybe, with some stimulation, Ms. Woodson's heightened memory might identify suspects involved in the homicide case. You never know. Evidence like that could stand up in a court of law with the help of a little white lie, of course. Happens all the time. "It's my duty to investigate the best leads available, isn't it?" I asked myself.

Okay! I'm as I appear to be… totally puzzled… totally confused. How should I handle this situation in the name of justice without violating the law? A gorgeous woman wanted to break this case wide open.

The truth? She's a lonely gal seeking a real man's touch… And, in a mighty fine apartment!

There's another factor to consider. I'm working this case alone. There's no need to send an inquisitive Detective partner to Starbucks for two coffees… no sugar. My free will decision-making took over. Should I stay with this woman? Should I not? What's a loyal cop to do? Ms. Woodson's silky fingers dimmed the apartment lights. I think she's not to be denied tonight. A shameful blush busted out over my face. My macho stance withered. I'd become weaker.

Barbara Woodson noticed I no longer controlled my rational self. She sensed my vulnerability and knew the time was right. I tried to run as fast as I could and take a quick picture of the second air-vent. It was too late. My ethics had vanished. I tried but I had lost this race. I was hers for the taking. I knew it. She knew it.

I slowly backed up to the front door. My right shoulder inadvertently brushed her soft left shoulder. The touch caused our knees to buckle. Neither of us said, "Excuse me," 'cause we enjoyed the touch.

Barbara Woodson weighed about 104 pounds. She stood maybe five feet tall on the tip of her toes. In addition to her pleasing nightgown, she was wearing the biggest pair of bunny-eared slippers I'd ever seen! I'd surely lost control of this situation. I thought the inevitable was no longer the inevitable.

I held my hand out to her. That's when it happened. My professional insanity vanished. My reality returned.

"Your help was greatly appreciated, Ms. Woodson," I shouted in her direction.

"I've gotta' leave... Right now!"

"If I have more questions I'll ring you tomorrow on the telephone. Thanks again!" I followed.

I raced like a wounded moose back to the entrance. Before I shut the apartment door, Ms. Barbara Woodson's little feet came sliding down the hallway.

"Please don't hate me, Mr. Policeman!" Ms. Woodson said.

"My begging was obvious, huh?"

"I've got this thing for cops! You know... men in uniform? Especially fine ones like yourself."

"No commitment's needed to be my friend."

"No commitment at all!"

"Don'tcha wanna' be my special friend, Mr. Shy Detective man?" she asked. Ms. Woodson waved her hand around her body. She acted like a game-show host introducing herself as the prize. I hesitated. I questioned my embarrassing conscience one more time. Unfortunately, I had scruples. I'm a better man than this most times. "Sorry, young lady. I'm outta' of here," I mumbled. Those were the magic words. Ms. Woodson pulled her gown to its original shape. "Now she wants respect?" I questioned.

I was thankful I hadn't acted on her propositions. It was too late in the night for such shenanigans. I shook my head. I walked away. No verbal response. No signs of macho stupidity. Nothing. I was a better man. I totally embarrassed myself over this cavewoman's ethics. My values, ethics, and everything important to my unshakeable character remained intact. Thank goodness!

I had considered solving a homicide case through this lady's vulnerability. I inhaled. I slowly released the air caught in my lungs. I drove away from the crime scene. I drove away from a multitude of bad investigative decisions. I drove away from an opportunity average crime fighters rarely declined.

I'll admit it. I'm a fool. A big smile captured my face. My lips poked out with satisfaction. I'd enhanced my sense of pride by rejecting Ms. Woodson.

Or, did I? Barbara Woodson would have been an extraordinary conquest. I needed no more skeletons in my crowded professional closet. I praised myself for not falling for her gestures. I placed this homicide case on hold. I headed back to my office glowing with a new personal pride. I've been bested by lesser temptations in the past. Some you win. Some you lose. This time I, Detective Bishop Calloway, was the winner.

I crossed the Shenandoah River Basin fifteen minutes later. I was heading east when my radio squawked like the world was coming to an end.

"The Detective assigned to the double homicide on Davidson... return to the scene on the double!"

"I'm on the way," I answered. "And, for the record, the name's Bishop Calloway!" There was a strange silence on the radio. I'd pissed somebody off. They'll get over it. They always do.

I arrived shortly thereafter. I re-entered the apartment building. A uniformed patrolman pointed to the hallway door right under the red exit sign. My personality changed that very moment. Nothing good was ever found on the other side of an exit door. A bricked stairway put me at the alley's level. Flashing patrol car lights were over on the left. A trash dumpster was open on the right. Streetlights were non-existent. Flashlights were shining into the dumpster from different angles.

A cop's demeanor tells the entire story. The way he stands... and the way he makes eye-to-eye contact are demeanors that reveal anxiety in the patrolman's next chosen words. A little red sneaker was found at the base of the dumpster. Well, I thought it was red. It was orange and its' shoestring was tied in a knot. A busted-toe sock was stuck to its inner sole. It was a sneaker size for a 7 or 8-year-old child.

"This evidence might assist in your homicide investigation," said Patrolmen Pitts. "We were canvassing for weapons used in those apartment slayings. We opened the dumpster. This is what we found," he added. Patrolman Pitts handed me his flashlight. I hesitated. I took a deep breath. What I'm about to observe would not be pretty. I waved the flashlight around the half-filled container. My light came to a halt on a naked foot. It was a foot of a youngster. I couldn't tell if it was male or female. The lack of toe-nail polish suggested a young male's foot. I couldn't say for sure.

"Push this trash aside," I said. "Let's find out who we got here." The body was that of a young male. He had been dead for a couple of days. The young child's mouth had been duct-taped.

His hands were tied with the single orange-colored shoestring from the other missing sneaker, no doubt. A skullcap twice his size covered his eyes. His clothing was wet but not with blood.

Trauma, or the expectations of death, forced his body's pores to open. A soap of some kind left a white faded color on his skin. "This little fella' drowned! He had lots of help!" I yelled to the nearest pair of patrolman's ears. "Leave him in this stinkin' dumpster for crime scene purposes," I sadly advised.

There was a sense of quiet. No one had anything to say. A young man's life had been needlessly eliminated. His eyes remained open. No telling what he saw in his last hours. No way to tell.

"Who'd do something like that to a young little fella'?" I asked myself.

The medical examiner had already left the scene after examining the earlier dead bodies. He, too, was ordered back to the scene to examine this new discovery. I'd wait for the official cause of death of this child.

At times, I looked to the sky… or to the moon if it's late in the day. Anyone who swears they've become immune to the horrors is a liar. No one ever gets used to innocent victims of death… no matter the age.

Something bothered me. It was right on the tip of my tongue as I gazed at the full moon. This dumpster sat right below the apartment where the double homicide occurred. It also sat directly across the alley from Ms. Woodson's rear bedroom window. Her bedroom lights were still on. I could see her little shadow peeking from behind her curtain. She knew I was looking in her direction. It was almost impossible for her curious eyes to miss the action around this dumpster. Ms. Woodson just turned her bedroom lights off. I raced back to her apartment before she had any chance of leaving. I kicked on the door… this time with more force. The pitter-patter of little feet was heard inside. Footsteps stopped at the door.

"I know you're in there, Ms. Woodson! Open up!" I yelled. "No more stupid games!"

Someone, again, was pushing an inquisitive eye through the peephole. I held my badge closer. The door opened. Ms. Woodson stood inside the door. She was wearing nothing but those stupid, big-eared bunny slippers.

"You've come to your senses, I see?" she said. "You came back for me, didn't you? You couldn't stay away. I knew you'd return. Cops always do," she reiterated. "You wanted to do the right thing but couldn't, huh? You didn't get a mile away. You turned that car right around, huh?"

"My love will control you from now on. I know it. You know it," she added.

"Using 'huh' to end so many silly questions must be a woman thing," I thought to myself.

Barbara Woodson moved closer as she talked. She grabbed my hand. My frowns turned to concerns. This Barbara lady would play with my emotions no further.

I grabbed her little neck. I wanted to squeeze the life out of her. Instead, I gently stroked her cheeks with my fingers. "Tell me what you know about the murders across the alley?" I softly screamed.

Ms. Woodson acted like she didn't hear me. She made eye contact and moved in for the kill. She tried to kiss me. I pushed her away.

"Excuse me… Ms. young thang! I'm a better man than that?" I shouted. What I repeated to her was a lie. I said it anyway. She backed away a step. She choked out a weak apology as tears started to flow. She thought my tender touches were foreplay. They weren't.

"I'm a cop first and always, little lady! I'm not here for your pleasure! Tell me what you know or I'm taking you downtown!" I said in a stern voice.

Ms. Woodson instantly sang like a bird. That murdered man sold drugs in his apartment. He'd been doing so for many years. He's from somewhere in the Midwest. Chicago, she thought. She didn't know for sure. His female friend discretely took care of his needs once a week. Same place… Same time.

"Who's his drug supplier?" I yelled into Ms. Woodson's swollen red eyes.

"He gets his stash from a group of nasty looking dudes. They are people you cops don't want to mess around with," she warned.

"Those nasty fellas visited him several times a month from the other side of the Potomac River. They drove solid black navigators with big spinning hubcaps and dark tinted windows. I've never seen them up-close face-to-face. They entered thru the apartment's lower level rear doors," she added.

"They're nothin' but 6-foot shadows to me. They always stared at resident windows when they left. The stares were like warnings that we should never be a witness to anything they were doing!" she finished.

A more believable Barbara Woodson fell to the floor. Her head rested in her hands. She kneeled in prayer.

She remembered hearing a bunch of gunshots on the night in question. It was after 11 PM… minutes before midnight. She nosily peeked out the window. The tall shadows were throwin' something into the dumpster. They drove off afterwards. She had no idea it was the body of a little person. She didn't want to get involved.

"Whatcha' want me to do?" Barbara kept asking.

"Those guys are natural born killers! If they knew you were here right now… I'd be dead by Sunday!"

"So, whatcha' want me to do?" she kept shouting. "That's why I make love to as many cops as I possibly can! I'm scared! I need round-the-clock protection!"

"Cops knocking on my door at all hours of the night keeps me alive! Don'tcha hear me? Huh, don'tcha hear me!" she continued.

I glanced disgustedly into those gorgeous hazel eyes one more time. Yes. If Barbara Woodson wasn't fraternizing with other police personnel I'd… well, never mind.

This selfish little woman cared less for a youngster killed over bags of white powder. I walked away. No cursing. No threats in a menacing manner. No more thoughts of neck twisting. Nothing! It was simply another distasteful day at the office.

Three people had been murdered. The dead man and hooker meant nothing to me. The death of an innocent youngster, well, it drained my heart. His name was Kevin. He had lots of bruises on his neck, hands, and feet. His head had been held underwater 'til he drowned. The Medical Examiner said it happened in the bathtub.

You've heard this kind of nonsense before. America has a Kevin in every neighborhood. I felt nothing right now. I won't say much more. It's 2 o'clock in the morning. My police shift is officially over. Emotionally, I've been bested. Mankind can be so brutal. I'll follow Ms. Woodson's leads tomorrow after both of us have had a good night's sleep. I gave the Woodson chick my business card. I promised I'd be back the next day. "Better put some oil on that memory of yours!" I directed at Ms. Woodson. "It better work a whole lot better tomorrow!"

I drove west on Parkside. Ms. Woodson saw more than she's admitting. Nothing happens in that alley without her bright eyes takin' notice.

I returned to my office the next morning. A trillion telephone messages screamed from my answering machine.

"Please come over, right now!" pleaded Ms. Woodson. "I know more than I said about those murders across the alley! Please come over, right now!" she yelled into my answering machine. She left that same message every half hour until about 5 AM this morning.

I expedited with red lights and siren back to Ms. Woodson's apartment. Foot patrolman were guarding her door. "What's going on?" I wondered… but really didn't. My jog to her front door slowed to a walk. My walk slowed to a crawl. My wobbling feet took me no further. I had maxed out on the horrible earlier this morning.

I knew this Barbara woman… but really didn't know her. She was seeking police help all along. I was too busy looking through that flimsy peach nightgown. I was too busy trying to get over as a lover. I was not doing my job and Ms. Woodson is gone. I didn't need to see what's left of her. Bad guys like that don't play. I needed one final look, anyway. I needed a peek evidence-wise and for professional closure. If only I had stayed? If I had stayed here last night she might be alive right now or… I'd be dead!

Captain Franks blocked Barbara Woodson's doorway. He had a box of cigars in his hand. He grabbed a fistful of my coat. He pulled me aside. He wouldn't allow me to enter the crime scene.

"Don't hurry, Bishop," he said. "I'll assign this homicide to someone else! I've over-worked you. Take the rest of the week off."

"Take the rest of the week off" were words never before uttered from the Captain's mouth. I turned as if leaving. Without warning, I quickly pushed the Captain out the way. I raced inside.

My actions startled Captain Franks. He raised his index finger. He pointed it at me. I'd get no more chances to disrespect him.

The crime scene was horrifying. Ms. Woodson's body was lying across the kitchen table. Her eyes were facing the ceiling. She'd been brutally tortured in a bad way. A bloody ping hammer was found under the kitchen table. The Medical Examiner said the skin, bone, and blood belonged to Ms. Woodson. Fingernails had been pulled, hands and feet held over a gas stove, and fingers broken backwards by a blunt instrument.

Tears fell from my macho cheeks. Det. Jenkins of Homicide had witnessed this kind of torture before. "This little gal died for withholding names of witnesses," he said. "This torture has drug dealer executioner all over it."

They held Ms. Woodson's hands palms-up over the edge of the table. Each time she didn't answer a witness question, the assassin struck down with the ping hammer finger by finger. And, as a calling card, her executioners shot her twice in the back of the head.

"It took more than one executioner to do this," Jenkins added. "Based on telephone records, Ms. Woodson named witnesses. She called your number many times. You never answered."

"How many times did she call your office telephone, Bishop?" Jenkins asked in a raspy voice.

"Ten or so," I returned.

"Lucky you never answered," said Jenkins. "Sounds like she gave the goons your identity. These playful little goons now know who you are!"

Jenkins' information meant nothing to me. The goons knew my identity. They knew where I lived. If my name was on someone's hit list... so be it. I fell to a chair with my hand on my gun. I wanted to kill someone... anyone... right now!

Captain Franks gave me that stare. He pulled me to my wobbling feet. He whispered an unrepeatable message in my ear and shoved me out the front door. I don't remember what he said. It didn't matter. I was a failure as a Cop. I had arrived too late... twice... in a short period of time! I'm sorry for all the Kevin's of the world. Forgive me, Ms. Woodson! I won't rest 'til someone pays for this! Somewhere, somehow... the future will avenge your deaths.

I returned home. My tears had vanished. I pulled out a little black journal. I swallowed yellow and blue pills I sorta' confiscated from the crime scene. Whatever my real thoughts were this terrible hour... they needed to be written down. I would write about Kevin's and Ms. Woodson's lost souls. I thought it would make me feel better. Was Ms. Woodson using my love for her personal protection? I simply had to know. I think I already knew. Weird, huh? As a wanna' be philosopher, I shouldn't keep looking for logic in an insane world. Yet, I can't help it. Logic might be my only hope at the moment. Would a coupla' unknown yellow and blue pills make my world a better place?

I'll give in to my demons this one time. I'll attempt to document my thoughts in my black book as best possible.

My trusted black book...

Make no mistake about it. Men are natural born hunters. I can't reject that DNA fact. The opposite sex, on the other hand, has no excuse for their unpredictable behavior.

Women continually hide behind that "I can be irrational whenever I want!" attitude. Maybe that's why good men are so hard to find.

Speaking of unpredictable behavior, several weird things happened today. It's uncanny how women lookin' for true love are attracted to my police status. Once they find out ole' Bishop's a crime fighter, anything goes. Their actions from that point on are downright pathetic. I don't feel sorry for them anymore.

Why the special attraction?

Is it the blue uniform?

Is it saving lives instead of hurting people? Or, are cops real good fantasy lovers?

As a badge holder in this big little city of Sircus Junction, do women see me as a human Band-Aid for love's hurts? Am I a non-

emotional countryside quickie minus the stalking personality? Are women that lonely?

Questions? Questions?And... More questions? I wish I had the answers. I don't. I loved a woman years ago. She knew I was a cop when we first started dating. She was honest and admitted she was more attracted to what I was versus who I was. Her statement meant nothing to me... 'til I stupidly fell in love. The pain from that nasty break-up still haunts my soul. I emptied my naïve heart of all the affection I could muster. The way she mistreated me at the end... well, I could never heal the relationship scars inflicted by her former lovers. The loss of her affection bothers me... cop or not.

I've since discovered something. True love is not to trust your heart to another. True love is maintaining a balance between your heart and head when challenged by love's common experiences.

Don't get me wrong. I believe in sharing my life with a significant other. After many disastrous love affairs, my significant other is my loyalty to police work. It is and will continue to be my best love! It's better than living with your momma'... if you know what I mean.

I'm an energetic crime fighter. My selfish ego challenges the criminal mind every single day. I know not where that Superman complex comes from. I don't really care. That same ego, however, rarely challenges my selection of potential lovers. I wondered why?

Does this concern affect my ability to find a soul mate? Does fighting crime replace the love I need from the opposite sex? The answer is affirmative on both counts! I'm not talking about neighborly-type affection. I'm talking about serious personal relationships.

I know. Who am I to judge? I can neither control love's jealousies nor a bandit's ability to not pull the trigger. I possess no urgency to change my cop's life to a normal insanity. What would I do to change things? I'd create a humanistic world... a world full of more love and less crime. I'm not too bright, huh? Would a stronger work-life balance introduce me to better relationship longevity? Would it allow more unpredictable women to enter my pathetic life? Don't really care 'bout either. Will my job always come first? Only time will tell. I've been overwhelmed on this day. My thoughts are wild. My thoughts are inconsistent. I've asked far too many questions. I've received too few answers.

What about the Kevin's of the world? And, what about that sexy, naive neighbor with the hazel eyes who lived on the alley side?

I've witnessed a drowning society over the last 24 hours. A social cleansing of 20th century culture is needed if this world wishes to survive itself! That's for sure!

Once I'm able to psychologically return to current-day realities, I promise to discover a way to put cleansing the world on my personal calendar! That's a promise I intend to keep!

CHAPTER 2

I needed a break. The assassins were killing an entire drug-happy neighborhood. Every lead was a dead end. Details of Barbara Woodson's torture hit the streets. A concerned neighborhood of witnesses shut down. I can't say I blamed them. A change of scenery was needed. The calendar is a detective's best friend, sometimes. Several nights later, my schedule placed me at a black-tie function. It was the 50th Annual Sircus Junction Gala. A black tuxedo was mandated so the rich and famous could open their wallets under a cop's stare.

I left the precinct at 4 PM. I had three hours to prepare for the function. The trek to my suburban home was a thirty-five minute drive. I had enough time to shower and make the drive downtown. I parked the unmarked police cruiser in the driveway. I walked up my red brick steps. The screen door was locked from the inside. Sondra was home already. Now I'll have to explain to her why I'm attending the black-tie gala alone.

I pushed on my half-broken doorbell. I pushed it more times than necessary. Sometimes it works. Sometimes it doesn't.

Sondra's shapely silhouette came to the door. Her hazel eyes peeked thru our double-laced curtains. She unlocked the deadbolts at her own sweet pace.

"You're home early?" she said with an attitude. "And... how are you this evening?" I responded. Sondra placed both hands on her hips. She turned her head slightly to the left. She nodded without saying a word. Her non-verbal reaction sent a chill down my spine. When our conversations began like this, a loose hair was ticklin' her bottom or something. I didn't want any drama… not today.

I walked towards the bedroom. My shoulder accidentally brushed Sondra's upper torso. Neither of us cordially said, "Excuse me." That's how it was with us sometimes. Whatever her attitude tonight, I will not be listening.

I quickened my pace to the bathroom. Sondra did, likewise. The back of my head felt her questionable scowls. I had no time for this. I had to get six hours of sweat off my stiffening back.

I continued through the house. Things were out of place. An over-scooped bowl of lemon sorbet was on the living room coffee table. It melted over the cup's edge into a smooth sugary mess. Sondra usually stays away from sorbet to fit a 34C bra. I think that's her size. I don't know if the number 34 is the cup size or the chest size? I guess today's not a good day to seek clarity. I kept walking. The television located in the parlor was stuck on a scratchy pause. The screen was cryin' out for somebody to turn off its unwatched agony. Sondra taped her favorite soap operas on Fridays. She watched them whenever she's depressed about nothing. Go figure. Depression was a normal part of Sondra's life.

Sondra spent hours watching the "Young and the Restless" soap opera characters change sexual partners every other month.

Okay. It's time for the truth about our relationship. Sondra and I are experiencing another trial separation. It's the eighth time, no less. We don't know why we remain together. We coexist in the same house. We're independent of each other's needs. We have our own space… I think. We've shared nothing intimate and that's enough of our "none of your business" highlights!

I'm glad this confession's out in the open. I refused to be the bad guy in this scenario. It's not fair to either of us.

I quickened my pace to the bedroom. I undressed. I jumped into the hot shower. I thought about our lives as the steam softened my skin. Sondra and I could've done things differently. No kids, we lived without a true connection. We discovered a lust for each other, married early, and took different career paths. We grew apart. We respected each other even without intimacy. There lies the problem. I deserved some passion. I needed passion as an everyday norm. The lie I've been living with Sondra had taken its toll.

Watch out! Sondra's shadow just pressed against the shower curtain. She followed me into the bathroom. I'll act like she's not there. I might escape this moment without a new bump on my head. "Come on in, honey?" I sarcastically asked over the steamy water. "Just like the old days, remember?" I added. Sondra didn't answer. Her shadow showed no signs of movement... only that of thought. My sarcasm intentionally agitated her. I could do that sometimes. It was one of my better talents. Sondra stormed out of the bathroom. Her exit was one of those "I'm leaving but I'll be right back!" exits. I leaned to the opposite wall of the shower. I stayed there for several minutes. If another episode of that "Psycho" movie became reality... I'd be ready.

I reduced the water pressure for better hearing. I wanted to hear Sondra's footsteps comin' back this way. She had a history of snatch and throw scenarios. Months ago, Sondra yanked open the shower curtain and threw an electric toaster on the shower floor. I survived. The toaster was unplugged... a fact unknown until surviving a possible heart attack! Sondra found my expressions hilarious. She giggled for days. She told her so-called bogus girlfriends. They laughed for months. They're still laughing at me. No biggie. A real gentleman will let that incident slide 'cause... only a woman deeply in love wit' her man would ever threaten to kill him! Yes. I was lucky to have Sondra in my life.

I double-rinsed Johnson's Baby Shampoo out of my hair. I could do so with one eye open 'cause it's mild on the eyes. I tiptoed out of the shower. I opened the medicine cabinet. I removed a red and white bottle. It had a Clipper Ship's insignia across its face. I needed to feel special tonight. I splashed on the after-shave lotion that drove women crazy in the '70s! It was the latest fragrance from... Old Spice!

Seconds later, Sondra reappeared at the bathroom door. Her keen sense of smell acknowledged that fabulous aroma. "Getting all dressed up with nowhere to go, huh?" she asked, rhetorically.

Sondra peeled off her clothes all the way down to her pink lipstick. She couldn't help it. I splashed on this same after-shave sex-trap the first night Sondra was championed. The stuff worked then. It's working now! I moved closer. I seductively whispered... "Thanks for the show, sweetheart! I've gotta' go!" Sondra went bananas over the timing of my not-so-important snub! The Gala was official business. It could not wait. I'd invited Sondra to many of my formal on-duty functions. I must be honest. Sondra always looked forward to dressing up. She's a very beautiful woman in heels. And, with the right hairstyle, watch out! Men were always whispering in her ear. They were only after one thing. They sought an opportunity to validate her well-gossiped history. Her history never bothered me. She handled her past reputation with ease. She was going home with me at the end of the day. The best part? I considered Sondra a non-date during on-duty scenarios. I didn't have to chaperone her all night long. Tonight would be a special night. I could feel it in my bones. I would not invite Sondra to the Sircus Junction Gala. This function was about business... personal or monkey business... whatever!

Why she could not attend would be a lengthy discussion. I tried not to have it. I prayed I didn't have to have it. That conversation is now a reality.

"I've gotta' work the Convention Center Gala tonight," I said as I stared at Sondra's right hand... the quicker of the two. "Without me?" she replied in her shaky voice. Sondra really wanted to go. Not to be with me but for old time's sake. "Yes, without you," I cautiously replied. Sondra acted like she didn't hear me. She ran into the bedroom. She emerged seconds later carrying a red formal and several pairs of black pumps. "It'll only take a minute for my make-up. You can give me a minute, can't you, dear?" she asked.

"Take all the time you need," I responded. " 'Cause your butt ain't goin' nowhere tonight!"

Sondra's happy expressions went blank. I prepared to duck the usual flying objects. She did a great job containing her emotions. She felt embarrassed for thinking we'd work things out. Her dress and shoes dropped to the floor. She tightened her right fist... the quicker of the two. Her left hand nervously tapped her shaking thigh. Sondra suggested we allow our love to grow stronger. She demanded it. We looked at each other... each waiting for something regrettable to happen. Nothing did. We spent the next minutes blaming each other for not satisfying the other's needs. I promised myself not to be denied passion I needed. I sought something more than that received from her... stronger than what I had for my work... wherever it presented itself. Tonight may offer that opportunity.

"We should get that divorce," I reiterated. I walked passed Sondra. I unintentionally brushed against her right shoulder. Neither of us surrendered a cordial, "Excuse me." It was like that with us sometimes. I placed a toothpick in my mouth. I headed out the front door.

Sondra clenched her teeth. Tears fell from her hazel eyes. "You really want that divorce, Bishop?" she asked.

"I can be the woman you need!"

"Tell me what you want. Open up. Let me enter your cold-hearted world!"

"I need to understand you better."

"Keeping me on the outside kills my affection. It kills my need to love and to be loved."

"Bishop, might we have another go at it?" she asked through her running eye shadow.

"Can't your heart seek counseling?" she asked.

"We can go together or go it alone. We don't have to end it this way."

I knew this lecture was coming. I never learned how to verbally express my feelings. Acknowledging a weakness made a man a sissy-boy in my father's eyes. I'm an apple from that same tree. My inability to be verbally expressive embarrasses me. I don't know how to do it. It was not something I learned at home. I've never had the skills to tell Sondra our love was over. I would immediately become defensive. It was easier to stay in my silent, destructive world.

Sondra was very long-winded. "I know you don't love me as much as I love you," she continued.

"If you did you'd remember what color shoes I wore on our 10th date that first year."

"What color were they, huh?"

"What hairstyle did I wear, huh?"

"Did I wear a wig that day? What color was my blouse, huh?"

"How many buttons, huh?"

"You can't describe the earrings I wore, can you?" she continued.

"Butcha' know what, Mr. Selfish man?"

"I could tell you what color socks you wore two years ago, Mr. Selfish man."

"I could tell you how many times you took out the trash without me asking... Mr. Selfish man."

"I know how many times we made love since we met. That's how much I love you. That's how much I care about you, Mr. Selfish man!"

"Any woman... any devoted woman... notices those things, Mr. Don't Want Me Anymore!"

Sondra's tears got heavier. Her mascara dripped onto the expensive blouse I gave to her on her last birthday. Sondra actually bought the blouse for me... to give back to her as my present to her. Ahhhh, it's the same thing, right!

Sondra was asking some wild questions. I shook my head. I stared at the ceiling. "Who remembers stuff like that?" I silently asked. "And, why does it matter?"

"It has to be a woman thing 'cause men barely remember when they last changed their underwear."

Sondra's verbal attack came to an end. "I don't ask much from you, Bishop. I want you to make me happy on a daily basis. Is that asking too much?" she added.

Ding! Ding! Ding! Ding! Ding!

Bells went off in my head. An alarm had sounded. I couldn't make Sondra happy on a daily basis? It wasn't my job to make her happy. My job was to make myself happy. Together, we could make each other happy. Isn't that how good relationships work? "Sondra, I have a full-time job! I can't spend the rest of my life making sure you're a happy camper!" I snarled.

A smirk came over Sondra's face. "You're unbelievable! It's always about you! Please leave!" Sondra yelled. She turned her back to me. She walked away. I waited a good minute for her return. I thought she'd return if only for a moment. I thought she'd do some more begging. She did in the past. Today, however, would not be one of those days.

Oh, well! Sondra shouldn't tease me like that. It's not fair. Her non-actions pissed me off. It shattered my ego. I stormed out of door. Sondra slammed it behind me.

Click! Click! Click... were the sounds of three deadbolt locks one by one. Sondra's silhouette wept against the laced curtains. My heart wanted to return to her feelings. My heart wanted another try to see if the love I sought could be found within Sondra. My feet kept walking. They've carried me through many situations. They refused to go back.

Teardrops escaped my eyes. I turned my head to the right to hide my vulnerable state. My ego slapped me. The reaction brought a halt to my emotions. I drove my good lookin' tuxedoed-self away from 4101 Braddock Lane. I made a left onto Rock Canyon Boulevard. I swerved left to miss a stupid jogger. "Where's your reflector jacket, knucklehead?" I shouted as I headed downtown. I felt less compassion for Sondra. I felt a basic friendship guilt... maybe? Okay. I can't tell the difference sometimes. Sondra was never one of those "love at first sight" relationships. We met several years ago. She was my friend long before becoming my lover. Our friendship turned to a relationship one night when I saw her... really saw her... at a business party. She was standing at a cash bar listening to everyone talk 'bout nothin'. Sondra was easily bored. Her mini-skirt, fortunately, was cryin' out for a man's attention. Sondra was tightly holding one of those fancy sipping glasses. It was one of those fancy glasses with lips on it. The kind used for dry martinis.

The more I stared at Sondra... the more I wanted to stare at her. She had to know she had my attention. She also had to know she was wearing a ridiculous Jesse James hairstyle. Duuuuh? It covered too much of her forehead. Was she hiding from someone? An old boyfriend, maybe? What's up with that?

Sondra stood there interpreting possible thoughts written across my forehead. She pointed her non-virgin self in my direction every so often. I would not be easy prey for that deadly spider. Not tonight.

When we did make eye contact, she dropped an ink pen from her purse. I'm too old for that trick, young lady. Let some other sucka' pick it up. I wasn't givin' up my seat at this crowded bar for a female drunk I didn't really know.

Sondra got rid of any man who fell for the ink pen trick. She'd look my way after each man disappeared into the crowd. Like clockwork, she'd drop the ink pen on the floor again. "At least she's persistent," I thought. Sondra finished playing her pen games. Our eyes finally locked as the restaurant's closing time neared. She silently gave approval to approach her. I had a few more lite beers. The rest was history.

Everything about Sondra was acceptable. She posed no threat to my ego. She was not the clingy type. I did, however, recognize the value she placed on material things. Material things were important to her. They defined her. They dictated her happiness and measured her successes. We had great jobs, good salaries, and supportive friends. That wasn't enough. Sondra had a "Keep up with the Jones" personality. The situation that broke the camel's back was the engagement ring incident. I'll never forget it. Sondra wanted a great engagement ring. I wanted to give her something special. Yet, where did that percentage of your salary rule come from? How could anyone spend so much money for a ring based on another's rule of etiquette? No one asked me. Sondra never asked me. She assumed any diamond with her name on it had to conform to that standard. It had to cost more than any ring given to a rude hussy currently in her social clique. The ring's price was a silent message she wanted to dangle in their upper-class faces. I researched the engagement ring situation. A good diamond... a real good diamond cost about $10,000.00 per carat. Adhering to that unreasonable percentage of your salary theory, Sondra was due a $40,000.00 ring. No way that's gonna' happen.

Sondra offered no alternatives. "If you truly want my love this is what it's gonna' take!"... A message clearly sent my way.

I told Sondra what I could handle financially. I'd do the best I could. She could take that crazy rule and shove it! My statement brought nothing but a blank stare from Sondra. She responded by flipping me the bird. I questioned the finger. I ignored the blank stare. Both caused me to reconsider her love.

Weeks turned into months. No ring had been placed on Sondra's third finger–left hand. I tried to locate one I could afford. Every diamond I thought satisfied her passion was too expensive. My shopping patterns were not up to Sondra's liking. She'd already bragged to her peer groupies about this fantastic diamond ring she was receiving. She made that announcement a tad too soon.

Sondra's patience reached its limit. She traveled to New York City recently supposedly on a business trip. She found her way to New York City's Diamond District. She returned nights later with a sneaky look on her face.

I approached for a welcome home hug. Three weeks had passed since we honored our friendship with intimacy. I was glad she returned. All was right in the world. She slowly reached out to me. Yes. She would break her bodily silence tonight. Sondra was all mine as we collected each other. She gave me a simple hug. She then placed her left hand on my shoulder. I said nothing. She placed her fingers on my ear. I still said nothing. I also had no idea what she was doing.

Sondra became agitated. She raised her left hand. She stuck her ring finger in my face. A 4-carat stone made me breathless. No... speechless is the word. It wasn't the quality of diamond I would have selected. It wasn't worth whatever the price she paid. I refused to break her heart. I would let her have her moment.

"Look what I accidentally found in New York City!" she shouted. "I hope you like it as much as I do! I know it looks expensive. Don't worry, dear. You can reimburse me later!" My pride was crushed. How could she do this to me? Why didn't she wait 'til I fulfilled my financial promise? I'm the man in this relationship. I looked into Sondra's eyes. I wanted her to see what I was feeling. I didn't want to lose her before she was legally my property.

"Wait a minute! Did she say I could pay her later?"

Wow! Our love had become twisted. This was a power play. I didn't want to mess things up. I didn't want to kill intimacy opportunities attached to that phony diamond.

Without too much fuss, I compromised. I would become Sondra's stupid fiance'. She could keep that faulty ring. The real me she would never have. Sounds dishonest? Sounds cold-blooded, huh? Whatever!

Call it ego. Call it selfishness. I called it saving a soul mate that can complete my life. The ring acceptance farce was based purely on personal gratification. Tonight will be a great adventure... all because of my humbled heart. Yeah, that's the ticket!

I took advantage of that stupid diamond. (No reason to expect otherwise.) It led to marriage. The marriage went downhill fast. Could we have rescued our marriage along the way? I don't know. Sondra and I never will. Our relationship's been in limbo. No reconciliation made by either of us. We loved each other the best we could. We lasted a full year on intimacy alone. As those feelings diminished, others couldn't be sustained. Thus, was my assumption accurate? As levels of intimacy take their natural course, must other parts of the relationship become stronger for any relationship to survive? Again, who knows? In my heart, my love for Sondra dwindled. I felt no need for her company... a prime example the effects of intimacy were stronger than I figured. What I did to Sondra was heartless, wasn't it? Get over it! I'm aware my feelings were unfair. I took ownership of them. I apologized to Sondra. I did so while sitting at a traffic light near Watson's Lane. Sondra wasn't sittin' in the car. I'm sure she heard my sincere apology wherever she was.

That diamond ring episode was a power play. Was it Sondra's way of showcasing her love for me? Or, was it an opportunity for me to showcase a 40k love for her? It mattered not. I didn't have 40k for a marriage commitment I wasn't ready to make.

I made that decision alone. Why didn't I get professional relationship help on how I felt and why? This was my personal baggage. Mine alone. Other issues affected our relationship. Sondra had affection for Koon Cats. I met those huge gigantic creatures the first time I rang her doorbell. These four-legged animals were bred mainly in the Northeast part of the country. They had personalities of real people. Her cats had a long list of do's and don'ts. I had to honor this list for Sondra's sake. Big kitty no-no's were: never enter their marked territory; never put them out of the house; never sit on their chair or couch; and, never force them off the bed. These rules were ridiculous. A real man should not be controlled by a couple of dizzy cats. I would play by the rules. Be a good guy.

I never violated kitty-cat rules when I stayed at Sondra's house. I could only watch as the cats controlled the entire living space. I freaked out. Things had to change. When Sondra left for work, I had those cats all to myself. I kept broom handles in the trunk of my car. I retrieved them before Sondra had driven a mile down the road. I chased those big-headed creatures all over that house. I whacked at them 'til Sondra returned. The cats cared less. It took a while before they got my balance of power-related message. I would always put the weapons back in my trunk before Sondra returned. Sondra would never know of my brutality unless these high society cats spoke English.

This was welcomed exercise. I loved whacking cats without bruises showing. Sondra assumed I had accepted her cat demands. Our intimate relationship was never better. The spanking went on a long time. An animal revolution was secretly in the works. One morning the cats urinated on Sondra's white furniture. It was the cats' way of telling Sondra someone had to go. Sondra witnessed similar cat behavior with her previous man friends. She now understood her cats were very unhappy with me... her latest beau. Without obtaining a search warrant, Sondra opened my trunk. She found a dozen broken broomsticks. Each broomstick was numbered. The words... "Use Only for Whuppin' a Koon-Cat's butt" was written in my handwriting. Sondra's search was illegal. Thus, I denied ownership of the weapons.

Sondra believed in her cat-people's messages. She berated me for abusing her animals. The woman I cherished chose kitty-litter love over a good strong man.

Oh, well.

The cat-people sat on top of the sofa moving their paws like they understood sign language. "See ya' later, sucka!" bounced off their front twos. The paw writing was on the wall. I had been bested by a couple of critters. Please don't share this pussycat story with anyone.

I refused to let Sondra leave me. I wanted and needed her. We got back together a few weeks later. Regrettably, it was after her people-critters were kidnapped by a mysterious Cat Burglar. I don't know who would do such a thing!

Local News Flash::

Sondra's Koon Cats have mysteriously disappeared. They were probably buried in unknown rose gardens four houses down the street. Nothing else was taken during a bold daylight burglary... 'cept broom handles containing a fingerprint, or two, or three!

"What a weird break-in, huh?" thought the neighbors and the police. Sondra stapled lost and found posters on every telephone pole in Sircus Junction. She posted a $10,000.00 reward for the return of Koon Cats known as Peaches and Cream, and the arrest and conviction of their cat-nappers! The cat and manhunt was nationwide while someone down the street was sittin' on the reward during a barbecue.

Sondra's cooking was another relationship issue. Don't get me wrong. I don't demand a hot meal every night. When a woman works, there's no reason for her to slave over a stove after her 9 to 5. Sondra thought cooking was a natural gift to women. If Sondra were an average cook I wouldn't complain. If her cooking skills were below average: Yet, she was above avrerage in other areas, I also wouldn't complain. Maybe I should be a bit more blunt. My sweet Sondra had few skills that were mentionable. None... other than you know what. Nothing she prepared was acceptable. I've seen Sondra burn a boiled egg. That's the nature of her skills. Sondra hosted Thanksgiving Dinner last year. She invited 25 of her closest friends. Only three rsvp'd... the two cat-people and yours truly! I sat quietly and ate an uncooked turkey. It gobbled every time I touched it with a fork. The cat-people had the better idea. They hid their turkey wings under the dining room couch when Sondra wasn't lookin'. Smart kitties, huh?

I'm a major part of this cooking fiasco. I had never told Sondra the truth 'bout her cooking skills. My appetite was nothing but a big fat lie. I have another confession to share. Living with a non-cooking skills chick is pure nightmare! There, I've said it! Insecure men will eat bad food for a lifetime. Sillier men remain quiet because of intimate goodies that come with unspoken loyalty. I'm on the record as being neither of the two. I must apologize to Sondra (And, to all of the naive, non-cookin' women in America!).

Thoughts of Sondra's and my past quickly came to an end. I arrived at the underground garage for the City's Gala. I parked and entered the Grand Ballroom. I tried to hide my relationship guilt involving Sondra. I tried to keep Sondra out of my mind. I would discretely seek the next love of my life. I would say goodbye to Sondra at the same time.

My security post was front and center. I noted if the rich and famous entered solo or were escorted by security personnel. My pocket notebook was running out of pages. Hundreds of celebrities later... there she was! This woman wasn't showing off. She was comfortable being herself. That was a trait I admired. She was wearing a black sleeveless dress up over the knee. A size 6 it was, I think. Everything from her hair to her feet was complimentary.

"Is she gorgeous or what?" I shouted for only my ears to hear. She had a special crease in her smile. It worked perfectly. It was a smile commanding a high level of respect. All she wanted to know about you was her first impression. Nothing else was sought if you were, in fact, a decent person.

Her hazel eyes were hypnotic. They reversed questionable thoughts as she approached. I really liked that. This lady stood strong in sassy French-cut heels. I think they were French... about four inches high. If her heels were another inch in length (5 inches) I'd have to leave her alone. Women of character know what I'm talking about.

The finest of leather wrapped around her feet. The leather anchored her graceful stance. Her body curved when needed. She had a posture that made a ballerina jealous. If someone were to become my lover... it's this woman!

Seeking answers, I followed her every move. She approached a reserved table filled with eager guest. Seated men graciously stood as she approached. They cared little about frowns from jealous significant others. Manners were not the norm from these so-called gentlemen. She recognized jealousy issues before she took a seat. This woman coupled her knees as she sat in the chair. Peeking at a great pair of legs was voided. I tried to imagine what she wore under that dress. I'm only a simple man. I'm not sure what women wore under black sleeveless dresses.

The room continued to fill with male and female guests. New eyes also watched her every move. Everyone waited for any opportunity to approach her 'bout nothin'. Men watched lustfully. Women watched with jealous eyes. I'd be lying if I didn't imagine myself making love to that black dress. It would be a normal response from a normal man. I'm… a normal man.

Her posture had dignity. She saluted every female respectfully and in a non-threatening manner. This act negated special attention given to her from rude, but suddenly well-mannered men.

No gentleman acknowledged ownership of her as of yet. No one gave this property a "Get over here 'cause you belonged to me!" welcome. Is it possible she didn't have a special man in her life? Stranger things have happened.

My heart vibrated for a lady I never met. My cop's eyes followed this treasure. I observed how she danced and with whom. She had to belong to a lucky man somewhere. Wherever he was… he was at the wrong place. This woman should never be out of her man's sight. She had exactly what men desired. Is that an insecure statement? Or, is that a sheer statement of jealously?

No. It was simply a fact of life! There's always a more handsome man out there. There's always a man with a better car, bigger house, lots of cash in the bank… and larger feet! These men wait for a princess like this to come along. They immediately pounce. They promise her everything they've earned in this whole world.

Yes! If she had a special man… he'd be sitting next to her. Wherever he is right this second, I hope he stays there. I smiled my crooked smile. This may be a chance at new love.

Another hour passed. I approached her and shyly ask for a dance. I was prepared to handle her denial with dignity. I expected the worst. God smiled on me. I extended my hand. She accepted. I placed her hand in my sweating right palm. I led her to a not so crowded spot on the dance floor. Soft music filled the evening air.

She allowed herself to be held. I introduced myself as Sir Bishop Calloway. My inquisitive expression waited for hers.

"I'm... I'm... I'm... Ms. Jillian Esther Carson!" she said after pausing. She clearly emphasized she wasn't a married woman. It still went right over my head.

The dance offered me the chance of a lifetime. Yes... I could legally touch her body without the police being summoned. I could tell this Jillian woman was seeking a real man. She truly wanted our bodies to touch. I dared not pull her too close. Something hard was protruding from my mid-section. It was my .38 Caliber Smith and Wesson. I kept an awkward distance during the dance. Too awkward, I suppose. The strange look on Jillian's face suggested I was afraid to hold her as a confident man. I ignored her look. It was too early to reveal my cop's identity. We glided across a crowded dance floor like Fred Astaire and Ginger Rogers. Jealous male eyes cursed my every step. The angel of my dreams might be standing right in front of me. This was so right. I stayed away from small talk. I feared saying the wrong thing at the wrong time.

The music ended. The musicians took a short break. I told Jillian how nice it was to dance with her. I applauded her gracefulness. I apologized for the distance I kept on the dance floor.

"I'm sorry I held you in such a delicate manner, Ms. Carson. Maybe next time?" I cordially asked. Jillian moistened her lips. She turned her head slightly to the left. She gave what I perceived to be a "You may hang out with me if you play your cards right" smile.

Jillian then whispered while gently blinking those hazel eyes... "I'm happy that bulge in your pants wasn't human excitement, Sir or Mr. Calloway... or, whatever you call yourself! You won't believe how many arrogant men violate my honor by attempting to penetrate me while on the dance floor," she followed.

Jillian's words left me speechless. I stared at her for the longest moment. She held my nervous hands. She was in no hurry to let them go. "Your dancing is pretty good!" she added. "Thank you," I returned in a knucklehead manner. Her comments sought a longer, more intelligent conversation. I wasn't ready to have one. I have to practice talking to women like her. This was a Sondra times ten. I had to be careful of what I said and how I said it. My heart beat insanely as I escorted this ball-buster back to her table. We were rudely interrupted on the way. Some guy asked if he could have the next dance with Jillian. I had no right to answer for her so I deferred.

Jillian stared at me with a questionable look on her face. She turned to the gentleman and replied, "I'm tired right now, sir. These shoes are hurting. I really need to sit down, but thanks anyway." Jillian repeated her answer a second and third time because this fella' wouldn't accept no as an answer. He begged, again. She denied, again. He stared at her in disbelief. He mumbled something that sounded like "witch" as we continued to her table.

My cop senses told me to leave this fella' alone. I wanted no part of him. I would not put my life on the line for a woman I met several minutes ago. Jillian was great... but wasn't worth dying over.

We arrived at Jillian's table. She still held my hand in a controllable manner. She gently squeezed it to get my attention. I leaned closer. I was a mere inch or so away from her pink slender lips. I hoped something sweet was verbally about to enter my ears. My hopes were dashed. "Sir Bishop, or whoever you call yourself, don't you know the basic dance floor rules?" she asked disgustingly. "Don't allow another man to touch your woman as you leave the dance floor! Got it?" she snarled. "I expected you to be more of a man. I expected you to deny his request as though I was special and you were havin' none of that!" she added. "I had no idea who that gentleman was. I surely didn't want him puttin' his fingers on me," she said while calming down. "I, Jillian Esther Carson, have a right to deny anybody! You've gotta' help me ignore guys like that! Remember that, okay?" she demanded.

I could only agree. My ears were ringing from being chastised by a woman I hardly knew. I showcased an apologetic "I can do better" smile. I may have lost this imaginary lover before I had any rights to her!

I returned my nervous self to the far corner of the ballroom. "What did Jillian mean by that handshake?" I wondered during the short walk. "Did I over-evaluate her warmness?"

I moved to a table closer to Jillian. I needed to see more of her. To do so, I discreetly utilized my stalking skills from yesteryear. I relocated to an empty table paid for by a no-show sponsor. I still had no one to share this great moment in time. "Was Jillian Esther Carson toying with my emotions?"

"Did she enjoy our dance?"

"Was her handshake the sign of a future relationship? Or, was she simply a selfish little flirt?" My heart was now under the control of Ms. Jillian Esther Carson! My nose was wide open as they use to say back in the day.

Jillian sent some nice smiles in my direction during the night. I quickly glanced around my sponsor's empty table. I wanted to make sure her smiles were mine. They were. I should, however, do a better job protecting my heart. I don't want to suffer when this lovely non-acquaintance dumps me. I broke out in a cold sweat. Remember that crease in her smile? It was working its magic tonight. After one dance, I had committed my life to her. I had envisioned our imaginary marriage of five years and her weight gain of 30 pounds. We had three kids, a house, a boat, two dogs, a nagging mother-in-law living with us, and a very good 540 credit rating. Our temples greyed from nothing more than loving each other.

I had since graduated to a higher level of coolness. My love senses were returning. I had no idea what my next pursuit of happiness should be. I didn't really know this Jillian woman. I'll let it go at that. I persuaded my psyche to be more aggressive when the inevitable occurred. Someone made a grand entrance into the ballroom. He was 6 foot 5 and weighed about 220. He, too, greyed around the temples. This fella's tuxedo hung well from his broad shoulders. A real looker he was. This caused me to bite my inner lip. Another glance found college rings on his fingers. And, for the record, his black tuxedo wasn't rented. It was personally tailored. Those of us who can't afford to purchase a tuxedo know the difference between renting and owning. It's in the trouser cuff stitching and around the jacket's lapel.

I know... don't be a player hater! This man walked straight into my angel's arms. A collective sigh of relief came from cautious women seated around the room. I recognized this fella' from somewhere. This familiar dude was breaking my little cop's heart.

"Yet, don't I know him from somewhere?" I kept asking myself.

Say it ain't so! This fella' was an old ladies' man from years ago. He was a person I disrespected. His arms were around the future mother of my children. Say goodbye to my dream of a white picket fence.

"Billy Credit!"... That's his name! My feelings of future love vanished. I could neither compete with this man nor did I want to. He stole every decent woman I had back in the day... Or, did I simply lose them? The latter truth scares me a bit. Credit's reputation was horrible. Love 'em and leave 'em was his motto. It never took more than a week before women surrendered to his pressure. He bragged about his conquest to anyone within earshot. Took great pleasure in it. Billy Credit had everything a real woman wanted. I don't know why the smart women couldn't see ole' Mr. Heartbreak coming. There's no such thing as the perfect man. That's the first mistake women make! Credit's

Doctorate Degree was purchased from a non-accredited college and women still didn't care. That was mistake number two! Mistake number three? His Mercedes and Jaguar belonged to his momma' and women still didn't care. With these glaring issues, his fellow competitors saw right through him. "Why do women learn the hard way?" I wondered. "Why do sweetly tainted words, a good strong body, and the appearance of success lead to easy sex?" It never happened that way for me. I was disappointed this man showed up. I would not dance with another woman the remainder of the evening.

I kept imagining Jillian in my arms. I closed my eyes and allowed Jillian to gracefully place her chin on my shoulder. We strolled over a floor tremendously envied by all. At the end of our imaginary dances, we French kissed to write home about. I no longer cared about Jillian's dashing Romeo. He could easily find another victim.

Jillian and I never spoke during my hallucinations. I interpreted her gentle touches to mean she enjoyed our conversations. I tried to enter her gracious heart at that very moment. I tried to enjoy her dancing and the memory of that initial handshake.

"Did I violate an unspoken trust by doing so?"

"Would I lose her to a man I despised?" No matter how I tried to slow the Gala's clock on the wall, the social event of my life neared its end. Jillian was ready to leave. I took a glance at Jillian. I wished an everlasting picture of her smile. I stared, helplessly, as old Romeo helped with her coat. I wanted to do so. It no longer mattered. It was an hour since we danced. She's probably forgotten my face by now. A woman like Jillian Esther Carson could have any man she wanted. I'm a cop for goodness sake. A good one... but just a cop!

Jillian waved goodbye to those seated at her table. She and that Credit fella' made their grand exit down the red carpet. Jillian stopped, suddenly. She intentionally turned. She sent a nice smile in my direction right in front of that Romeo guy. I returned a weak grin. I had nothin' to offer this splendid woman. "I'd never get closer to her than that smile." I accepted it.

Jillian's smile should have satisfied my needs for the night. It didn't. Instead, the finest of smiles created a big hole in my heart.

The function ended. My police powers were never needed, thank goodness. That's when my thoughts of Jillian became uncontrollable. The stalker within me was ready to explode.

"Where's Jillian Esther Carson now?" "Is she home in bed, alone?"

"What's she doing?"

"With whom is she doing it?"

"Where's that Billy Credit fella' right now? I know what he likes to do!"

"How did Jillian's ego fall to his touch?"

I'd bet a bag of 7-Eleven donuts she slept with slick Billy more than once.

Jillian wasn't that fine, anyway. She's just a good lookin'... classy tramp!

"Good riddance!" I finalized.

My ride back to the house was a quiet one. If Sondra refuses to unlock the screen door, I'd have to crawl through a garage window I intentionally left unlocked. Sondra secretly knows about the unlocked window. Making me crawl sorta' represented my begging apology for things I shouted earlier.

Sondra had no words for my return. Our lives were back to the norms of the night. Around 3:30 AM, our bodies would accidentally, unintentionally, intentionally touch. An hour or so of unscheduled intimacy would follow and I, we, had made peace with the world... NOT! I felt Sondra's love had now become nothing but a Band-Aid. Not a good thing. The reason? That Jillian witch's touch! My personality changed that night. I wanted to become a better man. I'd begin this personal transition by having a long, honest talk with Sondra. I moved out the next weekend. It wasn't Sondra's fault I felt the way I did. She was a sweet woman. I wished our relationship survived. I officially broke up with Sondra. We hugged goodbye to each other like never before. We cried together like never before. Prayed together like never before. I apologized for the mess I put her through over the years. Okay, I'll confess. It was really Sondra who cried. I did offer my shoulder, though. And, it was Sondra who really prayed for us. My ego wouldn't travel down my weaker religious side. And, finally, my apology to Sondra was a cleansing action for my life. I needed it. It helped me become a better man. I'm now a man of religion. My self-esteem has been elevated. My character is stronger and I talk to my mother every day to make sure she wants for nothing.

I was not good enough for Jillian Esther Carson's love. I wasn't in her social class. That weakness was evident when I didn't approach her on that Gala evening. Oh well, I'll never know. My brief encounter with her imaginary love taught me a lot. I've grown so much since the night my heart was broken. I ceased to recognize Jillian's existence. A man of my stature can't love a woman who doesn't even know he's alive.

"What will I do with myself?" "Can I satisfy a need to not be in her life?"

"What about my manly desires?" Duuuuh? "It's obvious I'm still fascinated with this Jillian woman, huh?" Later, I watched a rerun of "All My Children." I was seeking a way to mend my broken heart's spirit. Erica Kane's heart tends to heal soon after the next commercial break. As a loyal observer of that soap series since day one, why can't I learn from that show?

I realized how stupid this method of healing was. I sought the next best thing for my heartache. That was writing in my little Black Book! I reached into my bottom drawer. I grabbed my little book and my best Bic writing pen. It was time for me to share intimate man-stuff with my best friend and even better listener.

I tired from a long day. I swallowed a couple of those illegal yellow and blue pills I confiscated from the earlier double homicide crime scene. The dead man and his hooker no longer needed them. I fell asleep before I'd penned a word. I wanted to return to my days as a youngster. Whenever I needed a fresh start in life, I dreamed about my good old little fella' days. Those were the best days of my pathetic life.

My return to those days was based on illegal drugs I had available. Were those dreams wake-up calls from the Almighty? I didn't know. I swallowed more pills to immediately escape myself. I awakened several hours later. I remembered absolutely nothin' from my dream! "What's up with that?" I wondered.

The wanna' be historian in me wanted to document my religious escapades from way back when. My request failed me this time. I grabbed my pen and little book from the bedroom floor. I would document my old love for religion for my future self to read. Doing so would allow me to get as far away from my present police occupation as possible.

Another set of yellow and blue pills were consumed. They finally transported me to an unknown land far, far away. Control over my location was obviously based on the number of illegal pills. In my case, that meant wait and see!

My street-corner pharmacy cohorts advised further use of these pills would result in unpredictable behavior. Unlicensed pill doctors in my neighborhood also insisted I leave those yellow and blue amphetamines alone.

What do they know? How many times had they witnessed dead kids face-down in an alley dumpster? An unrestricted slumber from a triple dose of yellow and blue pills bested me in a matter of seconds. I've been transported to an era never before visited.

Hello, Strange World...

"Where am I? How did I get here?" I don't recognize my present self one little bit. I'm not as tall as I used to be. I barely weighed 100 pounds and my body strength's all but left me.

My knees are heavily bandaged. My blistered fingers no longer have fingernails. Both feet are bleeding and I am shoeless. The torn, sweat-soaked rags on my back are clothing, I guess. My eyes hurt when I stared at the Sun... or any light for that reason.

What has happened to me?

Why has God transported me to this location? Am I here for something... specific? When will my questions be answered?

A memory was restored from nowhere. The remains of my functioning-self resembled a body enslaved. I had traveled to an era where human bondage was the norm. I'm a servant of that bondage!

To stay alive, I'm required to push brick after brick into an allotted slot. I must surround each brick with a straw-based mortar. This same job must be completed day after day... after day... or I will receive a deadly punishment!

Guess what? I'm not alone! Hundreds... maybe thousands... make up this workforce. We actually resembled each other. We have the same eyes and the same broken bodies! Same broken spirit!

Depressed and bewildered, we, an apparently captured people, sought rescue through a certain cycle of death... a death that would propel us into a new life... a life welcomed as soon as possible.

Bricks pushed into pre-cut slots by my bleeding fingers were building mortared mountains. I would soon reach the apex of the structure my captors devoted my life to complete.

A voice from nowhere reminded me I'm not alone! Thousands of souls were pushing bricks into designated slots just like me. They cried out like I did. They moaned like I did. Their bodies were disabled and disjointed... just like mine. Yet, all have toiled on.

Constant, measureable progress was the mandate from my captors. Nothing must prevent my daily tally of brick and mortar. I've seen first-hand how daily tallies of brick are enforced. I've witnessed how concerns for humanity were completely disregarded for the sake of progress.

I've nodded goodbye to fellow laborers I knew... but really didn't know... as tons of mortared brick consumed their bodies. They had become immortal right before my very eyes. They had become a lost but permanent part of this historical structure. Each death took a part of my soul with it. These cries of sorrow would be heard throughout eternity, or until this man-made structure released their souls.

It won't be long before I have joined them. I, too, seek to join this mass of sealed spirits. Sooner than later, I wished! I'm not strong enough to take my own life. My captors, no doubt, will have little trouble doing so. It will be a blessing when this occurs. The end. My end.

Meanwhile, to make eye contact with anyone working on this unknown structure was against the rules. It's a treasonable crime to know what other fellow laborers were seeing, feeling... thinking. Solitude is all that's allowed. I could solemnly talk to myself as long as no others were listening! Otherwise, harsh disciplines were forthcoming.

The only successes left in this God-forsaken world were completing my portions of the construction. Each time I pushed a row of bricks to the structure's apex I received bread, water, and five gloriously short minutes of rest. That plateau was only a few minutes away.

The Sun's rays were softly calling down to me. They called but I've been stripped of my identity. I could only assume they were calling my name. This acknowledgement gave me strength to complete my brick assignment one last time. The bread rewarded was stale. It was infected with lice. My half-cup of water had to be immediately consumed or it would be poured on the ground by the hand controlling it. No matter. I've been to this plateau before.

Questionable rewards were expected and not an issue. The most important reward was the five minutes of personal time earned for reaching this height. Five minutes that lacked any possibility of torture.

These precious minutes were so... well... use your imagination. I always used them to relax my mind. I'd try to make sense of a reality I didn't deserve. I used those precious minutes to dream of another life... a happy family that used to exist. I even dreamed of strange new worlds I'd heard about rumor-wise but never visited.

My current reality was calling. It was time for me to go. My minutes were up. I gave thought to breaking my captor's rules. Yes, that time had come. I would open my eyes for the first time while standing on top of the structure. I would finally visualize the constant pain and suffering of my day... my life.

I tried to understand the reason for this structure. I tried to understand the use of my life and the lives of others to build it. My earlier assessment of laborers was correct as I witnessed the mass of controlled humanity. Huge labor forces were at work brick by brick.

The sounds of leather cracking the backs of enslaved torsos were horrendous. There were constant cries of pain. Screams indicated more deaths were imminent.

I said goodbye to vocal captives soon to die. They, too, had broken laws by surviving long passed the real. My urge to see all and understand all was cut short when a strange pain penetrated my feet. The pains were beyond my control. It was a sorrowful pain with a restless glory attached.

The human suffering I felt came from souls buried under layers of stone beneath my feet. I was disrespecting the entombed inhabitants by adding another 100 pounds or so to the structure's weight. I was disrespecting the burial of precious souls. This fact cut deeply into my heart.

Entombed souls were free of bondage! I, on the other hand, was not! I took this unwelcomed knowledge discovery to my new supply of bricks and mortar. They were stacked at the base of the structure.

I looked upward. My continued will to live had vanished. A will to live was now a plateau I would no longer pursue. Life was no longer necessary. The need to push another brick into another slot invalidated my sanity.

My new independence was a violation not tolerated by the ruling class. The death of me will no longer be my captor's concern. My rewarded bread and water could be given to another soul awaiting my similar destiny. Give my cup of water to the youngest in chains... please!

I took a gut-filled moment. I looked into several captured faces struggling to hold their heads high. I spoke to all with courage to listen. I made this decision knowing my life would come to an end shortly thereafter.

Respectfully, I begged for someone, anyone, to tell me what I'd spent my captive life building? Was this a temple of God? Was this temple built to worship some other kind of king? To what have I contributed?

"Someone... please answer me before I leave this place," I wishfully shouted, albeit solemnly.

The answer was on the tip of an unknown tongue when that expected song of leather... Crraaccckkk... viciously stung my naked back.

Sounds of mixing straw and mortar were noises no longer heard. My soul would get the final rest it deserved.

The unknown hand on the whip shouted, "We shall forever honor captors dedicating their lives to the Great Wall of China!"

Those words of honor, while sarcastic, were the last words I'd ever hear! Within seconds, my soul joined those forever bonded by this ancient ideology... a class system of construction that didn't have to be! The only so-called explanation came from a soldier whose whip controlled my existence. I wanted no other captives to speak to this soldier on my behalf. This soldier would be rewarded in another time and place. I would see him on the other side.

The pounding in my heart did so for the last time. It would breathe no more for this old warrior. I felt my soul rising. Knowing I perished in a holy way, I thanked the Almighty for whatever life he afforded me in this strange world.

Good or bad... didn't matter. I'd been joyously welcomed into His Glory... Forever!

"Amen to us all!" I thought as the effects of yellow and blue pills were wearing off. Questioning the truths of historical persecutions were always interests of mine.

"Why would such a dream come to me at this moment?" I wondered.

"Was there a humanistic message attached to my dream's political culture?"

"Was there a relationship between the Great Wall of China's labor pool and the horrific criminal activity in today's Sircus Junction?"

"Or, did those yellow and blue pills challenge my religious perspectives in some way?" Only time would tell. Meanwhile, capturing a group of murderous assassins was fresh on my awakening mind!

Gotta' go finish the job!

CHAPTER 3

Several years passed since my encounter with Jillian. I couldn't help but remember her. She was the finest woman I never wanted to love again.

Not bitter about it. I've grown into a more confident man. I've learned how to survive the loss of declined love. I've reconnected with my true identity… reclaimed my sanity.

I never sought out the infamous Jillian Esther Carson for another attempt at unconditional love. I don't think about the woman anymore. I've forgotten what that woman looks like. I would not, could not hate her any longer.

Okay. I've made that perfectly clear, right? The new me had become a very nice guy. Mentally, I'm doing swell (a 1960's word). Physically, I'm jogging at least 5 miles a day to relieve internal tensions.

Yes. It's true. While I'd never tasted the fruits of Jillian's love, no other woman lived up to the imaginary love-makin' we experienced after that Gala years ago. It's a traumatic experience to lose someone like her. Been there… Done that.

I've tried new relationships. No big deal. You know what? To truly love and lose a woman hurts a lot. Loosing a woman who doesn't even know you're alive hurts even more. When a woman is the first to leave a relationship… there's a giant hole in a man's gut nothing can fill. Ouch! Alternate life-styles were never options. I loved the opposite sex too much. I'm tired of talking to myself. I'll jog another mile. I'll call it a day.

I turned at Compton Lane. I stopped for a rush-hour crosswalk signal. I jogged in place awaiting the light to change. While waiting, an anonymous set of hands frantically waved from the other side of the intersection. A woman was desperately trying to gain someone's attention from inside a department store's giant window. From this distance, I appeared to be the object of that effort. The red light changed. Oh, my! I must be dreaming! I jogged closer to the huge window. Standing inside the front window of Margo's Bookstore was that wicked witch from the past. It was that woman I immortalized earlier in my life. It was Jillian Esther Carson in the flesh!

How did she recognize me from a distance? The girl's got a keen set of hazel eyes. I've gotta' to be careful. The truth be told... her fangs were still imbedded way down in my heart. I never wanted to become vulnerable to her touch again. I tried my best to avoid the finest woman who never wanted to love me. An evasive strategy was needed. I took a shortcut through the main entrance of Margo's Bookstore. It was an act of stupidity on my part. Duuuhhhhh? I pushed through the crowded swivel doors. I hoped for every chance not to meet this forgotten woman. I remembered too well the hurt she put on me several years ago. She didn't care then. Why should she care now?

Jillian's fantastic hairstyle looked the same. "Why fix what isn't broken?" I thought. She had gained a little weight. Once a perfect size 6... she had since ballooned to... a fat size 7-ish maybe? She gained all that weight after she dumped me years ago.

Yes! The stress of losing me had taken a toll on Jillian! I still recalled the dangers of her spider's touch. I promised not to go through that torture again. I shook my head in disgust. I would be less aggressive if ever we met again. This chick wasn't all that. Losing another round with a spider wasn't worth the pain.

The pedestrian traffic was horrible. Shoulder to shoulder, everyone forced a path through Margo's doorway to the Train Station below. It wasn't too late to change my mind... to not be bitten a second time. I made a decision to do just that. I turned to escape the pressing crowd. I would allow this spider no longer into my life. Thank God!

The pressing pedestrian traffic worked to my advantage. Tears of joy and relief fell from my eyes. My ego applauded this decision. I headed for the exit. A past life and over-valued lover would hurt me no longer.

In one gigantic breath, I exhaled. I waited for others to flash their transit-payment cards. My life will be back to simple in another few seconds. Stressful memories of Jillian exited my mind. I smiled. I had saved myself from a future of misery.

Just then, an unknown set of smooth fingers slithered down the back of my soaked jogging shirt. "Excuse me, young man?" said the blast from the past. "Is there a decent bookstore in this big small town?"

I protested the question. It was that Jillian woman. She'd snuck up on me again. I was not prepared. She never did play fair. Here she is, again, up-close and personal. She looked better today than the slut I never dated several years ago. She was wearing a familiar perfume. It was Old Spice for women. The aroma was knocking my socks off!

Jillian possessed that same powerful stance. She had those same drop-dead crazy, hazel eyes. "Wait a minute! Did she say... young man?" I questioned.

Everything great about this knucklehead of a lady started to return. Remember that deadly crease in her smile? It was ripping through my heart like a hot knife through butter.

This Jillian chick took a quick minute to tell me her life's story. She did so right in the path of the pedestrians. This came as a complete surprise because I barely knew her and I really didn't care!

Her words didn't register. Her lips were moving. Words were being spoken. I was somewhere else in time. Okay... a bad habit of mine. I drifted back to that special night years ago. I wondered what became of that black sleeveless dress. Did she still have those sassy French shoes? Where did she and Billy Credit go after that black-tie function?

These were questions I wanted to ask, but didn't. My nerves couldn't handle the truth. If Jillian cheated during our imaginary love affair, I'd have to shoot her in front of all these pedestrians.

Well... probably not. I've grown into a more mature person. I'd do it later when nobody's around. My memory was returning. This woman was still deadlier than ever. I was no match for her. She was and is too much lady for me. No doubt as dangerous. I had grown wiser when affairs of the heart were concerned. Yeah, right!

Jillian wasn't really looking for another bookstore. She asked about one but had a different look in her eyes. Frowns on her face yelled, "Hey! Mr. Bishop, or whatever you call yourself, a beautiful woman stands before you!"

"Talk to her, stupid!" she silently suggested. "I may be the woman of your dreams! This is your last chance to find out!" I acknowledged Jillian's invitation in a visual sense only. I would not respond verbally. I stood there, unresponsive.

Jillian became disgusted. "You can't do it, can you?" she asked. "My needs are too heavy for you, aren't they? I'm simply too much woman for you, huh?" she snarled. Jillian turned her back. She started to walk away. My destiny was leaving. I couldn't let it leave so easily. "Wait just a minute, my precious Darling," I shouted for all travelers to hear.

"Let's go somewhere! Look into each other's eyes!"

"Let's talk 'til an early Sun lightens your lovely face! Destiny, once again, has placed us together!"

Jillian came to a complete stop. She turned with the most curious look on her face... like she'd heard those lines before. I smiled. I squinted my left eye a bit and twisted my lips into a knot. The words were by Cary Grant in his 1950 movie. He was begging Deborah Kerr, Grace Kelly, or some famous actress not to leave his side.

I forced a few phony tears like Cary Grant did to save his lovers. It worked back then and it's working now. Jillian accepted my invitation for coffee. "I'm kinda' funky after jogging twenty miles or so!" I sorta' expanded. Sweat was drippin' everywhere. "I hope you don't mind my funky smell?" I said to Jillian in my best Cary Grant voice. Jillian then caught me completely off-guard. Without hesitation, she responded to my sweaty concerns in copycat fashion.

In her best imitation of a Grace Kelly like voice, she said... "I don't mind your offensive smell mister funky-man. But, please, enough of that Cary Grant crap!"

I was totally speechless. "The mouth on this woman is something special!" I thought. I wiped my forehead with the bottom of my sweaty cut-off jogging shirt. I wanted Jillian to witness the one new stomach muscle I'd developed at Champ's Gym. I used that arrogance to physically part the rush hour crowd and lead her out of Margo's front door.

Crystal's Deli was a great place to sit and chat. Fancy attire was never an issue. The place was only a few blocks away. So... off we went.

The ham and swiss on French bread... and I love French bread... was Crystal's best sandwich. There's a major problem when dining at Crystal's. The food's great but the place has too many mirrors! Mirrors are all over the place. Didn't matter where you sat. You still observed too much of everybody else's business.

It was not the greatest place to begin my next love affair. Who cares? It was just coffee. Didn't matter who saw us together this fine day. I'm gonna' love this woman for the rest of my life. What I didn't need was an ex-lover recognizing me and interfering with my motives. I desperately wanted no hussy from my past staring at my future wife with hatred in her eyes. That happened too many times. I lost every one of those episodes. I have the scars and restraining orders to prove it. No drama today, please! It's too early in the relationship. That kinda' stuff would be too hard to explain to a lady like Jillian. She'd never understand my past romances nor did I need to understand hers. Each of our lives, up to this point, would remain ancient history.

A man's credibility takes a hit when he's placed in that position. Old truths won't matter. Men are considered dogs 'til they prove otherwise. A fine woman like Jillian would leave me in a heartbeat. I don't wanna' take that chance.

I put on the biggest pair of dark sunglasses I could find in my shoulder bag. I did so as a precaution. Ironically, Jillian reached into her purse and did the same thing. "What the…?" I thought. We entered the coffee shop looking like the Blues Brothers from Detroit.

A hostess with… aahhh… borderline looks?… greeted us. Her name was Cindy. Cindy had a hair weave down to her shoulders. She kept trying to seat us in well-lit places. Not only did she need her ends clipped; she had no idea what two sets of dark sunglasses meant as customers. The store manager and her personal beautician needed to school her about certain things. I declined her first three table choices. Cindy had to know we sought a discreet table for two. The restaurant's front door had to be at Jillian's back. It was important to keep a proper distance between ex-flames and my future wife's eye.

Cindy finally offered the better table. She did so after accepting a twenty-dollar tip for doin' absolutely nothin'. She knew the deal all along. It was the most preferred table in the Deli. It was waaaaay back in the right corner. It leaned against a wall and had no windows or intrusive mirror angles. The table was square with two itty-bitty chairs. It sat directly under a framed support beam and, lucky for us, right next to two big ole' fat people! How convenient!

Jillian suggested I sit with my back to the door. That, of course, was never going to happen. Jillian finally gave in after my insistence. I could see she didn't like it. "Hold the chair for her, stupid!" my conscience commanded. Jillian kindly waited 'til my chivalry kicked in. She grinned at my awkwardness. She snickered at my attempt to demonstrate a level of social class I knew... she knew... I never had in the first place.

I held the lucky chair until Jillian was comfortably settled. I, covertly, took this opportunity to sneak a peek at those lovely thighs. No luck. She still knows how to properly bend those knees together when being seated.

The best part of my covert action? The fabulous Ms. Jillian Esther Carson caught me peeking at her legs outta' her left eye. She had to know I'd already secretly made passionate love to her! She loved the aggression displayed by the new me. She could tell by my crooked eyebrow she would escape my touch no longer! My strategy to stay aggressive continued. I am naïve but I'm learning fast. I sat with more confidence at the table. Crossing my legs made me appear a bit more in control. I held that pose for about two solid minutes. I pulled a muscle doing so. Jillian saw how hard I was trying to impress her. She ignored it. How sweet of her. It was time to champion the fine etiquette of Café dining. Ahhhh! Let's see. I'll let her order first. "If she ordered anything over ten bucks... the Golden Arches were in her immediate future!"... A thought I kept to myself.

I'd be polite. I'd allow her to be the first to taste her food. "What's the difference between the little salad fork and the big salad fork? Can I place my elbows on the table's edge?" I wondered.

"Decisions? Decisions? Decisions? What's a man to do?" I asked myself while staring at Jillian's cleavage. "Where's Emily Post when you needed her?" I'm glad I had basic manners. It makes a stupid man like me a classier fella'.

There's one last thing. A real man should carefully listen to how his date orders her food. If she orders anything cooked rare... her intimacy skills were limited. That means I won't be getting lucky any time soon. If she orders anything cooked well done... it means this gal's as horny as an Alaskan Moose! (I forgot where that propaganda came from!)

Our waitress arrived fifteen minutes later. She brought a nasty attitude with her. The waitress insisted I order first. She did so by ignoring Jillian. This was the beginning of consistent, bad customer service by this unscholarly winch. "Is ya' wanna' co-cola, coffee, or sumptin' wit' bubbles?" she asked while popping gum and twirling a kid's Barney pen in her right hand.

Jillian and I, flabbergasted, stared in disbelief. The waitress reshuffled her feet. She leaned her hips to the side. Her body language was one of impatience. She then placed both of her hands on her hips. She stared directly at me with the biggest hazel eyes I'd ever seen. Yeah... hazel. She winked, put her Barney pen to paper and, while locking eyes with me, asked... "So, what's it gonna' be, darlin'?"

Jillian quickly placed the menu above her eyes. She assumed the waitress and I were old school friends trying to politely overcome a botched not-so-recent booty-call. "Darling? Where did all this darling stuff come from?" I wondered. I never before laid eyes on this tall glass of fresh milk!... (a term I got from my younger brother). Not once in my life! I surely wouldn't have chosen Crystal's Deli if I had.

Jillian was only an arm's length away. She observed the whole episode. She slanted her eyes. I thought about complaining to the manager. I didn't. I wanted no more attention brought to this table.

This gal, unfortunately, was auditioning for the part of waitress in a scary movie! I... a real man... would take control of this situation. This little philly would embarrass me no longer in front of the woman I once hoped to never love again. I turned and faced the waitress. I would certainly recapture Jillian's honor. I turned to direct some foul-mouthed words to a set of virgin-less waitress ears. I turned to champion her customer service-less attitude. I turned... I turned... I turned and witnessed the shortest little apron skirt known to man... Hallelujah!

Her white and blue nametag read Beverley. It didn't reveal her last name. This Beverley chick knew her customer service skills were non-existent.

There was only one way to officially display my anger. I made it known to Jillian I would leave no more than a 50% tip for this foxy little thing. Jillian, for some unknown reason became outraged. She held the menu over her face while discretely evaluating my behavior. Seconds later she responded with a sharp kick to my shins. The immediate pain meant she wanted to love me... NOT!

"Why did my spirited little lady react this way?" I wondered. I hadn't a clue. Her kick had to be accidental. Maybe she didn't like the way her future Bishop undressed the waitress? No way she could've read my innocent mind, and I'd never admit anything even close to a confession.

Jillian's kick was way over the edge, huh? Jealousy must be a hidden asset of hers. My ego objected, again. "Don't let Jillian assault you like that, Calloway!" it silently yelled. "She challenged your manhood, dummy!" Meanwhile, I tried to hold my tongue.

I couldn't. I also didn't have the right to openly shout a very forceful message.

In my most masculine but lowered voice, I whispered in Jillian's direction... "If you ever want Calloway as your last name, sista'... you should better control those jealousies!" Jillian gently sat back in her chair. She had that "Oh, no you didn't!" look on her face. She said nothing for several minutes. She reestablished eye contact. She exploded verbally for only me to hear! This gorgeous woman silently cursed me like an old sailor. Although she, too, cursed at a whisper's level, I clearly heard every one of her vicious verbal memos. When Jillian finished, I knew... she knew I totally understood her direct messages!

I got it. Movin' on.

Our attention returned to the slutty waitress named Beverley. She'd personally witnessed our discreet yelling matches. She shook her head in disgust and said out loud for each to hear... "You little buttholes need ta' grow up!" She left to get two coffees... no sugar. Before she did, she winked at me outta' her right eye. This pleasant but crazy waitress had chosen sides! I was the winner!

The fabulous Beverley tippy-toed away. She returned a short minute later with two cups of Sanka coffee. "What in the world is this?" I thought to myself. "Nobody drinks Sanka coffee anymore. My great, great ancestors drank that stuff way back in the 1800's. What's up with that?"

Beverley cared less. She awkwardly leaned forward and placed two glasses of water on the table. Her filthy fingerprints smothered each glass. We asked for straws for obvious sanitary reasons. Beverley responded by pulling two "unwrapped" straws out of her hair. She placed them on the table. Jillian and I, again, stared at this Beverley gal.

Jillian's hazel eyes widened. They questioned the customer service of the also hazel-eyed waitress.

Both sets of hazel eyes stared at each other. "And?????" Beverley visually asked. Another quiet took over the table. Jillian and I were deciding whether to leave this joint or stay. Bev (we've secretly become old pals) dropped a packet of sugar under my side of the table. She made no attempt to pick it up. I would brighten up this little philly's bad day by being a man of scruples. I would retrieve the packet of sugar. I reached for the packet but stopped short of doing so. I stopped short because the packet had a telephone number written across it. I smartly decided not to pick it up with Jillian Esther Carson a mere three feet away. I would do nothing to offend the woman who wouldn't love me in the past. To save the evening, and eliminate another sharp kick on my shin, I tippy-toed the sugar packet further under the table.

Whew! That was a close call. The packet of sugar was now out of harm's way. My sweet Jillian would have to go to the powder room sooner or later. I'll retrieve the packet at that time.

The moment of truth had arrived. It was time for Jillian to order her meal. Beverley, again, tried to solicit my food order before taking Jillian's order. That's still not gonna' happen. "In case you haven't noticed young lady, I'm trying to be a gentleman. I never order my food before my guest does. So, please, start this process correctly by taking her order first," I said jokingly in my best Cary Grant voice.

Jillian heard my request. She immediately slammed the menu on the table. "Do we have to discuss Cary Grant again?" she asked.

"This is real life, Mr. Bishop Calloway! This ain't no television show!" she shouted. I shook my head apologetically. "I'll leave Cary Grant alone," I said. "I promise!"

Jillian calmed down. She wanted a meal with her coffee. "I'll have a nice rib-eye steak," said my sweetie pie. Nearby patron ears heard Jillian's selection. It was so quiet you could hear a pin drop. The anticipation was immense. Beverley, seated deli patrons, and I waited for Jillian's completed order. "I want that rib-eye steak cooked... well done!" she heartily voiced. "I also want a big batch of fries with lots of brown gravy on top!" she added.

The entire restaurant erupted with applause. I shook my head with great approval. Jillian was astonished at the applause. She didn't understand what all the fuss was about. She had no idea she had unknowingly declared a higher level of intimacy by ordering a well-done steak.

"What just happened? Why the applause?" she asked. I responded with a little bold-faced lie. "A famous movie-star entered the restaurant," I said.

Jillian grinned. "It must've been Cary Grant! I've been hearing his voice all day today!" I paused. "This woman's absolutely priceless, ain't she?"

I requested bread and butter as a start. This table's action was making me hungry. Fresh bread is a date crutch of mine. If this meeting turns disastrous, I'd have a basket of French bread in front of me. It gives me something to do with my hands. It's a conversation buffer of sorts and a way to display some manners.

Jillian will be offered the first choice of bread. I hope she doesn't pick the pumpernickel. That's another favorite of mine. If Jillian decides not to become my future love, at least I'd have a stomach of pumpernickel, an acceptable trade-off.

My God! Gloria what's-her-name walked through Crystal's front door! It was the loud and boisterous Gloria. The Gloria with the filthiest mouth in America! The one relationship experience every guy in America regretted his entire life. Every man has had one. Women too. Gloria was wearing a pair of dark sunglasses. How ironic.

I haven't seen Gloria since that ice cream incident at the Capital Sports Arena. It was playoff time. The Los Angeles Lakers were in town playing the Washington Bullets. During that game, Gloria's hazel eyes appeared outta' nowhere. She stood in the exit aisle several feet away. I remembered that day like yesterday. Kareem Abdul-Jabbar sky-hooked 25 points over Wes Unseld and it wasn't even halftime. Gloria shouted untruthful relationship lies to any ears that would listen. She claimed I abandoned our relationship after being intimate with her. She yelled these lies to a fast growing sports audience. Her accusations were absolutely false. I'm not that kind of guy. What really happened was… Gloria, a certified lunatic, wanted control of the relationship. I wasn't about to acquiesce. Unfortunately, I accidentally lost her telephone number on purpose. Yeah. I said it correctly. Gloria took this game's opportunity to beg me to come back to our relationship. Gloria wanted our love to begin anew. She wanted my embarrassment before a national audience to pressure a decision out of me. That was never going to happen. Gloria started crying before the whole world. She verbally dogged me out in front of 21,042 fans. I kept my cool. I'd heard those names many times before. I waited for an official time out in the Bullets/Lakers contest. Gloria, meanwhile, embarrassed me in front of my best-ever girlfriend at the time (her name escapes me).

Gloria's tirade caused me to miss key minutes of a great playoff game… sooooooo… I lost it! I gave Gloria the finger in front of her new basketball friends. I sat down in my seat. Seconds later, an ice cream cone hit me squarely on the forehead. The ice cream covered my eyes and nose. Strawberry I think. It dripped onto my new basketball jersey. I received that jersey as a gift from my best-ever girlfriend… what's her name… and she was pissed. She wanted no part of that crazy Gloria.

I still didn't lose my cool. I slowly emerged from my seat. Everyone in Section 224, Row 7 rose to their feet and allowed me to pass. They eagerly waited to witness what I was gonna' do about that ice cream cone.

Wes Unsel missed two foul shots during this nonsense. Elvin Hayes picked up a technical foul. And, Trinitron's roamin' camera picked up some domestic ice cream action. Fans thought I was a jerk and they didn't even know who I was. Boos came from every direction. "So what!" I said to myself. "If they only knew how weird Gloria was?"

The saving grace? The game went into overtime. Washington took the lead on a Bobby Dandridge bank shot. Nothing was more important than the game's final minutes. My new lady (aaahhh… her name still escapes me) and I watched the television monitor near the fire exit. We did so just in case there was a fire emergency. I had some scary histories with Gloria. I was afraid she might recognize me at Crystal's Deli. My fears were warranted. Gloria actually mooned me once. She bare-butt mooned me while at a Thanksgiving Dinner. This action was performed in front of everybody. Grandma… Grandpa… little Tommy and Tera… it didn't matter! She bent over and pulled her jeans and cotton-laced draws to her knees. She poked out a hairy lady's butt inches shy of the butterball turkey. I was told to kiss it along with other choice words. The incident was horrifying. Little Tera hasn't eaten turkey meat since that time.

The Bullets vs. Lakers basketball game neared its end. Gloria was canvassing the Sports Arena looking for me. I forced my new girl friend down the fire escape ladder before the final horn. For some strange reason, I haven't heard from what's her name since that incident. Maybe she was mad because she bought the tickets. She never asked for the return of the expensive Laker basketball jersey, thank God!

I haven't seen Gloria since that basketball game. Gloria really doesn't scare me. Not one bit. I just didn't want another drama scene.

Gloria met some goofy-looking guy in the other corner of Crystal's. He wore a rather odd toupee' and, he too, wore a pair of dark sunglasses. He should've opted for a shaved head. Some people. Gloria was really into that loser. She never looked in my direction. She would never let an opportunity for revenge go wasted.

I've got to find a mature way to relax when ex-lovers are nearby. Jillian saw how nervous I was about something she knew nothing about. Jillian gently grabbed my hands. She looked into my eyes. "Let's get something clear, Bishop Calloway... or, however you wished to be addressed!"

"There's no man in my life right now," she said. "I'm not dating anyone!"

"Remember how you acted on that black-tie night?" she asked. "You thought there was somebody special in my life, didn't you, huh? Didn't you?"

"You thought Bill Credit was my lover, didn't you? Huh?"

"You thought he personally paid for my dress, shoes, bra and underwear. Didn't' you, huh?"

"Everything I wore belonged to him. Huh? Didn't it? It was written all over your stupid face, Mr. Silly Man!"

"And, you know what, Mr. Silly Man?"

"I couldn't stand the thought of it! That's why you received nothing but a smile that night!"

"That's why you went home alone, Mr. Silly Man!"

"A more confident man could've had me!"

"I was looking for Mister Right that evening."

"I thought he could be you. Think about it. You let me walk right out of your life. You never even called!"

"Thanks for nothing!" she added.

"There's one more thing you should know, Mr. Ownership Man!"

"I'm not a piece of personal property!"

"I don't care about your previous relationships."

"And, for the record, I never slept with that Billy Credit maniac that night!" she sarcastically slammed.

I sat there in complete silence. This woman's got some kind of mouth! "How could hateful words come from a fine set of lips?" I wanted to ask, but didn't.

"Of all she highlighted, did I hear what I wanted to hear?"

"Did I hear correctly? That there's no special beau in her life, right now?" The answer was yes!

Fireworks exploded about me. The day had taken a pleasant turn. We talked while the food was being prepared. Jillian conducted some personal research after that special function. She thought well of my reputation based on her social network of spies.

Jillian was aware of my recent relationships. She quickly mentioned Sondra, Loraine, Ethel, Brenda, Sara, Gail and Barbara, and… Ethel… again!

She highlighted a different Barbara from Miami, Carol from Chicago, Naomi and Sara–a couple of twins from New York City, followed by Shirley from Toledo, and last but not least, Sheila… a super-model from Alabama.

Jillian repeated what the grapevine said about Gloria and the ice cream incident but… who cares?

Wow! Jillian's crew of nasty spies were pretty discreet. Word never got back to me somebody was investigatin' my personal closet. I'll surely remember she had good investigative skillsets.

We talked about what we wanted out of life. We spoke of goals. She wanted a business career or one of mother if the possibility presented itself. I had no reason to believe Chief of Police was beyond my reach. I told her braggingly and of my desire to attend Graduate School. Things were lookin' up!

The coffee at Crystal's Deli wasn't good. Sanka Coffee never was a good flavor for me. Jillian said she could make a better cup in her own kitchen. I heard that hint loud and clear and accepted! Jillian grinned with twisted lips. I returned a crooked smile. Men know what I'm talking about.

I summoned our nasty little waitress. It was time to bring the check. She saw me waving but wasn't too responsive. She was too busy flirting with the dark sunglasses near the window. He acted like he had nothing to hide. Yeah, right!

Beverley glanced my way two or three minutes later. She nodded then took her own sweet time bringing the tally. I had had enough of Beverley's shenanigans. I reduced her tip to 10 percent for obvious reasons. She deserved even less. I thought about no tip at all.

Beverley returned as cranky as ever. She leaned across the table and removed our dishes. Her tiny skirt rose several inches higher as she did. I would be a real man. I would not peek at what she was offering. Her actions were simply unacceptable. Jillian and I knew what she was doing. Her unchaste behavior was duly noted. Jillian observed me man-up to her episodes. I would not be party to this filthy behavior. It had nothing to do with impressing my coffee partner. It was simply the right thing to do. Bev's display degraded waitresses everywhere. She would get little or no tip from this smart guy. I left $40 on the table for a $20 tab. That'll teach this gal a lesson or two about customer service!

Jillian shook her head disgustingly. "Men!" she mumbled. I looked at Jillian and asked… "What?" Jillian rose to her feet before I could hold her chair. I guess she was still pissed off at the customer service. We took a couple of steps toward the front door. I remembered my car keys and a packet of sugar. I went back and retrieved my keys… alone. 'Nuff said.

We arrived at Jillian's house. She didn't live far away. I wasted a few minutes waiting for cats, dogs, or ex-boyfriends to make noises as we entered. If either did, I'd find a cup of coffee elsewhere. Been there. Done that! Jillian did make a great cup of coffee. We talked all night. We laughed about stuff 'til the wee hours of the morning. I didn't want to wear out my welcome. It was time for me to go.

Jillian offered a sweet peck on the cheek. Her caresses were strong and lengthy. Stronger hugs led to more passionate kisses. Only Jillian's recently purchased jeans from Nordstrom's buffered her intentions. I knew the jeans were recently purchased because the sales tag was recognizable. I did not forget what Jillian had at the Deli. She had a rib-eye steak. It was cooked well-done with a ton of French fries and gravy. This food combo suggested I was in deep trouble. A test of love was forthcoming. I wanted to back away. I feared sending the wrong signal.

Jillian held me a little bit tighter. "Was she sending me a signal?" I wondered.

"Was Jillian teasing me? How far did this princess want to go?"

My High School Dating Code instructed: "If you deny a woman's request for sex...while definitely honoring her virginity... she'll never go out with you again!"

Wow! My memory's pretty good, huh? I chose to honor my high school code. Jillian, meanwhile, wondered if I didn't like women 'cause "How could I refuse this gorgeous creature standing before me?" I had won brownie points by not forcing the intimacy issue. She knew how much I wanted her first-time love. I would wait 'til a marriage ceremony. I'd wait for the ring. The thought of that made me shiver. I'd never done that before. This woman had, therefore, put my sexual needs on hold. Am I crazy or what? Have I lost my mine? I didn't know if we were compatible? The rib-eye steak and fries test says we are. They aren't true scientific measurements. They're human emotions. Is Jillian intimate three times a month or once a year? It's not proper to ask her, is it? Wait. What am I doing? Intimacy can never be the foundation of love. Remember that relationship with Sondra? Jillian and I weren't intimate 'til several months later. She trapped me in a cabin somewhere west of the Rocky Mountains. We were attending one of those office retreats.

Jillian, all of a sudden, completely lost her mind. She locked the cabin door. She threw the card-key out the window. I felt like Daniel Boone on Sadie Hawkins Day! I fought her as best I could. Her charms over-powered my honor. I realized I would have a tough time waiting for our special wedding night. I pushed Jillian away. She had this look in her eyes. Something wasn't right. This seduction was taking on a difference direction. I am the Lion by virtue of my masculinity. I am the hunter. I'm the one who decides if or when intimacy occurs because... I am the King of the Jungle! My Lion frown delivered that strong message.

Jillian stared back. She turned her head slightly to the left. She folded her arms and tapped her sharp claws at the elbow. My ankles trembled. I tried to relax. A female now controlled me. I could yell for help but I won't. Before I knew it, I'd been manipulated, stimulated, and seduced to absolutely nothing! It was the best worst three hours of unwanted pain I never again wanted to again experience (Yes, I said it correctly).

I'd been slain by a beast called Jillian. I'd experienced every pleasure unknown to man during this gruesome ordeal. I am the Lion. I am the King of the Jungle. I was slain by the opposite sex.

Were there witnesses? I prayed not. No one must ever know. Jillian must never tell anyone she captured me without my consent. Doesn't Jillian know stop means stop? Doesn't she know I can refuse her touches whenever I wished? Didn't she understand the criminal consequences of not heeding my warnings?

"What kind of bionic woman was she, anyway?" I wondered. My useless torso fell to the floor. I had no energy to do anything. I breathed a sigh of relief. This fine creature finally let me go. If she were a black widow spider I'd be dead by now. The female black widow spider kills her mate right after being intimate. This spider's price was high... but possible.

I regained my composure. Where's my self-esteem? My dignity gave way to this distinguished jungle cat. She restored my faith in my power with one sentence… "You're the greatest lover in the whole wide world!"

"Okay…!"

"Did Jillian's statement mean I'm back on top? Have I regained enough respect to lead this family into the future? Or, will Jillian be the boss from now on?"

"Will she ever allow me to be a man again?" I have one last confession. "I, the great Bishop Calloway, had been conquered by the best of women!" I took out a handkerchief. I wiped the tears from my eyes. I even choked a little. The mere thought of this confession hurt. I'd never been bested before. I'd never been the hunted. I'd always been the seducer but never the seduced.

This was a very strange feeling for an experienced, ego driven, hard-nosed crime Detective.

"Where did Jillian learn those sexual skills?"

"Does she have a personal trainer?"

"Did she read a book or something?

"Did she learn them on a future Oprah TV Network?

She probably wanted freedom of intimacy and chose this time and place to fulfill that destiny.

Yes! Jillian chose me. I was the lucky one. A grin consumed me. The woman of my future proved she could love better than anyone. This answered our questions about each other.

Jillian starved for my touch. When I didn't respond right away, she took things into her own hands. She had to know if we were compatible. She wanted to know how she'd be loved in a long-term commitment. Wow! I'm the victor. The very fine Jillian Esther Carson had to know more than I. I am, therefore, more of a man than she is woman.

Jillian's ability to love is a forever kind of love. She was that good. I'd never find a better mate in life. I couldn't let her get away. I again referred to my outdated High School Handbook. It said: "Women will fall in love first and evaluate their partner's intimacy levels later. Men, on the other hand, will fall in love with anything crawling if the intimacy is fulfilling."

I totally agreed with the Handbook. Men are the smarter of the species. I dropped to one knee. I popped the question. "Popped the question" isn't a very romantic term. But, after magical sex... what is!

It worked! Jillian accepted! I vowed not to have a relationship like the one I had with Sondra. I bought the first gold wedding band I saw. This test of love was important to me. I waited 'til Jillian asked me out on another date. When she least expected it, I slid a solid gold band on her third finger, left hand. She cried and cried and cried. She and her mother were the happiest women in the world!

I would buy a better ring, soon. Jillian wanted no part of that suggestion. "This ring is what you offered. I'll cherish it forever," she shouted. Alas! My decision to marry was a correct one. On a sunny June afternoon, Jillian Esther Carson became Jillian Esther Carson-Calloway. She would move into the future as my forever partner. There wasn't a greater love in this world. My happiness, unfortunately, was short lived.

As I thanked God for Jillian, two forgotten faces came to mind. Those were the faces of Kevin and Barbara Woodson. Their killers were still roaming the streets of Sircus Junction. I took a vow not to rest 'til those murderers were brought to justice. I've yet to honor that commitment. Jillian interrupted deep thought lines across my forehead.

"What's wrong, Bishop?" she lovingly asked.

"I've had too much to drink, Jill," I answered. Jillian Esther Carson-Calloway didn't believe me. Not one bit. I had lied to my precious new wife for the very first time. Jillian knew it. It took only minutes of married life to lie to my wife! I'm a jerk!

Our wedding day was not the best time to share unfulfilled workplace promises. It was, however, my new wife doing the asking. My new marriage deserved trust and sharing. I should've been honest with Jillian. No doubt.

Oh, well. The wanna' be philosopher in me says a better world of more love and less crime must exist somewhere. I felt an immediate need to describe the world I so desperately sought. I felt the need to do so right here... church bells and all! I located an isolated room in the back of the church. Shamefully, my private thoughts did not include opinions from Jillian... the newest member of my life.

Where's my head? When no eyes were upon me, a handful of yellow and blue pills exploded on the tip of my tongue. The pain from daily criminal realities overwhelmed any thoughts of Jillian's future love. I left reality, again, for a dream of dreams. I knew not where they would take me. Far from here, I hoped.

Little Black Book...

It's been a while. I've missed you. I've taken a lovely wife. I wishfully assumed she'd take your place in my confidential world. My assumption was tested today. It failed.

I did not trust Jillian with my latest wanna' be philosopher feelings. I don't know why. I simply chose not to do so. It makes no sense. I make no sense.

I've shared with no one my dream of creating a sin-less world. It is a world requiring forty days and forty nights of a rain-soaked baptism. You've heard that rainy number before. The constant rain will prevent living souls from escaping this baptism. Yes... my so-called new world will be a special world.

The sky will never empty during this cleansing. Drop after drop will wash away previous criminal attitudes created by mankind.

A partnership will grow new seeds of life. I'm referring to a new Sun and Moon. No other growth factors will be needed. Just plain seeds growing new human beings.

Is such a thing possible? We'll find out. History says only one special man ever walked this Earth. That was two thousand years ago even though mankind existed much earlier. Researchers say this Earth is millions of years old. How could that be?

Many challenged the coming of Christ. Many do not. Who will be that similar special person to walk the new world's soil?

Will it be me?

Will it be a female?

Or, is that person already here waiting to be acknowledged? The answer's unknown. Anything's possible. Crime and love in my new world will be handled differently. Unwanted philosophies of each will disappear. Nothing would remain. No thoughts. No memories. No past descriptions of a criminal mind shall be written on secluded cavern walls for later discovery. A new learning will occur.

The rains of change will cease after forty days and forty nights. Another new world will present itself. How long will this new growth take? Only time would tell.

I'm talking about a pure beginning. What's the rush? Might mankind act right if true human growth takes its time?

A proactive chance for a new civilization is needed. There are no blueprints. Nothing will be guaranteed. Nothing will be brought forward because of too many self-discovery variances. Embarrassingly, the world we presently inhabit makes unwise choices when free will's available. Several free-will social issues have never been addressed. (1) Today's cultures still welcome economic gaps. Begging for alms occurs no matter what country traveled; (2) religiously, mankind scrutinizes the Bible too differently. So much so, certain cultures base acts of terror on its interpretation. How can this be? And (3), immigrant forefathers pioneered this world seeking a better land for a heritage not yet born. Huddle masses yearning to be free still seek that gracious opportunity.

Foreign populations seeking America's greatest gift of "liberty and justice for all" must do so over some other country's border. Based on America's history, isn't that a social double standard, maybe?

My new world will address those inequities. I intend to wash away all histories of mankind. My new world will address social pains attached to cultural differences. I'll research why they've become adversarial sub-cultures. I'll remedy them away.

Reborn from new seeds of life will come a better society. Hoped are mindsets open to lesser biases. Hoped are mindsets that reverse criminal behaviors.

My experienced cop's eye is excited about this new world. I can't wait to rewrite our questionable histories. Here's another chance to police us. Here's a chance to police our communities... our country.

This is one last chance to take ownership of our existence. We must create a better environment or die! Dare we set these new seeds of life in motion? Might we seek "life, liberty, and the pursuit of happiness" one more time? Should we cultivate them from a soon to be drowned-out world?

I think, yes! My optimism will be contagious. I'll push this perspective through the cultural lens of a competent new world. I'll do whatever to create more inclusive mindsets. Loving thy fellow man will take its rightful importance. My laws will mandate better use of free will options. My laws will force civilizations to take ownership of all future behaviors.

Does the new world sound realistic? Probably not if you don't think as a cop does. Probably not if you haven't seen the world through a cop's eye... day by day... 'til you've reached the point of no return.

Once that happens, welcome to the new world of Bishop Calloway... a world of social reality! Enough for now! Enough about the new world! When such thoughts capture my soul, I have to write them down. Establishing a new world requires more time and more thought. I had neither at the moment.

Jillian, my wife of several hours... just called out to me... Again!
I must leave my unfilled imagination and console her.
This... I must do. I owe her this!

CHAPTER 4

Sircus Junction is not the best place to be on hot steamy nights. It's not the best place because the humidity clings to everything it touches. When northeasterly breezes don't exist, the stagnant hot air promotes criminal behavior. It's a fact of life.

Even the leaves on the trees are affected. They hang there in the dark going back and forth... back and forth... awaiting their natural return to Earth's soil.

You can eliminate the wetness with your forearm. You could use the back of your hand. An old wrinkled handkerchief will do. No need to hurry. An abundance of sweat is on the way. Humidity is off the charts on nights like this. And, that's the point! When the humidity becomes unbearable on Shenandoah's River Basin, something bad lies just around the corner. The suspense is killing me. My police cruiser's faulty air conditioner was causing me to sweat. I needed water. I needed something cold and wet, right now! I've been looking for the nearest 7-Eleven. Those Orange and Green stripes would be a welcomed site. I've never looked hard to find them. I actually passed one a half-mile back. I decided not to stop. I purchased a small stick of deodorant from that 7-Eleven last month. I paid $4.99 for the smallest size on the shelf. That price was very unreasonable. It was a petty larceny crime. That same size was $1.99 at the Super Mart two blocks down the street. I would've saved $1.50 per city block if my math were correct.

How much of a convenience does the western world need anyway? Americans care not. I didn't care. I do, now. I would purchase a Super-Duper Slurpee when thirsty. I'd mix about 30 ounces of Banana and Lime flavors together, grab two gigantic straws, and find a shade tree somewhere. Within a few hours, my gaseous nature would have my nostrils screamin' for mercy! It was easier to simply pour 2 lbs. of pure sugar down my throat. My sugar high would last another four hours. I'd gained 5-pounds overnight. What's there to say? That nasty stuff tastes great. I still don't know how something that tasted so good could be so bad for your health? Whatever.

I kept driving. My last clean shirt was clinging to my sweatin' back. Hop Sing's Cleaning Factory was nearby. It was a short right turn at Stottle Lane and a half-mile down on the left. I take my uniforms there. They offer a police discount with no strings attached.

The City Council was attempting to close Asian cleaning factories down. The ability to charge low prices was forcing the higher-priced Mom and Pop voter-constituents out of business. Hop Sing hadn't needed any protection for a while. Suspiciously set fires had recently slowed down a bit. It's Friday night. They're probably closed by now, anyway. Small business owners and their profits wasted no time getting outta' town before the Sun went down. You get my drift? I'll drop by Hop Sings' first thing in the morning. Until then, I'll allow the humidity to control the sweat on my body.

Speaking of funky energy, pumping the brakes on this department owned Pontiac GTO takes too much effort. I don't wanna' kiss a utility pole anytime soon. This unconventional vehicle became police property several months ago. The driver failed to stop for a red light. When pulled over, the smell of an illegal weed escaped the driver's window. The Officer performed an illegal search and found 100 lbs.. Ooops!... I mean about 50 lbs. of Marijuana under the back seat.

The illegal search was challenged the next morning. The challenge was upheld and criminal charges were dropped. Returning the vehicle to the owner wasn't part of the deal. Racketeering laws are more serious. The owner refused to open that Federal Court can of worms. Thus, the vehicle became official police property.

This vehicle's bright yellow color can be spotted blocks away. It advertises against drug trafficking whether it wants to or not. Only supervisors or above can drive it, so I guess I'm the lucky one. Either way, it costs about $17.00 to fill this gas-guzzler's tank in the 1970's. That's an unreasonable amount for gas these days. That money could be better spent funding the latest pay raise I haven't received. Don't get me started on the need for a Police Union.

My destination was ahead. I dimmed the headlamps. I illegally turned into the dark alley behind some row houses. Resident streetwalkers scowled at my bad driving decision. I didn't care. I'm a cop! Nothin' they could do about it.

Rats scurried about like they owned the place. They were larger than the norm and smaller than a good size kitten. They weren't scary to me. I've seen them too many times up close and personal. I could probably teach them a thing or two about survival. These fellas' looked like the best fed creatures on Earth based on over-flowing trash containers. Tenants accepted the rodents because the tenants had nowhere else to live. I, fortunately, went home to the rat-free suburbs. I hoped the 4-legged monsters weren't as prevalent inside the building as they were outside. And, they too, thrived when the humidity was high.

I coasted the unleaded Pontiac shy of an over-used trash dumpster. Men were standing in shadows further down the alley. They had to be the neighborhood Vice Squad because they looked too much like the normal residents. They were making drug buys from around the corner.

I approached with badge in hand. I identified myself as Detective Calloway. A smirk crossed several faces. It was a good smirk though… possibly from something heard during a drunken all-nighter poker game.

"So you're the Department's latest hero, huh?" a voice mumbled short of a shout. "Give us a few heroic details while our last drug buy takes place!"

The voice was referring to one of my recent ordeals. It occurred five or six months ago. Police gossip had me labeled either lucky or a great warrior… depending on who said what. "If they only knew what really happened?" I said privately.

I was tired of hearing all of the false rumors. I realized this was a great opportunity to bond with these officers. If the truth needed to be told… why not now? We had a few minutes before the final purchase. I decided to go for it. I recorded such instances in my special black book.

It happened about six months ago…

Dear Black Book,

I, *Detective Bishop Calloway, now question this noble career of law enforcement officer. I have the honorable desire to be one of Sircus Junction's finest. Instead, my life does nothing but witness death and destruction.*

I've tired of dying faces staring up from the ground… anonymous eyes seeking a last minute chat with their God. I'm tired of the drift of their facial expressions when the God they seek doesn't answer. Who am I to accept their last rights?

There lies the irony of my situation. It has become increasingly apparent a holy presence of some kind is following me around! There are reasons why I think so.

Here's the first reason. The District Watch Commander assigned me to the Duty Clerk position. It wasn't a promotion. No one wanted the job. Energetic patrolmen felt station duty kept them from the street's real-life experiences. I'm referring to unknown challenges at the end of a radio call.

Patrolmen wanted the freedom of movement. They didn't want supervisors looking over their shoulders all night long. I didn't mind station clerk duty 'cause it increased one's promotional opportunity.

Officer Marion Dirkinson had similar administrative skills. Our versatility created a special kind of in-house respect. We administratively controlled the entire precinct. Many times our shifts over-lapped. When that occurred, we'd reassigned ourselves to a patrol car to stay in touch with real world criminal action.

On a frosty day last year, something happened. There were few requests for police service. On quiet days like this, it's easy to call it a day. That's exactly what I did. Officer Dirkinson filled my void by reassigning himself to my patrol car at 1 PM. I raced home for needed rest. I had no idea my early exit would affect so many lives.

The strong afternoon sun blurred my vision during the entire drive. I entered my home with burned-out eyes. I immediately fell on the bed. I turned the television to the best show ever... the "All My Children" soap opera.

Fifteen minutes later, a news reporter pre-empted Erica Kane and Phil with a late breakin' news story. The reporter announced a bank robbery just occurred in my Police District. I remained awake long enough to hear a few details.

As I listened, the news reporter was standing at a recognizable intersection. It was Mac Arthur and Jackson... an intersection I patrolled hours earlier.

I sat upright. I wiped the near-sleep out of my eyes. The following message rang through my ears... "A Sircus Junction Police Officer Responded to a Bank Robbery Moments Ago! He was Shot and Killed by Unknown Assailants!"

I immediately went into shock. I had entered that same set of bank doors hours ago. A Godly-like truth entered my heart. That call for assistance would've been mine had I not taken the rest of the day off!

I sat on the edge of the bed and put my head in my hands. I heard the lousy details over and over for the next thirty minutes. It took a while before I finally accepted reality. Officer Dirkinson was dead!

I fought the hurt I felt inside. I was Officer Dirkinson's friend. Why did he have to die? Did I cause his death? Would he still be alive if we approached this robbery as a team? If the shooter witnessed more than one officer, would he have hesitated before pulling the trigger? Was God sending me a message? This unfortunate action introduced new religious feelings into my life. I could only think what this truly meant. "Was I scheduled to personally visit the Almighty? Rarely had I requested an early check-off time. Why did I do so today?" I wondered.

"Does God have a master plan?"

No matter what I told myself... today wasn't a coincidence. The bank robber had a partner hiding in the bushes across the street. No one saw him before the fatal shot was fired. I would've died from that same shot. This assumption could not be denied.

"Why does it take a tragic incident to acknowledge God's divine work?" In the 1970's... "Why did this gentleman die for me? Have you ever wondered why things happen the way they do?"

Death was right at my doorstep. Whether I believed it or not, God had another destiny for me. What I shared was the first reason I believed a higher power was watching over me. Weeks later... I still did.

The second higher power occurred weeks after Officer Dirkinson's death. I was foot patrolling to reduce daylight burglaries. I walked into the back end of Elm Street. I observed several guys breaking into a '67 Ford. The Ford was yellow bearing Virginia tags. I became interested not only as a cop, but because this particular vehicle belonged to yours truly. I drew my gun. I continued my approach. Both men spotted me: neither attempted to escape. This non-response should've raised a big flag of caution. It didn't.

I concentrated on the closest individual. He was wearing a heavy coat on a very hot day. I ordered him to stand still. He did as I requested. Without warning, he pulled a sawed-off shotgun from his coat. He pointed it directly at my head. As I looked down the gun barrel, my self-defense skills had abandoned me. I tried but couldn't recall what the Police Manual instructed about such occasions.

That very second, a holy, unknown voice instructed me to look directly into the aggressor's eyes. I can't remember what I said. I had traveled somewhere else in time. I was in that alley spiritually and not really there physically. I can't explain it... not even to myself.

The one thing I do remember? The unarmed partner begged his cohort not to pull the trigger. "He ain't worth killing!" the partner screamed. Seconds had turned into an eternity. Again, a special voice took control of my lips. The voice urged my mouth to order the armed villain and his partner to "surrender" unto me!

I spent the next few minutes gazing into each of the aggressors' eyes. It took more begging by the unarmed partner before the shotgun was actually lowered. Once I had control of the shotgun, the armed bandit glanced into my eyes. He gave me a short speech right there on the spot. "Cops are being wasted all over America!" he loudly said. "I'm not wasting a cop anywhere near Virginia 'cause of the example Virginia's courts would make of me. Consider yourself one lucky cop!" the aggressor mumbled. "You're a truly blessed man! God must be with you today!" he added.

Somehow I knew... the armed gunman knew... I truly understood his special words.

The arrest required tons of paperwork. The shotgun and ammunition were in plain sight for all peers to see. A multitude of "job well dones" came from all directions. The district was buzzing as word of my heroism quickly spread. My ego as a crime fighter swelled to an all-time high. I had been over-taken by a brilliant sense of death.

The truth...? I was simply a lucky man! I felt no need to make this embarrassing fact known. I didn't finish the paperwork 'til around 1AM. I left the district. My drive home felt tremendous! I, the fabulous hero crime-fighter, had survived the largest challenge of my police career. I didn't know another religious check was forthcoming. It surfaced as I navigated Route 95... a very dangerous Virginia highway. My acceptance speech for surviving that shotgun encounter had been over-simplified.

The saving of my life hadn't been credited to the higher power. An awakening was needed. Shockingly, the super macho image I carried away from the job site completely vanished into thin air. Control of my hands, legs, and feet was nonexistent. My car veered sharply to the left... without any help from me! My vehicle then maneuvered a dangerous traffic pattern... "All by itself"... and came to a screeching halt on Route 95's median strip... again... "All by itself!" It dawned on me I wasn't in this car alone. God had decided He and I should have a more candid talk. Our conversation ended thirty minutes later. And yes, He did all the talking!

God eventually returned myself to me! I, a more humbled public servant, was praying on top of a '67 Ford, yellow, bearing Virginia tags!

"How did I get on top of my car?" I asked myself. I took a couple of guesses! When I lost control of my vehicle earlier, I had no idea I'd survive that deadly vehicular threat. Cars sped by at high rates of speed without knowledge I no longer was in control. The driver in me desperately sought the highway's right shoulder... the location I thought was the safer withdrawal. I tried and tried but my steering wheel refused to follow my instructions. Instead, my car drove across the more dangerous left lanes and stopped in the only safe location possible! The right shoulder of the highway, for some reason, was obviously the wrong way to go. When the use of my arms and legs were restored, I was allowed to finish the drive home.

It was a 10-mile drive I'll never forget! A Greater Power had saved my life! These miracles had to be the work of the higher power I'd acknowledged since a child!

I never told these stories to anyone before today. The Vice Squad was the first to hear the truth from my lips. How this will affect my leadership tonight? Time will tell.

Vice Squad ears processed my confessions. They had no more questions about my past history. My radio confirmed the latest drug buy was successful. We could concentrate on the task at hand.

Another thought came outta' the blue. Higher-ranking officers were nowhere to be found. They had tired of officially justifying questionable drug raids. Tonight, this responsibility would be surrendered to an unknowing rookie Watch Commander.

Another fact? Mayor Josh Harrison was seeking re-election. He was using police reform to motivate votes into another six-year term. So far his policies were working like a charm. His drug concerns were two-fold. He mandated better supervision of court ordered raids, and he pushed for a Citizen Review Board (CRB).

The latter's a kiss a death. Citizen Review Boards are as anti-police as they come. Cops rarely got a fair hearing when innocent bystanders had been accidently killed. This Mayor doesn't care much about the rank and file. Until the CRB becomes reality, no search warrants could be executed without the Watch Commander (W/C) leading the charge.

The W/C is the only official authorized to carry a shotgun during a warrant's execution. Ironic isn't it? Mayor Harrison is using Police and Fire Department votes to influence his re-election bid. Yet, he agrees to a CRB? What's he thinking? He's a jerk but I like him. I'd vote for him again. Don't ask me why. My promotion placed me in the middle of this urban nightmare. I must not falter. My reputation was at stake. The search had to be a legitimate one. Everything had to go by the book. I didn't forget to factor in hot weather. Humidity on someone's fingers could cost a life. The last drug buy occurred in apartment 313. No one had entered or exited since. The suspected drug pushers were inside. "Why did the drug pushers choose this location?" I wondered. A second escape route is a valid part of a criminal's thought process. Why none this night? There's one entrance to the building. There's one door to apartment 313. There's no other way to exit the apartment without a ladder.

Drug dealers are very intelligent people. They rarely make mistakes. Their strategies are far superior to what police agencies expect on a daily basis. They out-maneuver the police anytime they wish. I became cautious. "When faced with negative circumstances, the unknown has a propensity to become a deadly reality," was an old proverb that comes to mind.

I gazed into the eyes of each vice squad officer. I looked for weaknesses of any kind. Their faces must display levels of confidence I needed. I'd cancel this activity without giving it a second thought, if not. Uniformed cops required strong personalities. Vice Squad cops needed them even more. I decided to quickly re-assess my personnel. Randy was a middle-aged white man. He loved his undercover role. Infiltrating drug rings were his greatest thrill. Randy's family was envied by every member of the Vice Squad. He had the basic wish… a pretty wife, two kids, and a white picket fence. He lived every day as though it was his last. He focused on nothing but reality. "Strange guy, huh?" I thought.

Johnny… a black male… was only 22 years old. He barely passed the height and weight requirements. He wore a beard and sported a braided hairstyle. Johnny sought respect by abusing his police powers every chance he got. I had certainly heard about those police personalities before. Johnny over-reacted to anyone questioning his limited physique. His personnel folder was a lot thicker than most. He was dependable when it mattered most. His days as a police officer were numbered.

Gabe is the only Latino in the group. I could easily stereotype him. I won't. His car was an exact replica of the one used in that 1970's Hit Show, "Starsky and Hutch." This man loved the excitement of a police chase. He'd shoot anybody trying to evade the law. Need I say more?

Gabe's other problems were the off-duty kind. All-nighter poker games kept his marriage(s) in shambles. A dependence on the Daily-Double horse races didn't help either. He absolutely loved what he did for a living. Dying on the job was the only way he wanted to go.

The Vice Squad had a supervisory savior named Butler McKee. He was an up-front and responsible Corporal. McKee stood tall for this band of merry men when no else would. He was well educated. He disliked political bureaucracy. His writing talents easily validated questionable search warrants... a skill many department supervisors would die for. City politicians loved the way his bandits spearheaded the fight against drugs. The Chief of Police and Mayor took full credit for Vice-Squad raids... but only if everything went according to plan.

Corporal McKee resented hypocrisy. He supervised a squad no one wanted... within an environment no one sought. While his drug convictions were impressive, his search warrants resulted in the deaths of quite a few drug pushers over the years. This made the Mayor and Police Chief nervous at times. I wasn't about to enhance McKee's stats any further.

No one was more capable of pulling my butt out of a fire than this McKee fella'. I welcomed him without acknowledging his value. My ego was like that. Word had it he reported directly to the Mayor first. The Chief of Police was second on his list depending on his attitude that particular day. That's the kind of power he had.

My decision was final. The psychological edge I sought was found in this proud group of men. I wanted rational, controllable mindsets. Aaahhhh, forget that! I really needed a bunch of wild and totally committed... Crazy Cops! Normal-minded patrolmen would make the supreme sacrifice for their city. I don't doubt it for a minute. Today, however, I needed a squad of take-no-prisoner gun-fighters. I needed cops who'd already changed their death benefits from their wives to their mistresses. I needed veterans who didn't mind losing their entire paychecks on poker Fridays. And I needed foxhole free agents recently back from Vietnam… longing for a reason to kill someone again! You heard correctly. I needed unconditional loyalty to a rookie Watch Commander. I sought men who'd take a bullet so I could live another day. These thoughts were going through my mind as sweat poured down my face.

A previous question re-entered my mind. "Where did all the higher-ranking supervisors go?" I was at today's roll-call session. A Captain and two dumb Lieutenants talked a lot about leadership. I heard the Captain sign off at 6 p.m. He could leave anytime he wanted because he was the Watch Commander. The Senior Lieutenant yelled into the radio about 8 p.m. "Everything's quiet tonight so I'm outta' here!" he declared. Thirty minutes later, the lower-ranked Lieutenant responded to a call in another sector. I personally know this guy. He never commits to problems in another sector. "What's up with that?" I wondered.

Minutes later, the radio dispatcher placed the Watch Commander's status on my shoulders. He was the same dispatcher I've had problems with over the years. He yelled my new classification over the radio as loud as he could. He did so several times. No other police personnel pressed the talk button for the next couple of seconds. I could hear a slight laughter in the silent radio background.

"It's an honor to command hundreds of fine men," I said to myself.

I was naïve. I was given this assignment at 10 p.m. It was too late to worry about a suspicious chain of command. More important questions needed answering. I was prepared to lead this group of bandits into battle. I had reservations. Each Vice

Squad member also had reservations as they wondered about my leadership capabilities.

Did my sweating face give away my supervisory coolness? Did nervously taping on the police vehicle's hood cause a problem? I swallowed hard to negate any possibility of a mutiny. I took breaths of tonight's humid air. "Let's do this without killing anyone!" I uttered.

Cpl. McKee recognized the higher-ups had placed me in harm's way. He approached. He discretely whispered... "Boss-Man! If you aren't mentally prepared to do this drug raid thing, I'll understand. You might be tonight's Watch Commander... but you can see why I am the way I am, huh?" he sarcastically asked.

"Thanks for your love, Mckee," I replied. "Make sure these armed bandits know who's in charge. Once that's done... Let's go! By the way, no one's getting' shot tonight, right?" McKee rolled his eyes. He spit at my feet. He turned and walked away.

A brisk summer breeze came from nowhere. It was a welcomed break from tonight's scorching heat. It whistled through the red brick development. Members of the raiding party said a few prayers. I had already accepted my death as a possibility. Doing so privately was easier than doing it in front of these loyal men.

I wondered how I'd feel when death was imminent. I now know. It's a giant emptiness the average mind can't process. I've lived a ten-year oath to serve the public. The oath validated my decision to perish whenever the situation presented itself. I've placed my life in God's hands whether I wanted to or not. Sounds simple doesn't it? I remembered another thing. "To whom much is entrusted... much is expected!" This wasn't the best time to become my wanna' be philosopher self. My followers needed my strength. Car trunks were opened. Bulletproof vests and riot helmets were thrown to the ground. One vest was quite larger than the others. It resembled body armor used in bomb scare situations. I'm glad that's not needed.

I turned. I reloaded my Smith & Wesson. A hand tapped me on the shoulder. The armored car-lookin' vest mentioned was shoved into my arms! I hesitated. My comrades slid the heavy armor over my head. It had become quite clear. Because of the Mayor's new law, the W/C had to carry the dreaded shotgun. The W/C must be the first person entering the premises.

I gathered myself. I led this aggregate of nut cases through the building's front door. The hallway was mostly dark. The moon's rays peeked through several busted glass windows. A bunch of nothings streaked through my mind.

There's more bad news. The leader of this real-life Dirty Dozen movie had to place a copy of the search warrant directly into the hands of the resident owner!

"No Way!" I quietly mumbled, again. Whatever happened to the good old days when Watch Commanders yelled into a bullhorn from behind a distant tree? I guess those days are gone.

We secured positions. Chuck, one of my crazier cowboys, carried a heavy-duty sledgehammer. He positioned himself at the base of the drug seller's door. He held the giant hammer above his head and awaited my command to rip off the door's hinges.

Virginia Law mandates law enforcement personnel must yell "Police" before crashing through any homeowner's door. The Watch Commander is supposed to wait ten long seconds before destroying whatever's preventing legal access... yaadda, yaadda, yaadda!

Yeah, right! Maybe in somebody else's lifetime! That law was only applicable in a classroom setting. Search and seizure policies were very critical to this country's civil liberties. "But... not tonight!"

My soiled shirt was now a wet rag on my back. Perspiration flowed from my armpits into my crotch. The armored vest had me sweating like a pig. I moved into the hallway shadows to hide my wet trousers. I didn't want these brave men thinking I'd pissed in my pants… which wasn't far from the truth. It was time to do this thing. My rapidly fading voice yelled…

"Police! Open Up! We Have A Search Warrant!"

The pitter-patter of big and tiny feet scampered inside the apartment. Squealing voices were not of hard-core criminals. The voices were of older women and the youngest of child. This brought forth a reality. My fingers would not discharge a shotgun within these walls. Real people were a few feet away. Immortality was out of the question for me… for them… for all involved in this mess.

"How did I get here?" I wondered. I flashed back to the 1960's. In those days, it was I who was being pursued by the "Po-Po!… Coppers!… and… The Man!" I promised way back then never to put on a police officer's uniform. Where's that promise now? It's here and its hands are around my throat. I'm in a lost world of imminent death. I froze like a statue outside the thin wooden door. A first shot had to come from my shotgun.

Sweat ran into my eyes. "Darn humidity." I acknowledged. Without asking, I wiped my forehead on the chest of the cop directly behind me. It cleared the stinging sweat from my eyes. His stare didn't appreciate it.

"How did bad surveillance occur?" The occupants were five hardened felons with absolutely no reason to live. Yet, these so-called bad guys outsmarted a recently promoted smart guy… Not a good thing.

During today's earlier drug buys, mommas' and kids were solicited from other apartments to dine for free at the drug seller's apartment. Another invasion strategy was needed. My gallant ability to lead vanished. Meanwhile, the crazy cowboy holding the sledgehammer slammed it against the door locks before any command was given. Somehow, McKee had something to do with that action.

Door locks were demolished. Door hinges remained intact. The door now leaned to the inside wall. A 2 x 4 piece of wood had been nailed against the inside base of the door. It was an effective delay tactic. The next blow ripped off the remaining hinges. The door fell aside. It offered a 12-inch opening. It was, however, wide enough for an average man to shimmy through. Every inside light had been turned off. Nothing was visible from the hallway. I awaited sounds of gunshots. Streams of hot lead should exit the opening any second.

My mind was on overload. I tried to imagine the next action. My feet moved forward but really didn't. I didn't know who possessed what inside that stupid environment. My heart stopped beating. My shotgun lingered outside that apartment's door. A strange silence filled the air. The devil was about to break loose when, out of nowhere, a strong set of elbows shoved my body through the door's opening. I fell awkwardly. My head caught the hardwood floor. It bounced several times. I lost consciousness! A blast from my shotgun tore through the room! The last thing heard was screaming! My blackout took me to another universe. I was transported to another place in the history… this time without the effects of those yellow and blue uppers. The wanna' be philosopher in me took control.

To Whom It May Concern…

While I lay here unconscious, I'd like to schedule forty days and forty nights of rain to purify the souls of my new world. I'd like my final choice at free will to be a decision for all. I shall introduce new rules for a new existence. Every citizen will be asked, not ordered, to conform.

When my requested forty/forty rains were scheduled to finally end, only those who agreed to take an oath for a future mankind will survive. The oath will be a simple oath. It shall consist of the following:

"I solemnly acknowledge the birth of a new sin-less world. I swear to: (1) forgive all criminal behaviors and begin a new beginning; (2) learn to love my fellow man to the fullest; (3) come forth leaving all

personal biases behind; and (4), adhere to the new rules by allowing my conscience to be my judge and jury!"

This oath must be honored before the last drop of rain falls from the sky. No more oaths will be accepted after that time.

I don't know what would happen to those who refused to take the oath. I do know the new world would commence with or without those souls. No exceptions.

The first year of our existence will challenge a life of nuclear families versus nuclear weapons. I don't know where that challenge comes from. It just did. The thought of this futuristic endeavor is inspiring. It also scares me to death because... I'm no religious leader.

My consciousness was rapidly returning. I could go no further with these thoughts of a new world 'cause of a massive headache!

My sanity or portions of it had returned. A large knot on my forehead resulted from the fall. My latest religious journey seemed like an eternity when, in fact, it lasted only ten long seconds.

I remained staggered in the darkness. When I hit the hardwood floor, pressure transferred to my shotgun's trigger. The results were devastating. People were hit by the blast. Unknown drug sellers and hostages. Blood splattered everywhere. "What was that shotgun blast all about?" shouted a now interested drug dealer. "Isn't negotiation part of any raid process? No need being ridiculous!" the voice added.

I waved the search warrant with one hand. The shotgun was in the other. "Where did that dream of a forty-day rainy season come from?" I thought while waiting for my head to clear.

"Was it significant to this crisis?"

"Was it a precursor to my death?"

I didn't know. I knew my undercover crew and I were in total darkness. Amazing isn't it. The enemy of darkness minutes ago was now our ally. Meanwhile, men, women, and children scurried about. Mothers and babies screamed for their lives. "Down on the floor! Stay out the way!" drug pushers decried. Blinded by my life's uncertainty, I hollered... "Police! Don't Anybody Move! Nobody Take Another Step!"

My vision took its own sweet time. Toilets were flushing. Flash papers were burning. Handguns were heard falling to the floor. Silhouettes of bad guys hustled about using children as shields. Neither they nor their captives knew what to expect from cops who released a shotgun shell into a crowded room.

I crawled across the hard floor. My destination was the apartment's far wall. As I did, my knee struck one of the handguns on the floor. I wasn't sure of the caliber. I picked up the gun. I ejected six rounds of ammunition. The shells scattered like a bunch of marbles. Everyone recognized that sound. It heightened the sense of urgency. Babies. Women. Hostages... no longer mattered. This recently promoted Watch Commander would take no more chances.

A calming effect entered my life. The last time I felt this way was several weeks ago when I tried to stop a crazy bandit from stealing a car. Not any car... my car. I crept behind him knowing he was wearing a long heavy coat in the heat of summer. The bandit turned. He placed a sawed-off rifle against my temple. I had become the captured.

I had learned from that incident. Everything occurred in slow motion that day. I wasn't scared. It was a feeling few souls could describe. A sensible cohort talked his armed partner out of a 1st Degree Capital Murder conviction. His begging gave me another chance at life. I swore to stay out of harms' way in the future. In a world of criminal sins, it was a promise I couldn't keep. "Where do I go from here?" I wondered. The apartment was a dark hell. At that moment, unidentified knuckles struck me across the face. "What coward would do this?" I asked. A fight he'll get once I find out who he is. I wiped the blood from my nose. I looked around. It was probably that McKee fella'. Undermining my leadership would be worth the fight.

I had a new understanding of who I was. I had a renewed responsibility as a so-called leader. I released the shotgun's safety button! The menacing sound of *"Click, Click...Clack"* bounced off the apartment walls. My latest message was loud and clear. Cops, drug sellers, and to my surprise, several mothers recognized that another deadly shotgun shell just entered the gun's chamber. My valiant undercover crew sought protection wherever they could find it. Yes. I'd found the power of real leadership. I no longer cared for my life. I kneeled in the middle of someone's hardwood floor. I yelled for the attention of undercover vice-officers.

I waited for my fellow members' responses. I thought a gunshot would pierce my heart any minute now. I lived on. If it were my destiny to perish, it would've happened when I was shoved through that wretched door. Still unsure of the leadership in me, I tried to reset the shotgun's safety button. My first shot had already harmed people I'd never met.

Another shot would be unexplainable. "Do what you've gotta' do!" I told myself. Sweat from the humidity didn't keep my finger from releasing the safety latch for the third time. It was the easiest decision I'd ever made in my law enforcement life. Neither humidity nor a conscience would be a factor.

Adult shadows crawled toward rear bedrooms. The apartment had no back doors and this was a third floor unit. Outside of every window were uniformed officers. No escape was possible. If criminal mindsets were ready to die... I'm okay with that.

I shouted code names of undercover officers. Each answered without injury as they utilized my torso as a command post. The Vice Squad was now a bunch of scared little sissies.

"We've got your back!" one advised. "Don't waste time looking for us! You're totin' a shotgun! We ain't going nowhere you ain't been first!" another voice added.

"How can they joke at a time like this?" I wondered. All of the armed players had become one big huddled mass. I attempted to show an attitude of strength. I tried to restrict armed players from entering a loose cannon mindset. Another shot in the dark would cause a deadly ripple effect. Innocent lives hinged on this fact.

I eagerly sought help from whom else... the higher power from above! The important thing was protecting the abducted kids. "I've got to help those kids right now!" I told myself. I challenged all occupants to stay put. It took another thirty or so seconds for my eyes to adapt to the apartment's darkness. I couldn't identify any colors except dark gray or just plain black.

Human silhouettes scampered throughout the apartment. The occupants were different sizes, ages, and faceless. Innocent mothers and children became a reality as my eyesight returned. Those injured from my accidental blast gathered in the living room. Yes, the human element had re-entered this scenario.... with it a new pressure. There was an anticipated gunshot expected from a member of the drug gang. A thin wooden door separated life from death a short minute ago. With shotgun in hand, I stood seconds from innocent kids... imminent death... and, yes... another of Channel 9's late breakin' news stories!

Common sense tried to surround this dilemma. "Who dies so others may live?" I asked over and over. This wasn't a dream. This was as real as it gets. Armed villains and innocent families were intimately mixed. If gunfire came from this cluster, I could never press the shotgun's trigger. People are probably gonna' die before this is all over. That's the world we live in.

My sweaty fingers wanted no part of this deadly episode. My decision was to not make a decision. I hoped the lack of police advancement would make the armed felons feel less threatened. Thirty seconds later, a trembling voice from within the cluster challenged me to lower the shotgun.

"Put it down, now! Or, I'll kill everybody in this place!" said the voice. My response wasn't immediate. The cluster's voice baffled me. It didn't sound like a television's bad guy. It didn't sound like a notorious movie villain. The voice was simply... a regular guy's voice!

"But, was it one I could trust?" I wondered. I kept kneeling in case this voice belonged to an impatient man. I stayed low so the voice didn't use my silhouette as a target. Truthfully, I kneeled to the voice because I was scared to death. I never thought I'd see another day. Long forgotten was that body armor I wore. Not forgotten was the shotgun I carried. Please believe me. I really wanted to stand tall. I honestly wanted to man up to this request for forgiveness. Standing tall was such a simple way to die. All the voice had to do was aim at a 6 foot tall silhouette less than 10 feet away. I was too close for whomever to miss. I understood how death occurs. A single shot would come from the cluster as soon as I reached the five-foot height level. I'd drop to the floor. The shotgun would fall out of my hands in slow motion like it does in the movies.

A cry of pain would slowly escape my lips. Each slurred syllable would take a long time to be pronounced. Vice Squad faces would go into shock. They'd reach out to my fingertips. They'd console me. Gabe would place my head in his lap. His hand would support my chin. McKee would use both hands to pump my chest.

A radio call would cover the airwaves for "Man Down!" I'd hear the sirens coming down the street. I won't recall the drive to the nearest hospital. The last thing recognized would be a long line of badges, blue blazers, and white gloves' saluting as my casket slowly passes. My thoughts are so realistic because this is how death comes... when it comes!

There were other pressures on my backside. The pressures came from crazy cops telling me not to believe anyone seeking surrender. Time was of the essence. If it was my destiny to die, I would do so right here... right now. I swallowed hard. I started the longest upward stance of my short Watch Commander's life.

I moved to a one-knee position. I shouted to the unknown voice my intention to do so. I followed by bending at the waist. I would not drop the shotgun for any reason. There were no responses from the cluster. I completed my upward trek. I actually started to glow in the dark. Why would this happen to me? Why would my soul's target shine so brightly at this wrong place and time?

I waited for my childhood to pass before my eyes. I waited for my mother, father, and children to say goodbye before I entered the next world. They have yet to appear. I'm wondering why they haven't? My position was vulnerable. The shot should be forthcoming. I placed my life in God's hands. To live or die was his.

If I were to die I wasn't going alone. The shotgun's safety was off. My sweaty finger controlled the trigger. I, again, would not shoot into the cluster of children. If a shot rang out from any other place in this apartment, I'd return the fire. My decision was final.

A tingling sensation entered my body. A strength I knew not took control. My weak, tired voice became stronger. It commanded respect. My confidence to lead and survive grew with every second. I would take advantage of this new strength. I boldly ordered my sissy undercover cowboys to locate the light switches. Flashlights illuminated the room until ceiling lights were finally on. Once this was performed, my band of merry men stared at nothing but sweet, innocent, little faces. None had been hit by my accidental shotgun blast. One by one, mothers started to cry. Children followed their lead. They cried right along with their mothers.

Uncharacteristically, drug sellers and a bunch of macho cops wept simultaneously… a humbling experience if I ever witnessed one. Independent groups within the cluster required a moment to get a grip on things. Once that was accomplished, it was back to the business at hand.

Drug sellers held hands high. They surrendered without resistance. We canvassed the remaining rooms. Handguns, drugs, and cash money were confiscated, bagged, and tagged. Each vice squad officer evaluated the danger just survived. Relief was written on every forehead. Transports shuttled the apprehended to the precinct. The injured were taken to the hospital.

I was happy this warrant didn't result in death. The amazing journey seemed to last forever. During this episode, an unknown male vocalist sang ballads. I noticed his voice earlier while lying face down on the floor and made a promise to myself to buy that album if I survived this ordeal. The balladeer was, a then unknown, Mr. Peabo Bryson. The strong ballads were his first album. On a hot and humid summer night, "Who was somebody named, Peabo Bryson?" I'd never heard of him before this deadly search. Oh, well.

I discussed the drug raid with many of the naïve mothers. They had only agreed to an invitation for free food. They did not agree to buffer the police raid advances. The mothers witnessed their children being used as shields during the raid. They would testify on the government's behalf.

Crying youngsters sat free of harm. I felt an attraction to their innocence. One I'd never forget! Tears rolled off traumatized cheeks. I understood why. The kids were eight months to four years of age. Several were still shouting... "Mister... where's my mommy? Where's my mommy? I want my mommy!" Sensing upcoming abandonment, they knew a separation was imminent. Their tiny intuitions felt a more difficult hurt would occur if separated from mothers... drug users or not. These children were reared in drug environments. They survived.

I simply followed the State's Custody Laws. The children had to be taken from their present custodians.

"Would they be reunited later?" That goal was a long way off as each mother was placed under arrest. The Child Abuse and Neglect Unit responded. They took custody of the children. Juvenile Court hearings would be held the following day. Mothers cooperating with the Police were released. They were ordered to attend Family Court the next morning if they wished to regain custody. All came as requested. Janice Graves was a very outspoken twenty-one year old mother. Her children were ages one, two, and three. She had documented history of drug use. She was unhappy with the Court puttin' her through this process to get her kids back. The Judge, on the other hand, was furious. Upon learning of the drug raid, the Judge removed her kids from her possession. The Judge's decision was unacceptable to Janice. "Ain't no stupid Judge takin' my babies from me!" she screamed. "You might as well reverse that Court Order right now!"

The Judge resented the threat. She ordered the Deputy Marshall to place Janice under arrest. The Marshall grabbed for Janice's arm. Janice resisted. She bolted across the courtroom floor. She leaped over the witness stand and landed on the Judge's bench. The Judge ran back to private chambers 'til the situation was controlled. The US Marshall restrained Janice and placed her in the cellblock. A contempt of court charge kept her there for days. When Janice was released, the court initiated a six-month evaluation period to assess the future of the children. The last I heard, the children had not been returned to her custody.

Silvia Williams was another involved guardian. She was nineteen but a welfare mother for years. She had two boys... ages two and four. Both were present when the drug raid went down. Silvia denied knowing about the drug sales. She was there so her kids could play with other kids. Social Services had no records on her family. Slurred speech and highballed eyes, however, raised a suspicion she may be a drug user. A mandatory drug test was ordered. If tested negative, her children would be returned. If not, her kids would stay under the Court's custody until an intervention was completed. Silvia wasn't happy with this action but decided not to challenge the system. Unfortunately, Silvia tested positive. Years later, she still hadn't kicked her drug habit.

Sheila Canton, Buella Johnson, and Regina Edwards were parents scheduled to approach the bench. All did acknowledge it was irresponsible to accept those stupid dinner invitations. The Court had no histories on them. The Judge would return their children after a social services investigation.

I took the mothers back to their apartments in my effort to establish police rapport. Each accepted my offer. This was a mistake on my part. By doing so, I came to realize I could never accept their daily living arrangements.

Remember the rats I saw in that alley? They also resided in Sheila Canton's apartment. Buella Johnson had roaches by the thousands. All of Regina's utilities had been turned off. The stench of stale air, kerosene lamps, and soiled mattresses were the norms of each apartment. Attitudes of resident tenants were… "Please, stay out of my business."

"I've got enough trouble of my own. Keep me out of your police-related stuff!"

These mommas' made it absolutely clear they would do whatever I asked to get their kids back. "Please return my kids back to me!" each requested with that sexual look in her eyes. "Nothing must jeopardize those precious welfare checks!" I kept thinking.

Regina was the last mother I escorted back to her apartment. She was a good looker who would sell her body to the highest bidder when rent was due… but only if the rent was due. Otherwise, she carried her head high and was respected by those who didn't know her. Regina changed into something nice and short. It was a linen material… real easy to see through. The dainty material fell inches below her nice bow-legged self. "No kids around. Why don't you stay awhile?" she eagerly suggested.

I stared at Regina as if I didn't care. I would not be compromised... not tonight. Regina came closer. She gently touched me. I pushed her away... she touched me again and a kiss followed. Regina was a desirable woman. She extended her hand... and stepped backward each time I stepped forward. She kept her fingertips just out of my reach. Each step took me closer to her bedroom door.

"Mr. Policeman Bishop, you can have my body as my appreciation for helping me get my kids back tomorrow!" she whispered. "Not only tonight... but I will belong to you forever for saving the lives of my kids!" she added. "Please say you want me. You're the only real man I know!"

My commitment to this great big little town took control of my senses. I could not violate my sworn oath to protect the citizens of Sircus Junction.

If I agreed to please this woman, my name would be on the tip of her tongue every time she got in trouble with the law... especially in Family Court. I raced out the apartment door. Regina thought I was crazy to turn down her offer. I wasn't amazed at such gestures. Other mothers have tried before. I declined those offers with much less fanfare. More importantly, I witnessed an up-close and personal reality of each child's world.

My importance as a crime fighter diminished. I never thought assisting helpless children was important to Sircus Junction. It didn't take much additional thought. I finally decided what I wanted to do for the remainder of my police career. There I stood... a major crime detective... with many years of experience in a number of hell-raisin' capacities. Yes. It's time to make an interesting life change. Somehow, someway, I needed to provide a more valuable service to this community. The timing was right. Oh, so right.

I made my wishes known to the District Commander. He was in no hurry to support my career-changing decision. He now thought I'd make a great future officer. He did not want to lose me to another capacity. I had political pressure applied by an old golf partner... the Honorable Mayor Harrison. I discreetly mentioned an old friend of his... Ms. Barbara Woodson. The Mayor approved my transfer at a higher pay grade. He did so without too much hesitation.

Investigating the unknown was the best part of an officer's job. Never boring, each shift brought with it a new job description. Placing your life on the line night after night came with few "thank yous." The world of Child Abuse and Neglect would be a totally different experience. Baby-faced smiles were enough of a thank you for this veteran warrior. Their little frowns affected my daily levels of self-esteem. Baby frowns verified I had changed the course of someone's life.

These special children might become future policemen. Or, they might become dreaded politicians... all because a stranger showed them a little love a long, long, time ago. The children won't remember my assistance in upcoming years. They won't feel the warmth of my touch, the happiness in my heart, or the "Thank you, Mr. Policeman" they were thinking but were too young to speak. I will remember every one of them... forever! How could I not!

The greatest thing we can do in life is to help our fellow man! I'm simply helping my fellow... little man!

Wow! What a powerful feeling! I'm all in! No one died during that drug raid. My Mod Squad leadership spread throughout the Police District. I had become a great leader while actually scared to death. A respect I hadn't sought was commendable. Other officers expressed a desire to work under my supervision. Even McKee had good things to tell the Mayor. McKee tried to get me permanently transferred to his Narcotics Squad. No way that was going to that happen... especially since it was McKee who pushed me inside that door before my order was given. I've not forgotten how the Captain and two Lieutenants disappeared on that infamous evening? Am I stupid enough to think the first person through dark doors with a shotgun had a long shelf life? And, for what? To prevent ownership of the same weed and white powder found on tables at Friday night police poker games? No honorable longevity in that! None whatsoever!

My wish for a new beginning will be a healthy one. I embarked on a new career as a Child Abuse & Neglect Detective without further hesitation.

I needed some rest before my official transfer. I took time off to drift far away from the daily grind of everyday police life. I called these personal relief days... Criminal Holidays!

During this down time, I relaxed my mind. I got as far away from the stress of Cops and Robbers as possible. I would think only about social issues relevant to my sanity. I'd seek out the biggest shade tree in Lincoln Park and do more of my philosophizing... as I called it. I really loved my quiet time. I'd sit there enjoying nothing but freedom of thought. My mind would travel several decades ahead. I'd think about everything. Things like... "What did the world look like in the far future?"

Things like..."How are individual contributions to mankind measured?"

And, things like... "What kind of sin-free world could I really develop?"

That sounds crazy, huh?

CHAPTER 5

Jillian Esther Carson-Calloway was my second wife. I was her first husband. She's well educated. She hails from a family of strong values. Her parents have been married for forty-three years. That's a long time to love the same woman. Jillian wants our union to rival her parents. I'll give it a shot. Okay, there I go again… sharing too much of my personal life. But, I've gotta' talk to somebody, right?

I've witnessed stuff that's absolutely unreal since entering the twisted world of Child Abuse and Neglect. I never imagined children went through such horrors. There's much more to learn about these investigations. I thought I had witnessed child abuse situations in my old neighborhood. The batterings… bruises… and neighboring kids left alone without proper parental care were nothing new to me. Nobody advised me about other types of child abuse and neglect. Nobody warned me of psychological stuff like depriving basic needs from a little child. I thought I was a real man in a real man's world. I thought I'd seen everything that could possibly happen to kids from my neighborhood back home. I didn't. I've since learned I required a broader understanding of the child abuser's personality. I also sought a better evaluation of the mindsets of my new Child Abuse Detective partners. They are a weird but efficiently bunch of investigators.

Det. Jack Roy Charleston is an Ivy League graduate. He constantly gets on my last nerve. His written police reports had to be perfect. He's nothing but a stupid lawyer who couldn't pass the Bar Exam. Tried four times I've been told. He uses legal jargon to prove he'll actually pass the Bar Exam someday. He tries to impress the Juvenile Court by stretching basic words into pages of ridiculous mumble jumble. That's just a hunch on my part.

Det. Mike Johnson's another investigator I'm still trying to figure out. He carries a pocketsize calendar. He calculates his retirement benefits every day he works. His retirement life is already structured. He knows the kind of retirement home he wants. He knows which State has the best retirement laws... like Florida. His financial portfolio is based on today's most current stock market values. Kinda' weird, huh? This got to be a bit much.

On the professional side, Det. Johnson spends a lot of energy keeping valid abuse complaints out of Family Court. He never earns overtime. He places a timely eight-hour shift ahead of anyone to be served. Since child neglect work is very subjective, it is easy to twist the truth. Det. Johnson reported most of his investigations lacked evidence to be presented to court... something he thought was a social waste of time. He's a depressing maniac.

My favorite wanna' be partner is the one and only Det. Lola Reed-Fletcher. She's the finest female on the department. She knows it. Very aware our high-ranking officers are suckers for nice breasts and a decent smile; she uses her sexy power to get whatever assignment she wants. This woman detective, God bless her soul, never met a person of power she didn't like. Gossip had it all she's gotta' do is to walk into any District Commander's office with a certain smirk of her face. When her sexual politics threatened careers, she was either transferred or promoted to keep her mouth shut (pardon the pun). Lola cared less what others thought as long as she wasn't foot patrolling on a cold night. No need for subordinate police levels to complain. There are lots of tight, cotton-laced panties climbing the promotional ladder in this big little town. Sircus Junction's police environment is no different than corporate America, the military, or any other political arena. Rumor has it Det. Fletcher keeps a secret little file loaded with departmental relationships. I hope she never loses it. A promotion would accompany the discreet return of its' valuable information. Another issue? I tried to get into Lola's pants years ago before I married Jillian. I've never been successful. Not even a sniff. I'm secretly jealous. I was never good enough for her. I was of no personal value to her because I couldn't advance her police career. Lola constantly teased me with her sexuality. I took her precious bait every time. Naive me. I would've given her everything I owned. She could be cashing my alimony checks and living in my beach house by now. All she had to do was say those magic words. The L word never had to enter our picture. Liking me a little would have been enough.

During roll-call sessions, male and female cops eagerly listened to hear who'd be Lola's assigned partner that day. Most times, I was the lucky guy. Precinct Commanders thought I was least likely to aggressively approach her during a midnight shift. They sorta' trusted me without trusting me. I was assumed to have honor and integrity. Yeah… right! My feelings for Lola drove me crazy!

Patrolling with Lola was pure torture. She's nothin' but a sexual nightmare. She'd sit inches to my right on the unmarked cruiser's front seat. I'd make a hard right turn. Her hips would slide open to the left and gently touch mine. Her skirt would rise an inch or two. Moments later, her manicured nails pulled it back down. I intentionally made several more hard right turns. And, some more hard right turns. Det. Lola Fletcher and I would drive around in circles for hours.

I was a loyal partner. I would've placed my life on the line for her. Lola never let her personal guard down for a moment.

I, on the other hand, didn't care what other officers' thought. Lola could have lied. She could've secretly told me she wanted me. Who was I going to tell? She wasted no sexual energy on me five years ago. I do remember that. She affected everybody. I mean everybody.

I wanted Detective Lola even more so during hot summer months. When the humidity was sky high, she wore nothing that didn't stretch a man's or woman's imagination. You heard right. Masculine female cops wanted Detective Lola as much as the men. She was an equal opportunity ball-buster. She knew exactly what she doing. "You'll never get any of this!" was written all over her face. I was satisfied I would never have her. The fellas' wouldn't believe me anyway. My ego wanted her all to itself. Her glances were all she would give. I accepted them. She's been talking to me more lately. She heard about my promotion. She heard about me becoming an instant hero. It's too late, Detective Lola darling! As much as I want your touch, I want Jillian Esther Carson-Calloway's touch even more.

Didn't really matter 'cause Lola was makin' out with a different Captain every month. Others and I were jealous. I've shared more about Lola than necessary. It took me a long time to get over this policewoman. Surely you understand why. Don't hate me.

My final office partner was Detective Beau Rodgers. Beau was the recipient of an enormous inheritance. He didn't give a darn about anybody. Beau tried to validate his existence by saving the under-privileged child on a daily basis. He was trying to give back to a community he never connected with. At least his philosophy sounded right. These were my Child Abuse and Neglect partners. You can see why I worked alone, when possible.

I received a radio call a moment ago. It came from Columbus High School on the north side of town. Sam Jacoby is the Vice-Principal. He recently opened a student's locker. He found something interesting inside.

I arrived twenty-five minutes later. Mr. Jacoby hadn't seen a certain student for several days. He tried to contact the child via telephone. The telephone number no longer worked. Emergency notification forms are attached to the inside of each student's locker. As Vice-Principal, he could enter a student's locker anytime he wished.

Mr. Jacoby found more than he was looking for. He took me into his office. He shut the door. He took a large manila envelope out of a private safe. He handed it to me. I opened the envelope top-down. Ten color photographs fell onto his desk. I stared at the photos. My experience as a child abuse detective soared to the next level. Graphic prints portrayed nude teenagers having sex in the privacy of somebody's home. That wasn't the only problem. The real problem was each person in the picture appeared to be a member from the same family. Mr. Jacoby verified that fact.

Whatever you can imagine about family incest, these pictures displayed that sexual position. Pleasured faces meant the teenagers enjoyed what they were doing. No coercion appeared present. This action had been captured on film. This sexual display was… how do I say… well over the line?

Why were these photos kept in a school locker? Were they being shared with other students, or being hidden from mom and pop? Aren't there state laws against sexually exploiting teenagers? These questions needed answers. I needed to become an instant expert on Child Incest Laws. How did I get from drug raids to here? I confiscated the photos and responded to the address found in the locker. I knocked on the door.

A young voice from inside asked, "Who are you? What do you want?" I identified myself as a Police Detective. I asked to speak to either parent. "Neither are here," replied the voice behind the door. After a lot of threatening, the voice rendered a telephone number for the parents. The father was contacted. A meeting was scheduled for later that evening.

I interviewed the father at 8:30 PM. I asked him about the photos. He said he violated no laws by allowing his kids to participate sexually amongst themselves. The Police Department had no reason for any criminal investigation.

His children–ages 13, 14 and 15–have never been forced to do anything. "They love each other as siblings as well as boy and girlfriends. We've allowed freedoms with their bodies!" he shouted with a stingy growl. "My wife and I don't prohibit their sexuality. Nudity is not a bad thing around this house. Neither my wife nor I participate in any way whatsoever!" he added.

This father was, at least, somewhat honest. Or, was he? My conscience kicked in. My experience as a crime fighter told me differently. Where did these kids learn this behavior? The parents didn't deny how the kids were raised. Someone introduced incest behaviors to this family. The probable suspects were the parents, of course. Thus, no more excuses. I assumed during the kids' development, both mom and pop interacted with the siblings in a sexual manner. I tried to rationalize this situation. I couldn't arrive at any other conclusion. The father spent the next few minutes explaining how his civil rights were violated. "The photos were obtained illegally. No way did anybody have the right to force open my son's locker," he said. Trespassing was not an issue in this case. The issue was a sexual one.

I explained to Papa his actions as a parent violated Child Incest Statutes. If true, I'd return tomorrow with arrest warrants. I made this fact known to the father. He, unfortunately, wouldn't acknowledge the seriousness of my words.

I approached Family Court the next morning. I sought legal interpretation of this scenario and what to do about it. "Entering school property was a no-brainer. The locker never belonged to the student?" said Dave Williams–Assistant D.A. "Lockers are school property. Students sign a Waiver of Rights at the beginning of each school year. Entrance can be gained at any time by the proper authority. Anything found can be used as evidence," he noted.

Do their actions violate incest statutes? Does parental acceptance violate the Criminal Code? The answers to both are yes. "What do you want me to do?" I asked the ADA. "Satisfy the complaint through Family Court," he replied. Minutes later, Family Court's Honorable Judge Art Brennan agreed a violation of Incest Laws had taken place. He subpoenaed the entire family to Family Court. "The parents aren't trying to leave the area. We need a hearing on this matter. The Court needs to order some kind of evaluation, maybe?" the ADA added.

I obtained legal opinions but no actual warrants. I returned to the house. I advised the parents of the court's intentions. The father agreed to nothing I said. He ordered me out of his house. I obeyed but said I'd return. I obtained warrants that night. Detectives and uniformed officers would assist me the next morning.

It was 6 a.m. when I rapped on the front door. Both parents were surprised to see an army of police personnel. I placed the warrant in the father's hands. There was a long moment of silence and several strange facial expressions. Each time an expression came my way, I returned a goofy one of my own.

Other officers were puzzled at this point. I understood why. Experience taught them certain expressions could mean a number of things... many of which were deadly. With teenagers all over the place, I took a softer stance. I allowed the parents time to think about this situation. I had a few minutes but not a lot of time. My police department peers were here in force. My leadership skills were being scrutinized. This was not the time for questionable leadership.

The father made a decision. He agreed to his children's temporary removal. He stepped away from the front door. He spoke the words, "Okay, then." I could hardly hear him speak.

He took several steps backward to allow us to enter. I cautiously entered the home. A dangerous tension was in the foyer.

Daddy's approval didn't seem sincere. It was an approval with no real commitment. It was a commitment with consequences. Sometimes all a cop has is a gut feeling. He must listen to it whether he wants to or not. It's survival related. Whatever. The father irrationally roamed the living room. I kept a close eye on him while teenagers put on their clothes. Last night's sleep was still in their eyes. A cloud of uncertainty hovered over their heads. I tried to interpret their baffling frowns. I had trouble doing so. One was of sorrow. Another was of relief. The lessened stress of finality was in the air. The stress of coveting a sibling was coming to an end. I wondered what would happen to them? They were good kids. They responded, "Yes sir" and "No sir" if asked a question. How could they be bad kids? Their clothes now on, they collected whatever essentials needed without much of a fuss. One by one they assembled near the front door. They awaited instructions from people they've met for the first time.

I allowed hugs and family goodbyes before removing children. Momma' completed her hugs and kisses. She told them not to worry. They'd be together soon.

Tears flowed down teenage faces. But... where's the father? What's he up to? I raced into the dining room. I observed the father reach into a small file cabinet under his desk. He peeked over his shoulder at me. I was about fifteen feet away. The father pulled a .38 Cal. Automatic out of the cabinet. He turned in my direction and yelled... "How I raise my children is none of your business!"

Everyone within range of his words froze. The father held the gun high in the air. His sweating finger was pressing against the trigger. I explained to him this criminal complaint was only a minor setback. Pointing a gun was a totally different matter.

"No one's hurt! Let's stop now!" I shouted. Several Detectives surrounded the father. There was a funny frown on Papa's face. We had apparently entered his private domain. I've seen that frown many times. It was the dreaded "Don't give-a-damn if I die!" expression! Three seconds ticked off the clock. On the third tick, Papa fired one shot into an officer's chest. This action was totally unexpected. The shock puzzled my comrades.

The distraught Papa rotated 180 degrees on the ball of his foot. He deposited two more shots into the hip of Det. Johnson. The detective fell to the floor. He didn't move. The father displayed a life-ending smile. He held the gun to his head. It was too late. The next shots fired came from every direction. Death had raised its ugly head.

Medics raced the injured to the nearest hospital. I sat on the front steps with a lot to say but totally speechless. How could such an incident happen? I always thought Child Abuse investigations were less dangerous. Under closer scrutiny, I never included the emotions of losing a loved one—let alone three loved ones. I know parental emotions are unpredictable. They can introduce feelings more hostile than the norm. The family ran to their father's side. It was an uncanny display as they wept over the body.

Remaining onlookers stared. They wiped away the tears. They, too, tried to figure out what happened on this unforgettable day. I felt cold inside. The world had stopped at my doorstep. I checked the cabinet for other weapons. None were found. I did find more explicit photos. They were all over the place. Not well hidden. No need to hide them anyway. Not in this household. Photos were marked as evidence. The family was taken to the precinct.

The teenagers were removed from the mother's custody. They were temporarily placed in a foster home. The case remained in the Court System for five or so years. With each passing year, each teenager advanced in age. As each reached eighteen, each was released from the Court's custody.

Guess where each new adult returned to live? They returned to their mother's home. They violated no laws by doing so. While the teenagers were out of the mother's custody, the mother did everything mandated by the Court. The Judge suspended her sentence. He defended his ruling by saying there was never any coercion on the parent's part.

Good or Bad. Right or Wrong. This Court system did all it could in this situation. It removed the children from an incest environment. It gave them freedom of choice as adults. Once that choice was made, there was nothing else to do.

I'm witnessing some of life's twisted circumstances. I have lots of work to do. This job takes a toll psychologically. I'm mentally exhausted. I'm aging faster than the norm.

A rest break became a priority. I went home. I flopped on my king-size bed. Dreaming helps me escape the depressing world of child abuse. Before I knew it, my futuristic world was upon me again. The more I think about a better universe... the more I'm recognizing the reality of it all. "This can be a better world! If someone has to create it... why not a wanna' be philosopher like me?" I wondered.

Don't get me wrong. I'm not as smart as I think I am. I'm simply a fool thinking so. "Isn't it my destiny to establish a better way of life?" I again wondered. "There has to be a way to a new beginning. Maybe... within my dreams... I could find those answers. I know I could find the right answers if I took a couple of those illegal pills I'm slightly hooked on."

I did just that and fell into a deep sleep. I awakened twenty-four hours later. I needed a few more days off. I had vacation hours to use or lose. I decided to use some of that. Police officers place tremendous value on how days off are used. It's important not to waste them. Days off normally include a fishing excursion. The last one's been a while. It's time for another. I contacted a bunch of fellas' at the last minute. Away we went!

Weird things are discussed during fishing trips. Everything mentioned is strictly confidential. Today's conversations will be documented in my special little book. I broke the rules doing so but never told the fellas' about it. You know how I am about writing things down.

I hope the fellas' forgive me!

My Dearest Friend,

It's common knowledge policemen love to fish on their days off. It doesn't matter how many fish are caught. It's about the camaraderie of it all. The daily pressures of saving lives are set aside so the mind can wander without restriction. We can only relax when no bad guys are around the next corner. Getting rested mentally is a hard thing to do sometimes. But, not today!

I contacted several police pals last night. I finalized a fishing trip on short notice. I said yes to the dreaded police twins known as the Mustard Brothers. I invited them as a last minute thought. I was surprised they said yes.

The Mustard Brothers were rarely invited to social gatherings. Their uncomfortable odors and unsanitary functions... including their legendary snort-sniggle-sniggle-poof fart noises... are too offensive for fellow officers and the general public. The Mustard Brothers are police department canine handlers. It is the smelliest job a police officer can have regardless the extra monetary stipend. That's how they got the name Mustard Brothers. I probably made a bad decision inviting them... but oh, well; a fish cares less whose hook it is. I can see several apologies comin' from me in the near future.

Our rented black mini-van had a bad muffler. It noisily crept across the mountaintop to the precinct's secret fishing stream. I was the designated driver for the first hour of travel.

We had special rules for these trips. Rule Number One: All conversations were banned until we reached the fishing destination.

Rule Number Two: Any comments made while fishing for that elusive Northern Pike were strictly confidential. Rule Number Three: We promised to do nothing but serious fishing from 4 a.m. to... maybe, whenever the first can of beer was opened. These rules were always enforced. If anyone violated the rules they were never invited to attend future excursions.

Soon after we arrived, each of us found a special fishing spot along the scenic Hathaway River shore. The only grumblings over the next several hours were unrepeatable curse words. The cursing suggested slippery adversaries were outsmarting us today. The only things biting this early morning were buck-toothed mosquitoes.

We acknowledged our failure to catch fish for a tasty lunch. We did the next best thing. We eagerly unwrapped the fried chicken and baloney and cheese sandwiches (hold the mustard) we had slapped together just in case the fish were pitchin' a shutout today. Containers of hot sauce were turned upside down. Lite-beer emerged from the stream's cool temperature.

The real fun begins after a six-pack or two. The "8th Annual Caveman Fishing Convention" was officially in progress. Jake and Calvin Mustard, Robert Phillips and I, Bishop Calloway, were the only chartered members at this session. Female gun-toters, spouses, and significant others were never allowed to attend special fishing events.

Sooner or later, our unique problems with the opposite sex would pierce the group's shallow concentration. This would alter our focus from Northern Pike to personal relationships. Well, that's how it usually happened.

Jake Mustard, the older twin by about thirty-two triflin' seconds, was the first to break the verbal ice. He sought some brotherly advise about his diminishing sexual attraction to June—his wife for twenty years. When seeking intimacy, he has to guess when the wifee-gal was in the mood. Jake's been guessing poorly over the last year or so and he's tired of the inactivity. Jake saved this question for us fishing pals 'cause he knew we were well educated when it comes to talking 'bout women.

As an option, Jake decided to wait until his wife made the first move. That way, he could take advantage of her without having to guess. June, his wife, made no first moves and really didn't intend to. June told Jake she wanted no intimacy because his sanitary issues were embarrassing to her peer group.

"Wowwwww...!" we collectively mumbled. Jake talked to June about this nonsense. June indicated her desire to be loved on a daily basis, and not just when he wanted her to play a game of catch with his sperm! "Now, come on, fellas'?" Jake sincerely asked. "What does June mean when she says stupid stuff like that?"

Jake would never cheat on sweet June 'cause he loves her to death! Jake's given June everything a credit card can buy. If you include the value of maintaining a secure job for decades, Jake feels he has the right to her intimacies at least a couple times a month? "Okay, guys? My true-blue brothers?"... Jake struggled. "Are my needs out of whack or is June just crazy?"

Calvin Mustard, the younger brother, looked around the campfire. He wanted to see who'd be the first to verbally help his older brother with the right words. I couldn't be the first to respond 'cause... I accidentally spilled coffee on my shirt at that very moment. I really did. I really did... really!

Robert was our resident nerd. He sheepishly looked away and started pickin' his nose. I guess neither Robert nor I wanted any part of Jake's ridiculous problem.

Calvin finally spoke up to help a brother out... literally! Listening to two brothers have a decent conversation was always a real treat. It normally resulted in a "best user of very descriptive curse words" contest. Anyway... Calvin chimed, "That same kind of situation happened to me a while back."

"My funky first ex-wife kept telling me I was exaggerating. So, for the next six months, I kept a calendar diary. I wrote down every time she and I were intimate. I wrote down which one of us got things started."

"The next time we argued about the lack of intimacy I was armed with nothing but the facts."

"I was ready with my research and I successfully proved my side of the story," he added.

Calvin's first ex-wife went absolutely bananas. She couldn't believe he recorded their sexual history. She freaked out and resisted his approaches after that. Calvin knew the beginning of the end was near. He tried to save that relationship but nothing worked. "She became a witch on a mission to destroy!" he whimpered.

"It's been a while, though. I still don't understand why she left me," Calvin retorted.

He bowed his head. He became silent as a mouse. A sincere tear or two quietly rolled from Calvin's cheek onto his baloney and cheese sandwiches… hold the mayo. We, a loyal but concerned audience, honored his unspoken silence by throwing him an unopened bag of Sour Mustard Potato Chips and a flat bottle of Battlefield Co-cola. A crunch or two turned Calvin's smile from upside down to right side up within minutes. Our rescue team brought Calvin's damaged ego back to the real world. "Thanks, fellas!" he proclaimed. "I really needed your sensitivity when I lost it a minute ago!" We collectively shrugged our shoulders in buddy-like fashion… told Calvin he was loved and passed the pickled frog eggs without losing a beat.

Robert had the longest lasting relationship of anyone attending this convention. Yet, when he spoke about women issues, he was rarely taken seriously. In fairness, and because we only brought him along to drive us home, we voted to allow his ridiculous contributions to be heard. And, so they were.

Robert's suggestions about relationships were short and sweet. "Jake and Calvin should pay more attention to their lovers on a daily basis," he started. "By their own admission, the only time they paid attention to their significant others were when they wanted some nookie. There lies the problem." "Both were only interested in the results of a conquest. Neither Jake nor Calvin considered connecting with their woman's mind, heart and soul in advance," he added. A strange silence captured the fishing camp. Nothing was spoken until Calvin shouted, "Where did that Dr. Phil-like nookie stuff come from? You've been listening to that television, huh?" Jake asked.

Robert wasn't done speaking. He suggested the mighty Mustard Brothers do the little things most spouses would appreciate. "Do them on a daily basis. Not only when you seek attention!" he scolded. "Shower your women with love and appreciation… all the time! I'd bet a bag of 7-Eleven donuts they'll return that affection in more ways than one," he added.

"Being the recipient of a one-way love affair is not a very good relationship. And, there's one more thing, fellas'," Robert continued. "If you stupid knuckleheads don't want my two cents… keep your sloppy, insensitive mouths shut!" he screamed.

I twisted an apology from the Mustard Brothers for embarrassing Robert. It took a whole lot of beggin' for it to happen. I had to actually eliminate several poker game IOU's the Mustard Brothers still owed me.

The Mustard Brothers acknowledged the hurt they directed at this gentle, loving man. Jake did something I thought never he'd do. He leaned over and sincerely apologized. He put his hand on Robert's shoulder, looked him in the eye, and sarcastically whispered… "Robert, I'm sorry if I twisted your little cotton panties in a knot! Please accept my apology. I'll do better, okay?"

Not to be outdone, Calvin followed with… "I'm sorry too, Robert! Here's ten bucks. Go buy yourself a box of butterfly tampons! You little sissy!"

The Mustard brothers turned and simultaneously flipped Robert the bird. They fell out laughing! I sorta' snickered too. I tried to conceal how funny the Mustard Brothers truly were. I wasn't successful.

Everyone agreed Robert had some pretty good points. As the group's registered nerd, "What could he possibly know about relationship intimacy?" we wondered. Robert turned. He caught my eye and stared at me with a frown as if to asked... "Why did you invite the Mustard brothers on this fishing excursion? You know they ain't worth the time!"

I shook my head in silent agreement. Robert's eyes were absolutely right. The Mustard Brothers were a mess. It was too late to do anything about it.

Calvin again asked for our attention. He wanted to discuss another situation affecting his relationship. His request was granted. To obtain a specific number of monthly intimacies with his second ex-wife, Calvin designated Thursday nights as official intimacy night.

Calvin and his second ex-wife, Mary, thought this would take the guesswork out of the best time to feel intimate. When those weekly scheduled dates arrived, Mary wasn't necessarily in a romantic mood. If her mood wasn't right that day, Mary didn't feel she had to substitute another day within that same week.

Based on previously agreed upon rules, Nancy incorrectly assumed she could wait 'til the following week or for the next Thursday to arrive. She would honor that date, again, but only if her mood was right. "At times, Mary's mood didn't kick in for several weeks," Calvin added. "She's not keeping the weekly schedule like we agreed."

Calvin said Mary agreed to the schedule because she thought it would work. She now swears the truth is that... it hasn't. The arrangement virtually eliminates spontaneity. It has hindered her ability to feel intimate at any given time.

"Predicting attractiveness is hard to do. I rarely felt horny on Thursday nights," Mary griped. "I don't know why. Maybe because it's the best cable-tv watching night? You don't even remember I'm a woman until ESPN goes off!" she added. "When I do feel hot, you've shown no interest in me." "Approaching intimacy this way seems to be nothing but misplaced lust. It's not a loving, tender, or special moment between two married people. It's easy to turn off my fantasies. So, why bother?" she added.

You can imagine the response Jake and I had to Calvin's punishment. We voiced our displeasure. His wife's reluctance to live up to her womanly expectations was a bogus move (especially for not doubling up the following week). What kind of wife was she anyway?

We chastised Calvin for only seeking Mary out once a week. Mary and he should've scheduled intimacy a minimum of three times a week and then... maybe then... they would've been successful at least once... Duuuuuh? No sireee! Weeks without intimacy are socially intolerable.

Robert, our resident nerd... disagreed, of course. He reinforced the desire for two loving partners to interact emotionally and physically on a daily basis. Robert said making love doesn't always have to mean being intimate. It could mean touching, hugging, kissing, and many times just talking to one another.

To prove his point, he suggested we experiment with his theory. The next time we were in a loving atmosphere, we should attempt to make love to our partners without actually performing any intimate acts. A questionable... "Yeah, Right!" slipped off our lips at his funky suggestion.

"Passionate words will surely excite your mate," Robert guaranteed. "Caressing her with no hidden agenda will stimulate her even more. If acts of kindness were consistently given, even losers like you fellas' would have fewer problems to complain about. Good social intercourse skills normally lead to consistent sexual activities," insisted a goofier Robert.

"This occurs because one partner wishes to please the other. Even if a partner's lust isn't raging on any particular night, it doesn't equate to a hand's off sexual approach by the other," added Robert.

Jake, Calvin or I didn't care about Robert's opinion on this delicate matter. We acted like we were listening so he would finally shut up. Now that Jake and Calvin had finished their confessin', I reluctantly decided to share a problem of mine. It wasn't a sexual question. It's one that directly affects having a more pleasant relationship with my spouse.

"*Here goes, fellas'*," *I shared. "When my wife asks me to wash dishes, take out the trash, or cut the grass... why does she get so moody when I don't do it right that second?" I asked clinching my teeth.*

"*These untimely requests are really startin' to get to my nerves!*" *I moaned. "Everybody knows the trash truck won't arrive 'til 7 tomorrow mornin'! Another hour or so won't affect how long the grass grows! And, as for the dishes, I'll wash every one of 'em after tonight's football game! Okay, maybe my actions border on being inconsiderate of her wishes. Yet, why do these discussions turn into such huge arguments?" I asked by now big-eared comrades.*

I waited patiently for valuable feedback from my fellow caveman fishermen. All three were as quiet as a church pew on Mondays. Even Robert, the nerd, was speechless. "Okay. Maybe you guys didn't understand my question?" I surmised. "Yes. That's it! You simply needed more information! Well... it's like this fellas'. If I don't jump exactly when she wants me to do something, seconds later she'll start washing the dishes herself. She'll immediately take out the trash. And, she'll start mowing the grass... all without any help from me!"

"*This reaction isn't the norm. Does her patience need to be addressed?" I asked. "I'd then begin to feel guilty for something I knew nothing about."*

"*So, I'd go do those things she requested. I'd do them that very moment."*

"*But, get this, guys! While I'm outside mowing that stupid grass, or takin' out the trash a day earlier than necessary, she's inside the house cheering for my local football team! There's something's wrong with this picture, right?" I asked. "Don't women understand that football games have a scheduled time? Don't our wives understand the game won't wait until minor chores around the house are completed?"*

Another quiet hit the campfire. No one had anything verbal to offer. Minutes later, still no response to my issues. "Ok. Here's an easier question for you bone-headed group of law enforcement morons!" I yelled.

"*What does it mean when Princess, my little wife's nickname, snatches the newspaper out of my hands, or turns off the television during an overtime game, and demands quality time? We've been together for five years. What kind of quality time is she be referring to?*"

I finally got some body movement from these pinheads. Jake and Calvin shook their heads in utter disbelief. "*And, we thought we had female problems, huh?*" *said Jake as he sarcastically winked at Calvin and Robert.*

"*Our problems are only about intimacy! Yet, yo' precious little wife Princess won't even let you watch a football game? Maybe you need to play a game of tennis with her head! You ever heard of a... backhand, huh?*"

"*Jake! I'm not finished!*" *I yelled.*

"*My Princess... she'd sit right next to me on the couch. She'd look directly into my eyes and calmly say... Let's talk!*"

"*I, stunned at this request, honestly responded... Okay. Whatcha' wanna' talk about?*" *She'd then scream,* "*About us, stupid! What else?*" *My macho ego would then take over. I'd counter with something like...* "*Oh, no you didn't! If I had something to say I would've already said it!*" *And, that's when our relationship started dissolving.*

"*For the life of me, can you fellas' shed some light on my situation? Can't anyone tell me what it means when a woman says, 'Let's talk?' And, you really don't have anything to talk about?*"

Jake and Calvin called my situation a bad case of spousal nagging. They chalked it up as a natural disrespect found within the hearts of all females.

"*Hummmm?*" *I thought.* "*That's not a bad response from two fella's who flunked High School Cafeteria... Twice!*" *I'll give it some thought.*

It didn't take long for Robert to open his nasty but brilliant mouth. "*When Princess requests your help, you must satisfy that request at that exact moment. She very well knew the football game was in over-time. That football game was only a coincidence to her request.*"

"Look here, Bishop," he continued. *"A valuable component of real love is sacrificing something for the other. It matters not what you're doing at the time. Women love the fact you're making an effort without griping. They view your efforts as a true statement of caring! Admit it, guys. Aren't women more important than a stupid football game? Satisfying them should always be your most important issue!"* he concluded... *but still wasn't finished.*

"In retrospect, what if your woman was enjoying a good book when your manly urges kicked in? Wouldn't you feel more loved if she put the book aside and responded to your needs? That novel she was reading was as important to her as that football game was to you!"

"For you knuckleheads who never took time to learn this fact, women feel lots of affection at times... but other times... they need a refill of love's emotion from us!"

"Here's an example," he said. *"When you're readin' the sports page, she might feel loved watchin' you read that crappy newspaper. Her internal love tank's full when that's happening."*

"There are other times, however, she'd rather spend that precious time talking to you. That same newspaper will not be appreciated at that moment? So, if you don't put that paper down, she thinks the paper is more important to you than she is! When that happens, she'll yank it from your hands and scream... Let's Talk! This simply means her love tank needs refilling!"

"There is a caveat," said the now smarty-pants Robert fella'.

"Filling her love tank doesn't mean being intimate in the next 60 seconds! It takes a lot of effort to fill a woman's huge love tank. Otherwise, she'll know you're only trying to get back to that stupid football game or crappy newspaper. Your women are not that dumb... and, neither are you! I hope!" he shouted.

"I know we're all goofy cops with twisted theories of what love's all about. We gotta' understand what it takes to refill a woman's love tank! If you do it right... she'll read that newspaper and watch that football game with you."

Robert had everybody's attention. He was startin' to sound like a robotic Dr. Phil. "I want all of you to add value to your relationship's love tank by eliminating the attention you might direct to that television. And, here's the trick!" he whispered.

"Start filling her love tank while watching a TV show she wants to watch! Or, tell her how much you really love her while she's reading her favorite novel."

"If she pushes you away... remember the exact words she used to defuse your approach. Repeat them out loud so she knows you clearly heard what she said. Then say something nice to let her know you value her time... even though 'your' macho love tank needs re-fillin' also! Got it?"

"There is an astonishing Catch 22," he kept goin'. "You can talk to her about anything... as long as the conversation is strictly between the two of you. As you hug, chat, and do the rest of that honey stuff, you're rapidly refilling her need 'to be' loved and her need 'to' love energy levels. Neither process takes all day! It's something you must do... especially if you desire more moods of intimacy!" Robert decried.

Jake, Calvin and I listened with open minds. "How does Robert know so much about women?" we wondered. "Since he knows so much about chicks, why doesn't he share one of his relationship problems?"

Robert heard our thoughts. He chimed right in. He never gave it a second thought. He told us about a past situation involving he and his one and only wife. When they consummated their marriage years ago, they'd never before discussed their intimacy needs. They experimented a little bit to learn more about what the other wanted but gave it little thought.

Robert enjoyed all types of touching. His wife, in retrospect, did not. This was a major problem but they married anyway.

To make his marriage work, Robert suppressed his desires for the next couple of years. Margaret, meanwhile, was satisfied with their status quo. She never knew Robert's needs were unfulfilled.

Robert finally asked her for a more exciting relationship. Margaret refused. She said certain acts of intimacy were things she'd never do. *Robert should have made those desires known while they were dating. Somewhat devastated, Robert stopped seeking intimacy from Margaret. Robert would love her regardless. This fascinating cop now had the attention of everyone on this fishing excursion. His problems were more interesting than any bold-faced lies we could offer. We couldn't wait to hear how his situation ended. We asked Robert tons of serious questions like... Wasn't the lack of intimacy unfair to him?"*

"Isn't it difficult when a woman doesn't care?"

"Didn't Margaret know you could seek satisfaction elsewhere?"

The final, stupid question shot out of Calvin's mouth... "Does your wife have any sisters who like getting drunk at frat parties?"

Duuuhhh?????

Robert heard every one of our questions. He shook his head disgustedly. He refused to answer any more questions until our ecstatic cavemen ears had calmed down.

We opened the last 6-pack of Miller-Lite Beer. We patiently sat on the river's edge with our mouths wide open. We looked like kids about to learn new stuff in kindergarten.

Robert took a deep breath. He appeared thankful to find a group of loyal fellas' he could share things with. We recognized a bit of un-trust in his voice but... then again, we were his best friends, right? He must have known we had his back. We, too, felt the psychological pain he's gone through over time.

By sharing this pain with us, maybe Robert wasn't such a nerd, after all. Huh?

Yeah, Right.

The conclusion we waited for soon came. Robert thought sex of any kind outside of marriage wasn't the correct way to fix his problem. He approached his wife. He stated how certain intimacies were satisfying. He asked why they weren't desirable to her.

Margaret started crying. She told Robert any touching was considered taboo during her younger years. Intimacy was never an open conversation in her household.

She didn't mind being in certain positions. She would never, however, reciprocate. Robert was a sensible man. He immediately suggested marriage counseling. We, a band of irrational cavemen cops, suggested he seek out a blonde who wasn't inhibited about nothing!

Either way, Robert and Margaret worked hard to solve their problems. Through counseling, Robert found out hurtful family memories were a major part of Margaret's life. Those memories had never been addressed so a healing could begin.

Robert went silent. We tried to coerce more secrets out of him. His facial expressions refused. He'd already shared too much of his private life. He did remind us about our Oath of Confidentiality.

Robert smiled a brotherly smile. He tearfully sat down for an internal thought. All of us, again, were quiet. A new love for our brotherhood clouded the naïve mindsets of three out of four cops. The sunset reflected off the special stream. A long day of fishing or... confessing... was coming to an end. Sandwich bags were empty. Beer bottles were restocked in their returnable cartons. Only one netted 5 lb. Northern Pike snuggled between an abundance of melting ice cubes. We would eventually flip a coin to see who took that lone ranger home.

No one felt like talking. There was nothing else to say. Each fisherman processed the day's value. We wondered how much of this newly learned relationship stuff would affect the lovers we're going home to see.

The Mustard's rehearsed a sure-fire forgiveness plea while repacking the mini-van. It was an apology taught to them by Robert... Mr. Know it All.

I sat alone. I calmly wrestled with my "best way to love a woman" guilt factor. I had to do so all by myself.

Robert tried to get a tan with the last Sun of the day. He had a sarcastic smirk on his face. He'd finally collected long overdue I.O.U.'s from knucklehead cops who would no longer call him a professional nerd. I'm sure he'll never let us forget this educational day.

We completed the packing. I watched under the tip of my baseball cap as Robert, our newest leader... followed a secret gravel road to a familiar turnpike merge.

The Mustard Brothers, never satisfied, fought over the remaining leg space in the vehicle while pushing out more unwanted poof, sniggle, sniggle, fart, and gag bodily sounds.

Robert was warned time after time to drive carefully during the return trip home. After all, the only reason we originally brought that nerdy sucka' along was to drive us back after a very tiring day.

Okay... you know that's a lie! The truth's obvious, isn't it? We, an unbearable group of city cops, annually fished Robert's brain tryin' to find a way to enhance personal relationships we're afraid of losing!

'Nuff said! Having achieved that goal... the "8th Annual Caveman's Fishing Convention" officially came to a close!

We arrived safely back in the city. Unspoken anticipation was already on the faces of my fellow fishermen. The Mustard Brothers quickly exited the mini-van. They raced home to demonstrate newly learned philosophies of love to their significant others.

Good luck to them. They'll need it. I, on the other hand, headed south on Main Street to Jo-Jo Baxter's Fish House.

I'm a very faithful husband. I shouldn't have to buy some gilled evidence to prove I've been fishing all day. I will because my marriage has been kinda' shaky lately. Jillian is starting to question my hours away from home. No way was I going back into that house empty handed. Jillian had pretty good investigative skills. I'll take no chances.

Jo-Jo Baxter's Fish House had lots of seafood on ice but no Northern Pike. Didn't matter. Jillian loved any fish as long as it was fresh. She didn't care if the fish was from freshwater or saltwater. She doesn't know the difference. No need to explain today.

I purchased 25 lbs. of anything slippery enough to turn the grease brown. I had the heads yanked off. I split 'em right down the middle like always.

Explaining why I netted nothing but burps, farts, and empty beer bottles was not something I felt like doing. I'd never returned empty handed. No need to start now (Thanks to Jo-Jo Baxter's).

The remainder of the evening was calm as the wonderful smell of hot grease filled the air. A lightly battered white fish was being fried on high. I surrounded each piece of fish with my grandma's secret cold slaw. It's a messy combination or herbs and spices. It's been a family secret for years. Please don't ask for its' ingredients. Never gonna' happen! Like I said. It's an old secret.

My inquisitive Princess found it hard to argue on a stomach full of fish.

Oh yeah... I forgot something. If you cook the fish just right... it kinda' fills up a woman's love tank. I had Jillian licking cornmeal off her fingertips by her second piece.

Thank God! That special crease in her smile I hadn't seen in awhile had returned. It probably didn't mean too much so I won't over-react. I eagerly washed the dishes. I took out the trash without being told! No biggie. I cut the grass even though it didn't need cutting... it wasn't too dark.

And... you're so right! I'm doing this because... I am the man I am! Never said I wasn't.

Jillian's intimate responses were truly welcomed. She didn't know it but she never had a chance to decline my subliminal advances. I had filled her love tank via unsolicited considerations around the house. You could say I'd learned a valuable lesson. I know other kinds of communication are very important to the sustaining of real love.

Also, if you wanna' think as a caveman, you can say a stomach full of fish, grandma's slaw, and dish washin' chores were decent forms of approved communications! You get to make the call! I did. Tomorrow's another day. With it comes other challenge of life.

Peace!

I went to bed that night with a smile on my face. I closed my eyes. I swallowed no pills… yellow, blue, or otherwise. I was proud of myself!

CHAPTER 6

Months went by. I've been too busy to think about a new world. I still investigate Child Abuse Complaints for a living. Included in this group are the Abandoned Child Complaints. There's never a day without one. I'm referring to kids left unsupervised. I'm referring to kids left on somebody's doorstep. I'm talking about discarded babies found face-down in neighborhood trash dumpsters. Such calls are common in this big little town.

I'll spare you the grief of describing each situation. I'll talk about them another time. Please forgive me. I don't want to appear rude but Jillian Esther Carson-Calloway... my lovely princess of five years... is on my back again!

I know it sounds like I don't care. I do. She wants to have an honest discussion about our personal relationship. Tonight's the night! Sooooooo... I selected a great restaurant to satisfy Jillian Esther Carson-Calloway's selfish request. I tend to use her full name when she's pissing me off! Tonight I'll take her to *IBERO's*—an expensive Spanish restaurant located in the center of town. I need to make something perfectly clear. Jillian has been the foundation of our marriage for years. She anchored everything we've accomplished as husband and wife. I mean this emotionally. I mean this religiously.

I work long hours for the sake of the family. I do so for the overtime money. The extra cash keeps things afloat. I'm proud of myself as a provider. Working long hours are things good husbands do to become better fathers. These traits are needed for a relationship's survival. I also do this so Jillian can concentrate on her motherly responsibilities. She surely must know this. Having made this confession... "Why does Jillian Esther Carson-Calloway want to talk to me?"

She's the best mother a child could have. She finds time to take care of my needs as a husband... as a man... a very sexual man. She enjoys the fruits of our intimacies. She seems pleased with her life so far. What else could be out there?

Jillian can shop for clothes whenever she desires. She hangs out with her girlfriends any night she chooses. She doesn't even get interrogated when she returns! I do trust her. I wish I knew more about this upcoming discussion. I could better prepare for it. I think I know what it is. I'll bet her motherly responsibilities are smothering her. I'll bet her personal identity needs more nurturing. She has little opportunity to do so because of the kids. I betcha' that's what this lovey-dovey talk's all about.

Sacrifice is the name of the game isn't it? Sacrifice. If you look in the dictionary under that word... you'll see my picture. I give the ultimate sacrifice. I gave up my identity to give this family all it needs. Jillian, likewise, may have to put her personal growth on hold. It's nothing more than another's sacrifice. I hope I can explain it to her as easily as I just did to myself. There's one way to find out so... off we went... to *IBERO's*.

I started the evening correctly. I complimented her outfit. Shoes. Hair. Fingernails.I opened the passenger door. She really liked that. I kept a smooth, non-threatening conversation during the ride. This made her smile.

I inquired about her day with the kids. I forced her to laugh every now and then.

I talked about the value of family. I talked about the value of love. Things like that were easy to do.

Jillian Esther Carson-Calloway was a gorgeous woman. She was more so when her hairstyle perfectly surrounded her face. I helped her with that a lot. I loved calling her full name even when I wasn't pissed off. It was such a great name. It was a name with character. It was a loving name. It was a proud name. It's... well... ahem... actually an extension of my name! It stimulates me sometimes just saying it.

I loved this woman. I always have. I always will. What else could a husband ask for? The anticipation of our dreaded talk was killing me. Okay. Maybe there's another child on the way? Maybe my dragon-lady mother-in-law was visiting us again? What the heck could the important issue be? I'll find out pretty soon.

We arrived at *IBERO's*. Jillian was wearing the shortest skirt and blouse combination I'd seen in a while. She was very appealing on this special occasion. The parking attendant stole a glimpse of her personals as she exited the car. A quick rise in his pants became apparent. I'll let this dude's wishful thinkin' go tonight. I've gotta' be on my best behavior. No tip though.

We entered the front door. Everybody gazed at my little princess. I paid the host fifty bucks to seat us at the best table. The table, of course, placed Jillian's back to the front door. I thoughtfully held her chair. When the waiter appeared, we started the evening with a bottle of *Restarente' Chianti*. Jillian loves that stuff. It's expensive. She drinks it like water.

I smirked. It stimulates the sexual nature in her. Who knows? I might get lucky later.

We quickly consumed several bottles. And... It happened. The discussion. The discussion I didn't want to have was on the way. Here it comes. Jillian sat back in her chair. She held my hands and started speaking. I listened with open ears. Jillian didn't understand why our personal time had dwindled to nothing. "Since you transferred to that Child Abuse Unit... I never see you anymore!" she said. "Every time we're about to be intimate, that stupid beeper explodes and off you'd run... chasing some crazed child abuser!"

Jillian wasn't finished. She rolled her eyes. She added... "Your discipline towards the kids has eroded. Their respect for parental authority is at non-existent levels."

She quieted down, leaned backwards, and twisted her lips. She awaited my response. I simply sat there, totally amazed. I was dumbfounded. The expression on my face showed it. I didn't agree her accusations were valid. I truly loved Jillian. I needed her. How could she say I had no time for her and the kids? I worked a minimum of seventy man-hours every week. I worked a double shift on most days.

I did long hours so Jillian could watch soap operas during the day. I did this so she could visit shopping malls when she wasn't watching the kids. When I wasn't chasin' child abuse complaints, I was always in her arms at home. There were a few precious minutes I was sleeping. But, for the remaining seconds of every day, I was in her company. As I saw it, her complaints were... *BOGUS!*

I did agree on one thing. My level of discipline was nonexistent, but justifiable. My constant interaction with neglected children caused said reductions. I observed parents charged with child abuse violations every single day... even if abuses were unintentional. As much as I wanted to discipline to the kids, I'd die if an abusive incident found its way into our happy home.

I'd become too afraid to lay a hand or anything else on the kids. I'm afraid of the consequences of an injury. A criminal complaint is attached to a parent for life! I would not let this happen to me. To us!

Jillian was speechless for a couple of seconds. She suggested we revisit the discipline problem another time. I agreed in my silence, I guess. We ordered and finished several more bottles of Chianti. Jillian's hazel eyes took control of me. I knew something else verbal was on the way. "I need more of you if we're to keep this marriage alive," she whispered. This comment caught me off guard. I, motionless, had no immediate response. Jillian was the woman of my life. I needed her special kind of love. I needed her presence to balance my emotional mindset. I needed her gentle touch so I could be successful in my line of work. I worshipped the ground this woman walked on. I really did. She needed to know this fact in the most sincere way possible.

I reached across the table. I grabbed her tender hands. I softly stroked the middle of her palms. (Errol Flynn did this to Betty Davis in a movie. Jillian didn't know Errol Flynn the actor. I was safe.) Sorry, I digressed. I gazed into Jillian's adorable hazel eyes. I seriously apologized for being inconsiderate of our marriage vows. "I will always... always... always... and another always... love only you!" I said in my sexiest voice.

Jillian smiled. She actually squirmed a sensual acceptance. She tightened her knees. She swiveled back and forth in her chair. "What is she doing?" I wondered. "Why is she so antsy?" My cool demeanor allowed Jillian to regain her self-control. We started communicating again. She spoke of breaking the marriage longevity record held by her parents. We had no realistic chance of doing that 'cause her parents were still alive and kickin'! (I didn't mean to say it that way!) Jillian said she was all mine if I truly wanted… "To have and to hold 'til death do us part!"

Ah-Ha! That's what this personal chat is all about! Jillian's love tank is empty... again! I must thank Robert the next time I see him. Jillian's smile resurfaced. Remember that dangerous crease in her smile I saw way back when? It was back! It's obvious. I've gotta' recapture the love we had at the beginning. Yes. True love has to be a very big part of our future! I must do something out of the ordinary right now. I must demonstrate to Jillian she's as special now as she was years ago.

IBEIRO's was getting crowded. Conversations within earshot were similar to mine. Lots of the fellas' were holding another loved one's hands. Loving couples were peering into each other's eyes. Special bottles of whatever were constantly being uncorked. Words of appreciation flowed from everyone's lips... not caring who was overhearing the content of conversation. The strength of my marriage recommitment will now be tested. A willingness to say personal things in front of unknown ears was and always will be a true test of love.

Several romantic phrases I intended to use tonight had already been stated by that jerk sitting right behind Jillian. I had to change my verbal attack 'cause of that fact. Nope. I would not go there. Tonight is supposed to be Jillian's and my special night. "Those other knuckleheads should've chosen another date night." I sneered. I looked around the restaurant. Many smiles were recognizable smiles. Twenty tables or so were talkin' about love. It dawned on me that half of the tables were off-duty cops and their significant others! I kept this observation from Jillian. She shouldn't know this location was a cop thing. I made eye contact with recognizable police officers. I gave them the magic wink-wink. The magic wink-wink is an unspoken personal alert. It means... "Please don't acknowledge me as a fellow police officer! Not tonight, anyway!"

Jillian quickly turned her head. She wanted to see to whom I was wink-winkin'? I grabbed her arms before she completed her neck twistin'. I pulled her out of her chair to my lips... forgetting 'bout the short skirt she wore. My across-the-table hug raised Jillian's skirt up her backside. The restaurant patrons' "never miss a thing" eyes saw what I go home to every night. A pair of high, white, cotton-laced stockings was the only thing covering Jillian's personals. She wore them for this special occasion. Somewhat embarrassed, I didn't know what to say or how to react. I was proud to own what was now everybody's eye candy.

Jillian pulled her little skirt down. She smiled and proudly, but uncharacteristically, yelled for all big-eyed observers to hear... "This body belongs to nobody but you, Bishop Darling! It's all yours... I'm all yours... forever! Please don't take me for granted, Bishop. I love you waaaaaay too much!" Her statement silenced the restaurant. You could hear a pin drop. Patrons' wondered how much more of our soap opera they'd see.

"Was that a threat from Jillian? Or, was it a loving gesture delivered in a strange way?" I asked. Seconds later, patrons stood at their tables. They began to clap their hands. They cheered as though Jillian's panty-less bottom was nothing but an example of a woman's commitment to true love. On-looking patrons wouldn't stop. They rendered a standing ovation over two minutes long. We responded with glances of gratitude. We pleaded for everyone to return to his or her own business, thank you.

This excitement wasn't planned. This night was about dinner, discussion, apology, forgiving, and if lucky... maybe a little bit of nookie. It was never about inspiring unknown juices. I sought another passionate kiss from Jillian. She graciously had another to give. I conspicuously placed my left hand on her right thigh. I wanted to restrict that tiny skirt from rising up her back.

We kissed each other as we desperately wanted. You know what? Jillian was absolutely right. It's been years since we touched each other in a loving way. For the first time in a long, long time I felt kinda' giddy inside. She, too, bubbled with love's special feeling. That third bottle of Chianti had something to do with it.

Jillian leaned closer to me. She whispered into my ear... "I... need my man, right now!" Her fingers turned my head. She looked directly into my eyes. "I wanna' be satisfied like that first time! I wanna' feel like I'm your new woman. Please take me back there!"

"Remember way back then? We've gotten away from those fantasies. I want them back! I want you back!" she said. "I don't wanna' be just some woman who cleans your house!"

"I won't be some old used-up chick who changes your kid's diapers!"

"I don't mind placing my career on hold."

"I can never be placed on hold... if you want me to continue being your wife... that is!" she finished.

Jillian kissed me gently on the cheek. She held my hand on her thigh. I'm so naïve. I didn't recognize that certain look in her eyes. It was one of concern. But, maybe not! Those frowns had been there before. Had I refused to honor them? Did I take Jillian's love for granted? It hurts to even think about it. I know it might be true. Was this discussion another attempt to right this relationship's wrong? Jillian apparently loved me regardless of my non-attention to her needs.

"What's a fella' to do?" I wondered.

"What do I say?"

"How do I react?"

I had no valid answers to these questions. Tears trickled from my eyes. My ego quickly slapped me. It put a halt to that emotion. I, a macho cop and the police department's latest hero, was showing signs of weakness. I'm weakening to the L word. Jillian reacted to my unusual sensitivity. She placed her head on my chest. She put her hand over my heart. It reminded me of her touch at the black-tie function years ago.

The restaurant went quiet again. I looked around to see who the fool was this time? I didn't have to look far. It was me... again! As I dried the tears on my face, my life and reputation as a fearsome cop probably came to its end. Remember those policemen I wink-winked at earlier? They had eyeballed my softer side. The entire department would know of my episode of sensitivity by tomorrow morning's Roll Call. I was as they say... dead meat!

Jillian understood my situation. She attempted to come to my rescue. She called for the check. We thanked the waiter for the temporary use of *IBERO's* best table. We summoned over the owner. He was a close friend of ours. We thanked him and apologized for leaving early. I left everybody a hefty tip. We headed for the door.

Before exiting, Jillian came to a halt. She called for the attention of every patron who could hear her. In front of the same eyes that observed her short skirt episode, she seduced me with the juiciest French kiss ever. I'm sure this was done on purpose. She wanted the police department's new gossip to be about something most of them would kill to have... her love... and not about insecurities I might have.

See what I mean? This woman was not only gorgeous; she was downright adorable! All eyes were on us as we left the premises. Cops and significant others now realized one thing... this Jillian Esther Carson-Calloway lady was the most desirable woman on this planet. And... She was all mine—short skirt and all!

Jillian did well tonight. Her plan to save face for me was a successful one. We left *IBERO's* atmosphere full of envy, erections, and inquisitive stares. We didn't ask the valet to bring the car around. Instead, we gave him a $20 bill to not do so. We ran hand in hand to the old red Lincoln Mercury in space 42. We sped away from the parking lot. We headed west on Kennedy Avenue.

Safety would not be an issue. Seat belts weren't fastened 'cause foreplay was definitely expected. Jillian jumped on me like "white on rice" before the first traffic light. Her hands were all over my body. I tried to reciprocate but had to keep my eyes on the road. Sensing my frustration, Jillian made herself more available to my touches. As she did, dangerous light poles were calling our names. I chose to abuse my police powers. I violated a long avenue of red traffic light signals. If traffic lights were armed with those stupid cameras... I'd lose my driver's license for sure.

Jillian cared only for her pleasure. She was on cloud nine. She laughed about showing her personals to an unknown public.

Every subsequent traffic light violation enhanced Jillian's level of excitement. She said some private things to me I can't repeat 'cause you ain't no close friend of mine. Was this the new Jillian or the bottles of Chianti doing the talking? I wasn't sure.

The ride home didn't take long. We undressed before reaching the top of the stairs. We were locked in each other's arms shortly thereafter. My caresses were sincere. I wanted to reproduce the emotional love she experienced at that retreat cabin. I am referring to when the Lion King intentionally lost his crown to a devil of a she-lion.

I smiled. I smiled and loved Jillian like I did that very first time. I could tell she, too, wanted to regain our lost love of yesteryear. Jillian was and still is the love of my life. I think she was giving me a wake-up call. I think, non-verbally, she demanded I realize the fruits of her soul would not be wasted on just any man! This wasn't a hidden message. Jillian kept her eyes open while making love to me. She'd never done that before. I've never observed hazel stares like those I'm witnessing right now. Her fingernails were never as sharp as they were tonight. Don't get me wrong. She was definitely enjoying herself. But, at the same time, she was acting sorta' psychologically indifferent? Does that make any sense?

I transitioned back to her feelings. The time was right. Jillian Esther Carson-Calloway needed to be loved more like never before. Her uncontrollable moans meant satisfaction was imminent. I would deliver her as requested. I was gonna' come along for the ride, concurrently. (Nice semantics, huh?)

Unfortunately, at that precise moment, a loud vibration-like noise came from my discarded clothing. The more it buzzed, the more I tried to talk to Jillian about her feelings. It was kinda' funny, but not. The buzzing occurred every so many seconds. I tried to camouflage the buzzing noise by moaning at the exact time the beeper sounded. I prayed Jillian didn't hear the noise.

Stupid me. While pushing Jillian's spirit to the fullest, her psychological feelings came to a screeching halt! I slowly turned, inquisitively. I peeked into Jillian's hazel eyes. Her face was now emotionless. Her twisted smile questioned my loyalty to our marriage. Right here! Right now! I knew the coldness in her heart was about to make a giant statement. I was scared for the first time in my life. I wanted Jillian to reconsider any diminished love she no longer felt for me. I wanted this evening's good times to overshadow that black beeper instrument lying a mere seven feet away. I could feel the instrument noisily eroding the ambiance of this night... this relationship... this marriage.

Who am I fooling? Jillian and I, and the whole wide world knew who would win this contest between love and booty... err, duty. The buzzing was too noticeable. Each buzz killed any chance of recapturing opportunities offered a few minutes ago. Each buzz announced to the world a great woman was about to be lost by a jerk.

Minutes elapsed. Neither of us spoke a word.

I was still holding Jillian in a very healthy position. "Was there a chance?" I thought to myself. "Would Jillian allow the buzzing instrument to win but still continue to love me?" The inevitable occurred. Her body temperature cooled like the North Pole. Within ten seconds, I was hugging an icicle.

Jillian vigorously yelled... "Get off me!" Her demeanor registered that message loud and clear. If I chose to answer that beeper... there was nothing else to say. I knew what this was all about. It was about freedom of choice. A choice afforded to no one but me. Nothing would make Jillian happier this moment than winning over the buzzing.

I had the hammer. I desperately needed to choose my love for Jillian over any love for a foolish job. Jillian knew the upcoming answer. Her mind understood my truth. She wanted no part of it. Who was I kidding? I knew the truth after buzz number one.

Jillian understood me better than I understood myself. No need to procrastinate. Bring on a decision! I exercised my freedom of choice and answered the stupid beeper. Did I think I wouldn't? I excused myself from my relationship's interlude. I tried to honorably slide out of Jillian's cold clutches. Her arms and thighs tightened each time I tried to pull away from her torso.

I thought I'd lost her mentally. She was fighting against her own feelings. She was making a few last efforts to keep me with her in her heart of hearts. I gave a serious thought to not leaving Jillian tonight. The beeper's muffled vibrations... kept calling out to me! I now had the "beeper jones." It resembled my dependence on those yellow and blue demons. They just kept calling out my name.

Louder!

Louder!!

Louder!!!

They kept calling me. They called as though I hadn't made my decision. Give me a break, please!

I stopped breathing. Another moment of truth was upon me. Jillian was holding on for dear life. It was my life she was trying to hold on to. Her body's demeanor was tearing at my heart. "This is really not the best time to leave!" she begged. "I need you more than you need that police job!" she added.

I didn't respond. I said nothing. I neither moved nor uncurled my limbs from her popsicled clutches. It became clearer and clearer. My decision was destroying a once in a lifetime relationship. I remembered a comment made years ago. It validated how I felt right now.

"A cop's life can easily resemble a bunch of crap!" I used to say.

I'm bringing this all on myself. The decision to leave or stay was a no-brainer. I needed Jillian. She was the only positive thing in my life. I couldn't continue on without her. I could always get another job. My education credentials easily qualified me for other opportunities. Jillian's love would easily justify any career transition I made. It would allow more time for us to truly love each other. If any woman was worth such a sacrifice it was Jillian Esther Carson-Calloway. I tried to validate the best decision on my part. If my life was worth anything, the buzzing from my clothing could not be a factor. I pulled Jillian's soft, cold hands over my shoulders. I kissed her smooth forehead. I tenderly brushed strands of hair away from her eyes. I wanted absolutely no barriers between us.

Sensing the return of a reconsidered decision on my part, her hazel eyes lit up like a Las Vegas casino. Her touch softened. A tender warming returned to her fingertips. She was biting her top lip awaiting that victorious reply–the only reply she thought I could give. "My Darling!" I whispered as sensitively as I could.

"I'm sorry! I've gotta' get my butt out of here!" Jillian didn't move. Not one bit. A mini-second later her body fell limp to my apologetic touches. She uncurled from the awkward warmth of my arms. She walked into the next room. Most times she'd pack a small bag lunch or perk some fresh java to take into the night's cold.

"Tonight? ... Jack-dog nothin'!" I dressed in her silent absence. She re-entered the bedroom. She stared in my direction. She had disbelief in her heart. I tried not to glance into those hazel eyes. If I did I know I'd change my mind. Her head slowly turned away from my presence. I had ceased to exist. She knew it. I knew it. I gave Jillian the best kiss she'd allow her cold shoulder to receive before leaving.

I voiced my tremendous love for her. I reiterated no choice had to be made on our relationship. This was merely a decision to do my job! She accepted my apology. She denied my words at the same time. Something special was missing from her eyes.

It was something I didn't really want to see because the truth would've killed me right there! Jillian's touch was one of reluctance. Her unspoken attitude was even colder. That special crease in her smile totally vanished!

"I'll recapture her love later!" I kept telling myself. "Women always over-react when love's the issue!" As much as I wanted to stay, I had to go. I blew my selfish but lucky wife a goodbye kiss. I exited the front door. I sped into an early morning cloud. I left behind more than I realized.

The office was overwhelmed with child abuse and neglect complaints. I was near the Chester section of Sircus Junction. I took a child abuse complaint nearest that part of the city. An anonymous telephone voice kept reportin' five young kids being left alone every day while the mother worked. "Okay, no biggie," I told Sgt. Joy… Sircus Junction's only female dispatcher. "I'm on it!"

The neighborhood snitch said the mother worked Monday to Friday from 7 AM to 6 PM. The children's ages were about one to 4 years old. The caller further indicated the mother was home at this moment. "The mother would, unfortunately, be leaving the apartment in less than an hour!" the dispatcher followed.

I parked my police cruiser about a block from the address given. I'd wait 'til the unsuspecting mother left for the day. To kill some time, I opened a Washington Post newspaper. I wanted to read about that questionable Washington Redskins football victory. They barely beat the Minnesota Bears or Vikings or somebody. Quarterback controversies were destroyin' the team's chemistry. The quarterback controversy was between Sonny Jilligan and Bill Jilmer. Ooops. I really meant Sonny Jurgensen and Billy Kilmer. Still got Jillian on the brain. No use calling her. She won't answer the telephone. If she were calling me in reverse fashion, I wouldn't answer the phone either.

I gotta' talk to somebody. I needed to talk to somebody right now. Whoever it is must be a good listener. I needed someone to tell me I was right in my decision. I needed someone to blast my sweet Jillian's selfish attitude. I didn't need anyone to fix my problem. I could do that all to myself. I could do that by simply apologizing to Jillian for absolutely... Nothing! Been there. Done that.

Where's my best friend in the whole wide world? Where's my... little black book? It always serves me well. It's always there when I needed it. I wanted to speak the truth to my trusted friend. A blank sheet of paper will do. I'll transfer my written thoughts to my official friend later.

Yes! That's it!

Hello... my long lost friend,

Why are women so fickled. I've been nothing but the best to Jillian. Unfortunately my best hasn't been good enough. When the going got tough, my precious Jillian put me down. She could've been more understanding. This was not the case? What else could I have done? The answer's puzzling.

At the end of the day, this woman—my exception to the rule—was just like all the rest of the dames. I'd fallen into the same old trap when communicating with her. I now realize the only way to win an argument with a woman is by not being logical.

I have, once more, learned way too late that logic has nothing to do with opinions concerning love. What could I have done differently? What could I have shown Jillian character-wise to make her understand all the good I had in my heart? All the love I wanted to share?

Oh, well. Surely it wasn't the number of "I love yous" sent her way. I had "I love you" coming out of my mouth at least once every week. Jillian still wasn't satisfied. Said she needed to hear those words more... much, much, more. I lovingly obliged even though those three little words were hard for a macho fella' like me to say. Yet, I said them anyway. Can I get a little thank you for my effort? I couldn't win. This fact was amazing to me.

When crazy women hear the words "I love you" from dedicated dudes like me, the longevity and value of those words should last for several weeks at least! Selfish women continue to complain when not told time and time and time again! Over and over! Those same old words! Over and over! Time and time again! Get my drift?

In reality, those same old words tend to lose their value the more they're repeated. The more they're repeated… the less value they hold; hence, the fewer times real strong women needed to hear them. Right? I paused a second. I tried to understand Jillian's thinking.

Nope. Wasn't happening. I couldn't figure out why she felt badly about the hard job I performed. Go ahead and sue me! I'm a dedicated professional. What else can I say? I shouldn't have to apologize to anyone. My job was to serve and protect the citizens of a big little city in a small valley in Virginia.

Jillian was nothing but a spoiled brat. She lived a charmed life before we married. She never wanted for anything. Her silver-spooned history was nothing but a future kiss of death to any man. I'm sure you know what I mean. To never want for anything means to have never lived for anything. She had lived nothing but a charmed life. No strife. No hunger. No turmoil. No normal verbal or physical abuses. No wearing of used panties passed down from an older sister. Nothing! Absolutely nothing earth-shaking ever caused her a normal moment's pain or drama. The rest of the world should be so lucky.

I've come to a valid conclusion. Women ain't nothing but a basket full of trouble. All they do is nag… nag… nag… nag… nag… take a short break… and nag, nag, nag some more! Real men try their best to live without them. Then we realize we can't live without the opposite sex. Wow! We're trapped either way!

There were times I couldn't stand Jillian but… I loved her anyway. I hated a lot of things she stood for but… I still loved her. One week out of every month she's as moody as all get-out! Even those days didn't make me want to adjust the love I had for her. That's why I've told her I loved her more than any man's norm. I did so even when I didn't want to. When I didn't feel the need to say those redundant semantics of luv', I said them anyway.

A special feeling came over my soul just this minute. It affected my heart. I wish I could explain it. I can't.

The more I remembered repeating those three magical words... "I love you!" to Jillian... the more my heart desired to repeat them again. And, again!!!

And, again!!!!!!

For some unknown reason, the more those stupid little words came outta' my mouth... the more my marriage to Jillian meant to me! As I continued to pronounce those words... well, do you know what I'm trying to say? In a nutshell, the more I told Jillian I loved her, the better I felt about the universe we'd created for each other.

Here's another thing! The more those itty bitty magical words went into Jillian's ears, the more love I got from her! There was absolutely nothing Jillian wouldn't do after hearing those words. Nothing! Nothinggg!!!!!!

I can't explain it. I wish I could. My current image of Jillian's love was changing by the minute. She wasn't this scary, selfish person anymore. She was the wonderful, thoughtful person I loved long before we married. My mindset about love started to change. Every time I told Jillian I loved her... a special kind of warmth filled my heart. You may not believe this but the more I told her... well, the more I felt I needed to tell her. No way!!! "Love is an uncanny emotion isn't it?" I asked and answered.

I needed to tell Jillian how I felt about her every second of every day! Every minute! Every hour! I wanted to tattoo the words–I Love You!–On my forehead. I wanted her to know how I felt every second of my life. I'm becoming a wimp, huh? Stay with me, though.

"Where's Jillian right now?" I wondered. I've got to find that woman. I've got to get her to return my love for years to come. It may be too late. It may not be too late. I truly did need her. I wanted to love her 'til death do us part. I wanted her by my side so, together,

we could break her parent's stupid marriage longevity record. "Yes...
Jillian!" I silently screamed. "Where are you, Jillian? Let's go get that
longevity record!"

The police dispatcher–Communication Specialist Ivan–busted up
my depression. He yelled at me to let go of the radio's microphone and
stop puttin' all my personal business over the air. I guess I got carried
away. It was Jillian's fault.

I refocused on the present. Reality and a massive headache had
returned. So did several of my little yellow and blue friends. It's been a
while. Thank goodness! At least, I'm still in control of somethin'!

The ratted-out momma' was in her mid-twenties. I witnessed
her catch the #34 Primrose city bus at 8:12 AM. It was goin'
downtown. I waited a few minutes. I wanted to make sure
no late-arriving baby-sitter was on the way. I watched the
windows for movement. Small-headed silhouettes flashed
across a rolled-downed window shade every now and then.
Children were definitely inside that apartment. That was all the
validation I needed. "What would I do if these children were
left unsupervised? How should I communicate with them?" I
pondered. Disneyland immediately came to mind. I'll use some
of my Disneyland impersonations to enter each child's heart.
Donald and Daffy Duck never let me down. Snow White and
the Seven Dwarfs' were too complicated. I only used them when
the neglected family was seven or larger. My ability to duplicate
voices was dependent on how I felt on a given day. Today, my
throat was kinda'... ahhh... Buggs Bunny-ish!

Before exiting my police cruiser, I practiced an assortment
of Disney voices. You never know. Mickey Mouse's voice had
opened as many left-alone doors as his girlfriend who wears
those big black pumps. Her name is Mindy... or, something like
that.Persuading abandoned kids to talk to a total stranger is a
tough task. Most kids don't even realize they've been abandoned.

As they see it, momma' simply went off to work. That's nothing new. She'll return when the Sun goes down! I don't fake the truth unless it's necessary. I sometimes act like I'm the child's mother. I do so when privy to momma's real voice and habits. Other times, I'm a fireman trying to evacuate a building. I rarely do that anymore. It caused too much paperwork the last time I carried a wheel-chaired grandpa from a non-burning building.

I feel clueless this morning. Jillian is still on my mind. Losing her was far more important than a bunch of little brats. I really didn't mean it that way! That last statement was a little selfish.

I cleared my head. I knocked on a door full of questions. A little voice from inside innocently asked... "Momma', is that you?" Police skullduggery is a shameful tactic but legal... soooooooooo... I used one of my Mickey Mouse voices to imitate her momma's voice—one I'd never heard before.

"Yes, my beautiful baby girl! I forgot my peanut butter n' jelly sammich! Will you please open the door?" asked the questionable Mickey. The child cared less for my verbal disguise. She didn't move an inch and strongly reminded me... "You ain't my momma' talking out there! You sound like that little mouse on television!"

"Wow! My imitation of Mickey must've been really good!" I silently chuckled. I still needed to upgrade my covert skills. Goofy's voice would be my next attempt to shackle this big time tiny bandit in my small town. Goofy's voice just might do the trick... "I'm sorry I lied to you, little girl, Aaaahilt! I'm Goofy, your new neighbor from next door! Can I borrow a cup of sugar, a bar of soap, or a sock with a hole in it, Aahiiiilt?"

There was absolutely no response from this precious big little sister. I did, unfortunately, feel a sarcastic little smirk on the other side of the thick wooden door. Her dangerous sarcasm silently instructed... "Please... Mr. unknown man tryin' to break into my momma's house while she's at work... can't you do better than that?"

The momma' who abandoned this child should be proud of the child's maturity level. I'm proud of her maturity level! She could watch my bad kids any day of the week! No cost would be too much! I stopped what I was doing. I looked around. I had to make sure Jillian didn't hear that last comment. Returning to the present stalemate, I've now become an impatiently pissed-off detective! The caretaker's challenge has escalated to a personal one. I've got to find the right words to champion the little Ma Barker! At times, in a vain cop's world, the best direction for success is a straightforward one. The maturation process of this little girl had to mean she was a street-wise kid! "Duuuuhhhh????"

Yes! I'm Sircus Junction's best investigator for a reason! I smiled, internally. This humiliation has to end before my peers stretched the truth a tad. The remedy was right on the tip of my tongue. I, again, knocked on the apartment door! I used my natural voice and yelled... "Hey, little girl! I just found five dollars in front of your apartment door! Yo' momma' must've dropped it when she left this morning! Open the door. I'll give it to ya'!" All of a sudden, the pitter-patter of little feet gathered together on the other side of the door. "Is it a $5 dollar bill or... is it five $1 dollar bills?" the voice enthusiastically inquired. I snickered... 'cause victory was near. I reached into my pocket. I pulled out some cash. I slid a new dollar bill under the door and responded... "It's five, new, original $1 dollar bills! Okay, 'lil Miss Knucklehead?" Thirty seconds came and went. She finally responded... "Well, all-righty then! But, if you don't mind, slide the rest of those little puppies under the front door and... thank you very much, Mr. Po-Po!"

"Well, I'll be a mother's...!" I thought to myself. The official investigative score was "itty-bitty" abandoned child... 3! The department's hero, watch commander, and veteran child abuse detective... 0!

I was obviously dealing with a very intelligent child. A mere tiny-tot, she probably graduated from Harvard and was home on Spring Break. I've got to play hardball with this kid. Sooooo, I lied for the fourth time! "Hello, again, little girl. I'm your momma's latest boyfriend and probably the father of at least one of you in there! She sent me over here with some food for everybody!" The sound of little feet again started to shuffle. The little smart-mouthed leader then asked... "Do you have enough food for everybody?"

"You gotta' be kidding me!" I mumbled. "This little girl has an adult-like vocabulary! How bad can her momma' be?"

It mattered not. The only important thing was the movement on the other side of that door. I finally, finally, hit the right nerve! Several motivational speeches were needed to persuade Miss Smarty Pants to open the door. Once I saw her cute little hazel-colored eyes, she was all mine! Her facial expression indicated she now knew I had lied about the food.

"Oh... no you didn't!" she shrieked. "Please, Det. Mr. Po-Po, don't come in here. Okay? Please go away. Okay? Momma's gonna' get real mad at me if you come in here," she begged. This child was the trusted four-year old caretaker of her brothers and sisters.

In neglect situations, I always tried to make a conscious effort not to scare the youngsters. They committed no crime by being under-aged. I spent a good half hour apologizing to Sara—the mighty itty-bitty caretaker—in my best Pluto voice. I'd become a hit television series as each little face wanted to own one of my Disney characters. It took a little more time and effort to finally gain Sara's confidence. Her first smile came. Younger brothers and sisters followed her lead. I had everybody's trust.

Unsupervised children readily accepted their living conditions as reality. Knowing this, I would try to hide any expressions of disgust. I canvassed the entire apartment. While doing so, I kept a smile on my face as I stood ankle deep in Saltine cracker boxes and empty dog food cans. I took normal breaths of air in my attempts to disregard a bedroom filled with hundreds of this month's soiled pampers. I completely ignored a bathtub filled with long-standing urine. I didn't get outwardly depressed when over-flowing human waste didn't flush away properly.

There's another depressing issue about this place. It hurt more to discovery improperly wired hotplates and leaking kerosene heaters... fire hazards waiting for the best opportunity to consume these valuable lives. "Who's the momma' of these kids?" I silently asked knowing she was nowhere nearby. "Why did it take that nosy anonymous neighbor so long to call the police?" Maybe I'll never know. It didn't take a rocket scientist to realize each child had a different father. I warned you. These situations are my worst nightmares. I rounded up the kids. They totaled five... three girls and two boys ages 1 to 4. Wow. That equals five kids in four years... gotta' be a set of twins somewhere in this bunch. Most had no clothing to wear. I had to utilize my apprenticeship as a father. Boy's pants or girl's pants... at this age... what's the difference? I prepared children for a ride that will most certainly change their lives forever. Like most kids, they sensed an unsolicited help that meant nothing but trouble. They started crying at the same time. Imagine five little knuckleheads cryin' 'cause a stranger stuck his nose in their business? I didn't have to imagine it. It was happening in real time, right now! To calm their fears, I summoned that Black Magic of all Black Magic tricks. It was within that secret world all kids loved and understood... "McDonalds!" An imaginative version of "Muck-don-nals" with ketchup and fries easily coerced this clan into my unmarked police cruiser.

These uncontrollable infants were all over the car. I couldn't get 'em to sit down. But, wait! Over there, just across the street!

There goes those life-saving Golden Arches! The tiny foreheads could barely see over the car's dashboard. Their big eyes and fantastic hearts honorably held me to that promise of... "Burgers, fries, and apple pies... along wit' a couple of small co-colas... five straws, please!"

All was right in their world! Those kids were happy. I mean really, really happy! Food can do that to you. I could've driven to a Texas-based "Muck-don-nals." The kids didn't care as long as they got the chance to waste Mickey-D's mustard all over my suit! Several youngsters used the cruiser's back seat as a potty! I made a pit stop at the police department's car wash. I got the inside-the-car people to hose down the whole smelly family for a few extra bucks. We just lined the kids up like a game show and let the water fly! The carwash people did what I asked but didn't want that kind of business any more. Okay, whatever. The children were placed under the Court's custody. Later that evening, momma' found the summons I'd left on her door. She responded to my office. She explained why she abandoned her kids. I searched old files under her last name for past histories. My search was negative. Several apartment fires, however, had occurred in this same building. A different family of children started those fires. Two infants perished. This history, and leaking kerosene heaters, raced through my mind. A no-brainer... Grace Porter was arrested. She was charged with Willful Abandonment under the Sircus Junction's Neglect Statute.

As angry as I was, I was just as sympathetic. Ms. Porter was a previous prostitute and a recovering drug addict. She re-dedicated her life a year or so ago. She was simply trying to survive. She loved her children. She never asked the government to help with their upbringing. She'd made her peace with God.

"Didcha' really look at my children?" she asked.

"They have no material possessions. Yes, daily meals were always questionable. But, can't you see how happy they are wit' life itself? That's most important isn't it?" she added. Ms. Porter performed as best she could as a mother. That wasn't good enough. I had to remove those children even though her love was all they had. It wasn't easy.

I gave Ms. Porter my final decision. I prepared the paperwork. Ms. Porter dropped to her knees. She pleaded for mercy. She requested an unofficial release of the children. She requested an official warning... a legal option at my disposal. Even though Ms. Porter had a questionable background, her life had become meaningful. She could not exist without her kids.

We made eye contact. I could only refer to the moral support I'd give her in Family Court. She fell to her knees... again. She begged God for forgiveness once more. She prayed and cried. Prayed and cried... until taken away to Central Lockup. Sometimes doing the right thing hurts. Unfortunately, Social Services said this same family had been abandoned at least once in each of the last four years. The Judge had little trouble rendering a verdict. All five children were permanently removed from the mother's custody.

Grace Porter performed the unimaginable. She committed suicide as soon as she was released on bail. She died from a self-induced cocaine over-dose. A hand-written note was taped to her chest. It was addressed to me! It read:

"Detective Calloway,

Guess what happens to my will to live once my world has been yanked from under me? I tried to live without my kids... but why should I? You personally made sure I was a parental failure. You could've easily afforded me a second chance to succeed. You made a bad decision to not do so. I will always hate you.

By my own hand, I'm going to another world. You can bet I'll wait for my children there! And, you can bet I'll see you there, also.

*Nobody made you God. I hope the rest of your life is a bunch of crap!
You ain't nothin' but a scum-suckin' police pig!"*

Grace Porter was gone!

Her suicide took a precious part of me and a piece of each child with her. As an honorable law enforcement officer, I've asked myself something over and over. "Were her children better off with her alive versus her dead?" Time will tell. The children were separated. They were placed all over the small town of Sircus Junction. Some, luckily, found a loving foster family. Others weren't as fortunate.

I passed by those foster homes a lot. I constantly wondered if they remembered that special day of crying and laughter, burgers and fries, the car wash and, of course... the loss of their mother.

Maybe I'm the only one! I'll never forget the look on that young girl's face when she found out I lied about the food. I still imitate silly Disney voices used to break up this otherwise loving family. When reality finally set in, I thanked God my sons and daughters are in better situations. I've gotten too personal with my neglected family cases. Yet, how could I not? I probably treated each child as my own... a tremendous no-no.

And, honestly, Ms. Porter, if you wanted me to suffer for removing your children... Your wish is being fulfilled!

My time-consuming investigations and court appearances made it harder to be there for Jillian. I'd get home about 3 AM in the morning. I'd have to leave at 6 AM to go back to court. I would snuggle against Jillian's body regardless of the time I arrived. Those days are gone. Our king-size bed has grown a lot larger. It's more spacious now. Jillian looks at the clock every time she hears my footsteps enter the front door. She pulls the covers over her cold shoulders like clockwork. Her body language screams... "I've a terrible headache, tonight! Please don't touch me... please, don't put your cold heart on me!"

Jillian understands the importance of my work. She doesn't understand the importance of my choice! I loved her as much as I loved this rewarding work… even if it agitates our relationship. She wanted a fair marriage–nothing more or nothing less. I think she's done her part in keeping that delicate balance.

Who knew what God's destiny was for me? I hurt badly when I observed abandonment expressions on Jillian's face. I hurt just as much when I looked into the eyes of abused children needing my help! I shouldn't have to choose one over the other. I haven't. Jillian has stayed by my side because of our children. There's no other reason. If I could get Jillian to love me one more time… I'd be a happy camper! She wouldn't have to show any love until it truly returned to her heart. Couldn't she do that for old time's sake? She's lying right next to me. I can feel her body heat. Nah! She might as well be a thousand miles away. I want you in my life Jillian. Please return to me before I, too, mentally disengage.

I turned my back to Jillian. I pulled the bed covers over my shoulders. I summoned the only positive thing left in my life. It was an old dream of a newly sought world. I wanted desperately to return to that secret place. It never happened. Instead, another nightmare brought me to a questionable place in religious history. It was a depressing place. It was during a time when…

All Roads Led to Rome…

Dear Black Book:

When I closed my eyes this night, I found myself drifting somewhere within the Roman Empire. It was during the late 4th Century. Why and how I got here is beyond me.

Am I reconsidering my decision to be a Christian?

Will this dream totally commit me to a more spiritual life?

Why else would I have these thoughts tonight… within this historical era of all places? Here I openly stand worshipping a

God who scares so many. To do so is absolutely the kiss of death. Christianity is not accepted in this stagnant empire. History knows, however, the next Caesar will embrace Christianity as an option to his own religion. That's a long way off. I can't be too vocal about something that may or may not be on the horizon.

So, "Why am I here?" I kept wondering. Within seconds, I was acknowledged as one of many being delivered to a newly built Coliseum. Our trek was long, deliberate, and a consistent one. No one was allowed to stop for any reason. A similar crack from a whip enforced that rule. Hymns of Prayer caused sympathetic Roman heads along peasant-filled roadways to bow to those about to unknowingly fall.

Rome's ruling class, however, cried out but only in laughter at those destined for a Lion's belly. Roman leadership couldn't understand why Christians perished over a ridiculous belief... an intangible assumption that could only be found in a new kind of world?

Rome's facial expressions inquired why Christian death marchers showed no fear? Where did such inner-strength come from? Would this questioned faith eventually change the world for non-believers? I was a true Christian. I was a true believer. I honestly didn't ask to walk the stones of Rome's business district. Then again... maybe I did! I wanted to understand the holy differences that brought me to this religious caravan. I questioned not why I'd honor my religious belief 'til death... or why to honor it as a future glory?

Several other thoughts came to mind. I was worshipping a man, a thought, a belief nobody could see. All were intangible to man. Romans, in retrospect, worshipped the Great Caesar as the Almighty. It was the law. It was a serious Roman law. To voice otherwise was absolute treason. You'd be banished from the Roman Empire, used as bait at the Coliseum Circus or, even worst, sent to warship gallows 'til death!

Roman society worshipped huge temples of stone. Huge idols were built representing their Gods. During my barefoot walk, cobbled-stones led me passed numerous Roman idols. Each towered on nearby hillsides. Each stood higher than the *next closest honoree. Each idol structure attempted to out-do those who'd already passed on to the next life.*

Hypocritically, I think they were seeking the same God Christians knew existed. Good luck with that, Romans! Our journey through city streets came to an end. We had reached our final destination. The gates to the Coliseum sands slowly opened. We entered as a group. No force was needed. There was a slight applause from the crowd. It wasn't one of praise. It was one acknowledging a right to die for what we believed—a silly thought indeed.

Bunched in the center of this coliseum, Christians voluntarily submitted to the Lions' vicious attacks. We dwindled slowly in number... one by one. The beasts chewed away our defenseless circle at the applause of elite social classes. It soon became my turn. I would validate the new life I believed in. A Lion's hunger set upon me from my blind side. Surprisingly, I did not cry out for mercy 'cause... I am the man I am! My quiet deliverance was imminent. Wait! Isn't this where I'm supposed to wake up from my dream? Isn't this where my dream ends? Isn't this where a cold night's sweat from reality ends? Shouldn't I open my eyes right now and thank God the Lion's belly was just a dream?

Oh, well. A true reality or whatever wasn't happening so I prepared for the Lion's breath. The next thing I knew a warm morning sun was in my eyes. I raised my hand to shade its' glare. Somehow! Someway! I was no longer afraid of dying. I'd been spared from the Lion's jaws! Or... had I really? Had I been spared from the Lion's rage or did my actual death release my soul? My reality must've been the latter.

Why would it not? No one had ever been spared from this Circus. I certainly would not be the first. I opened my eyes one more time. I had been returned to the present day and time. I desperately tried to interpret a dream that took place... today... hundreds of years after the fall of the Roman Empire.

Was this a dream or a religious warning? If so... a warning to what? Does this dream have anything to do with my wish to establish a better World? History apparently holds the answer. It's a well-known fact. All master civilizations rise and all master civilizations fall! The western world... this western world… shall be no different. Others and I will not see that day. "Will Christianity play a key role in that transition?" I wondered out loud. "Cause… somehow… I know it will but don't know when!" (300–400 AD.)

CHAPTER 7

I sat in the back of the courtroom. My beeper sounded. I thought it was on the silent mode. I was wrong. The offended Judge glanced my way. He gave me that stupid jerk look. He's thrown people out of his courtroom for less. I didn't like his frown nor did I care so I flipped him the bird. Fortunately for me, my hand was under my briefcase at the time.

The call was from Ardie Calloway... my wonderful mother. Whenever she called it was normally bad news. Somebody... somewhere... died. Somebody... somewhere... was divorcing. Or, her injured leg wasn't responding as she wished. I'd return her call a.s.a.p. You can't keep her waiting. If you do she'll quickly move to the next number on her irrational speed-dial setup.

She doesn't get angry. She simply assumes you don't care about her questionable conversations anymore. There's a little bit of truth to that statement. Not much.

She left a valid message this time. It concerned the health of her husband, my father, the great William Green Calloway. A life of non-filtered Camel cigarettes and Jack Daniels "straight-up" had taken its toll. His physical capabilities were rapidly dwindling. His health had never been questioned. His doctor appointments went unfulfilled time after time. His male ego couldn't or wouldn't handle mortality, I think. This man... my father... his caveman ego... wanted it that way.

Ardie Calloway was his wife of forty years. She constantly prodded him to visit a doctor concerning his health. He finally acquiesced. Every member of our family gave a sigh of relief 'cause he'd soon be under a real doctor's care. What we never knew, however, were the true results of his medical tests? William Green Calloway was too macho. He would never portray a beaten man.

We assumed his mandatory medical prescriptions addressed any illnesses the doctor may have found. That was not the case. I finally realized how vulnerable his health was. Such news hurt deeply 'cause I never pushed for a more rewarding father-son relationship. I wanted to. It never happened. Life in general got in the way.

Over the last twenty years, we spent little time together. I wondered if his time left on Earth would expire before this would happen. My job allowed me versatility to travel when emergencies occurred. I could spend time with my mother and father without my work being compromised. And, that's what I did.

Jillian and I were having problems. She urged me to take care of my parents. She understood the value of family support. "I'll take care of the kids. Go do what needs to be done!" she would always say. I had an up-close and personal observation of my powerful father's decline. I watched him change into a totally different person during the last days of his life. His mannerisms were no longer selfish. Regardless of his past, his caring for others increased ten-fold. He became very appreciative to anything done on his behalf. This was not the father I remembered from yesteryear.

"Are unknown aspects of his medicine creating this person I hardly knew?"

"Had a close call with death inspired his awakening?"

These questions I pondered. Something was very wrong and I didn't know what it was. I've always believed... "Better late than never!" So, I decided to satisfy an old promise I made to William Green Calloway a year or so ago. This man was never one to force an issue. Promises directed at him were never forgotten. He'd silently wait 'til that promise became a reality. Whenever that gesture took place, a geeky little smile was the only thank you he portrayed. His smile was more than enough.

He was happier with the thought of being asked to participate more so than satisfying the promise itself.

Yes, something about him definitely changed. Remember that special voice watching over me in the past? While driving to his house last week that same special voice called me. That voice told me William Green Calloway had accepted God in his life. I found that hard to believe. My father was not a religious man. Neither was I at one point. I kept this thought to myself. Getting closer to him became important. My latest unfulfilled promise was one of fishing. Fishing had always been a major part of my father's life. We hadn't fished together as father and son since I was knee high to a tadpole! There was no better time to deliver this promise… especially one that included a large mouth bass!

Erwin–a younger brother–and I forced Pop to visit his family in Charleston, South Carolina. This was a great choice because his brother (Thomas) lived on a coastal inlet–supposedly considered a fishing gold mine! My father could visit his family and maybe catch a striped bass or two. It excited him to know such a trip would take place. He'd merely smile that certain smile. It was all he would give. It was all we needed.

We wanted Mom to go along for the ride. She refused. I guess she knew how important it was for her husband to have this time with his sons. Time was short. I think she knew more about her husband's health than she acknowledged.

Anyway, off we went in a rented mini-van. For old time's sake, we took the same interstate roads Pop took long ago when he visited his Virginia roots. Each time we passed an old landmark brought back his greatest memories. These landmarks allowed him to share his life.

He was so proud. His face beamed like never before. It was important to capture this day… this week… this man. I leaned back in the passenger seat. I recorded everything that would fit in my diary.

Dear Diary,

Pop's eyes widened. He proudly pulled back his shoulders and spoke of his twelve brothers and sisters back home. "We grew up right in the middle of Pittsylvania County, Virginia during the 1920's and '30's. Our town was full of nothin' but good soil. Trees were everywhere… and lots and lots of gravel roads!" he mentioned anytime he thought somebody would remotely listen.

"My family lived a sharecropper's dream!" he used to say. "We had everything God had to give! Yup! Everything we ever needed 'cept clothes was right there on the farm! We were nothin' like you selfish chillen' are today!" he mumbled shaking his head side to side. He twisted his lips and rolled his eyes. He quieted down.

His verbal reminiscing came while sprawled out over a nicely unbuckled seatbelt. Seatbelts were a no-no back in his day. They were mandated for the new generation of drivers. He was a veteran driver and felt he didn't need them.

"I left the farm and became a soldier at age seventeen!" he boasted. His proudest military achievement was surviving France in World War II. He reminded us… again… and again… and again about a big ole' bomb that fell into a hole filled with water. That hole was only several feet to the left of the jeep he was driving. The bomb–a 500 pounder–misfired and didn't explode. The impact, however, flipped the jeep onto its side. He was driving around one of General Patton's Commandin' Officers when this happened.

"We were lucky," he reminded. "The only harm from that definite round trip to heaven was a face full of mud and Army boots filled with piss!" ("And... Yes! After 30 years, this story still sounded fishy to me!" I thought.)

You couldn't tell if Pop was stretching the truth. Nor could you tell when he was serious about his exploits in World War II. What made him believable was that big box of World War II Medals on his clothes dresser. I sometimes snuck into his bedroom and stared at them. I wondered how he truly earned them.

As a regular kid, I thought real bullets and bombs and rifles and grenades were part of his military memories. The biggest unanswered question I always had? "How many enemy soldiers did you kill?" Silly me. I guess I'll never know 'cause he never shared those kinds of memories.

Erwin and I continued to follow his earlier life down memory lane. Our van passed a little schoolyard just over yonder. For those who don't know, over yonder is country talk for... "Right over there, stupid!" Several kids were playing baseball behind an old wooden structure. A closer look revealed it was an old, leaning, baseball batting cage. It must've been used at least fifty years ago. The baseball being tossed around by the kids was actually a stuffed sock filled with a little sand and other useless socks.

You could play with this imitation baseball forever. No matter how hard you hit it... it was going nowhere. A real baseball... one with stitches and everything... was a rarity for country folk.

The sight of the aged baseball diamond dwindled as we motored on down the road. Silence had, once more, captured the van. Everyone knew what Pop's next conversation would be about... what else? Baseball!

Pop never had to brag about his baseball accomplishments. We witnessed his super-star talents many times. Third base or Shortstop. Wherever... it didn't matter! His posture in the van told it all. His body sat perfectly upright. His head was tilted slightly to the left. Soon we'd hear that sucking noise he made whenever he picked his teeth with a match book cover. These bodily functions were how he bragged when he really wanted to brag! He did so without speaking a word because he knew... you knew... how great a baseball player he truly was! His baseball achievements were unforgettable. "Nuff said about that!"

Obviously, the old man was startin' to feel pretty good about just everything. He was feelin' good about how he'd lived his life. As a pleasant surprise to his memory, I spoke of several childhood incidents involving the two of us. These were incidents Erwin had never heard before.

Quietness returned to the van. Pop, eager to hear this dialogue, leaned forward from the rear seat. His ears would not miss a single word. In the old days, I never could have had a conversation like this with him. He and Erwin anxiously waited for me to begin. "Remember that time we fought over the best way to eat an egg?" I asked.

A curious frown appeared on his forehead. I was in the 4th or 5th grade, I think. I came home for lunch one day. I was minding my own business trying to open up a can of spam to eat with my scrambled eggs. You, Pop, for some unknown reason, turned to me and demanded I start eating eggs like a Man! "Scrambled eggs are for little sissies. It's time to grow up!" you yelled. "From now on, you're going to eat your eggs sunny-side up just like I do!" you demanded.

Making your comments more sickening, you always fried your eggs in grease found in that old coffee can on the stove. "Pop!" I remember shouting, "That grease is full of bacon bits, pig feet oils, pork chop run-offs, and last Friday's fish bones." The thought of cookin' my egg in that mess caused this little elementary kid to vomit.

"So, as slick as I thought I was, I resorted to childhood trickery," and I smiled as I said it. "I waited until you weren't looking. I, a 4th or 5th grader with my entire life ahead of me, threw that sunny-side up stuff directly into the trash when you turned your back to me!"

"I rubbed my stomach like it was a yummy treat. I gestured loudly so you could hear how much I liked your style of runny eggs. I fooled you until today, huh?" I laughed. Another silence filled the van. This old man... my father... stared at me in the van's rear mirror.

"I knew all along your little butt wasn't going to eat those eggs," he sarcastically mumbled. "I was simply making it necessary for you to get your next belt-whippin', little fella'! Discipline was mandatory once you threw those good eggs in the trash. Besides, I ate those eggs later regardless of that stupid yummy noise you were making." he stated as a matter of fact. "And, I do remember beating your tiny butt after school that day, right? I bet you forgot to mention that, huh?"

I quickly switched to another memorable incident. "Remember the infamous ice cream caper, Pop?" I asked. Another frown captured Pop's forehead. "Your company had a Christmas Party one year. The food was free so I tried to stuff as many ice cream cups in my pockets as possible. The weather outside was so cold. There was no possibility they'd melt before we arrived at the house," Once home, I was gonna' hide the secret bounty on the roof of the back porch."

"Unfortunately, you took the entire family to meet your boss at his private office. We gracefully stood at attention like little toy soldiers. The room temperature and my body heat started to melt the ice cream cups. Within minutes, vanilla, strawberry, and chocolate ice cream started oozing out of every pocket in my brand new suit. The Neapolitan ice cream mess spilled onto your boss's new floor. It was a floor just painted for the office party."

"Your spineless other kids wanted no part of my covert action. They slowly moved to the other side of the room. I remembered your expression when you saw my embarrassing mess. It was one I'll never forget. Hahaha... You remember that day, don'tcha, haha? I tried to explain to your boss I was the chosen ice cream carrier for the entire family. Nobody bought that explanation. No one at all!"

Pop chuckled for the next fifteen miles. He did remember that ice cream caper. He said his boss told everyone in the company about the *funny Calloway family (Pop didn't think it was funny after he got me back home. I think that was butt-whippin' number 344... and I was still just a little fella'!)*

Despite what the 1950's and 1960's offered, my father was the leader of my life–even in his own non-loving way. I, an innocently misguided child, couldn't properly evaluate parental love as it applied to my father. I actually hated him at times. I thought he hated me all the time. I later found this not to be true. What he disliked about me was that tremendous cloud of deviant behavior constantly following me around. There's no need going there. Let's return to our trip to South Carolina.

These vacation moments were so special. I looked at the old man in he mirror. I told him I loved him. I hoped it wasn't too late to finally say these... oh, so right words. He didn't answer. He said nothing. I looked into the rear view mirror again. A sleepy smile was on his face.

My old man... my father... never heard me say those precious words. He didn't hear my last sentence. I'll make another attempt before he leaves this world.

Pop needed more than a few rest breaks. I attributed that need to a secret illness he wasn't ready to share. We had hundreds of miles to go. With some luck, he'll tell us what those illnesses are.

We crossed the border into South Carolina. It became evident to William Green Calloway this trip wasn't really about South Carolina. It really wasn't about fishing. It was about life! The beginning of it. The ending of it.

Erwin and I were happy and sad at the same time. We were proud to know that God was not only in the van, but had somehow entered Pop's life, as well. This excursion has been so rewarding, so far. Would fishing surpass any feelings we, as a family group, experienced? Only time would tell.

We arrived in Charleston on a Thursday night. We would fish all day Friday and Saturday. We'd return to the Northeast on Sunday. This was Pop's first visit to South Carolina. He was overjoyed to hang out with Uncle Thomas—his older brother. As luck would have it, the first day of fishing landed no fish in a nearby Atlantic Inlet. This day of disappointment did nothing to damper our spirits. Uncle Thomas guaranteed fish on the next day. The next morning came. The location of my uncle's guaranteed fishing hole wasn't far from where we anchored yesterday. We launched his 17-footer and motored to the clearest blue water I'd ever seen.

"The South Carolina Fish and Game Commission will eventually mandate a permit for these waters! None were required until next month!" said my trusted old Uncle. We anchored at a location where the Atlantic's salt-water fish lunched on the Inlet's fresh-water fish. Droves of fishermen were taking advantage of this unique water combination.

We made sure Pop caught the first fish. It was sorta' a reward for his life. Once that was done, everything was perfect. We waited to catch the gran-daddy of all bass. Across the Inlet, a small vessel left the dock. It headed in our direction. Minutes later, a nicely creased Game Warden insignia became visible. He cut off his little motor. He drifted several feet to our left.

Outta' nowhere, the warden unhooked his gun's trigger guard. We, therefore, awaited that famous request never wished to be heard by serious fishermen... "May I see your fishing permits, please?"

Collectively, Pop, Erwin and I turned to Uncle Thomas. We waited for a much needed clarification on this fishing permit issue. Uncle Thomas didn't break a sweat. He calmly dug into his wallet. He produced a South Carolina fishing Permit for this special body of water! The Game Warden used a much sterner tone for the rest of us. He requested the required fishing permits. And, again, he received an aggregate of negative responses.

The Warden placed his hand on his gun. He smiled a bit. "I know you'all didn't travel way down here to fish without a permit, didcha'?" he asked with a sly grin on his face.

We northern fellas' needed immediate support from our quiet relative. None came. Not even a peep. Erwin and Pop looked at me as though I was now the elected leader. Democratically, I became the mouthpiece for an unlicensed group of bass anglers. Not knowing the Warden's name, I sarcastically said, "Excuse me Mr. Barney Fife, this waterway is still unlicensed territory!" The Warden placed his hand on the trigger. "No Siree! Taint so!" he shouted back. "Not any mo'! The law changed this same mornin'!"

Three soon to be locked up fishermen from up north smirked at the warden. He kept his hand on the trigger and generously smirked right back. Thirty seconds later he declared, "I'm gonna' lock up all unlicensed people in this boat!"

Six hundred miles from home brought another moment of silence. Somehow, we knew another statement was on the way.

"Let me tell you people from way up 95 north what I'm gonna' do," he timely shouted.

"Your state is a long way from here. If I let you go home, I gotta' feeling you won't bring your butts back down here for the court date."

"How true! How true! How definitely true!" thought three pissed-off northerners? We respected the Law as well as any other citizen but he was right on target with that assumption! William Green Calloway, on the other hand, verbally exploded about the unfairness of this whole situation. The warden felt threatened. He upholstered his pistol. With a big Boss Hog smile, the warden calmly stated, "I'll let you go... but a monetary fine of $243.00 must be posted!" "And, just so you know... that's $243.00... Per Person... CASH!!!!!! That'll teach you all people from up north a valuable lesson, won't it, huh?"

Before I could say a word, Pop shouted... "Hey, Buster! That's highway robbery! Take me straight to jail! I'll do the time before I give you that kind of money! Nope! Not today!" Erwin and I tried to quiet the nasty mouth of our father. We also knew there wasn't a Small-mouth Bass anywhere in America worth $243.00 per person!

There was another silence on the water. "Take one cash payment of $243.00 and we'll get off the water." I said. Again, we played the waiting game with the Warden 'til he finally shook his head up and down... accepting the offer. I dug into my pocket only to hear Pop shouting, "Don't pay it! Don't pay it! Let's all go to Jail! It just ain't right! "So, %$%&*# you, Barney Fife! I don't have lots of time to live anyway. Whatcha' gonna' %$%&*# do? Arrest an old dying man because he didn't have a fishing permit?"

Pop quieted down after he realized what he revealed. Not about the fishing permit but his remaining time to live. The warden came to a valid conclusion. Something else, something special, something religious had occurred in my Uncle's illegally anchored 17-footer.

The warden holstered his weapon. He extended his hand. I quickly placed the money in his greedy fingers and asked no receipt-like questions. Uncle Thomas started the engine. We motored on out of there. We were without the massive catch we expected. No biggie. It was time to get outta' good ole' South Carolina. We had, as you now know, more serious medical realities to deal with. We said goodbye to Uncle Thomas and his gracious hospitality while silently thanking him... for nothing fishing-wise!

In retrospect, without his knuckleheaded non-licensed help, we wouldn't have found out the truth about Pop's medical condition. We left several hours later. The constant elimination of road mileage couldn't make me forget what I'd heard in the boat. I decided not to talk about it in the van. Pop stretched out on the back seat. I noticed he needed to spit in a coffee can every several minutes. This didn't make matters any better.

The dark liquid dripping from his mouth truly bothered me as we headed north on Interstate 95.

I know what tobacco juice looked like. This was not tobacco juice. This was something else. The mixture was directly attached to whatever ailed his insides. My brother and I were quieter during the return trip.

I did the driving. My brother did the snoring. Uncharacteristically, Pop did most of the talking.

He never did consider sleeping. He was too busy enjoying this excursion. He talked... and talked... and talked some more. He talked about anything and everything interesting in his life. He took full advantage of this opportunity to relive his life in the presence of his sons—even if the younger one was snoring.

Guess what neither Pop nor Erwin knew? Neither knew God was riding in that van with us! (Or, did Pop really know? Yet, how could he have known?) The religious feeling was so strong it was unbelievable. That's when I knew Pop's secret illness was terminal.

We motored on up the Interstate. The best of the entire world was riding in this van. Nothing else mattered.

Allowing William Green Calloway to enjoy himself, to speak of things never before shared, and to be a good listener were tremendous bonding experiences. Whatever Pop wanted to do and whenever he wanted to stop was okay with me. We stopped every other hour, on the hour, as we drove the vehicle north. Pop took his time exiting the van's side door.

He slowly yawned. He stretched his rapidly aging body for a couple of seconds. He entered the Rest Stop's door and headed directly for the men's room. Before returning to the mini-van, he walked around the knick-knack shop 'til he found something resembling that far off location. Most times it was something as simple as a cigarette lighter. He had affection for fancy cigarette lighters. I never commented on this choice, especially at this time in his life.

Pop looked like a kid in a candy store. These were the final purchases he'd ever make. He had accepted the fact his world would end soon. I tried not to cry. I understood why he was enjoying himself so much. What I didn't know was how long he'd have to do it?

Our return trip was coming to an end. We laughed about that entire stupid trip to South Carolina. The fishing thing... That Boss Hog situation... My uncle's lie about the permit... Pop found nothing but humor in it all! Hearing that much laughter from your sick father, well... the love between us couldn't get any better. I thanked God for allowing Pop to feel so good one more time.

Pop crashed from pure exhaustion in his special seat in the van. It was the seat he occupied from day one of the trip. He stayed awake as long as he could. I, in turn, appreciated whatever company my dying father provided. While he slept, I remembered all I could about this man who was about to join the Lord. As the story goes, Pop heard of jobs available in a Virginia town 300 miles north of his birthplace. Ignoring my grand-parent's opinions of finding nothing but heartaches away from sharecropper's roots, Mom and Pop loaded three young kids into an old, broken down Chevy and headed north. I remembered the car's oval-shaped rear window. It corralled three little faces and a chicken box as we sought uncharted territories up near the Mason Dixon Line.

After arriving in Sircus Junction, Virginia—a suburb of Washington, DC—Pop found work at a paper plant until he retired forty years later. He was so proud of this feat. I remembered some of his caveman's features. William Green Calloway was a father you could admire and dislike at the same time. As an example, the few times we played catch were some of our greatest and worst moments together.

To misjudge a tossed baseball from him meant total embarrassment. It meant certain death to a little fella'. Who knows? Maybe he thought baseball was some kind of an upward opportunity? At eleven years of age, I pitched a perfect game in Little League. I also hit the game winning home run to win that same game 2-0. When Pop heard about the game, he became a spectator at my next contest. It was the first time he came to see me play. His presence caused such nervousness; I struck out on three straight pitches in the dirt.

I never saw the pitches coming my way. I only saw my father's high esteem before my plate appearance, and his disgusted frowns after he observed my pathetic attempt to follow in his footsteps. As the son of a local All-Star Dad, I totally destroyed the famous cliché'... "An apple doesn't fall far from the tree!"

Pop witnessed one of my Adult Baseball League games fifteen years and sixty-seven championship games later. I homered twice and hit two doubles on that special day. I had hopes of redeeming that old horrible childhood performance. At the game's end, I could only lovingly smile at his assessment of my current talent... "You still can't hit the curveball! Huh?" he mumbled. If you knew my father you were aware of several caveman-like facts. First, a man never cries and second, a man never shows his vulnerabilities by acknowledging worthless little compliments. If this were true, his curve ball comment was the only honorable caveman response he could muster while silently... saving face! Pop smirked because he knew... I understood.

His love for the game of baseball never stopped. I surprised him on one of his birthdays with tickets to a Philadelphia Phillies game at Veteran's Stadium. We had great seats right down on the field. I wish I had a recorder for this event. His expressions of joy brought tears to my eyes. We knew this was as close he'd ever get to professionally playing on that darn, silly, artificial turf. Years later, he was inducted into the State's Baseball Hall of Fame.

He was supposed to deliver a speech at the ceremony but refused once in front of the crowd. He sorta' ordered me to do so on his behalf. I remembered how proud I was to speak for him. Once in front of the microphone, I disregarded a normal speech because I'd never told him how much I loved him—in any forum. Okay. He wasn't the greatest father. He was, though, the best one I ever had.

This moment in time was chosen for some reason. While his peers applauded his tremendous baseball talents, he cherished the first time in thirty years he received an "I love you" gesture from me. I looked for him after the speech. I wanted to show the world that we—a bold family of Calloway cavemen—could honestly display love and affection in public and not feel wimpy about it.

This never happened. This never happened because my proud father... a dying man... was hiding in the atrium performing things banned by society... smoking and crying! Yes. It was a proud day for the Calloway family–on both sides of the Mason Dixon Line!

Reliving old incidents made the return trip a more enjoyable ride. The trip was a total success. Everyone loved the time shared together. Days on the calendar were quickly passing. It soon became obvious William Green Calloway was dying of lung cancer. Without too much detail, my trips from Sircus Junction became a daily function. I traveled to help my mother whenever I could.

I witnessed Pop's body deteriorate each week. I watched his strong will to live dissolve. He was bed ridden and would die any day now. Each night he said goodbye to whomever at his side. The next morning it astonished him to see he was still alive. We chuckled about it all the time. In fact, we bet on it.

He'd bet God would take him during the night. I'd bet his eyes would open the next morning. I kept winning. I kept winning because he loved to play the state's lottery. The first question out of his mouth each morning was... "Did I hit the lottery last night?" I had to show him the legitimate lottery ticket. He wanted to hold it in his hands. I reminded him those lottery tickets were purchased with somebody else's money. He chuckled. At the dying age of 67, he was trying to cash in on his last bit of luck. "True luck doesn't work that way," I thought to myself. "True luck occurs when maximum opportunity meets maximum effort."

William Green Calloway's true luck occurred when he accepted God into his life. No greater luck would ever be needed. The inevitable occurred. William Green Calloway died one night as I returned from a business trip. He actually died in the arms of a younger brother.

I cried. I cried because I wasn't there when he said his final goodbye. Somehow, I felt kinda' cheated. I watched this great man slowly die every week over the last year. I really did want to be there at the end. I deserved to be there at the end.

Maybe... just, maybe... he may have wished so also. Several nights before he died, William Green Calloway gave me a certain look. It was one I'd never seen before. He had called for the Almighty. He did so proudly. There were no last minute lottery jackpots. He sought no extension to his valuable life. It was time. Jack Daniels and unfiltered Camel cigarettes had won this personal battle. His request was granted at 11:07 PM.

I arrived at his side about an hour too late. My brother mentioned how a mysterious gust of wind pushed against the window curtain the moment he said farewell. That particular window had been tightly sealed years ago. There was absolutely no way a breeze of some kind could occur at that very moment.

I smiled. I looked to the sky. I whispered goodbye to he I learned so much about in a short time. If I had one last question to ask, I'd ask him why he made certain decisions during his life. I didn't take advantage of that opportunity. Now, I never can.

I can never ask why he left the family when I was twelve years old? I can never ask if eight children and working double shifts for food was too much pressure on him as a father? And, I can never ask if he truly loved his kids? All of us... 'cause we never heard him say those magical words... to any of us... ever! Oh, well. Whatever. Since his death, there have been instances where someone has been watching over my travels.

God and his Angels come to mind. Pop's face comes to mind. I wondered if they're working as a team? Before Pop died, I thought my grandfather, Grandpop Charlie, was watching over me. Strange observation, huh? Not really. Life beyond this world has to be a very special place. Like others before me, I shall receive answers when the right time comes. My journey to understand God's lessons must continue. And, so they will.

Do you ever wonder why things happen the way they do sometimes? I do all the time. I became depressed over this significant loss. I took a handful of yellow and blue pills and tried to sleep. Too many pills, actually.

My ability to return to a safe place was pushed to the max. My promise to establish a more fulfilling world over-powered me once again. A developmental model of a sin-free world was forming in my head. Describing it would be the first time I attempted to do so. It would be a start to something new!

The parameters of a new world without Sin were on the tip of my tongue. I reached for my special listener. I reached for my best friend. My thoughts must be recorded before they disappear into thin air. They must be edited... and re-edited... and re-edited... until they make sense. It will not happen any time soon 'cause there's another child abuse assignment waiting for me.

CHAPTER 8

Psychological child neglect and abuse occurs all the time. A well-known memory came to mind. I'll never forget that Upper Eastside home. I remembered stopping at the entrance gate. I was astonished. A magnificently landscaped driveway led to nothing short of a gorgeous mansion. The mansion was surrounded by a row of sculptured trees. I'm sure the home commanded a price tag larger than anything I'd earn this lifetime.

It was odd I was sent to this location. A concerned neighbor reported... "A seven-year old retarded child had been abandoned by his parents. The child was hidden somewhere inside that ten thousand square foot house!" The dispatcher was very aware this was a wealthy neighborhood. The caller had to be mistaken. The dispatcher ignored the anonymous complaint several times. The caller complained a third time. I was dispatched to investigate the complaint.

I arrived at the front door of this lavish estate. My attitude concerning upper-class entitlement needed adjusting. I had stereotyped the response I'd receive from this influential family.

I rang the doorbell. I waited for a butler-type fella' wearing a black dinner jacket and bow tie to open the door. Minutes later... no answer. I rang the doorbell again. Minutes later... still no answer. Every time I rang the doorbell, a barking noise came from inside the mansion. "Guard dogs, no doubt," I surmised.

I grabbed the large doorknocker. I slammed it against the thick wood at least nine or ten times. The only response was a dog's bark. It sounded closer. "That's odd!" I thought. Mansions like this don't allow animals to run loose when no one's home. My thoughts on barking dogs ceased. No one was home... on the main floor or the second floor. I would come back another day.

I headed back to my cruiser. The dispatcher shouted for my attention. "An anonymous complainant is observing you from her window. Don't leave," he suggested. "The neighbor suggests that if you seek... you shall find," the dispatcher added. "Those were her exact words!" I canvassed the nearby residential properties. Maybe I could see a shadow in a window. The caller was obviously using some pretty good binoculars or a telescope of some type. Therefore, I must give this investigation a good effort in case this whole scenario is being recorded.

I checked and re-checked ground level doors and windows in this mansion. The mansion sat on five acres of real estate. I expected to see a dog kennel because of the noise I heard earlier. I didn't. As I walked around the mansion, barking noises from inside became louder. I peeked in the smaller windows nearest the howling sounds. I observed an animal leaping as though I was a trespasser. The windows were secured. I wouldn't have to dance with that irrational dog.

I'd seen enough. It was time to leave this place. I was embarrassed for even being here. I returned to my police cruiser. I advised the dispatcher this might be a prank telephone call.

"No Sireeeeeee!" he hollered back. "Please, check that mansion one more time, Det. Calloway! This time, take a pair of sunglasses! Take a better look through that same window!" the dispatcher screamed.

"What does he mean by that?" I asked myself. Enough is enough. This was nothing but a Senior Citizen complaint from someone who knows the Police Chief. I'm being pushed to satisfy the old geezer. So, for the last time, I checked the same window as though I really cared. This time I checked with sunglasses.

I spotted that same noisy animal through the Sun's bright glare. It resembled a strange looking dog wiggling a heavy chain. My written report had to be thorough 'cause I know it's gonna' end up on the Chief's desk. I would leave no investigative questions unanswered. I gazed long and hard through the window to identify the pooch for the record. The pooch spotted me. It charged forward as though I was entering.

"While standing outside the window, the dog-like animal stretched his chains as far as humanly possible!" Another question from the dispatcher forced me to accept the truth.

"Cruiseeeeeeeer 507!"

"Have you found what we've been looking for?" he again shouted. "No! I haven't found what we were looking for... dispatcher!" I shouted back.

"But... send me the highest ranking official you can find! Pronto!" I responded. That sector's Watch Commander arrived minutes later. He observed the situation. "You're the expert on these matters!" said the Watch Commander. "Let's do what you do best!"

"Let's go in!" I bellowed. The cheapest windows we could find were broken with the help of nightsticks. We entered the room with the questionable howling. We found the dog-like animal we sought. He was sitting on his hands and knees amidst excrement, old food, and over-turned water bowls.

That wasn't the main problem? The main problem was the dog-like creature was a brown eyed, black haired, seven-year old... male child! The chain's lock was a simple one to take off the special needs child. His turtleneck sweater buffered the chain's weight around his neck. His neck was completely raw. The sweater didn't do its job. Another reality? The precious youngster had mental issues. This little fella' had an "it's about time you found me" expression on his face! Tears filled his eyes. His baffled rescuers released him from horrible bondage. He leaped with joy. Jubilance would be an understatement.

The youngster tried to communicate to us. His slurred pronunciation was impossible to understand. The child suffered from bone growth disorders that forced him to a hands and knees walking motion. "What kind of parents would put a chain around a person's neck?" we wondered. I've described the value of this estate. Appropriate care for this child wasn't financially motivated.

The Watch Commander was a crafty veteran. He had seen every criminal scenario possible. Once he observed the child's predicament, another set of feelings took over. His usually strong voice wilted. Uncontrollable tears found the bottom of his tiny spectacles. I, on the other hand, used up my emotions on other cases. My investigative feelings had already hardened like the Rock of Gibraltar. This unwanted maturation was another of my problems with Jillian. She thinks I've lost my capacity for caring! That's another story.

"What kind of parents are these?" asked the Watch Commander. "You can keep this sick child abuse job of yours!" he shouted. "Give me a nasty gunshot-wound case anytime!" The Watch Commander quickly left the scene. He had to give a personal account of this situation to the Chief of Police before the media got involved.

Just when you've seen it all, along comes another psychological bashing. My further investigation revealed the child's parents were on vacation in Europe. They knowingly left him in this situation. They left the child enough water... but he turned over the buckets. They left him bread and rolls of salami for each day they'd be away. Unfortunately, the child ate more than his per-day amount. The parents left cardboard boxes over in the corner. The boxes were within the chain's reach for toilet-reasons.

The parents were legally notified the court had taken custody of the child. They refused to cut their vacation short! They'll be back next week! The child was placed under the court's protection. The parents returned six days later. They marched into Juvenile Family Court with the best lawyers money could buy. Huddled in the courtroom, no players exited for several hours.

Legal representatives of the parents introduced reports on the true psychological mindset of the child. They wanted their child returned that same day. Their attempts were fruitless. The courtroom doors finally opened. I was asked to enter. All eyes followed me to the seat of testimony. I described the home environment where the child had been rescued. I was descriptive. The Judge excused me from the room. The parents appeared to be ashamed of their disabled child. They intentionally hid him from neighbors, relatives, and their entire social world. The youngster, without much doubt, was permanently removed from his parents' custody. Other felony child abandonment charges were levied against the parents.

A two-year Court of Appeals dogfight followed. Parents were found guilty. The child was placed in a loving foster home environment. He was never reunited with his parents. Years later, the parents were allotted visitation rights while on parole but only within a supervised arena. Contrary to public opinion, money isn't always the best defense. At least, not this time!

I tried to control my feelings about children being left alone in situations like that. It didn't matter how or why kids are… it's wrong no matter how it's perceived. Sleeping with Jillian weren't the only differences we were dealing with. During the child-rearing era of the 70's, we had difficulty with the term "latch-key." I saw it as another reason to leave children alone. I saw it as a willful act of abandonment. Jillian thought it was nothing but a new social norm of the 1970s.

Latchkey. The word just kills me. If I had to define it, none of my words would be positive. Isn't it the parent's responsibility to create a safe haven for their children? Putting a key chain around little Johnny's neck is not creating a safe environment even if they're responsible and cautious kids. Allowing this action is not acceptable. Mrs. Holly Smith, the neighborhood gossip, always sits in her front window. She is a neighborhood watch participant. She is not an acceptable reason to abandon your kids.

To allow the child to carry a telephone is not a valid exemption. You've gotta' remember Murphy's Law is always just around the corner. When children are left unsupervised, negative things are going to occur. How can they not? A child learns by his or her mistakes. It's a natural process of maturity. Parents need to minimize those opportunities by not accepting this latchkey stuff.

This is my opinion... not Jillian's. Jillian wants me to acknowledge the higher level of maturity our children have demonstrated. She sees nothing wrong with trusting kids at early ages. In fact, news worthy stories on Channel 7 tends to only happen to other people's kids. Our son's school is two blocks away. He walks home with neighborhood friends everyday. He checks in with his pal's mother before entering our house. He does his homework 'til we arrive from work. I'm totally scared to death.

The Criminal Court is full of neglect situations. I couldn't live with myself if something happened to our children. This latchkey topic was a constant thorn in our love. Jillian's child rearing philosophies were certainly skewed. They must be addressed if this marriage is to survive. "Right?"

CHAPTER 9

That last fiasco stressed me out. Before attending the next morning's roll-call session, a child abuse complaint was waiting for me on the Captain's desk. I wasted little time. I drove my unmarked police cruiser in that direction. Traveling across town took me right pass my home. I was hungry. I might as well get something to eat.

Jillian would surely be there. Maybe... sharing a surprise breakfast meal might strengthen our marriage. Yes. That's the ticket! I entered our squeaky front door. Jillian had a surprised look on her face. "What's wrong?" she asked. "Not one little thing," I replied. "I was in the area. I thought I'd have an unscheduled meal with my beautiful wife."

"How thoughtful!" she sarcastically replied. "I admire your initiative. I am, however, leaving for a committed nail appointment. And, I'm running late!"

A quiet fell over the room. Silence was the only conversation we had for each other. Her mute message was loud and clear. Fingernails were more important than a few minutes together. Her fingernails were more important than a co-cola and over-cooked French fries... wit' gravy. Jillian followed the deadly silence with, "Don't look surprised. This is the first time you've ever been denied something, isn't it?"

"How does it feel, huh? How does it feel?"

"How does it feel to be on the other end of a non-consideration issue?"

"Huh? Speak up, Man?"

"I've given in to your needs for a long time. It's time for a change, Mr. Bishop Child Abuse Calloway!"

"Your needs are no longer at the top of my list!" she continued. "I still love you and all that!"

"I care but I really don't know where our relationship is headed."

"Our present love is not the love we used to have!" she screamed.

"Wow!" I said to myself. I came home for maybe some peanut butter and coffee foreplay. I didn't need all of this grief from Jillian. It's probably a mood she's in right now. It must be that time of the month. She'll be her real self in a few days.

Tears fell from Jillian's eyes. At times, Jillian cries because of the happiness she feels inside. She apparently realized how selfish she sounded during her rage. "I see the pain in you, Jillian. I'll not stress you any longer!" I whispered. I smiled. I started to leave the house.

"You're so unfeeling!" shouted Jillian. "I'm standing here crying. Instead of asking me what's wrong... your reaction is to go back to that lousy job? What a jerk you've become!" Another silence overcame me. This was the first time she's ever called me a Jerk. Whatever the problem, it surely had nothing to do with me. What could be bothering her? I've done nothing wrong lately. I've not broken any marriage vows. We've not been intimate lately. That decision has been hers and hers alone. Could she be upset about that? These questions came to me as I stood in the front doorway. It was not a good time to leave. I shut the door from the inside. I returned and faced Jillian. My attempts to hold her were denied. She ran into the bedroom. She locked the door. "Oh-oh!" I said to myself. Does she want me to break down the door? Does she want me to capture her? Does she want me to fight for her love? Or, can she no longer stand the sight of me?"

I softly called out to her as a macho man would. I wanted to talk to her. I needed to feel her in my arms. I didn't know how to do something tender like that. "Why do women always do this to men?" I wondered. I sat at the base of the bedroom door. I moved every so often to let Jillian know I was still on the other side of the door. I would cheer her up anyway possible.

I hoped Jillian would let me re-enter her world. "Jillian, please open the door," I lovingly asked. "You know I love you. Please open the door. Or, tell me what the problem is. Whatever. I'm sure I can fix it!" I added.

Stupid me. I heard her footsteps approaching. It's about time. My sweet Jillian had finally seen the light. Her nice voice was forthcoming. "If I wanted something fixed I'd call a carpenter... you stupid knucklehead!" she yelled. If my memory is correct, that was the second time in our history she's used the K word. She only uses that word when she's really pissed off. My demeanor went from victorious to loser. I came home for a jelly sandwich. Forget the peanut butter. And, I have to deal with this?

I tiptoed to the front door. I made a private call to my office. I told the dispatcher to test my beeper this very minute. I returned to the base of the door. I waited for my beeper to buzz. The beeper was placed on the hardwood floor. The floor would magnify the buzzing sound throughout the house. Seconds later, that sucker rattled like a rocket launcher.

I didn't shut it off immediately. I let it dance a little across the floor. I knew Jillian hated that buzzing sound. Her footsteps again approached the bedroom door. I'd used the buzzer as love bait and it was working. Jillian was dangling on the other end of my hook. I peeked under the door. Two perfect feet were leaning her body against the door. She, no doubt was all-ears. I talked into a cell phone to no one on the other end. "She's more important than any child abuse case! Tell the Captain to reassign that complaint to another Detective. My wife is more important!"

I hung up in an agitated manner. I walked back to the bedroom door. I resumed my seat on the floor.

Several minutes later, a sweet voice asked, "Bishop, did you do that just for me? Did that conversation mean you've changed?" I started smiling behind the door. "It surely does, baby." I answered. "I'll do whatever it takes to love you the way you want to be loved!"

"Please come from behind that door."

"Take all the time you want."

"Get that fingernail thing done, right now."

"In fact, get your feet done. Get your hair done. Get everything done," I added as I looked at my watch.

The policeman side of me should've arrived at that child abuse complaint at least ten minutes ago. I've got to leave without it being an issue to Jillian.

"I'm sorry for how I made you feel, Jillian," I said. "I'll leave you alone so you can get yourself together. As much as I don't want to leave, I'll do so to make you feel more comfortable."

"Do you need any extra money for the day?" I asked as I headed for the door.

"No, dear." she responded.

"I, too, don't want to leave at this moment... but my nail appointment won't wait." Jillian said.

"Can I make it up to you tonight, my caring husband?" she asked.

"When you return tonight, can we rekindle that love we used to share?"

"I want to do that so very much, dear," her magic voice added.

I looked this beautiful woman in her eyes when she came from behind the door. "Thank you for accepting my apology, Jillian! I'll be home about midnight! Bye!" I said.

I ran out the door. I put the police cruiser in reverse. I turned for another look at my personal property. Jillian was standing in the bedroom curtains... nude. She had a smirk on her face I hadn't seen in years. She unwrapped her intentions for later. I'll certainly take full advantage of those intentions when I return. Yes sirree... buddy. This is one night I would not... could not... work late! I left the house. I hastily resumed my journey. It would be difficult to alter my mental attitude on child abuse after this surprise visit with Jillian. I must if I wish to keep her love. My attention returned to my abuse and neglect complaint investigation. I arrived at Gregg Elementary School. I interviewed Ms. Thompson. She knew one of the students very well. She gave a history about the child. The last time the child performed poorly on a test, her mother tied her up. The child was locked in a dark closet. The child reluctantly approached authorities back at the school for documentation purposes. Ms. Thompson personally knows the child's mother. Based on the mother's mental past, Ms. Thompson fears for the health of the child. The student's name is Nancy Boston. She's a fifth grader. I agreed a further investigation was warranted. After conversing with the young child, I felt she told the truth as she knew it.

The fabulous Detective Lola-Reed Fletcher will assist me with the child's supervision. Detective Fletcher was my first choice. She's very effective with teenage girls. I did not seek her assistance for other selfish reasons.

Nancy cried uncontrollably. She told us how she was tied up in the coat closet for 48 hours because she didn't receive a top score in math. Nancy's mother duct-taped her mouth to prevent the sounds of screaming. Nancy's arms and legs were also duct-taped to prevent movement. Nancy remained in that situation without lights, food, or bathroom privileges.

The mother never checked on Nancy until the discipline period expired. "This closet thing has gotten outta' hand!" Nancy added. "I'm only 10 years old!"

This parental action surfaced over the last twelve months. Nancy had no question about her mother's love. "My life was much better before my father moved out last year," Nancy added. "Bingo!" I thought as a possible motive came to mind. "Something in momma' changed," the child offered.

"Unfortunately, momma's been doing irrational things since then."

"She's been bursting into tears for no reason."

"She's talking to herself at weird hours of the night. Now that my report card isn't straight A's, the sky is the limit as what she'll do to me next."

I had much to think about as I drove to Nancy's home. I was sure I'd learn something new today. A parent's response to grades can be negative while in a positive sort of way. Nancy was in an uncanny predicament. Her complaint was exactly the reverse of how it normally occurs. School-aged children are normally afraid to explain why they failed a class. They file these types of complaints for protection purposes. This child didn't flunk her coursework. She simply didn't attain the highest grade possible. To be bound and gagged was socially unreasonable. Some cultures don't see this as a bad ordeal. How would I evaluate any family's level of discipline? Maybe I could evaluate the neatness of the child? Maybe I could evaluate her ability to speak proper English? Or, by other visual factors observed in the home? The two options were acceptable at the highest level.

Once inside the home, I'll try to address the third issue. "What would I actually search for?"

"Who knows what's real and what isn't?"

I entered Nancy's home. A fine home it was. I sought the same thing her mother wanted... total perfection! Perfection was what I saw. Pictures on the wall were perfectly centered. Throw rugs were perfectly spaced over beautiful hardwood floors. Absolutely nothing was out of place. Testing my theory a bit further, I asked to see the child's room. As I walked through the home, I glanced into the mother's bedroom. It had the same personality as the mother... sheer flawlessness.

I asked to see the closet where this misery supposedly occurred. I followed Ms. Boston down a rear stairwell. She stopped short of a door bearing locks... too many for a room to hang coats. I slowly opened its door. The hinges squeaked a dooming squeak like that we've heard in scary movies. It was dark inside the 5 x 10 foot room. Stagnant air overwhelmed my nose.

"Once my visibility improved, would I see old bones or an old skeleton?" Were there splashes of dried blood on the walls of this downstairs cave? I looked deeper into the darkness. Was there another body bound and gagged? This nightmarish vision might sound weird to the average parent. But, within the ruthless world of child abuse, absolutely nothing is impossible.

I had to perform a basic investigation. I needed to prove Ms. Boston was not a parental lunatic. I put on a pair of white latex gloves. I swabbed between the cracks of stained wood. I gathered whatever was or wasn't there. If any of my captured samples indicated a presence of blood, the level of this investigation would increase several notches. I peered into the face of Ms. Boston. I wanted to see if she displayed any level of guilt. I wanted to know if she feared the results of this examination more than I. I did this discreetly.

After a few minutes of no questionable frowns, I felt at ease with her demeanor. I felt lab tests would reveal no evidence to any wrongdoing. I spotted a yellow broom handle in the far corner of the closet. Half of the broom's straws were missing. There was no evidence this cleaning utensil was used to discipline Nancy. If so, loose straws would show on the closet floor.

This complaint was no more than a suspect report. In my face-to-face encounter with Ms. Boston, I asked if her daughter's allegations had any truth to them. Without hesitation, she responded, "Basically, all of them are true. My daughter is very proud of her honesty. The whole truth is that Nancy has bad study habits. When her scholastic scores decline, I'm going to discipline her until she drops," the mother added.

I discussed the harmful side of physical and psychological abuse with Ms. Boston. She wasn't listening. I then asked, "What can a child learn by sitting helplessly in the dark without life's normal necessities?" "Total Concentration!" Mrs. Boston yelled. I then interrupted, "Suppose she needed medical assistance while you had her locked in a closet?" Based on past history, you wouldn't know it until the discipline's expiration. By then it could be too late!"

"I want only the best for Nancy," Ms. Boston shouted. "Look around this house! She has everything a child could want. I'm sure you've noticed no father figure around here. Give me some credit as a mother. Nancy and I have made it even though her father left us!" she continued.

I sat Ms. Boston down. I admitted if Nancy was telling the truth, I had a problem with the discipline she received. "There's nothing wrong wanting the best from a child," I said. "To be gagged, forced into a closet for two days will never be acceptable."

As of this moment, I'm petitioning the Family Court on this matter. Ms. Boston calmed down when she heard my last comment. She agreed to do whatever it took to have her daughter returned without any court intervention. This was easier said than done. Family Court has a rule, "A child cannot be returned to any home if he or she totally refuses to do so. This rule is obeyed regardless the child's age." When this situation occurs (it occurs more than the culture thinks), the child is placed under the custody of the court. Children declared psychologically balanced are capable of telling the truth. If a child feels safe and not threatened by the parent, they can tell that to the judge personally when he inquires. If a child is untruthful, this fact, too, will be discovered.

Thank God the judicial process worked in this instance. Honesty is important when addressing neglect complaints. Ms. Boston had no problem being just that. She described her love to the judge and the need to raise Nancy as best she could. She felt she'd done nothing wrong. After all, no physical injuries were inflicted. Ms. Boston was remorseful and attentive to the judge's instructions. Social Services had no documentation on this family. To satisfy the neglect complaint, the judge ordered a Social Services investigation by the end of the day. It was presently 10 a.m. At 4 p.m., the judge conferred with Social Services. Nancy was released back into her mother's custody.

The Court instructed Ms. Boston to ease up on her search for scholarly perfection. A Court Psychologist explained that the hurt Ms. Boston was experiencing from her marriage break-up was transferred to her daughter. Ms. Boston, not previously aware of that finding, agreed to on-going professional therapy. Hate for her former husband manifested the perfection forced on her daughter.

Ms. Boston desperately wanted to provide Nancy with the best education. Nancy could then learn to care for herself and never depend on a man. This transference of pain was a major problem. I learned seeking the best sometimes brings out the worst in caring parents. I was happy to see Ms. Boston and Nancy reunited. It was great to witness the court system work in this regard. I have a strange feeling there are similar cases I've yet to find. Thus, the challenge goes on.

The day had ended. I rushed home to satisfy Jillian, the love of my life. I wanted to rekindle that we have been without. I wanted us to look into each other's eyes and bring back magic from the good old days. I was mentally prepared to be the man she wanted. I'd practiced asking her to be the woman I sought on that first date. That first dance. Forever and ever.

I entered my house, on time, with flowers. I found Jillian... nowhere. Jillian had left the premises.

No note.

No children.

No nothing. Just gone!

"What did I do now?" I asked myself. I dropped to my knees. I started to weep. I was an empty shell of a man. No soul whatsoever. It was time to write something in my diary. I needed to take my mind off of my latest emptiness and I had exhausted my supply of yellows and blues.

"Where's my Jillian?" I wondered. "Where's all I have in this world?"

CHAPTER 10

My daily assignments only magnified the negatives in my marriage. Jillian and I sought counseling. We wanted our relationship to survive.

I was asked to consider another occupation. I was asked to transition to a more family oriented job. This was an unrealistic request. I was locked in to my occupation as a Child Abuse Detective. Changing jobs was never a consideration… not for me anyway. I made the biggest mistake of my life. I chose a law enforcement career instead of a life with this wonderful woman.

While the issue was heavy on my mind, a friend offered advice I didn't heed. "A good wife is the best thing a man can ever have!" he stated. "I know your wife's character. You should never let anything interrupt the love you have for her. A job can be found anywhere," he added. "You'll never replace that particular woman!"

You know what? He was right. I didn't listen until it was too late. My police career continued to flourish. My marriage didn't. Jillian followed her better senses. She chose a life of certainty over one of unknown. I entered my unhappy home that memorable night. The sounds of "Honey, I'm home!" ricocheted off the walls like I was in the Grand Canyon. Jillian didn't simply disappear. She was too full of character to do that. She left a voice mail telephone number. She welcomed future conversations if I promised to control my emotions. "Wow. That's generous of her," I thought.

I finally found myself face to face with Jillian. The apologies I practiced all week long didn't surface. I thought all I had to do was look into her eyes. All I had to do to gain her return was tell her how much she meant to me! All I had to do was drive Jillian and the kids back to our happy home. I was wrong!

I peered into Jillian's hazel eyes. Nothing happened. She'd heard many of my "honey, pretty pleases" in the past. They, too, fell on death ears. I realized my life was pretty much over. A separation was foremost on her mind. When the separation date arrived, I fell into the courtroom's chair with nothing to say. The only reason people separated or divorced was because of infidelity... nothing else! This was my basic defense. Yet, when the judge acknowledged the Separation Decree, a terrible emptiness entered my heart. There wasn't an outward sadness between us. I wondered why?

Sadness was slowly seeping into my bones. My soul was void of any feeling. Reality had set in. A handshake opportunity from my lawyer went unreturned. Jillian sat at the other table. I made eye contact with her to visually say I'm sorry. Her face went blank. "Nope! Not today mister! I'm not accepting apologies today!" was her returned look. We met at the courtroom's doorway. She tried to hold back the tears from her marital failure... a personal and generational one... for her family had been divorce-free until now.

She could hold back the hurt no longer. She grabbed me to steady herself. She placed her head on my shoulder and held on to me. She sobbed uncontrollably. I offered to return the hug. She pushed me away. "I can't believe you chose your job over our lives!" she sobbed. A lump in my throat joined the emptiness in my heart. Sadly to say, it was too late to save the only woman in my life. But... I'll survive. I've got to! My career would become my total mistress. Women I dated afterwards were substitutes trying to fill the void left by Jillian. My dating practices were so weird. It never took much to eliminate a possible new mate. My dating age group had children in their lives. I'd evaluate the woman's child rearing skills. If they weren't similar to mine, or Jillian's... there were no repeat dinners. This irrational thinking kept me depressed. I finally accepted therapy. I recaptured some of my sanity. I neither found Jillian's special kind of love nor stopped trying to find it!

Unbelievable, huh?

My life had become a bunch of crap! I made it that way. I know you've heard me say that before. It's true. The more I became involved in police work, the easier I handled my separation status. Or, so I thought. I was having no dating luck with my new dating evaluation process. I was looking for that next special woman in all of the wrong places. Ardie Calloway, my nosy mother, suggested I seek out a relationship with someone under God's roof. "God already helped me in so many ways," I recognized. "One more time might be possible," I conceded. "How do I get introduced into such settings?" The last thing I needed was to date a woman from the same church. That's like committing suicide. I couldn't approach a woman at Jillian's church, tell her I've made terrible relationship decisions with Jillian, and ask the new woman out to dinner? Or, could I? Shy in this regard, I asked the wise one... my momma'. She confidently mentioned the Adult Choir. "Those choir members know everything about everybody in the church!" she added. "Seek them out wherever you go."

Accepting her advice, I reluctantly joined a new church. Sircus Junction Baptist Church was its name. It was on Williamson Blvd way on the other side of town. I immediately interacted with its choir members. Within a month, I gathered more info' about its membership than I ever imagined. I did so by introducing myself to Sister Sizemore.

Sister Sizemore was the choir's elder spokeswoman. We bonded. I asked her to help me find that special woman. She agreed. We began that very evening at Crystal's Coffee Shop. And, yes, her back was to the door. Sister Sizemore said I should seek a woman who was secure, independent, and scholarly. She said I needed a religious woman who was true to herself. "Seek a lady you could trust in a relationship," she directed. "You should seek one who keeps God as an important part of her life!"

Sister Sizemore blinked her left eye several times but I knew not why. I did agree those characteristics she mentioned were admirable. I told Sister Sizemore to continue whatever strategy she had on my behalf. The following Sunday morning arrived. Sister Sizemore nodded as a certain worshiper entered the church. The lovely woman sat in the second row–left. She removed her coat. She was, indeed, beautiful. She had a gorgeous smile... not one better than Jillian's... but good enough. Her smile was one much younger than forty-nine, the age Sister Sizemore indicated.

She was a recent widower. Her late husband was a respected member of the congregation. There were no rumors she sought another partner. "Mrs. Harrison hid her loneliness for the last two years!" Sister Sizemore informed. "The good thing is that her former husband had characteristics similar to yours." My hopes improved. I had never met this woman before.

Sircus Junction Baptist Church had a late Sunday program that day. I'll officially introduce myself to Mrs. Harrison at the evening program. The opportunity presented itself. I nervously approached. She was cordial in every way. Her smooth voice sounded of Angels. I immediately knew I was in good company. She welcomed me to the church. We did the small talk thing for a few minutes. I then asked... "Do you need a ride home?" "Not really... Thanks anyway," she said. She turned. She made her way to the door. I followed with my nose wide open. When she hesitated at the door, I asked, "May I call you sometime in the future?" This question brought her to a complete halt on the church steps. She apparently had hazel eyes in the back of her head. She knew I had followed her. She knew another question would soon fly out of my mouth. "She's good!" I mumbled to myself.

Mrs. Harrison stared at me for a moment. "I'm can't date right now," she bluntly stated. "I'm still mourning the loss of my husband!" Stunned for a moment, I wanted to say... "You're a beautiful woman inside and out. It's been two long years! You've got to be a horny son-of-a-gun by now! huh?" That's what I wanted to say, but held my tongue. "Relax!" I told my ego not to let my underwear get all twisted up in a knot. That was simply a verbal thought crossing my mind.

What I actually said to her was... "I'm sure your husband wanted you to share your love with another deserving man! I'm the lucky man and I'm right here! Right now!" I said this with sarcasm while opening my arms for an approval hug.

Mrs. Harrison turned her head to the left. She gave me a look that could kill.

"Okay...?" I thought. I probably crossed the line. Perhaps I put my foot in my mouth. I was sure the next words spoken would negate any desire for a returned love. She placed her hands on her waist as if to say... "You must be kiddin', buster!" Yet, her next words didn't chastise me. They were words certainly unexpected. "If I'm ever interested in a new relationship, the man I choose must be committed to God! You might be that man," she said questionably?

She politely smiled. She gave final goodbyes to other exiting worshipers. I waited patiently. I wanted to see if she'd look back once she reached her car. It didn't happen. I waited patiently, again. I wanted to see if she'd look my way while navigating the parking lot. It didn't happen. I wasn't stunned by her bluntness. I was nothing but a stranger. I felt she was cold-hearted. She needed no one else in her life. I wasn't put off by her posture or that princess-type halo surrounding her fat head. "Why would a religious chick rush to satisfy another man's needs?" I asked myself. "Where's the rush!" Mrs. Harrison exited the parking lot. She made a right turn at Galaxy Road. My first attempt at new love was a failure. I sought out Sister Sizemore... my relationship Guru. She sat with me in the church pews away from nosy ears. Her explanation was pure and simple.

"Mrs. Harrison enters these church doors twice on Sundays and three other nights per week!" she said.

"She comes to do the Lord's work and whatever else the church asks. The man courting her must be dedicated to the church. Otherwise, he should look for somebody else!" I thoroughly understood these words. They didn't scare me. I desired Mrs. Harrison's love. Sister Sizemore's next words stung a little bit more. Gossip had it that this woman winch was involved with a married man.

Sister Sizemore looked into my eyes. She wanted to see if her messages were bothersome. "I said a man of 'this' church. Not a man at a church! Don't let me confuse you!" she reiterated. I slightly grimaced at Sister Sizemore's interpretation. How can a special woman like Jacque Harrison not attract any unmarried man she wanted? I returned the stare. It was a stare of jealousy. I would not be afraid of another man's want for Jacque.

Sister Sizemore looked around to make sure we were alone. She pushed herself a little closer. "Listen carefully my new friend," she whispered. "There's a possibility your precious Jacque is involved with a married man of the cloth!" she said in a more harsh tone. Sister Sizemore twisted her smile as if to say... think, fool!

A puzzlement clouded my face. Sister Sizemore took my hand. She gave me the answer to her riddle. "I think your future love is personally involved with the Pastor. How do you feel about that?" she frowned. "How could that be?" I asked. I've attended this church for several months. The one thing I know is the Pastor is happily married. I've talked to his beautiful wife several times. Both welcomed me to the church.

Sister Sizemore slapped me on the top of my head... in a loving kind of way. She didn't want me wasting time on a lady deemed untouchable.

"Where's the truth, Sister?" I asked. "Church gossip is far from the truth most times. The closest thing to reality other times," I added. "If I didn't believe this gossip was true, I wouldn't have brought it to your attention," she said. "Remember. You came to me seeking a friend. I want to keep it that way. If I can't tell you what might hurt you, I wouldn't consider myself a friend."

"Sister Sizemore!" I whispered. "How could a Pastor be connected to such rumors?"

"Pastors are human like everybody else. There are no witnesses to this rumor. Only gossip talk!" she mumbled.

I'd heard enough. I would continue to pursue this woman for a permanent relationship. It's possible she never met a good man since her husband died. No one she could really love. Maybe the Pastor was simply a religious connection? Maybe she confided in his religious ears. I paused after that last maybe. "Did he take advantage of her after her late husband died?" I wondered. We need someone to talk to during a grieving process. "Did something else happen between them?" If you needed direction after your spouse's death, is there a better person than your Pastor? You surely can't call on a previous lover. Too much touching... too many old memories. Been there. Done that. I'm sure Mrs. Harrison loved her late husband. I'm pretty sure she could handle the pain of loneliness. The pain of never loving that person again may never go away. If she decides to love another man, it'll be a different kind of love. Any new love will be the here and now. It has to be learned minute by minute. Second by second. Touch by touch.

I was talking too much. When I realized it, Sister Sizemore was staring at me with her mouth wide open. "Have you ever thought about becoming a preacher?" she jokingly asked. I thanked Sister Sizemore for being honest with me. She didn't have to be. She could have steered me toward a much less desired church momma'. There were lots of sorry ones to choose from. In fact, Sircus Junction First Baptist had lots of fancy hats and money from life insurance policies. I named this group of wealthy ladies the "Hat Connection" 'cause they tried to out-do each other hat-wise every Sunday.

At least Sister Sizemore's selection of Jacque was easy on the eyes. Others had to get up so much earlier on Sunday mornings... if you get my drift?

During our discreet conversations, I think Sister Sizemore considered herself a candidate for my heart. I gave it some thought, several times. There simply were no personal attractions. No love jones about her brown eyes kept me awake at night. The one time I expressed a possibility of developing a relationship with Sister Sizemore, she dropped her blue, cotton-laced panties faster than a speedin' bullet! I remembered that day like it was yesterday. Sister Sizemore invited me over for dinner to discuss other female possibilities. She knew the religious history (and bank account balances) of every widowed woman in this congregation.

It was an early Saturday afternoon, about 3 PM. When I arrived, Sister Sizemore had recently returned from the beauty parlor. She was wearing a sorta' loose fitting top-shirt and some overturned flat shoes. I absolutely hated over-turned flat shoes! She was showing lots of cleavage but... who cared. No one else was home. And, yes, way too much perfume and lip stick.

I felt awkward. Naïve I am but I can recognize a love trap when it's obvious. No matter how hard I wanted to consider Sister Sizemore as a future lover, I knew she'd end up another unwanted sexual conquest. I knew it. She knew it. She knew but wanted to be pleasured anyway. "Please make love to me for old time's sake!" she quivered. "No one needs to know!"

Sister Sizemore made a huge mistake in my character. I would not... could not... be that guy who needed a sexual outlet. I could never betray the woman developing my religious future. Friends are so hard to find. She meant more to me as a friend than as a nasty one-time lover. As soon as I was finished, I'd let the door hit me where the dog should've bit me thing... or however that saying goes. Loving her was not meant to be. I'm no different than most men. We run as fast as we can from an unwanted lover's bed. We do so to prevent the greatest relationship misgiving of all time... the unwanted possibility of looking directly in a woman's eyes afterwards and flat out lying about the L word!

It's a known fact! We don't know how we feel about any woman 'til we've been intimate. Afterwards, we'll make that dreaded fall in love decision. If we love the way a partner makes us feel in the bed, a further commitment may be easier to make. In retrospect, most decent women fall in love first (at least a little bit) before dropping their panties to their ankles. I'm not totally sure about this theory... it seems to work out that way.

My mother, Ardie Calloway, could add some clarity to this situation. If I approached her, I'd change my wording just a tad 'cause my momma's from the old school. Then again, I think I'll leave my momma' out of this discussion. The toughest thing to tell any woman reduced to a sexual object is.... I love you! It's really hard to say. It's even harder to say in a sincere way.

Women know the difference. Sister Sizemore... with all of her wisdom... would know the difference. If we'd made love, one of us would have to change churches. That person would likely be me. I liked the new church. I didn't look forward to another change.

I remembered what my mother told me about the Adult Choir. If I became Sister Sizemore's new beau, she'd have me marked as her personal property quicker than the reading of the

Twenty-Third Psalm! It's not a good feeling to be religiously owned. Been there! Done that... too many times! I gave Sister Sizemore an honest opportunity to enter my life. She loved to laugh. She wasn't controlling. She was well off financially (not that financial stability was a prerequisite). The honest to God truth... I couldn't go there with Sister Belinda Sizemore 'cause she was 4 ft. 8 inches tall and weighed 300 lbs.!

My decision to pursue the elusive Jacque Harrison was kept alive. I would do this in a passive aggressive way. I would do this in an "I need you but won't act like I need you" mentality. This will be my strategy.

As each glorious Sunday morning arrived, I'd say hello to Jacque, religiously. I'd then move on without any additional verbal fanfare. Other times, I'd complimented her hair... and then move on with my business. Sometimes, her dress... then move on. And sometimes, I'd say nothing and unintentionally send one of my wink-winks in her direction.

I always sat in a church pew that allowed direct eye contact. I did this to show a little interest every now and then. I canvassed the male attendees in the congregation each Sunday. I wanted to observe other beaus possibly interested in Jacque. I wasn't successful. I remembered her husband was one who visited the church on a daily basis. Her new man had to be someone totally committed to God. I now wondered? I now wondered if this woman was sending me a secret message? Was she asking me to leave her alone? Was she really committed to Pastor you know who? I became more observant of the Pastor each Sunday. I watched for eye contact between he and my Jacque. I watched for body language.

I watched for anything leading me to believe I was wasting my efforts. I didn't recognize anything obvious. It was probably stupid gossip. I decided I would approach Ms. Harrison, again. I would ask her out one more time. I wore my best suit that

Sunday. Got a haircut. Shined my shoes. A good impression was imperative. I approached her at the end of the sermon. "Excuse me, Ms. Harrison." I mumbled. "It's been a while. I thought it wouldn't hurt to ask you out one more time. Would you have dinner with me?"

God smiled that day. "Oh, my! I thought you'd never ask that question again!" she said with a big smile on her face. I, and my ego, was speechless. I never thought it would be this easy. "What's a good day?" I followed. "Well, I'll select a day I have no commitments to the church. I'll work it out. Here's my number," she replied. She placed her business card in my hand. Her work number was on the front. Her cell number was hand-written on the back. "I've been carrying this card around for a long time," she added. "I'm glad you came to your senses." She turned a gracious turn. She walked that woman's walk. It was the walk of curious satisfaction. A walk that made me believe she was sincere. I could do nothing but stand there. I watched her prance away for now. I've been blessed again with a human gift. "Jillian... who?" I remembered asking myself.

Thursday of the following week was chosen. Jacque liked seafood. The wharf was nearby. She shared what she'd heard about me. I shared, likewise. I didn't, however, share any gossip placing her in the Pastor's bed. To never ask was bothering me. I was not a very jealous man. Slightly insecure, maybe.

Within days, I developed feelings for this woman. She was very desirable. My fantasies were working overtime. I had to know the truth about the Pastor. Why couldn't I want her regardless of any past or current love she had for the Pastor? Did I feel injured because she slept with him? Or, did I feel injured because I knew about it? I think there's a difference. I don't know what it is. How could any real man follow the exploits of a married Pastor? A better question is, "How could any woman sleeping with a Pastor get into heaven?"

Great question. Answers are needed. Pastors talk about forgiveness. They talk about forgiveness all of the time. If there was indeed a past relationship between the two of them, I think each has forgiven the other. Each had moved on with their lives. Yes. Something happened and then it was undone. Case closed.

Weeks later, Jacque prepared a magnificent Sunday dinner. She invited me to stop by for a plate or two. She changed into a something seductive at the end of the meal. We snuggled. "Sir... Mr. Calloway... Whatever you like to be called... what are you motives?" she asked.

"My motives?" I repeated.

"Yes. Motives?" she reiterated. "Exactly what do you want from me? I've done my homework. You'd make a nice man-catch for lots of women at the church. You've sought me out. What I'd like to know is... why me?" she asked.

I became silent. I could not answer her question. I sought her out because of what she could be to me. What we could be to each other.

I really sought her out to take the place of my long gone Jillian... the woman I'm legally separated from at this time. I told Jacque I wanted a long-term relationship. I would go only as fast as she allowed me to go. Before I spoke another word, she kissed me. I kissed her back. "I've not been with anyone since my husband died," she whispered.

"I waited for someone special."

"I hoped you could be that someone. I left church that first day we met hoping you could be the one for me," she said.

"I waited to see how many within the secret Hat Society you seduce."

"Never a word of gossip, though."

"Mr. Bishop Calloway. Can you be the man I need?" she sensually asked. She squeezed my hand. She slowly led me to her bedroom. I desired this woman. I had no idea intimacy was the dinner she sought. If that's the case, "How many other men had she entertained for the sake of a Sunday dinner?" I wondered. "Is this how a woman of God acts?" Does this widower have an uncontrollable sexual appetite? Are churches filled with women freely expressing themselves? Questions… questions… questions. What I did know was I never thought Mrs. Jacque Harrison would allow me into her bedroom before she knew how to spell my last name. The rumors were obviously true.

If not with the Pastor… Was she with others under that same church roof? The heart I wanted to give this woman had disappeared. Jacque fell from a major desire to a mere conquest. I was ashamed of her. I was ashamed of myself. I'll make this fact common knowledge as soon as our fourth session of love had bottomed out. Thirty minutes later someone opened her front door. I heard keys rattlin' so it wasn't a forced entry. This unwanted entrance froze our passions.

Footsteps slowly headed for her bedroom door. I grabbed my gun. A burglary-in-progress was takin' place. I quietly asked Jacque if someone else had a key. She didn't answer. She sat on the bed's edge staring up at me. She had a dumfounded look on her face.

The footsteps stopped on the other side of her bedroom wall. I stood inside the door. My badge was in one hand. My Smith and Wesson in the other. An unwelcomed man's silhouette entered the room's darkness. I could see the fella's shadow. He, too, was armed with a handgun. Whoever this felon, he would be no match for Det. Bishop Calloway. Not tonight anyway. A brief scuffle took place. A knockdown knuckle or two… or three… and lights turned on… The Pastor!

"I'm not impressed with your boxing skills, Pastor." I said. I dumped his gun shells onto the floor. They rolled around like marbles on roller skates. "Jacque!" he yelled. "Why is this fella' in your bed? Our bed? You're mine and always will be. You know that, don't you?" he sobbingly yelled while rubbing his jaw. Jacque tied her lips in a knot. She silently wondered how much of this mess I'd leak to the Adult Choir's spokesperson. I put the Pastor's hat back on his head. I kicked him out the front door... naked. Before I did, I threatened to tell his wife about this incident if he bothered Mrs. Harrison again.

Jacque watched me work my discreet magic. Now that I've given this situation more thought, I think she used my police talents to break away from the Pastor's clutches. Jacque asked for and was blessed with my forgiveness. With a smirk of relief on her face, she embarrassingly invited me back to her bed. She wanted to finish what we'd started before the Pastor's intrusion... an intrusion I now realize she knew was forthcoming. This pious than thou slut apparently misunderstood me. She was sleeping with the church's leader. She was sleeping with a man of God who was in a holy marriage. She was sleeping with a special man who was married to a great woman. She, therefore, would sleep with me no longer.

Jacque admitted the affair was nothing more than a sexual one. It began a year before her late husband died. He knew about it before his death. He took the secret to his grave rather than embarrass the church. In retrospect, the truth was probably what killed him. That truth would not be my fate. The fine Jacque Harrison would kill the hearts of no other men.

She would harm innocent church wives no longer. She would move to another town. She would take her secrets with her. This was one promise she would surely keep. "Good riddance!" I said as I left her bed the next morning. "Jillian, where art thou!" I asked as I drove Interstate 66. "My life isn't working without you." Several hours of sleep relaxed my yearning for Jillian. My late shift would begin soon. Maybe lying next to an old girl friend might take my mind off of Jillian and Jacque? Besides... who would I call? I fell asleep wishing for a woman's touch. I found several of my old yellow and blue friends. I knew they would never let me down.

I'll dream forth and find that promised new world I've been seeking. I'd do it this very second!

My Holy Friend,

It is very important several social issues be changed for the better. Some are more critical to the new world than others. I'll try to concentrate on a few this second.

Newborn babies, the elderly, and a rapidly growing prison population must be given considerable thought if they are to be a prominent part of my new world.

On the issue of newborn babies, a law will be adopted to safeguard the new world's most valuable asset... human life in its earliest form.

Steering young minds away from sinful attitudes will be mandatory. I will attach an identity-coded microchip to the hipbone of every newborn child. The microchip cannot be removed until age 21. The only obstacles validating early removal are criminal convictions of any kind. Removing the chip before age 21 will invalidate life-long social entitlements such as the right to vote, free health care, etc. Yes. There will be a public outcry about this invasion of privacy. It won't matter. Not in my new world.

I will mandate each child be placed in a random selection pool. If a child's id number is chosen, caretakers and custodians must present that child to a designated health control center within four hours.

A special team of doctors shall make sure the child's mental and physical well-being has not been compromised. The penalty for violating this mandate is death. This new world... our new world... has to be a very serious world.

Once a child passes health-related tests, he or she will not be re-entered into the Selection Pool for a period of five years. If a child fails any of the tests... stringent interventions will be introduced to further protect the child. This protection should help eliminate child-abusive mindsets. We'll have to wait and see if it works. I hope so.

A government-backed retirement system for the elderly will be offered to men at age 65 and to women at age 75. The age difference is based on a female's ability to live longer than a male. Retirement compensation will be based on three categories of life-long behavior. The first behavior category... "How much did you help your fellow man?"... generated 50% of a retirement package. The second category... "Have you respected your parents over the years?" will generate 10% of the overall retirement package. The last behavioral category... "How many people have you forgiven over your lifetime?" will command a retirement value of 30% in the new world.

These behavioral categories will acquire their independent compensation values by evaluating your past conscience. Whatever life you've lived... how you've treated your fellow man... are personal issues found deep within your souls. They remain a part of you, forever.

The growing prison population is another social issue our new world must better address. Answers are hard to find even for a proactive world not yet born. Mainstreaming the criminal mind was good in past cultures as long as a halfway house wasn't placed in a nearby neighborhood. So, no more Halfway Houses... Please! Let's face it. No matter where you reside in this current world, crime has continued to increase. I've heard no innovative responses for addressing an over-crowded prison system. The new world will be open to recommendations.

Maybe something similar to the newborn baby's identification process could be utilized? The new world could place a microchip in the body of all criminal offenders. Whenever a crime is committed, simply check the grid to see which offenders were within that crime scene environment. Such measures might be considered barbaric... but they'd be great deterrent factors.

Researchers say as long as there's a Class System, criminal activity will be a part of any society. If so, whenever anything is identified as having value, a new class system can't be far behind. New haves and have-nots' create new criminal activity: Hence, more arrest, convictions, steel bars and concrete prisons. The moral here is that I don't have all the answers needed for my new world! Creating a new world totally without sin has to start somewhere. Maybe I should get into the steel and concrete business! The new world could simply build one very large prison city for the entire new world. Am I throwing stones while livin' in a glass house?

A weird buzzing in my jacket pocket expects me to return to the present. I gotta' go. The buzzin' might be Jillian. It wasn't. It was someone selling lower home mortgage rates!

CHAPTER 11

I tried to take my mind off Jillian. I fumbled through an unpacked box of old stuff sitting in the garage. I kept boxes packed in case Jillian came to her senses. I found my old High School Yearbook. I inquisitively flipped the pages to see faces of those I may have fondled in the back seat of Pop's '59 Chevy. I shouldn't waste my time. I knew the answer was nobody! I was the only guy in high school to graduate as a virgin. This fact still embarrasses me years later.

I didn't act that way back then. I gave my peers the impression sex was a daily ritual in my young life. Rachel, the girl I dated, gave that impression, too. Our sexual image made for a hot high school scandal. I had plenty of opportunities to score and Rachel Duncan was a fox. She was ready and willing.

Unfortunately, Rachel had the meanest grandma' East of the Mississippi. This custodian allowed Rachel visitors as long as everyone remained in her sights. Grandma' was determined to keep eager male hands off 'lil' Rachel. Rachel was a devil when grandma' wasn't around. She sought as much kissing and petting as you could give. She really did! My life would've drastically changed. All Rachel needed to say was yes… one time. I chuckled over those unfulfilled memories.

I dug deeper into the box of memories. I pulled out an old black book. It contained telephone numbers of acquaintances from long, long ago. When I reached the R's, Rachel's name appeared. Yes. The same Rachel from my high school days. I've kept in touch. Her telephone number remains a good one. I dialed it without hesitation.

A sweet voice answered after the second ring. It was the matured voice of Rachel Duncan-Spinner... now divorced. "Hello, Rachel!" I said in my sexiest voice. A quiet came across the telephone. "Is this Bishop Calloway? Oh my goodness! Tell me this isn't the ole' Bishop Calloway!" she screamed. "I'll be darned if it isn't!" We laughed for several minutes. "Where have you been? What have you been up to?" she asked. I didn't tell her the real reason I was calling. How could I say I pulled her name out of a hat? How could I tell her I desired her to be my next sexual conquest? I could no longer demand what was rightfully mine so many years ago? Her grandmother kept me from being the first real man in her life. I think I now deserve to be the next one.

"Rachel, can I talk to you about what never took place between us years ago." I asked. "It still bothers me to know we never made a go of it. Let's have lunch on that same park bench. Let's do some reminiscing?" I asked. I could tell Rachel Spinner was smiling on the other end. "That would be so fantastic! I'd love to do that! The sooner the better, my old love!" she added.

"Did I hear her correctly? Did I hear her say... Old Love?" I silently inquired. How could she nonchalantly call me her old love after ... let's say... 5 years had gone by? "Sounds like Rachel wanted more than I intended to give. Better be careful," I told myself.

Several days later, Rachel and I met on that same park bench where we kissed in the past. Keystone Park was made for lovers: and lovers we were back in the day. I tried to be respectful. No touching occurred as we sat looking into each other's eyes. We remembered the high school graduation ceremony. We received college scholarships to Centennial University.

College life was all that and more. We expected the unexpected. We were not disappointed. As freshmen, we were a young man and woman struggling to grasp a new educational lifestyle. We sought new expressions of freedom… expressions never before experienced. We laughed again. We recalled how much time we spent deciding on a college major. That was nothing but wasted time. Most freshmen had to take similar foundational courses anyway. Another learned lesson? Sixty percent of all students changed their majors several times.

We also remembered our first campus party. The faculty tried its best to make all incoming freshmen feel at home. They thought a welcoming party was a good way to start our college careers. It was a total flop. Wrong music… and most dormitories weren't co-ed back in those days. Rachel's roommate was Darcey Hammonds. I roomed with a guy named Gregory Munn. "There was an immediate problem between Darcey and I." Rachel recalled. "Darcey was more mature. She was from New York City. She had more beauty than I… a whole lot more."

"She was smarter, had a better wardrobe… and she arrived on campus in her very own car!"

"It didn't stop there," Rachel added. "Darcey walked like she attended modeling school. She came from a family of old money! Need I say more?"

"It took a while. We became the best of friends," said Rachel. "We ended up with identical courses."

Rachel said she and Darcey pranced around the campus like they were God's gift to men until something became clearer to them. It became obvious at Centennial U. that hundreds of princesses roamed the campus streets. It wasn't like it was back in our respective towns. Back home only a handful of girls were pretty enough for that distinction. "That was our first campus lesson," Rachel chimed. "Every girl on campus was as pretty as we thought we were."

"As for the young men on campus, the more handsome we thought we were, the more disrespect we had for you campus chicks!" I chimed. "We were taught by the upper-classmen to be true gentlemen until you gave us the green light to champion your virginity".

"I was not a part of that group, of course!"

"That's the kind of guys you silly girls wanted!" I added. I thought Rachel would respond to my statement. She didn't. She turned her head. She looked down to the sidewalk. I then remembered something that happened during those campus days I would share with Rachel.

Shortly after registration, we attempted a casual double date. It was a date with no commitment attached. Darcey was a very confident young lady. She was too independent for either one of our freshmen male mindsets. This fact scared us. Darcey turned heads of seniors without trying. That wasn't a good thing. The powerful clout seniors had on this campus was unreal. As a rule, any female accepting a date with a senior shouldn't waste any time puttin' on underwear. They were definitely comin' off!

Young ladies outnumbered men five-to-one on this campus. Most fellas' did the choosing. This observation did not affect Darcey. It did affect our double date. Gregory sat next to Darcey 'cause he was assumed to be her date. Her strong personality rendered him invisible. He was overshadowed by this tigress he never had by the tail. Darcey could be very sexy at times. She could call every man to attention and not let one touch her.

She knew the tricks men fell for and when to use them. Gregory, observing Darcey's demeanor, excused himself from the double date. "I've got to write a letter to my momma'!" he said as he ran from the room.

Nobody challenged him. Why should they? I, the young Bishop Calloway, was left with two gorgeous freshmen and nowhere to hide.

"Centennial's environment scared me to death back then!" said Rachel. "I wasn't ready for a prime time intimate environment. I was prepared, however, to let you introduce me to womanhood. It never happened," she silently mumbled in my direction. "You found some fellas' talking about ancient Roman history. You fell in with them. You never came back to me."

Rachel didn't get much privacy that night. Darcey entered the dorm room accompanied by a gorgeous hunk of a football player. The size of this man-ster was intriguing. The one thing she talked about all the time was dating larger men if you know what I mean. "I love everything about a larger man!" she's been saying. "Everything!" she reiterated as though I was naive.

What Darcey didn't know? Senior fellas' had wagered on her. The wager was to see who'd be the first to get into her pants. The footballer was Frank Kearsey. Rumor had it he was a 1st Round Draft pick... soon worth millions. The other rumor had Frank in more than half the girls on campus. Every time we saw Frank in the hallways he was whispering in some country chick's ear. He wasn't talking Biology 101 either... or, maybe he was?

Darcey said she could handle him if he got out of control. Rachel worried about Darcey that entire evening. She stayed awake until crazy Frank left the dorm.

Rachel heard the dorm's door shut. She raced into the next room. She found Darcey all curled up in a knot on the bed. Her eyes were pushed into a pillow. Something bad had taken place.

"I'm gonna' tell you how that horrible story ended!" Rachel cried out. "It's been years. I'm sure Darcey won't mind. Please don't tell her you know! Okay, Bishop?"

"Darcey Hammonds wasn't a virgin!" said Rachel. "But Frank's actions were a border-line case of date rape!" Before

Darcey could shut her private bedroom door, Frank became very active. Darcey wasn't ready for this action but didn't say no. She wanted to fit in with the campus in-crowd by allowing him to touch her," said Rachel. "Darcey knew she was in trouble but he was so much stronger. A minute later, Frank abruptly stopped. He left the dorm. He was only after the sexual aggression that accompanied rape. He didn't want love from an inviting woman," said Rachel as she turned to me. "How could a man do that?" she asked. "During those college days, did you ever desire me in that way?" she asked.

"Rachel, I tried to make love to you before we got to that college campus! I thought it might happen after you arrived on campus. Vietnam called me several weeks later. So it never happened," I said.

Rachel said, "I'm sorry about that time in our lives. We went our separate ways after that, huh?"

"The last thing I needed was a girl back home worrying about me dying in a far off land," I said. "Having my parents go through that was bad enough! My tour of duty in Vietnam lasted eighteen months. I returned without injury. A new GI Bill financed my college education. The rest was history."

"By the way, Rachel. On my way home from Vietnam, I ran into Henry Barker at Kennedy Airport in New York City. We talked over beers between planes. That's when Henry told me about the drug problems of Troy Williamson. Drug use forced Troy out of college. He was in a drug rehab place somewhere in Sircus Junction. "Troy was back dating his old girlfriend. I think you know her name. Her name is Rachel Dunlap, Dunson, Duncan… something like that. She graduated with us," Henry finished. "Rachel, please don't tell me while you were dating me, you were doing Troy?" I inquired. "If old blabber mouth Henry knew more about my business than I, who else knew?" "The thought of our romance did, however, keep me alive in the dark jungles of Southeast Asia," I added. "I'm sorry about that time in our lives," Rachel said over and over. "I did like you a lot."

"Your grandmother knew... didn't she? Have you been with Troy since Junior High?" I asked Rachel. Rachel sensed it was time for the truth. "I'm sorry, Bishop," she responded. "Troy and I were secret lovers since I was 12 years old. He was my first. My grandmother caught him with me way back then. I had a baby at 13 and gave the child to my aunt in Los Angeles. Granny made me promise no other man would touch me," she added.

"Both of you are going to get married as soon as you finished college. I'm going to initiate rape charges if you don't," Granny mandated.

"Troy was my only lover, never my love!" Rachel shouted. "That's why I needed you! I needed you for the psychological love you provided to me! I was already Troy's property! Any pressures you placed on me... well, I could handle! You were the safest person I could date!"

I sat on our special park bench with nothing to say. I sought out this woman to freak her out. It was I who learned something new. I'd been a fool in a situation I never suspected. How many friends knew this was happening? Why didn't someone drop me a line? The thought of sharing Rachel's love was hard to swallow. "So it was Troy all along, huh?" I asked again.

Here sat Rachel Duncan-Spinner. She had come full-circle. She was ready to do whatever I asked. She was prepared to solve this mystery in the most appropriate way possible. "I want to make love to you right now, Bishop. The past is the past. We can forget about other men. We can forget about other women. Let's move forward right now," she begged.

"What's the big deal?" I silently thought. I summoned Rachel for an intimate fix anyway. Here she is. Ready and willing to take care of old business. My old business.

I was a very proud person. I had feelings like other men. Now that the truth is out, an apology from her is supposed to right all the wrongs? It won't be as simple as that. I continued talking about the good old days with Rachel. I took her to my place. We were together for the very first time. Her skills were magnificent. I could see why Troy never wanted to let her go. "Who am I kidding?" I said to myself. "I might as well be honest! There's no way I could have satisfied Rachel's needs back in the day!" Rachel was a conquest long overdue. We wanted each other but in the old way. We wanted to turn back the clock. We wanted to laugh like we did during those great days at the High. If we'd made better choices, our lives could've been more rewarding.

So much for the dream of a lifetime. So much for my old love for Rachel Duncan-Spinner. We saw each other for another couple of weeks. It was never the same. We stared into each other's eyes and saw nothing. If we had it to do over again we'd do it differently. Life doesn't work like that. I became depressed. Depression was not a new word in my life. It affected me about one weekend a month. When it affected me, I stayed in the house. I'd sit in a special chair given to me by Jillian. Jillian understood the significance of that chair. She allowed me to keep it.

I sat alone. As I tried to regain my psychological edge, something always reminded me of Jillian. A remission to some degree and there I'd go again. Sitting in that chair. Wondering what I did wrong? Wondering how to correct it? Wondering if Jillian gave a darn?

Jillian had to at least care about me. I was the father of her children. I was no longer the love of her life. What I needed the most from her was farthest from my reach. The chair, on the other hand, I could touch. It was real. Her spirit was all over it. We made love in that chair during happier times. She'd assume a position most satisfying. Some memories just don't go away. Memories of Jillian don't go away. I unwillingly lost control. I called Jillian's number. She answered. I remained quiet. I knew she had caller id. I had nothing to say. I just wanted to hear her voice. I just wanted to hear her inhale and exhale... a heartbeat maybe. She easily recognized the owner of the silence. She stopped hanging up on me long ago. Jillian was allowing me to heal. I think she was healing also. It was a mutual thing. Not abusing her honor, I stayed on the hook for 30 long, silent seconds.

Guess what else was in reach? My personal Mr. Smith and Wesson! Several times, I held the telephone in one ear and Mr. Smith & Wesson in the other. I gave lots of thought to ending it all. My life was no longer valid. I'd lost it all for the sake of my job. The job I sacrificed everything for now caused me to consider suicide. I dared not. What would my children say? What would my mother say? More importantly, what would Jillian say? If everyone thought my life were no longer important, suicide would mean nothing.

Fortunately, that's not the case. I love you Jillian. No matter what I do, the value of my life is attached to your needs. Without you, I'm nobody! "Come back, Jillian! Please come back to me!" I cried out in vain.

I pushed the redial button on the telephone. Like clockwork, someone answered the second ring on the other end. This time I spoke.

"Jillian Esther Carson-Calloway? This is Bishop!" I said. "I know who you are," she cautiously replied.

"Would you consider dinner to talk about some things?" I asked Jillian. "I'm not asking for a date. Just dinner," I clarified.

"You must have been reading my mind, Bishop," Jillian replied. "I was just going to call you. I have a favor to ask. If you don't mind, that is."

I suggested we meet in one hour at *IBERO's...* that special Spanish Restaurant she loves? She agreed. My demeanor changed to one of wonderment. What could my Jillian want from me?

Has she finally come to her senses about our relationship? Is this her opportunity to say "Hey buster, bring your butt home, right now?" I couldn't wait. I was full of smiles at *IBERO's*. We faced each other for the first time in a long time. Her back was still to the door! I'm not crazy.

Jillian was as gorgeous as ever. Guess what Jillian was wearing? Yes. She was wearing that same short dress that got us into trouble the last time we ate here. This was a good sign. We finished off several bottles of Chianti she loves. Jillian asked the favor.

"Honey pie, my younger sister, Sugar, is missing!" she said. "She fell for some actor/director guy from New York City. She fell hook, line, and sinker." Jillian started to cry. Her parents tried everything possible to locate the sister. They haven't been successful. "I thought… since you're a super detective… you could go to New York City. You could bring her back home? Would you do that for me Bishop? Would you do that for us? Please?" she whined.

I needed more information about this scenario before I answered. I didn't want to make a promise I couldn't keep. Jillian shared as much as she knew. Sugar Carson met a guy at one of those Lower Manhattan acting studios. His name was Harry Wishbone. One thing led to another. They started sleeping together. Sugar is 19 years of age. She is old enough to make her own choices. This was not the Sugar I knew. She's a responsible young lady.

Sugar mentioned Wishbone's promises to make her a famous actress. This Wishbone fella' told her things to keep her under control. To keep her snuggled closely under him every night in his bed. He filled her young mind with promises of bright lights, mink coats and stuff like that. Knowing Sugar, she'd do anything to reach the level of superstardom. She's already Wishbone's love slave… not only for him; but also for profit from his friends. She drinks. She uses drugs. And… now… she's a high-priced prostitute!

Jillian said her mom received a call from New York City several weeks ago. The voice on the other end was slurred. It was Sugar's.

"Please come get me?" Sugar cried. "I have no idea where I am. Harry forced me into a drug life. I've tried to fight it. I need help. I need my family back," a slurred voice continued.

"If Harry knew I called you he'd kill me," Sugar added. "I make too much money for him."

Jillian started to weep for her little sister. "As you can imagine Bishop, this call destroyed the Carson household," suggested Jillian... the mother of my children... children I haven't seen because she curses my overall existence! "Don't get started," I kept saying to myself.

How could I say no to Jillian? She found the nerve to ask for my help. It's the first time she's ever done so. If this situation with Sugar was important to her... it was important to me. I had vacation days coming. I was going to use them for a fishing trip on the mountain with the Mustard Brothers. Oh, well. "I'll help your family anyway I can, Jillian," I said. "Get me that New York City telephone number. I'll do the rest."

Jillian exhaled. She sat way back in her chair. She poured another glass of Chianti—one for both of us. "Bishop. I love you for doing this!" she said. The remainder of the date went smoothly. There were no serious talks between us, just respect between two separated partners. She never told me she loved me. I, respectfully, never asked. I moved up the dates of my vacation. I had no idea how long it would take to track down Sugar's whereabouts. I packed my jeep. I prepared to head north to the Big Apple. I had to go pass my house—excuse me, my old house—to get Sugar's contact telephone number from Jillian.

I pulled up to the front door. My adorable children were leaving in the opposite direction in their grandparent's station wagon. I didn't get a chance to say hello and goodbye to them. I still needed their assurance we still loved each other. I have not nor ever would abandon them. I blew my horn as they passed by. They didn't hear me. A weird thing occurred. Jillian ran out of the house with the telephone number in one hand… a suitcase in the other. "No way you're searching for my little sister without me!" she screamed.

Her voice indicated it was no need arguing. "I'm going to the Big Apple with you! Case closed!"

I was speechless. Astonishment was written on my face. My heart missed a beat as I accepted the fact Jillian would be in my presence. She would sit right here next to me. She would be a silly arm's length away. Amazing, huh? Simply amazing!

The ride to the Big Apple took five hours. During the trip, Jillian cried for her sister while sharing as much family information as possible. There was never an opportunity to talk about our relationship. Rarely did I look into Jillian's sobbing eyes. I intentionally placed my right hand on her thighs to console her. She rapidly removed it between tears. She was havin' none of that! I never told Jillian about my dreadful life since we separated. Her baby sister was more important. My Jeep entered Manhattan's Holland Tunnel. A homeboy dispatcher friend traced the call from Sugar to a lower east side location. The address was off Chambers Street in the SoHo neighborhood. I knew that area from past visits.

The closer we got to Chambers, the more upset Jillian became. The observed street-life was questionable as we drove closer to the suspected address. "This is not the best of areas," I acknowledged. Jillian had no more tears to give. Deplorable living elements were observed at every turn. The streets were filled with the homeless and other wild-looking personalities. Kids of all ages roamed the streets. We saw no parents other than those seeking their missing children. I pulled into an alley about a block away from the address. "I'll be right back. You stay here. Keep the doors locked," I said. "Not on your life!" she yelled. "I've come this far. I'm gonna' do everything you do. Go everywhere you go!"

What could I say? This was not a normal woman. This was Jillian Esther Carson-Calloway... if only 'til the final divorce papers were official. She's a person not to be denied. We walked out of the nearest alley. We entered a dark stairway. It led to a second floor of apartment doors. I had a name and number for this address. It was not the name of John Wishbone. Janet Bouware or a similar name was listed.

We took one step at a time. We stepped over drunks, the homeless, and drug addicts on our way to the second floor. As we progressed, Jillian's hold became tighter and tighter. I tried to look like I wanted to illegally buy something or someone. Jillian, trying to blend in, fluffed up her hair to look like a hooker. The disguises allowed us to go unchallenged by those whose job it was to keep the unlawful peace in this place. I wanted to tangle with those guys... NOT!

A woman grabbed Jillian from behind. "Looking for female companionship?" a dark voice inquired. Jillian, horrified, didn't respond to the woman's inquiry. I took an aggressive stance toward the sweet-talkin' brunette wearing a lengthy wig. "Back away! This woman's mine! I bought her for the entire night. I'm not sharing her with you or anyone else. Not tonight!" I shouted. The stranger released her grip on the front of Jillian's tight sweater. She did so, reluctantly. She seductively licked Jillian's face and asked, "Where you be from, darlin'?"

"The upper east side," replied Jillian. "I could've guessed," the woman answered. "You uptown dames think you're all that 'cause your strange daddy left you money when he died. But you ain't nothing but prostitutes like us!" she added. A business card with a Wall Street address was forced into Jillian's hand. "When you're ready to be loved like a woman should, I'll be waiting," said the woman. She moved on. The weirdo' headed down the steps. She disappeared into the night.

I showcased one of my twisted smiles to Jillian. If she responded to that hooker differently, we could have died a few moments later. This environment takes no prisoners. If you don't belong here… the back alley claims your corpse by morning. No questions asked. I smiled a thank you to Jillian. She understood.

I found a corner of the hallway that was presently unoccupied. I wrapped my arms and legs around Jillian whenever an unknown silhouette came from either direction. I pulled on Jillian's dress and pretended we were gonna' get busy right there in the hallway.

Jillian caught on to my act. She quickly responded in the appropriate manner. It brought back nothing but great memories of how we used to be together. Her touch. Her smell. Her body movements. Everything blended like it really mattered. "Was she doing this for me or for her lost sister, Sugar?" I wondered.

Moans and groans from different pleasures bounced off the walls of every corner of that hallway. Everybody, somehow, was being satisfied. I had a recent picture of Sugar. I had not seen her in several years. Teenage faces change so quickly. I wanted to make the correct identification the first time. We'd only get one chance at this. I wanted to be sure.

We canvassed the second floor. It was getting dark. Most drug or prostitute related activities occurred after sundown. The time was right. There were no other stairways down to the street level. Anyone coming or going used this hallway.

Visitor traffic picked up about 1 AM. All sorts of people came and went: each never staying more than maybe 20 minutes. They were there for the obvious. They were there to score cocaine or for human trafficking purposes. The stairway became so dark we could barely see silhouettes of men and women. It would be tough to identify Sugar in this darkness.

Thirty minutes later Jillian tugged at my coat. The shadow of a woman looked to be the size and shape of her little sister. She and a man we didn't know disappeared into a door several feet away. We made our way to that doorway. I placed my ear to the door. A few minutes later, sexual comments like "I love what you're doing to me, Sugar!" shouted for all to hear. Jillian started crying. I'll rephrase that statement. Jillian went bananas. "Open this door, Sugar!" she yelled at the top of her lungs. Jillian never waited for that to happen.

She pulled a big ole' giant handgun from her purse. She shot the lock off the door just like John Wayne in the movies.

I was stunned. I didn't know Jillian was armed with a gun. Nothing but bad things could happen, now. "Where did you get that gun?" I shouted. Before Jillian answered, an unidentified man raced out the door. He ran down the hallway wearing no pants.

I removed my gun. I ran into the room expecting the worst. There laid Sugar in her gorgeous birthday suit. She was in a state of shock. She was looking up at the ceiling. Jillian followed me into the room. She grabbed pieces of discarded clothing. She wrapped them around Sugar.

Sugar was totally whacked out. She had no idea she was the object of a daring rescue.

A gentle punch motivated Sugar's revival. "Sugar, do you know who I am?" Jillian asked.

"Where's my man? Where's my man? Harry Wishbone, somebody's stealing from your girls!" Sugar uncontrollably screamed. Above the noise, heavy footsteps raced down the hallway towards the room. No need to ask. I sorta' knew who it was. A tall male shadow stood in the doorway. He pointed something in my direction. "No one messes wit' my business," he shouted. I, on the other hand, had grown tired of this bull! I immediately assessed the danger. The probable danger lurking in front of me was Harry Wishbone. Three shots rang out from my pal–Mr. Smith and Wesson. *Bang! Bang-Bang!* Harry's shadow fell to the floor. More footsteps headed in our direction.

I grabbed Jillian and Sugar. We raced down a rear fire escape. We ran through another alley to temporary freedom. If only we could reach Broadway safely...? We'd stop to answer no questions. The apartment was too dark for identities. Nobody really cared about the shooting other than he who would lose financially. That Wishbone fella' was up in the room... feet facing the ceiling. Jillian pushed Sugar in the back seat. She hopped in with her. I jumped into the driver's seat. We sped off into the night. I said nothing 'til we exited the other tunnel... the Lincoln, I think. Throughout the tunnel, all I heard in the back seat were hugs, kisses, and I love you stuff. Both women were all tears in a sisterly kind of way. I gave a quick thought to a three-some... Nah!

Once on the New Jersey side, I used alternate routes in case NYC cops were lookin' for a fella' and jeep fittin' my description.

Finally, Sugar spoke. "Jill, is that you?" she asked over and over. "Yes, baby girl! You're gonna' be all right!" she lovingly responded.

"You're gonna' be alright. Big sis and Sircus Junction's best detective is here with you. You're gonna' be alright!"

I loved hearing that conversation between two sisters. That scene was touching. It even got to me. I, too, was crying. I turned my head to the right so no one would notice that emotion. An hour later the sisters were still crying in each other's arms. They were crying and laughing and crying and laughing. It got to a point where I yelled, "If you don't give me a break I'm gonna' take you back to New York City!"

Jillian looked at me in the front mirror. Sugar, still slightly bombed out of her wild and beautiful mind, thought it was funny. "Women!" I mustered, softly. We stopped at Taylor's Diner. I picked up a couple of food plates for Sugar and Jillian at a Diner. I got three orders of Rib-eye steak sammiches wit' fries 'n stuff... to go! Sugar ate as much as she could. She vomited the rest. She fell into a deep sleep. Jillian stretched Sugar's torso across the back seat. She jumped into the front seat with me.

Jillian was mentally exhausted. She'd witnessed Sugar's predicament in a drug and prostitution arena first hand. She witnessed a shooting that most likely killed a man. Yet, there she sat. Looking straight ahead. Attempting to keep her eyes open as a lookout for the law. She placed her hands gently on my thigh. "Thank you so very much, Bishop. I know a lot of things happened back there. Things that would derail your career. Things that could place you in jail for a long, long time. Please believe me. No one will ever hear about tonight's escapade from me. Sugar's too far-gone to know anything. We won't have to worry about her. I want you to know how grateful I am. I love you Bishop Calloway," said my soon to be ex-wife… and stealer of my children.

All of a sudden Jillian's touches ceased. Somewhat disappointed, I turned to visually ask why. Jillian had collapsed from tonight's rescue efforts. She had fallen asleep in an awkward position. I pushed her off me. I tightened her seat belt. If personal love was tonight's reward, I'd have to wait another day to collect. Jillian's love, without saying, is always worth the wait!

I called ahead to enlighten the Carson family. They were pleased to have their baby girl back. They wanted her admitted into the Creative Rehabilitation Center 50 miles outside DC–a location no one would ever look for her. Jillian stayed until Sugar was admitted. "Take me home with you, Bishop," Jillian said in a pleasing tone. "You don't have to stay with me, Jillian. I understand," I responded.

"Bishop Calloway. Take me home with you. Don't say another word!" she demanded. The world was now a better place. I saved a young lady's life! I ignited her big sister's love in the process. Jillian entered my place. She pulled me into her arms. It had been a while. I forgot how great a lover she was. She fascinated me the remainder of the night. The morning arrived faster than normal.

My life would go back to the way it used to be. Jillian and my children would return to their rightful place… closer to my heart. The sun appeared. I turned to welcome the first day of my new life. I found Jillian only in written form. The note stated, "Bishop darling. How can I tell you how much I love what you did for Sugar, our family, and me? As much as I wanted your love this morning, I still had to leave. It was the right thing to do. I needed your love for the moment. I needed you to touch me like you've done so many times. To please you and be pleased by you."

"Our rescue efforts placed us together at the right time for the right reason. I must return to our separation status. Even though I love you more. I hope you'll understand," signed… Jillian.

I left my bedroom. I sat in a special chair. It was the one that meant so much to my past relationship with Jillian. I had the telephone in one hand. My recently used Smith and Wesson in the other hand. I hit redial and waited for someone to answer the other end.

Two rings later, her special voice answered. No conversation took placed. Nothing but quiet was heard over the next 30 seconds or so. No use identifying myself. The person on the other end surely recognized my quiet. I shook my head depressingly. I hung up the telephone. "Life is definitely not fair," I said to myself.

I drooped into a posture of despair. I smirked and smiled at the same time for I, too, was exhausted–physically and emotionally. Sleep became inevitable… and, so it was. I dreamed of my earlier "little fella'" life without the help of my yellow and blue demon friends…

…Welcome back, my old religious days!

I remembered the torn pinstriped suit I inherited for an upcoming Easter Sunday. It had no chance at being a 1950's fashion statement.

The jacket sleeves were too short. The trousers were poorly hemmed. The waist was three sizes too large for an old belt bearing one last hole.

Yes. A tailor's touch was imperative if this polyester ensemble was to survive its' annual hand-me-down ritual. These were nothing but fashion casualties, anyway. I never complained because the clothing had historical value. My older brothers proudly wore the same jacket, vest and trousers.

Throughout the years, my brothers and I attended Shiloh Baptist Church. We always sat in the same pew. I, the youngest Calloway, was a mere 10 years old. I was the fifth of six brothers born in six successive years.

These were very hard times. Economically, anything Pop bought at the Robert Hall Men's Clothing Chain in the mid-1900's was passed down until the youngest child outgrew it. Honorable hand-me-down suits were good enough for each of my funky brothers. Hand-me-downs would surely be good enough for me.

The quality of my over-sized footwear was also questionable. Our family's cheap shoe polish couldn't cover the scuffmarks on my worn down heels. Double-folded cereal box tops pushed into each shoe couldn't keep the April rains out of our flappin' soles. Broken shoestrings were only long enough to reach the second row of holes in each shoe. But, what the heck? A torn suit and worn out shoes were normal economic realities. Few neighbors did better. Personal embarrassment would be oh so slight if any.

I wasn't going to church to have my wardrobe scrutinized. I was going to church to uphold my religious upbringing (And, because of strap ultimatums from my mother, Mrs. Ardie Calloway... God Bless her soul). Ardie was the strictest of mothers. She was also an active member of Shiloh Baptist Church. She had been so for thirty-odd years or more.

During that Christian time, Ardie used her special religious talents to introduce each of her children to the Lord. She did so by matching our religious personalities to her many spiritual strategies.

She was so creative in this regard... I never agitated her because of her Godly ability.

Easter Sunday finally arrived. I carefully dressed in my newest hand-me-down suit. I presented myself for Momma's inspection. She didn't like what she saw. She completely rearranged my Easter look by discreetly placing safety pins here and there.

"Be a nice boy and behave yourself today!" she whispered in a stern, loving voice. She placed a fistful of pennies, nickels and dimes in my hand. "I don't want you empty-handed when you walk to God's table at the front of the church," she added. Yes. This momma of mine knew exactly what she was doing. I didn't always agree. I never had no problems attending Easter Sunday Celebrations (forgive my double negatives. I'm only 10 years old and flunkin' 5th Grade English). As a compromise, I told momma' she needed to take a chill pill on the other fifty-one Sundays of the year. You know what I mean? "The Lord needed to give this little fella' a break!" I urged. My bold proposition fell on deaf ears. It did, unfortunately, win me a trip to the woodshed where I was professionally entertained by my old man's strap-happy methods. Enough said about that!

I welcomed Fridays the most. That meant Saturday... the best day of the week... was just around the corner. My momma'... the family dictator... disagreed with my best day of the week selection. I didn't care. I chose Saturday as the best day of the week 'cause anything my imagination could do in one day... from swinging like Tarzan to a Richie Allen home run... was accomplished.

I'd perform my childhood magic all day Saturday 'til that expected motherly yell... "It's 8 o'clock! Get your little butt in this house! Right now!" I silently protested her Saturday night screams for two reasons.

First, after several of my older brothers finished serving their jail time, they were allowed to stay out much later at night. Second, I was a very mature 10 year-old. I was able to roam Sircus Junction streets with no threat of injury or otherwise. Nothing gang-related was happening on my side of town anyway!

Tomorrow is Sunday. I needed more Saturday play time to mentally prepare for Sunday's three hours of worship. You know I'm right! Not only that, I was going to miss Washington's Baseball Season Opener! This commitment showed my dedication to my religious roots.

The truth of the matter? My newfound religion was not as clean as it sounds. No one ever suspected I spent some of my church funds at Chucky's... the local candy store at 3rd and Lloyd Streets. Each Sunday, like clockwork, I traded some of God's money for some quietly chewable candies. Goobers, licorice sticks, and other stuff like that.

I never discussed this candied evil with momma'. She really didn't need to know. Or, maybe she already did? Either way, I solemnly repented this sin while sitting alone in the back pew. I'd do this repenting right after consuming the entire illegal bounty... a plateau I usually reached after the first hour of prayer. My time management skills sorta' left two remaining hours of prayer to ask for the Lord's forgiveness.

There's a major caution attached to this covert activity. It was important to never make eye-to-eye contact with Reverend-Pastor Smokem! His special chair sat high over the congregation. He could look directly down into your soul wit' no effort at all! He could stare the truth out of you whenever he felt like it. He didn't have to ask a single question. He somehow knew if you were truly a disgusting little dude.

I was scared he'd stop right in the middle of his sermon... grab me by the ears... and pull me right up onto God's holy stage. The Pastor would twist my nose in front of the entire congregation. He'd force me to confess to the misappropriation of religious funds. Elder worshippers would shake their heads in disgust and call me every name in God's book.

I had a plan. My plan was to confess I'd become spiritually weak from watching too many cartoons. I'd roll across the church floor like I was crazy and ask the holy members for mercy. I would admit to being guilty as charged. I'd be forever banished from Shiloh Baptist Church. This would surely embarrass the entire Calloway family.

So, please! Never make eye-to-eye contact with any Pastor... especially after you've spent some of God's money on goobers and licorice sticks! Simply apologize to the Lord and holler "Jesus" with a big smile on your face!

Come to think of it, "What did Jesus or Moses look like anyway?" At the age of 10, I had a choice. I could envision Jesus as I wished or accept those versions of him portrayed in several blockbuster movies. Actors playing the role of Jesus and Moses commanded different looks.

They did have several things in common. They were all sun-tanned dudes... and very tall in stature. Each sported white beards and shoulder-length hair. Several portraits of these great men of God were on display in our church. I guess their pictures were acceptable replicas of those I mentioned.

It was humanly impractical for a very young fella' like me to distort that familiar image! Two blockbuster Charlton Heston flicks like "Ben Hur" and "The Ten Commandments" had validated Jesus! These double-featured portrayals were the accepted American images. "Who in God's name dared challenge this truth after all the Oscar Nominations these movie flicks received?" Not this little fella', for one.

Charlton Heston easily resembled the man who parted the Red Sea River and swallowed up Yul Brenner's Army on two wheels. Gracious! Those scenes alone were good enough for solid spiritual validations. What other proof would a religious person need? I was definitely satisfied. Enough about that!

My intuitive momma' never knew I took short naps during the church service... or, did she? The Calloway clan is a Baptist family. Sunday services were very long days. Three hours or more was a normal Sunday. My neighborhood friends attended other churches. Yet, they were home playing in the backyard an hour or so later. I felt kinda' cheated in that respect. My neighborhood pals were Cathlecs... Moochlems... and Jewush... or, somethin' like that. We were *a cultural mix of great pals, to say the least. Friends belonging to other religious denominations never missed baseball or football games on Sunday afternoons.*

They felt privileged because they had shorter religious services. We wondered why Pastor Smokem needed several hours or more on Sunday mornings? Don't start me lying 'cause I don't know.

It bothered me that my pals had more time to wear the Washington burgundy and gold on Sunday afternoons. It bothered me a lot. How could I talk about this religious unfairness with my momma'? I still haven't figured out the best way to do that. Sounds too much like another professional conversation with a strap if you asked me.

As usual, I'd catch a nap right near the end of the sermon's second hour. Did anyone really expect a little kid to stay connected to the Lord for three solid hours? Nah! Ain't happening. I dreamed about a lot of things during church hours. My best dreams took me to Heaven where God lived. My worst dreams traveled to Hell where the Devil called his home.

Whenever I visited Heaven, the atmosphere was bright, warm, and inviting. I could eat all the ice cream I could find. I received a tour of this graceful golden residence by God himself. He led me around Heaven by the hand. I couldn't see his face directly. I knew he was there by his awesome glow. While walking, I listened as he reminded me of the long list of sins man continues to violate. Commandments like "Thou Shall Not Hurt Nobody Else" and "Yee Shall Not Covet Another's Momma" were several sins he was concerned about.

I remained quiet. I had nothing to say to His Holiness. I prayed he wasn't secretly asking me to surrender names of sinners from my neighborhood 'cause... I was pretty sure he knew a lie when he heard it. My list would be pretty long. Then where would I be? I wasn't ready to throw away my young soul.

Guilt surrounded my heart. I walked hand in hand with God but knew I was in big trouble. Dream or not, God had to know what I did with some of the Pastor's money. His punishment would surely be extreme. I had to act quickly. I decided to do God a favor. I'd punish myself for all the past sins I've committed. I'm sure God had more important things to do with his time. My punishment had to fit my crime so… I decided to surrender my eyesight. And, I did.

Thus, in my dream, and for the next ten years of my imaginary Heaven, I walked around Heaven bumping into everything not nailed down. I re-learned the differences between Cheerios and Frosted Flakes. I re-learned how to tie my Ked's sneakers in the dark. I could play no more on the red merry-go-round at recess-time. And, I definitely couldn't use the swings on school afternoons. After surviving ten years of this dream, I felt God's glow in my presence again. I asked why he let me go on for ten long years of dreamin'? His response? He never punished me. In fact, he forgave me ten dreamin' years ago. It was I who was punishing myself. "All I had to do was to call out to him… or, open my little eyes and heart to His Glory," he reminded.

The big guy took my hand. "Since you're young and inquisitive about how the devil works, here's a closer look," he added. He snapped his fingers. I hadn't moved an inch but immediately found myself flappin' around on my stomach. I felt like a corn-mealed fish waiting to be deep-fried in hell's kitchen.

One thing was certain. It was definitely time to thank the Big Guy and end this dream! I wanted to travel back to reality before my little tender self was flavored with hot sauce. At that precise moment, a pair of strong hands grabbed me by the jacket. They shook me a little then propped me up on the wooden pew. "This isn't the right time to sleep in church!" an unknown manly voice said.

Strong hands became gentle. The hands fixed my jacket and tie, tucked in my shirt, and disappeared in a crowd of song. I… was totally embarrassed, of course.

I peered at the group of patrons sitting closest to me. Everyone was singing, standing, and clapping from their hearts. Nobody seemed to care about my little catnap. "Yet, who owned that strong pair of hands?" I continued to wonder. "Where did he go?"

Meanwhile, the choir was rockin' down the house! All church goin' eyes… "Were on the Sparrow" sorta speak. Not wanting to miss another covert candy-eating opportunity, I finished off most of the Goobers. I also prayed I hadn't sat next to any old lady vigorously fanning herself. A currently hand-held fan with a picture of Lee's Funeral Home on it meant it was definitely time for me to slide to the end of the pew. Any minute now, Pastor Smokem is gonna' ignite some poor female's soul for the entire congregation to witness.

This action occurred not only on Easter Sundays. It occurred every Sunday! Once the Pastor's speech and the heavy fanning began, hats, pocketbooks and shoes are gonna' be thrown high into the air. This religious hoopla' would be followed by a yearning for the Holy Ghost… then followed by the ungodly sight of gigantic white cotton-laced female bloomers squirming all over the church floor!

Yucky! What's up with that? Why would His Highness allow these old women to show-off their huge white panties to the entire congregation?

Couldn't they squirm uncontrollably and keep their legs closed at the same time? It must be possible 'cause I never saw any of the finer, younger girls doin' any squirmin' around with their panties out… not that I would look. And, why didn't older women wear longer pants?

This religious loyalty must be a woman thing. I've attended church for over ten years now. I never, not once, witnessed a male worshipper roll around the church floor displaying his boxer shorts. Obviously, men must have had a better relationship with God than women. After all, God is a man. Jesus was a man. Moses was a man. Charleston Heston and Yul Brenner were men. Pastor Smokem is a man. And, Richie Allen, the best home-run hitter during the '64 National League pennant… was a man. What other proof was needed?

My Sunday school teacher, a real bold fella', said my momma' actually came from my pop's ribcage or something like that. These factors shaped my young thoughts on the issue of Godliness. "It would be a good subject for my next Elementary School's Book Report!" I eagerly thought.

Did the Pastor evaluate his preaching talents by how many women lost control of their church goin' souls or from donations from the pew? I didn't know the answer nor did I ask. Based on the number of women flappin' about the floor, big bloomers and all, this Pastor had it going on! I watched how he acted when this religious turmoil was happening. He was as cool as a cucumber.

He just sat there sitting high in the biggest chair on stage. Every now and then he'd take out a used white hankie and gently wipe the perspiration from his forehead. This was puzzling to me because he wasn't doing all the work!

He nodded to somebody in the choir and a loud song slowed to a hum. Church nurses in white dresses sat the squirming females back into their seats. Something special was coming. I sensed an explosion of some kind.

The Pastor's blessing was about to unfold. God was truly under this roof. A demonstration of salvation was welcomed.

Did it mean the Pastor's sermon was coming to an end? Not on a special day like Easter Sunday! Today's sermon had already reached its normal three-hour limit.

The Pastor, in his questionable wisdom, added another hour to his message. He didn't ask for anyone's permission. He also didn't let anybody take a ten-minute break like we received in kindergarten. And, to my surprise, no patrons got up and walked out.

The Pastor wanted to preach some more to faces he'd never see again 'til next year's Easter Sunday... or, the next funeral... whichever came first. Meanwhile, closure was on the faces of everyone in the church.

It didn't matter. The mighty Smokem took the extra time anyway. And, you know what? When he finished that extra hour of prayer, I felt much better about myself.

I was, in fact, so honored. I was blessed he kept me under his direction a little longer than the norm. I was so caught up in his *continued message I forgot about my covert candy experiences. I forgot about the first inning of today's baseball game. Those were small issues.*

I forgot because the Pastor had taken me on a four-hour picnic with the Lord. I never realize how it would benefit me later. Mrs. Ardie Calloway, my strong momma', must have known. Or, did she really? I was now full of life. I pranced passed the offering table for the fourth time... confident with my new self. I looked directly into the Pastor's eyes. I gave him a holy wink-wink. I gave him a visual thumbs-up for the message he delivered this fine afternoon.

I was offering him an opportunity to bask in his own glory. The Pastor returned my glance. I'm sure he appreciated my small gesture. A holy thrill passed through my body that very moment. The Pastor's smirk told me he knew about my covert candy sins. As Pastor, he's aware of every little thing that happens in this church... and our lives. His eyes were so revealing. Regardless of where I sat, how the Lord's money was spent, or whatever ball game I missed... once I entered this church, my soul was completely in his hands. These thoughts penetrated me as I walked before him.

I, now having been captured by myself, felt even guiltier. I reached into my secret pocket. I placed my last quarter and licorice stick on the offering table. I looked back as I returned to my pew. My offering was an act of gratitude for the church and church alone. It was not an act of gratitude for the next set of little fella' hands following my footsteps to God's table. Thankfully, the right person accepted the bounty. The Pastor threw the quarter in a basket and started chewing on the licorice candy. He did this right in front of the congregation. Wow! That took some guts! Paster Smokem's a cool dude, huh?

I left the church shortly afterwards. The morning's wet sky had turned to a radiant sunshine. I removed my fashionable hand-me-down jacket. I threw it over the shoulder of a shirt two sizes too large. The warm spring breeze made my walk home seem shorter. The clatter of my flapping soles wasn't bothering me anymore. I didn't care what people thought about my economic plight. I was poor; yet, felt just fine.

I entered the glow of my momma's house with a religious look of acceptance written all over my face. For some pious reason, I sat next to momma's love for the next few minutes. "Should I tell her what happened at church? Should I tell her about the Pastor?" I wondered.

I needed a clear conscience. I needed to disclose what's been happening to God's money. "Was this the proper time to test my religious self? Did momma' already know?"

This was so much for innocent little me to figure out. Thirty minutes later I admitted to falsely using the church's offering. I waited for a yell and some very harsh discipline. Yet, neither came. Instead, momma' hugged me.

She admitted knowing what I did with some of the money all along. Deacons and other members of the church were close spies of hers. I never knew they were secretly keeping an eye on me. I, Mr. Little Slick, never knew lots of people were watching. Their comments must have been pretty good. Mom enhanced my religious awareness. She stressed the importance of attending church and believing in the Lord.

"Goobers and licorice sticks were very small prices for the religion you've learned so far!" she said. "What's in your heart will never leave you," she insisted.

These were great words spoken by a great woman. I normally awakened from my religious dreams right after hearing momma's special words. Momma's preaching soothes my heart. Her words refreshed my soul every time. They made it easier to move on with the real-world mess I've made of my life. I thanked God for these valuable dreams. I thanked God for Mrs. Ardie Calloway and her magical words.

I smiled. I, again, said goodbye to my holy memories of the mid-1900s. I should've become a pastor. I was easily influenced by my earlier religious life. I was easily influenced by my momma's teachings. And, you know the effects Charleston Heston, Yul Brenner and Richie Allen had on my younger life! Enough said 'bout my good old religious days!

I awakened from my deep sleep. I returned to reality with a terrible migraine headache. Darn those illegal yellow and blue pills! I enjoyed this dream. I was not ready to return to reality. If only I had more pills... I could extend my trip back to the good ole' days!

Can I go back home, again! Please!

CHAPTER 12

The midnight shift was uneventful. The rookie dispatcher I despised (Communication Specialist Ivan) rarely interrupted the airwaves. It was 3:15 AM. The 24-hour Coffee Shop on Paxton Ave became a valuable midnight pit stop. I hoped the morning's roasted java hadn't been brewing since midnight.

Burnt coffee is a norm at this rat hole. This store had "Will somebody please rob me!" written all over the front window. I never directly entered this or other convenience stores. I parked in front of them for a long sixty seconds before entering. I adopted this ritual several years ago to maintain a longer life span as a police officer. This professional action gives hold-up bandits' time to re-evaluate future crimes... especially while I'm inside.

This deliberation allows me to decide how much coffee I'll put in my sugar? And, which sugar-free doughnuts I'll ignore? I can do this without constantly keeping an eye on the cashier.

Guess what usually happens right after I've placed a coffee or short breakfast order? A rookie dispatcher's voice will soon yell, *"Cruiseeeerrrrrrr 507...for a message?"* There it is. Just like clockwork. I interacted with the heavy squads from downtown when persons under age 18 are involved in criminal activity. The Heavy squads are Homicide, Robbery and Sex Investigative Units. You can always identify those guys by their Kojak-type hats and double-breasted suits. Det. Blair Howard is a member of the Sex Crimes Unit. He recently arrested an adult male for raping a 16-year old girl. The adult male is the resident boyfriend of the child's mother... for Christ sake! The daughter told her mother about the boyfriend's seduction several times. The mother seemed not to care. No responsible action was taken by momma' to personally or legally address the criminal acts. Det. Howard will process the paperwork on the adult male boyfriend. I was asked to respond and assist with possible Child Abuse violations. I arrived thirty minutes later. I read the signed statement given by the arrested boyfriend of the mother. George Samuelson was his name. George denied all criminal allegations. "That young lady was always after my body!" he said. "I denied her the first time her body was beggin' for my attention," he wanted us to know. "After that sexual episode, whenever her momma went to work, the little scarlet pranced around in a thin cotton gown to get my sexual attention. Sharon's momma' never complained so… what's the big deal? I thought having sex with Sharon was okay. We were only intimate about five times," George admitted.

The assaulted youngster, Sharon Munson, was at City General being examined. Sharon Paulette Munson, her full legal name, was a mature sixteen-year-old older-looking young lady. She had a body supporting more than enough womanhood.

Dr. Robertson's report suggested Sharon was a very sexually active girl. There were no signs of force around her vaginal area. Sharon was asked for her side of the story. Her first incident occurred several months ago. Sally, her mother, went to work one evening. Sharon took a shower. She found George in her room when she exited. Sharon asked George to leave. He refused. George grabbed her and forced himself on her! "My first-ever penetration took place that night. The rest is history," Sharon explained. Sharon said she struggled but George overpowered her.

"Once George started my sex life, he showed me how to enjoy it! I welcomed his touches from that point on!" Sharon added. "The sexual urges were strong feelings I could no longer ignore."

"I know this sounds questionable," Sharon moaned. "I tried to stop him, but at the same time, well, I'm very much approaching womanhood as you can see. I now have my sexual needs, too!"

"George and my mother make love all the time. I watched when her bedroom door wasn't closed," Sharon shared. "I've always wondered why George made momma' scream and act that way in bed?" she whispered.

Sharon eventually felt guilty. She telephoned her mother at work and told her about the sexual escapades with George. Sally didn't immediately come home from her job. She came home six hours later after her work shift expired. Sharon thought the slow response by her mother meant she didn't really care.

Sharon didn't know what to do. Her conscience told her she shouldn't be sexually active with her mother's boyfriend. "I finally learned it was definitely wrong to be screwing George at my age," she said.

Sally finally confronted George about Sharon's allegations. George denied everything Sharon reported. The truth was he found Sharon in bed with a neighbor's son. "Sharon was scared to death I'd tell you she was screwing around," he softly yelled. "Your 'hot in the pants' little girl begged me not to tell you!"

"My mother believed George over me… her own flesh and blood!" Sharon said. Sally dismissed the whole situation. It was like it never happened. She cautioned me about a baby. She gave George that old look of hers. The look meant… "I'm hope nothing my little girl said is true. Not one single word of it."

Sally went into her bedroom. She shut George out.

"George! You're sleeping on the couch tonight?" she yelled through the door.

Sharon completed the sexual scenarios. "George approached me. We got busy again. No force or aggression was involved. He simply asked if I wanted him again. My sexual feelings took over. I couldn't refuse. I was dressed in a loose half-slip. My body offered no resistance to this man. I possessed no guilt... nothing but young desire." Detective Hunter thought it best to cease any further description of the crime scenario. This little gal was way too graphic for a 16-year old. "Young lady... Why do you have to be so, ah, expressive?" asked Det. Hunter. "I'm not, really," she answered. "Don't you want the truth, the whole truth, and nothing but the truth? I know I'm embarrassing both of you cops. Your personal demeanors' are tellin' it all. I just feel good when I'm under a man's control." Sircus Junction's best two detectives went silent. Was this little girl playing us for fools? Or, was Miss Thang discovering womanhood before her time? We stopped interviewing Sharon Paulette Munson. We stepped outside, smoked a pack of cigarettes, bought several ice-cold co-colas, and started typing the paperwork. Sharon was age 16 going on 30. Sharon asked if we wanted her to be descriptive of other sexual acts? "I watched him teach my mother," Sharon mentioned. "I wanted to learn everything he taught her!"

The two smartly embarrassed detectives, again, ran from the interviewing room. Det. Hunter and I had heard enough. Sharon was certain her mother would take criminal action against George... whatever that was. I contacted Sharon's mother at her job. She came to the office as fast as she could. Sally listened to her descriptive daughter. Sally tried not to cry. She did both.

When advised of her daughter's latest sexual activity, Sally shouted... "You danced around naked to get his prick hard, didn't you? You're nothing but a little slut!" Sharon wept. She wept because she really loved her mother. She wanted nothing but her happiness.

George denied sexual wrongdoing. The crime came from his confession. We charged George with many lesser charges. He posted bail. He was released later. Sally knew George would be charged. She refused to ask him to leave her side. Sharon, the daughter, felt at fault.

The night passed. With sexual allegations weighing on her mind, Sally came home unannounced after the next morning's rush hour. She entered the home. She couldn't find George downstairs. She quietly tiptoed to Sharon's bedroom. She heard George making love to her daughter.

She tried not to open the bedroom door. She didn't want to witness the sexual truth she's denied for so long. Would this sight push her over the limit? Would this deadly truth push a knife into George's sweating torso?

To obtain these answers, Sally pushed on the bedroom door. Sally screamed. She'd seen enough. "She begged me this morning… so, why not?" George sarcastically uttered.

"She's as good as you are… now. It was never love. She wanted me to teach her how to be a real woman."

"Don't get mad at us, please?" George continued. "I promise never to touch Sharon again." The unthinkable happened. Sally looked at Sharon and scolded her for having sex with her man. "I've finally found a good man! You've intentionally ruined our relationship!" she bellowed. "Call the cops right now! We can get rid of this guy forever!" Sharon requested. Sally wasn't hearing it. She was blinded by her love for George… a man who didn't respect her own flesh and blood. Tired of this nonsense and the threat of losing her man, Sally threw Sharon out of the house. Sharon contacted the Sircus Junction authorities. A complaint of Rape was made. Detective Howard arrested George without confrontation. Sharon's signed statement charged George with assaulting her on three different occasions. I asked Sally to come down to Police Headquarters. When she arrived, I asked about Sharon's allegations.

"I didn't know who to believe when first told!" she replied. "Even when I found them in bed, I couldn't tell if the sex was forceful or not. Sharon wasn't screaming or nothing so I told George to never touch Sharon again."

"Why didn't you call the police?" I asked. "You obviously know Sharon's age?"

"Yeah, but like I said, Sharon wasn't yelling for help or nothing. I thought they were just screwin' around," the mother answered.

I was flabbergasted by this mother's responses.

I spent the next half-hour explaining her responsibilities as a parent.

The mother questioned my legal ability do so.

I chastise her for choosing another man over her daughter… for being non-responsible. I had no choice. I charged Sally Jean Munson with a Child Abuse violation for allowing her daughter to remain in an abusive situation. Sally broke down in tears when told of her criminal charges. I didn't feel sorry for her. I awaited the end of her tearful episode. She stood and hugged me as though she was thanking me for my support.

"There, now," I said. "Parenting can be tough, sometimes."

Sally's weeping eyes made contact. "My dear sweet man," she said. "Isn't there something I can do to avoid criminal charges?"

Sally, unexpectedly, placed her hand gently into my trouser pocket. "What is this woman doing?" I silently thought! "I'm in deep trouble now!" I quickly stepped backwards and tried to remove her hand.

"Just forget those rape allegations against George!" she begged. "Charge me if you want but please let George go!" The office door opened. Detective Lola Reed-Fletcher entered. Her inquisitive eyes stared at a woman controlling my zipper. Det. Lola frowned.

"Just think!" Det. Fletcher said disgustedly. "I was waiting for your final divorce papers! I thought maybe you and I had a future together. If this is the kind of woman you like, you'll never have me! You're no different than the rest of these department dogs!" she screamed. Det. Fletcher stormed out the office. I cannot tell a lie. Sally was a good lookin' woman. I would not accept any favors from her. I convinced her to back off. What I didn't understand was her willingness to seduce me for the sake of her precious George?

"Do what you want with my slutty daughter," she stated. "Save my George!" she said.

Life is not unconditional is it? I placed Sharon in a foster home. When the court date arrived, Sally admitted that she, herself, was sexually active at age fourteen. She thought the court was over-reacting over her daughter's sexual history. The Judge thought otherwise. "Everybody's got a social story," he decried. "Yours is unacceptable!"

A Social Services investigator interrupted the hearing with some additional information. "Your Honor... this mother has accepted George back into her home while he awaits trial. Not only that... she has agreed to testify George never raped her daughter!"

"I'd like to recommend other sanctions for the daughter!" asked the Social Worker.

"Sanctions granted!" ordered the Judge.

Sally didn't care about sanctions. She appeared relieved. Sally only cared about George… her rapist-boyfriend.

Sally was found guilty of Child Neglect. Sharon was removed from her custody. George was also found guilty of several rapes. He was incarcerated.

"This case was simply unreal!" I said to myself.

"How can any mother make such choices?" It dawned on me this society makes those choices all the time.

Was Sharon fully mature at age sixteen?

Too bad Sharon was not old enough to take care of herself. That way, Sally could no longer interfere with Sharon's personal life?

Sally, as a young child and in her defense, was pushed out the door at age 14. She did whatever it took to survive. Did her nurturing clock terminate several years ago? One thing was definite. Sally loved George so much she was willing to give up everything for him! Actually, she did just that!

Go figure!

CHAPTER 13

I received a welcomed call from Jillian last night. She asked how I was doing. She wanted to make sure I was okay. I didn't know she cared. Did she have a lonely moment? Did good truths about me return? She didn't mention the kids. How could she not? They're all I have in this world. If she needs an excuse to call, tell me something great about Marla, Rick, and Stanley. Give me a precious memory or two on each child. Allow me to smile about issues never to be Kodak moments. That's why she should call. I hung up and thought about it a bit. Jillian was the mother of my children. She deserved better. I called back. I apologized. Jillian wanted a meeting as soon as possible. I took a long minute before agreeing. She would not be allowed back into my life so easily. What other reason is there for an emergency meeting? All of her personal calls were saved within my telephonic storage.

My Trusted Friend...

Why is our world so complicated? Does God have a way of evening out the negatives of life? Does destiny run so true it's impossible to change? Can personal apologies restore faith when needed most?

Why do I ask? The worst news I've ever received came today. Jillian, my lovely but separated companion dropped a bombshell on me! She has Cancer. She's known about it for a long time. She never told me what was going on medically. Was I too blind to see it? Probably, so. More medical tests are scheduled three days from now. She's scared. I can hear it in her voice. She doesn't want to do this alone.

She wants me to accompany her to the doctor's office. She's asking for some mental support, I guess.

How could this be? Jillian ate the best of foods. She never smoked a cigarette a day in her life. Her heart was strong. She could run around the high school's track several times without breaking a sweat.

Her parents are living a long life. We're not talking about something passed down from previous generations. Is this a sick joke to get my attention? I should wake up because this is not about me. It's about her. I knocked on my old front door. Jillian answered. She immediately placed her head on my shoulder. Distress lines raced across her forehead.

I felt indifferent. This woman turned my life upside down by leaving me. I've been to hell and back twice over her loss. It hurts every time I think about what I no longer have. And, don't even mention the kids...please. Now she's asking for my undivided attention. Where do I draw the line? Was the hurt so bad my heart can't do this favor for her? Okay. She's the mother of my children. Does that justify the pains associated with this forthcoming mess?

I'm between a rock and a hard place. My feet told me to move on 'cause they always think they are right! My head wouldn't let that happen. Whatever decision made, I'd stick by it. I'll not run for the hills when the going gets tough. That's the kind of man I am. So be it. My cards are on the table. I'm all in psychologically... until her end if necessary.

I placed my arms around Jillian. I welcomed her fear by squeezing her as hard as I could. Her body was strong. My body was even stronger. I wanted to share the pain she was feeling at the moment. She reciprocated. She knew what I was trying to do. I never could fool her. I never tried. She knew me too well. That's probably why I'm here right now. She already knew I couldn't say no. She knew darn well I would not let her handle this cancer thing alone.

Was she taking advantage of me? My kindness? My medical plan? Only time will tell. Was she preparing me for the return of kids if she died? She placed her arms around my waist. She pulled me so close I could hear her heart beating. The unthinkable occurred. The dog in me became aroused. Jillian kinda' knew that would happen. She responded by kissing me tenderly on the cheek. "It's been a long time since we've loved each other hasn't it, Bishop?" she asked. "What's this dying woman trying to do?" I asked as I looked to the ceiling. As much as I wanted Jillian, I did not want her in that way. Especially not now.

Other things were more important. Okay. My excitement should not have occurred. It doesn't mean I had to act on it. Neither should she. I pushed her away. I was a better man than that. I would not take advantage of this vulnerable period. "Jillian!" I whispered. "I love you in the worst way! I'll be there for you. Your health is more important than sex. You know that!"

"But, your smile? That crease in your smile was doing its dirt again."

"Remember the good old days?"

"Remember that black tie function? Sure you do."

"I couldn't let you go then. I can't let you go now," I muttered softly.

Jillian took a step backward. She glazed into my eyes with a puzzled look on her face. "My sweet, sweet Bishop," she said. "There's something I must tell you. Listen very carefully, my darling. You gotta' keep that personal stuff to yourself! I'm depressed as it is."

"I need your shoulder and what's in your pants... not your heart!"

"I don't love you anymore, Bishop! Please believe that. My last days may be approaching. I want to experience your tender touch before I leave this Earth," she followed. "I want the man who knows me the best. Knows my body the best! I don't want a stranger, dear. I want you!"

An Elmer Fudd look of puzzlement captured my face. "Yes. I know," she added. "You're a jerk in so many ways. But, no one loves me like you do. That's something I'll not forget! You know what I mean, don'tcha' baby? Can you do this for me, Bishop Darling?"

Jillian smiled a smile I hadn't seen in a long time. I didn't respond to her statements. I was in another world. I saw her lips moving. I didn't understand a word she was saying. Well, I did but it was soooooo not Jillian. I agreed to be the best man she could want during this bad time. I didn't share with her that I, Bishop Calloway, would not stimulate her soul.

I am the man I am. I totally controlled the dog in me. It was not the other way around. That statement didn't sound like the real me. It is. Get used to it. The doctor's office was crowded. Cancer patients were everywhere. Cordial smiles were flashed wall to wall to unknown patients. There were no clocks on the wall. There was no need to get too neighborly… if you know what I mean. There were no sign-in sheets taped to a receptionist's window. The future wasn't promised to anyone visiting this office. It was a bland atmosphere if I ever saw one. People were here for a specific reason. No personal questions, please!

Jillian took her turn with the prerequisites. The results of more tests were completed. Jillian held my hand. She wanted me to go behind the second door with her. We entered. We sat there. Jillian was only a number on a blue folder. A white medical jacket controlled the remainder of her life. The news wasn't good. The cancer was rapidly spreading. An operation was needed, soon. Like, tomorrow! Jillian became uncontrollable. She cried and cried and cried. I tried to console her. A tear or two tried to escape from my macho eyes. It didn't matter.

I cared not what others thought. This was about Jillian. It was not about me. The kids were taken to grandmas for a couple of days. Jillian didn't want them to know the truth. She didn't want them to worry. I had to promise not to tell them about the cancer. I would honor my promise.

The operation took place 7 AM the next morning. Jillian looked to me as they wheeled her into the prep area. She squeezed my hand. "I love you so much, Bishop. Always have, always will."

"I'm so sorry I hurt you. I made you choose between your family and your job. That wasn't fair. I apologize, baby," added Jillian.

"We can make it as a family. Will you please come back to me, darling? I need you. The kids need you. We can start all over again. I promise I will love you, forever. Will you please say yes?" begged Jillian. "Come back to me... Okay? Your face is the only thing I want to see if these eyes open again."

A joy and sorrow filled my heart at the same time. I bowed my head. Our new life would start soon after this operation. I was thrilled. Eleven hours later the cancer was successfully captured. Jillian would live a long life. We would be a family again. Thank God. He answered our prayers.

A week went by. Jillian recuperated at a rapid pace. Each day brought new hope and anticipation. I felt like I was getting married for the very first time. The only thing different was our ready-made family.

The intimacy would be good. It's been a long time. I can't wait to tenderly touch her again. I'll get another chance to express my love for her every chance I get. My words were welcomed before, and right after the operation. However, during the recuperation period, my precious words tended to now fall on deaf ears. The more I declared my love for her, the less it meant to her. I was getting on Jillian's nerves. I could tell she tired from my anticipation to love her more. I saw that same look in her eyes when she awakened yesterday morning. It wasn't one of affection.

I grabbed her hand. I asked her to share her honest feelings with me. "Bishop, you've been so great during this ordeal," she lovingly whispered. "I love you so much for that. I know I've said a lot of things about our future. I know you can't wait for us to renew our vows... taking the kids to the movies again. Stuff like that."

"But, listen carefully dear. That lovey-dovey stuff ain't never gonna' happen… 'cause you ain't never gonna' change!"

"I ain't never gonna' let you change."

"You are who you are!"

"You're Sircus Junction's most famous Detective!"

"You only love the idea of making love to me on a permanent basis! You love that stupid job so much more than any of us," she cringed. "I'd be nothin' but a second place sperm receptor again!"

"You know it. I know it! I apologize for giving you false hopes. I wanted it to happen. Believe me, I did."

"What changed your mind?" I asked Jillian while trying to hold back my tears. "You know how much I needed this to happen. I've never wanted anything as much as I did this. For us to be a family again!" I returned.

Jillian gave me a disgruntled sneer. Her next words cut me to the bone. "Remember the first night after my surgery?" she asked. "I reached for you in the dark of the night. I wanted to hold your hand… together, as one, but you were not there. The night nurse told me your beeper sounded. You wasted little time running out the hospital's door."

"Something about a child in trouble," she mentioned. "Something about an emergency at work."

"I made up my mind at that very moment you'd never be mine. All mine."

"I can only be your mistress. And, a mistress I will never be!"

Jillian's demeanor turned sour. She had become another personality. "Please leave right now!" she demanded. "Go ahead and stay married to that relationship killer job of yours. Our days are over. I no longer need you. In fact, I despise you even more! See ya!" she said.

I turned… I attempted to explain my leaving the other night. She wasn't havin' it.

"And, by the way, Mr. Can't Keep Your Promises… let the door hitcha' where the dog shoulda' bitcha'!" she yelled. I stood there in amazement. How could she say something like that to me? Jillian stuck her foot out from the bottom of the bed and slowly shut the door right in my face! Another lousy chapter in my life closed. There was nothing else to say.

I would not beg for her forgiveness. I would not challenge her feelings. With tremendous regret, I'd never get another opportunity for our souls to merge. Stupid me!

Several days passed. The telephone rang. The caller ID indicated the call was from a local hospital. It was Jillian. I didn't want to answer it. I tried not to answer it. Why should I? I didn't like the way things ended the other day. Maybe she wanted to apologize for her behavior? Maybe drugs and other prescribed medications blew her mind? Was there another chance for our new family after-all? I'll give her the benefit of the doubt. I answered the telephone on the fourth ring. Jillian's voice jumped right into my heart. "Why are you not here?" she started. "I've under-taken a traumatic cancer operation. It was one that could've killed me. I politely asked you to help me through this ordeal. You said you'd be there for me even if the going got tough. I yelled at you one time and what did you do? You ran like like the devil!"

"What kind of shoulder is that? Huh? Tell me why I should trust you with a rebirth of our family? Speak up, fella'! Huh? You haven't shown the strength to withstand a family crises, huh?"

"Tell me why I should place my life or the kids in your care? Come on, simpleton! Tell me why? Huh? Tell me why?"

I could only listen with my heart. Jillian wore me out for easily giving up on her situation. I guess she had enough reasons. She was right. I failed to do what I promised. I was a loser in this instance. I felt so ashamed.

Her new silence on the other end of the telephone said enough. I didn't respond to her silence. There was no proper thing to say. I screwed up another chance at love. I hung up the telephone. I started thinking. Perhaps I'm not being the man I should be in this situation. I should prove I could accept all the verbal abuse she's giving out.

I'm a man of a man. My ego can handle her harshness. I'm stronger than that. It was she who had the surgery. It is she who was, maybe, under the influence of drugs. Be there for her stupid. She'll love you more for it later.

I acquiesced. I called her. My Jillian answered. She was glad I was on the other end. "I'm so, so sorry, dear," I said to Jillian. "Please allow me to make it up to you?"

"Let me come back to you right now?"

"Let me hold you right now? Let me... Let me...! Let me feel your heartbeat one more time?"

"Give me another chance to prove my worthiness, please!"

"Let me be there for you when you truly need me."

"Can I run to your arms, right now? Please? Please? Pretty please?" I begged.

"Okay, baby," she replied. "Bring your dumb butt over here... Right now!"

"Come to me! Prove your love!"

"Provide some substance to that you definitely want. Show me what's in your eyes and what's in your heart. I lay here wanting your touch. I'm still touchable, darling. Nothin's wrong with my sexuality. Many a night I've awakened hoping you were sitting in the chair next to my bed. That chair's empty, baby. Come sit with me. Be there the next time I reach for you. Love me mentally until I can share the physical love we both need. I can wait. We can wait. Get here as fast as you can. I'll stay awake 'til you enter the door. I miss you so much. I love you. Come to me, now!" Jillian insisted.

"Wow!" I said to myself. "Jillian sure can talk when she wants to, can't she?" I couldn't get a word in.

I don't remember her mouth being so wild. It must be the medication. She's got to be depressed after a major operation and all?

She probably won't be her real self for a long time. I'll get there as soon as possible. I'll prove to her I can handle the bad times as well as the good. Hold on baby. I'm coming! I love this woman. She's the greatest!" I arrived seventeen minutes later. Jillian's door was open. She was sleeping. One hand was falling off the bed. The other hand was tightly holding the emergency nurse's call-button. I sat in the special chair next to her bed. I wanted to surprise those hazel eyes when they opened.

Jillian slept well into the night. The hazel-eyed nurse, friendly and sympathetic, allowed me to remain in the room. 4 a.m. rapidly approached. The love of my life stirred a bit. She finally opened her eyes. She turned her head to the left and then to the right. There I sat, in the dark, awaiting that crease in her smile. You know the crease I'm talking about.

The unthinkable happened... again! "Gregory, darling... is that you?" she whispered. "Nah!"

"Jillian didn't say Gregory, darling... did she?" I asked myself.

"Jillian. It's me. It's Bishop," I mumbled.

"Bishop? Bishop who?" she weakly asked. "What the heck are you doing here?"

"Didn't I throw you outta' here a long time ago?"

"How dare you show up... here of all places? This is my room. This is my life. You don't control me or the kids anymore!"

"Nurse! Nurse! Get this Bishop maniac out of my sight!" she screamed.

I could only look at this woman. The pain-related drugs must be eatin' her up. Minutes ago she wanted me in the worst way. Now she can't stand my guts. Oh well. Here I am so here I will stay 'til she comes to her senses.

I must keep the promises I made to her.

Jillian fell asleep again but not for long. I held her hand. I gently brushed her forehead. I tried to get closer to her. I needed to get closer to her. When her eyes opened again she would thank me for being here. The love of my new life opened her eyes a few minutes later. "Bishop Calloway! Why are you still here?" she asked. "What do I have to do to get you to understand you're no longer wanted? Get Lost! Please leave me alone!" she reiterated.

"Okay, Jillian."

"But, before I leave, who is Gregory?" I asked inquisitively.

"He's none of your business!" she answered.

"I didn't know there was someone else in your life?" I said. "Why didn't you tell me? I could handle it. I could handle your new life... if that's what you have."

"Just get your dogface outta' my sight," Jillian blurted. "Why are you so hard-headed? Do I need to call hospital security?" she asked.

"No dear," I said. "My eyes are totally open now. I understand what's happening. Sorry I bothered you. I'll not do that again. Take care of yourself. Bye."

I headed out the bedroom door. Jillian staggered to the side of the bed. She grabbed one of her crutches. She used its' long reach to slowly push the door closed. And, with it, another final chapter of my pathetic love life. Jillian has acted this way for the second time. Stupid me. Will I ever learn?

A week later the telephone rang. The caller ID indicated it was from a local hospital. I answered it anyway. It was Jillian. "Come back to me baby," she commanded. "I've got that feeling."

"You know what I'm talking about. Don't you? It's time for some lovin'. Let's do what we do best! Let's do it, now!"

I hesitated. It was no longer about Jillian. It was about me. I hung up the telephone. Good riddance.

"Jillian... please don't call me... No Mo!" Good riddance!

Migraines were not my norm but this one's rippin' my head apart. A bad diet and stupid round the clock hours were the causes of my unbalanced system. Wham! My forehead explodes when this happens. I know a quick way to eliminate the pain... it's illegal. I won't tell if you don't?

I made a telephone connection with the Pill Doctor. His office on wheels is way over near Paris Heights. This guy has a remedy for any physical discomfort known to man. He owes me big-time 'cause I looked the other way when I passed by his outdoor medicine show.

I pulled up to his "ask me no questions" office. I rolled down the curbside window. "Hey man! Give me something quick for this migraine and I'm outta' here!" I shouted. No other conversation was needed. He reached into his back pocket. Several bags of white powder came flyin' through my front window. They landed on my passenger seat. "Take care, man!" I said as I pulled away. I didn't want to have a traffic accident so I waited until I reached my bed. I downed the powder with 22 ounces of a week-old 7-Eleven Slurpee drink. Seconds later, my head exploded like an atom bomb.

The reality was obvious. The pill doctor sent me on a trip back to whom knows where! I tried to sit up. I couldn't. Each time I sought a balance... my equilibrium forced me upside down in a place called nowhere. I was down for the count. There was only one thing for certain. Christopher Columbus, the Wizard of Oz, and Hitler were in a world of trouble! "Thus, where am I?" I wondered. I awakened 72 hours later. I still didn't know where I'd been.

CHAPTER 14

I'm two years into my attempts to successfully create a sin-free new world. Public concerns over my new world issues had turned pessimistic at the very best.

Protecting newborns? Identifying and tagging newborn children was absolutely resented. It took on a strong opposition after the first random baby selection process was instituted. The downfall? No one could predict which level of a parent's love was deemed acceptable.

The elderly? The elderly resented the creation of another class system for seniors based on how they'd lived prior to age 71. Everyone in this new world would begin anew at the same time. Measuring personal attributes from previous years was a tainted method and thought to be too subjective.

Incarceration issues? Building prisons for criminals not yet identified were too costly a logistical burden. Social opinions were to wait and see if developing newborns naturally challenged a criminal mindset.

A needed question about newborns, the elderly, and incarceration issues was… "Who said my new sin-less world would be a democratic decision-making process?"

My failing new world then brought forth something that was timely unexpected... It Started to Rain!

Not a normal rain. A rain similar to the forty-forty wetness experienced years ago during the initial onset of my new sinless world. Current new world leaders were trying to identify where our new civilization went wrong. We're eagerly addressing humanistic problems I might have overlooked.

This kind of knowledge was scarce. No new religious format's been discovered to explain why the questionable rain has again started to fall. The rain calendar stands at 10 consecutive days. Rivers and streams are now low-lying lakes. Highways and airport runways are underwater. Commercial traffic is at a standstill.

Food sources are drying up and crime, yes I said crime, has started to take over mankind's fate, again. Even the most innocent of people were hoarding anything they could find. This is where my new world has evolved to... and after only 10 days of constant rain?

"What's next on the list of unexpected for my new world?" I wondered. I'd better find answers to new world development very soon. There's another thirty days remaining!

....

The rains continued. Drop by drop. Minute by minute. Day after day. The rain calendar was now at 20 days and counting. How to survive twenty days of rain is a constant thought. Many new world lives have been washed away.

The population has decreased by 25 percent because of the constant rain. That figure increases each day. There are no answers as to how to stop the rain. There were no innovative discoveries for bringing the rains to a halt. Scientific minds merged in a gallant attempt to pray the wetness to a halt.

Neither the new Sun nor Moon has been visible since the rains started. The clouds are becoming ever so thick with moisture. So dense it's getting darker by the hour. I predict total darkness across this entire new world within the next 8 hours.

Total darkness, however, occurred at 12 noon... four hours earlier than predicted. There's no way to cope with the rains and the darkness. Fuel is non-existent. The rains shorted electrical and gas support systems. *Burning anything is not a true reality. Combustion cannot occur until the rains stop… if then.*

Worldwide, millions of people are in the dark. Feeling the curse of the inevitable, masses are locking doors to keep criminal elements out. The near future is not one the most imaginable scientist could forecast. Even I, the creator, didn't see this as the new future. My dream of a new sin-free world is coming to an end. My dream's over! This may be the last you hear from this world and me.

I'm late for roll call!

CHAPTER 15

Am I snake-bit or what? I got no respect afterwards when I placed my life in danger. I'm talking about a little of love's reciprocation. Just a tad. Is it too much to ask for tender loving care for my efforts? I put my life and career on the line for Jillian's family a while back. The only thank you I got was one night with Jillian. Lust was not what I wanted. Love is what I now seek. The longevity that comes with love has become the desperation my life needs.

Maybe I'm searching for love in all the wrong places. Church Choirs, Singles Bars, Supermarket Produce Sections... asking unknown women to identify a Yucca Root of some sort is not the best way to go! I tried all at one time or another. They're over-rated in terms of positive hook-ups. There's one place I haven't tried... the Internet.

I've been getting lots of inquiries over the Internet. I never gave them much thought. Who'd share their experiences with a stranger? Is meeting someone face-to-face that traumatic? Are we ashamed of our real selves to the point of dating a hand written message? Yet, we hear so many success stories. Does love's hurts push people to the Internet? There are millions talking all day long to people they don't even know. What's up with that?

Spare me the thought there aren't enough men and women available. That's nothing but a bunch of crap. There are plenty of potential partners out there. There's probably a shortage of men and women who'll never adapt to a theory of personal change. Think about it. I'd bet everyone lookin' for a partner on-line is lookin' for someone who falls under the perfect category. No one's seeking that guy or gal who needs to make a change for someone else. There lies the marketing strategy. The Internet's strategy is to entice participants who are egotistical, vain, and selfish to a personal fault. It gives them hope that such a perfect person exists for them. Yeah, right! The search for this complete one's self is a doosie. I laugh every time I hear those famous words, "My life without a significant lover is fine. When I do select a lover, it will be because I've chosen to share my life with someone. Not because I simply had to have a man or woman in my life." Well, if that's the case, why are people using the Internet to find a partner? If you are choosing a partner right now, have you really looked within your peer group? Can you accept change or not? Only you know the answer. It's true you must first love yourself before you can love someone else. If not, no one's ever going to fit into your pathetic love life.

Thus, a meeting is arranged to put an end to your mismanaged communication skills. You find out she is not the picture of beauty shown in her recent bio. She finds out you're much shorter than described. She's much wider than expected. Your old Buick is not the Mercedes you repeatedly bragged about. Her shoes are turned over a bit too much. Neither of you have enough money to pay for lunch. Dutch comes into play.

Ouch! Stalemate! The shock of reality withers. A decent, yet, respectful verbal intercourse tries to take place. Or, maybe not. Your double negatives challenge your college degrees. Her dangling participles place her in a California Valley... not the noted city of Boston. You still push on. Seeking a deeper reality. Internet relationships break down at this point. Trust is a killer! There's no patience involved by either person known as Mr. and

Mrs. Perfect Like Me! You aren't for me and I'm not the one for you. Regrettably, any relationship between us would take too much energy.

I'm exhausted just thinking about what I'd have to do to make an Internet lover happy… even in my dreams… and even without taking drugs. Whew! Wake me from this on-line debacle when it's over! Please! And, I apologize for getting off track with this life of mine.

I had several vacation days left. I spent all of them in the same place… that special chair. There was no place to go. No one I wanted to talk to. I used all of my Pizza and Chinese food coupons from that seat. My appetite was nonexistent. My stomach did not agree. I wasted most of the food. I am a mess. I didn't care.

I responded well enough from the latest Jillian affair. I returned to work on the midnight shift several nights later. During roll call announcements, I am constantly waiting for a lookout for a homicidal maniac killer on the loose from New York City. It won't take a rocket scientist to figure out the pimp shooter may have been from Virginia. Luckily, nothing was mentioned.

"It's good to have my best detective back!" shouted the Watch Commander.

"I missed you too, Sir," I sarcastically replied.

"That's good 'cause I have in my hand… another child abuse complaint. Right up your alley. No need waiting around here. Skip the remainder of this roll call session," he countered. "See ya' later!"

I headed to an unknown medical center listed on the complaint. It's a fact parents seeking medical attention for questionable injuries seek it during the late hours of the night. Stupid parents are under the impression that doctors, police personnel, and social workers have nine to five banker's hours.

They are not available to investigate questionable injuries once the Sun goes down.

Thirty minutes later, I was reading the medical chart of Sissy Thompson. She was a pretty seven-year old black female. Sissy's Stepmother brought her to Beckford Medical Center several hours ago with multiple burns on her hands. The burns occurred when Sissy accidentally touched the hot iron grills on top of the electric stove.

"Are these burns consistent with the explanation given by the child's Stepmother?" I asked Dr. Gloucester.

"The linear burn marks across the child's hands can happen that way," he explained. "If that's the case, why did you call us?" I asked the doctor. He removed the young lady's hospital robe. While holding back his tears, he simply counted forty-seven darkened circles on her torso. "Doctor, in your professional opinion, what caused these dark spots?" The answer to which I already knew. "These spots are circular cigarette burns," he responded. Without hesitation, I initiated a Court Hold procedure. I took some photos for future reference. Public relation skills my forte'… I rarely had trouble obtaining critical information from kids. It wasn't long before Sissy Thompson enlightened me. "When I'm a bad girl, my Step-mom holds my hands over the stove!" she said. "Have you been a bad little girl, lately?" I asked little Sissy. "Yeah. Today. I was bad today," said the seven year old.

There's a legal caveat involved anytime a child's answers might incriminate a guardian. It's one of credibility when comparing a child's testimony versus a mature adult's. If this complaint involved linear marks across the child's hands, this would be a more difficult decision. This was obviously physical abuse. I would make sure she did not endure another burn.

I didn't have to document the circular marks. An injury report signed by Dr. Gloucester validated them.

I asked the child, anyway. Upon understanding the question, the child knew she'd get her Step-mom in trouble. And, more trouble meant more burns. Sissy started crying. She changed into a different little girl.

Armed with this information, I responded to the child's home. I would interview the parents and personally check the stove with the parent's consent. Some parents can't tell a lie. Others don't know how.

As I completed my incident report, I strategically stopped talking. I peered directly at the parents. In a stern voice, I advised them of my personal opinion. "Mr. and Ms. Thompson, I know its quite possible Sissy touched the stove by accident. But it's absolutely unbelievable she burned herself with a cigarette forty-seven times... don't ya' think?"

This statement normally causes parents to look at each other. Remorse is what I'm seeking. These crimes are different from others. I draw on the parents' inner guilt. This was not a stolen car, bank robbery, or white-collar crime. This was flesh and blood. They affected a different set of human emotions.

"We can do this several different ways," I added. "I've placed Sissy under a Court Order. She won't be released from Beckford until the Court instructs it. Because of the severity of what Sissy has endured, I have to criminally charge both of you."

"I can do this with your co-operation or come back in the morning with a warrant! But, it shall be done," I said.

In Child Abuse cases, its better if a warrant is secured. Crazy parents of injured children rarely skip town without the kids in their possession. I've learned it's the caretakers who really seek help through these misguided disciplines. If the truth were known, many caretakers chastise children as their parents chastised them in earlier years. Parents need recovery interventions, too. Without question, the parent who placed Sissy's hands on the stove is probably the one who burned her with cigarettes.

It's a simple act of progression. Each time Sissy needed supervision, a cigarette burn was administered to get her attention. Whenever Sissy needed a larger dose of discipline, a harsher burn was warranted. The guilty Step-mom felt the need to better control the child, hence, the stove.

The father didn't commit the crime. He was involved, nonetheless. There's no way those burns weren't noticeable. And, by not reacting? He was definitely guilty of Neglect. The Court understands abuse phenomena better than most parents suspect. Thus, the Court's main focus was to re-unite the family–this I know to be absolutely true. Without much fanfare, the stepmother was found guilty of administering the burns. She received a five-year jail sentence. She was released after six months of incarceration. The child's father was convicted of Child Neglect. He allowed the burns to occur. His penalty was the removal of the child from his custody. The child was assigned to a foster home until Social Services contacted her natural birth mother. As in the past, these incidents left me flabbergasted more than ever before. These investigations taught me how difficult parenting can be. Yet, if acceptable parenting was never taught, "How can it be introduced to a child?" many wondered. Regardless how injured the child, I do observe elements of parental love in the hearts of perpetrators. "Can parental love eliminate the guilt of committing the act itself? Is a parent guilty if the thought behind the act was simply to be a parent?" These questions must be answered. Until then, I'll keep trying. The child needed an official transfer form for Sissy's medical file. I responded back to Beckford Hospital to complete that assignment. While talking to a nurse, I received a call from the dispatcher:

> "Detective Calloway, since you're already at Beckford, contact Dr. Brookshire on 555-7833 or the 3rd floor room 3A10."

Dr. Brookshire was in his office. He sadly told me about a two-month old named Corey Smith. The child had been a patient at Beckford since birth. The child's medical condition was unstable. He needed a blood transfusion or he was going to die. Because of religious reasons, his parents wouldn't consent to a blood transfusion. The child was born with medical complications. His health continually declined. Denying the blood transfusion would be a fatal decision. Making matters worse, it had to occur within the next few hours... by 7 AM. The parents were waiting in the hospital's cafeteria. I ran to discuss the health of their son. On the way up the elevator, my beeper went haywire. It almost jumped out of my pocket. I stared in amazement. The number belonged to Sondra, an old flame. I returned the call. It had to be an emergency. She answered on the first ring. "Bishop?" she murmured. "What time does your shift end?"

"You know the nature of this job, Sondra. The day isn't over 'til it's over. Not until," I added. "Can you drop by for a moment when you've finished?" she asked. "For me, this once?" I reluctantly agreed. My thoughts returned to Willard and Florence Smith. They were aware of the medical condition of their child. Each recognized the consequences of their decision. Both knew possible death was at issue; yet, indicated blood transfusions were against their religious beliefs. "If death resulted because of a lack of consent, it was simply the Will of God!" they added.

I spoke about the legal ramifications as I saw them. I, a member of the Court, wasn't letting a child die because of a religious affiliation. Little Corey had rights like any other citizen. I would protect those rights. If the child had an opinion, I'm sure he'd agree to the procedure. I tried to convince the parents to give written authority. After gaining no progress, I submitted the Court referral paperwork. My signature gave the hospital permission to keep the child in protective custody pending a court hearing later that morning. The time on the clock was 6:10

AM. The Court wasn't in progress until 9 AM–three hours from now. The blood transfusion was needed within the hour. I needed a higher decision on this matter. I needed one, right now.

I had a list of judges on stand-by. Judge Lora Shannon was awakened at 6:45 AM. She prepared a legal writ after a short discussion with Dr. Brookshire. The writ eliminated approval from the parents. This case would be presented before Family Court as a Neglected Child Complaint.

At 7:15AM, the child received the court ordered transfusion. When the judge heard the case later that same morning, the child was no longer in danger of losing his life.

The parents, displaying a demeanor of great relief, approached the bench. The father said although his permission could not be given to save his only son's life, a higher power could intervene and take that responsibility off of his religious shoulders. The entire courtroom fell quiet. Mr. Willard explained that the court's intervention was really God... or an act of God simply delivered through the Judge's decision.

The courtroom again fell silent. Everyone, now flabbergasted, didn't know if the Neglect Statute applied... or if this case should go to the Criminal Court system... or leave it as a Godly intervention.

The only thing real? Little Corey was no longer in danger of losing his life. Social Services found no prior issues in the child's background. The court monitored the child's condition until he was capable of being released from the hospital. Another hearing was held in front of Judge Shannon prior the child's release.

The Court declared if similar instances came before it, a child's health would always take preference over religious beliefs. "When a child is too young to make a decision, the court will make it for him," the Judge added.

"If parents attempted to violate court ordered transfusions, contempt charges would be assessed."

Having made this statement, the child was released back into the parents' custody. The court wanted to be notified anytime the child needed medical attention. The case was closed until its next review.

I learned a lot from this situation. I learned religion is given a high priority in this country. Parents do have a right to their own religious beliefs. As an investigator, where do I draw the line? Although the court intervened, it wasn't denouncing anyone's religious preference. It was simply acting in the best interest of the child. If a patient was of age and expressed similar views, such a request would have been recognized. In those circumstances, I wouldn't be involved. There are scenarios where an external decision must be made. The best decision for little Corey was made this morning.

I sat in the back of the courtroom. It was hard to believe the course of events I'd encountered over the last couple of days. The New York City rescue... the shoot-out in the dark... Jillian's love... to little Corey's transfusion. It was an unbelievable chain of events. I couldn't believe religion would allow a life to expire when a remedy was known. "Whatever happened to a child's right to be free of physical, psychological, and emotional pain while simply... growing up?" I wondered. No one told me about the psychological pain an investigator must endure to be good at this kind of challenge. How can these situations continue to happen?

I'd be lying if I said it didn't take its toll on Virginia's best Child Abuse investigator. I'm tired. I'm too tired to even complete my promise to Sondra. I tried to contact her over the hospital telephone. She didn't answer. I tried to talk to her again by office telephone. She didn't answer. Several hours later, my paperwork was done. I left the office. A mile down the freeway I tried to call Sondra, again. No answer.

I'd seen this behavior before. The woman on the other end hears the telephone but refuses to answer it. She refuses to answer so you can't tell her you've changed your mind about coming over. I felt this was one of those times.

I headed in that direction, anyway. I arrived at her home. Her car was still in the driveway. The door was ajar. No key would be needed. I pushed the front door open slowly. "Sondra, are you home?" I shouted inquisitively. No answer. Nothing was heard but voices of a television located in another room. "Sondra! Where are you?" I shouted. Again… no answer.

The house was familiar to me. Some things had changed. Other things moved here and there. To my surprise, pictures of Sondra and me were still hanging on the walls. Thoughts of the good old days went through my head. Thoughts of old love. Old kisses. The newness back then. A tap on my head disturbed my memories of the past. I looked around. I found nobody. There was another tap on my head. Again, no one was in the same room. The next tap wasn't really a tap at all. It was a drop of water falling from above. I looked upward. Drops of water were falling through the cracks in the ceiling. My God!" I said to myself. "Sondra apparently left the water running in the bath tub."

I raced up the steps. I lost my footing and slid down the slippery hardwood floor towards the bathroom door. I crawled through the standing water to turn off the faucet. I entered the bathroom. Someone's wrist dangled over the bathtub's edge. The wrist supported a Timex watch I gave Sondra during our relationship years ago (Well, I gave it to her after she purchased it for me to give back to her). The unreal entered my mind. "Sondra!"

I grabbed her hand. I pulled myself to the edge of the tub. Sondra was submerged. She had no movement. She was dressed in a sexy nightgown ensemble. It was sheer with black colored lace along the borders. The wetness caused both pieces to cling to her body. Its' revealing nature suggested she wanted to be impressive tonight. "But, to whom?" I questioned. I yanked the bathtub stopper. I released the water. I pulled Sondra from the tub. I dialed 911! I started an Emergency Medical Service vehicle in this direction. While awaiting its arrival, I forced air into Sondra's lungs. She was not responding. I saved several lives during my career. "How could she not respond?" I yelled to myself. "Sondra… wake up!" I yelled. "Sondra… please wake up!" I kept yelling. The more I yelled… the more I knew Sondra was gone. "Why would you do something stupid like this?" I asked the silence in the room.

Sondra never answer. Her eyes were wide open staring at the ceiling. No matter what position I placed Sondra's body… her eyes followed me. She had that "I'm never leaving you" look frozen across her face. I could hear sirens racing down the street. They would arrive too late to save my old love.

I held her in my arms. My life with her came forward. It was like yesterday. It was like yesterday we loved each other. Like we met for the first time. Everything we learned about the other was new and exciting. I yelled Sondra's name over and over. I cried in the process… similar to the way that Marlon Brando fella' cried out for "Stella!" in that movie. I didn't feel the hurt Brando did. When he did it… it was just a movie. This was not a movie. This was the real deal. The true pain was unbearable. "Sondra, why did you do this?" I asked the silence again. The EMS workers raced into the house. My ego tried to capture itself. I didn't want to show my private emotions. I tried to stop the tears. I could not do so. A saving grace? I was drenched from all the water. No one knew the wetness on my face wasn't water from Sondra's attempted rescue. Several energetic EMS officials yanked Sondra out of my arms. They performed their expertise on her. They tried everything. Nothing worked. Sondra was lost. Crime scene experts took pictures of the bathroom.

A very important factor went unnoticed. Balled up in Sondra's right hand was a pill container. Her hand was peeled open finger by finger. The container rolled onto the floor. I'd seen those pills before. I called them suicide bridge pills. Distraught others swallowed them before jumping off the bridge crossing the Pointer Ridge Parkway. This bridge was famous because of the numerous jumpers on a monthly basis. Autopsies usually found this barbiturate in the deceased's blood system; hence... suicide bridge pills. These pills were the barbiturates of choice when people wanted to end it all. Take a couple and off into wonderland you'd go. Never feel a thing. Not even death.

The pill container was from a street sale. No identifying names or numbers were listed on the container. Where the pills were purchased wasn't the issue. Why she took them? That's the real question.

I gave a personal statement for the record. After all, I had a past relationship with this woman. And, I was the first person on the scene. More questions were coming from Homicide, I'm sure. No way to get around that. I'd respond as best I could. I'll be questioned for foul play. This fact didn't bother me. I was a fellow cop.

Sondra's death had unanswered questions. Her telephone records indicated several calls to me earlier this day. This validated statements I'd made in my report. It validated I had not talked to Sondra any time in the recent past. The cause of death was drowning. No suicide or homicide labels were associated with Sondra's death. I wasn't worried. Det. Ron Mason, an old police buddy, will inform me of any new changes in the investigation. Ron said the initial investigation found no other person to be involved. "Right now the only name in the ongoing investigation is yours," he added. We're doing our best to clear your name... To declare this incident as a suicide," he added. "What's takin' so long?" I asked. "The official time of her death was several minutes before your documented telephone call to the EMS dispatcher," he replied. "Why is that a questionable issue?" I asked. "Well, the autopsy revealed the barbiturates in that container were not effective. They were taken but didn't have time to affect her health," he said. "So, there's a question as to how she got into the tub?" I sarcastically asked. "Well, Bishop. You know the nature of our business," Rob frankly stated. "Do your best. I've nothing to hide. Call me if you need answers or whatever."

Sometimes the easiest cause of death is the hardest to validate. I had nothing to do with Sondra's death. Yet, I find myself questioned by my fellow workers. The Watch Commander called me into his office." Bishop. You know the drill. Those Homicide fellas' think its best you take a few days off. While they finalize this investigation... that is," he said.

"Nobody questions your involvement. I certainly don't. Put your Smith and Wesson in the safe over there. You're on Administrative Leave... with pay. God knows you deserve it. Get lost for a week or two or three. I'll personally call once the investigation's closed," he quirked. I placed my gun in the safe. At the door, I turned... I shouted, "What's the real problem here? Is there evidence I don't know about?"

The Watch Commander looked up and hesitantly shared, "Your old girlfriend made a call to her mother before you arrived. She told her you were harassing her over the telephone. You wanted her back and were coming over like old times. You wouldn't take no for an answer. That drowned gal's momma swears to this conversation. Add today's calls to her number before her death, and it places you in a stupid situation. Doesn't it?" he solemnly asked. I had no response to the Watch Commander.

"Sir," I replied. "You'll find I had nothing to do with this death. Suicide is the truth regardless of how it looks. I'll stay by the telephone to help if needed."

"What am I going to do with myself now?" I wondered several hours later. I could only sit in Jillian's special chair for so long. I stayed in my house until the walls started closing in on me. The mental part of this was unbearable. Regardless the level of my innocence, my love for Sondra challenged the legitimacy of my professional character. After I'm found innocent, the thought being psychologically guilty will haunt me forever. I'll feel it everywhere I go. I'll feel it everyday I wake up and put on my shoes. I feel it now. I see it in the eyes of those who stare at me as I pass them on the street… at the bank… and at the grocery stores. My old friends knew Sondra as a good woman. Although it's been years, many feel I hurt her deeply and she never recovered from that hurt. My ears are burning from follow-up talk about our old relationship.

Jillian won't return my calls. The kids had to be transferred to another school district after the local newspapers got wind of this story. Those thought to be friends abandoned me like I had the plague. I tired of looking at reruns of Gilligan's Island and Hogan's Heroes. I tired eating in the fast lane of McDonald's… the carryout window of Chin's Chinese Restaurant. I started drinking to ease the loneliness. I took out the blender and tried to measure the proper ingredients for a heavy Fuzzy Navel. I over-measured the Peach Schnapps Liquor and under-measured the orange juice. I didn't like the combination. The tenth attempt had me buzzing to a new tune. I quickly ran out of the each ingredient. I called Bolar's Liquor Store. More mixers were on the way.

The doorbell rang.

I grabbed my wallet. I ran to the door eager to continue my Fuzzy Navel binge. The sweet taste of peach would be my newest friend. I opened the front door. A stunned look was all I had left. The visitor was Jennifer… Sondra's crazy, identical twin-sister from Chicago!

"Where's my Smith and Wesson when I need it?" crossed my mind. And, "Why was Jennifer so cordial?" I wondered. I thought she was at my door for revenge reasons. "May I please come in?" she asked. My house was a complete mess. I was wearing the same cut-off shirt and dirty jeans I'd worn the entire week. I had the same underwear on for Christ sake! I'm embarrassed. Yet, standing at my front door was the sister of a girlfriend many think I killed.

"Jennifer. Why are you here?" I asked. Jennifer stared at me. Didn't say a word. Seconds later she asked, again, "May I come in, or what, Bishop?" I peeked outside. I looked up and down the street to see if nosy neighbors were about. The last thing I wanted was another questionable murder attached to my name. Thus, I reluctantly allowed her to enter. "This place looks and smells like a pig sty! You should be ashamed of yourself!" she smirked. "Wow! How fast her demeanor changed," I thought to myself. She was sweet as could be outside that door. Once inside, she became instantly negative. I wanted to say something apologetic but couldn't. "Bishop. You're in a heck of a bind," she stated. "You know my sister's life ended when you left her. Don't you?"

"Sondra talked of committing suicide since that day you didn't take her to that black-tie gala, remember?" said Jennifer. She poked her index finger in my chest over and over and over 'til it pissed me off a little. "Remember that day she called? She asked you to come over? That was a very tough day for her. She had previously called me and momma all week long," said Jennifer. "Sondra tried to live without you. She just didn't know how."

Jennifer was now eye-to-eye. Neither of us blinked nor took a deep breath. At that exact moment, tears flowed simultaneously from each of us. Jennifer and I cried together. I placed my arms around her as she did. We stood in the same spot—crying together for the same reason. We were feeling the same loss. "I wanted to see you in the flesh. I needed to look in your eyes. I must hear why you wanted to end my twin sister's life!" she said.

"I loved Sondra so much. She told me you loved her just as much," she added. There was another ring at the door. Probably the liquor store delivery... yes. When I returned, Jennifer was still crying. She looked for a clean place to sit. She found the only one available. It was Jillian's special seat. I threw another measurement into the blender. I whipped up another, stronger load of my special mixer.

"What are you drinking?" Jennifer asked. "I'm not a hard drinker but this Fuzzy Navel stuff tends to ease my loneliness," I responded. "Would you like one?"

"Yes. Please!" Jennifer answered. Jennifer and I drank Fuzzy Navels until the cows came home. Six hours later Jennifer gave me a great big hug. "I'm sorry for accusing you, Bishop. I know you could never do anything so gruesome as committing a murder," she said. "Sondra spoke so well of you. Even after you left, she never had a bad thing to say." Jennifer poured another Fuzzy. "I envied Sondra," she whispered through her tears. Jennifer nibbled on my neck. She tightened her hug. "Bishop. We've had a lot to drink. I want to get closer to you. I want the love you gave my sister. Such affection has eluded me over the years," Jennifer stated. "Bishop, you could never harm Sondra. She took her own life. You, however, need help with the police investigation. I'm here to give you that help," she followed.

"But first, I wanna' feel as my twin sister did. I want the love she described in your love sessions. I want you to hold me like you held her," Jennifer continued. I was dumbfounded. What was I to do? Here was the key to my legal vindication.

Before I could answer, Jennifer acknowledged another truth. "Bishop. I wanna' share a secret nobody knows but my mother, sister, and me."

"You were aware Sondra and I were twin sisters... but not as 'true' twin sisters. As true twin sisters, we shared certain strong feelings."

"Where are you going with this story?" I asked Jennifer.

"Bishop. Each time you made love to Sondra... I felt your love touches, too!"

"When she screamed your name out loud... so did I way back in Chicago. When she fainted from exhaustion... so did I. And, when she fell asleep, afterwards... me too!"

A frown captured my face.

Jennifer continued... "My darling Calloway, I've loved you from the very first day Sondra met you! When Sondra fell for you... you became the love of my life! I tried to disconnect from Sondra. Her feelings were stronger than mine. Your love for her was stronger than anything that came my way. I looked forward to being loved by you... even if it was... through Sondra."

"And, yes to your next question!" she added. "Sondra was aware you were making love to both of us. She encouraged it 'cause she sorta' knew your relationship wouldn't last forever."

"Being twin sisters was hard on her. Before you, we were just a pair of freakish sisters. We were always depressed. We had each other's love... in every sense of the word. Need I say more?"

"We trusted only each other for comfort. We feared others might learn the truth. Only our momma' knew. We didn't like our incestuous urges. We tried but it was hard to deny our needs. It was a passed-down-from-ancestor type thing," she finalized.

"Sondra tired of the pressure. She wanted to end her life. She found your love... a great love. It bothered her to share that special love with me!"

"Bishop, I was her unwanted outcast sister. She didn't want you to know about me. I pressured her to love you the way she did," Jennifer added. "Sondra knew I couldn't resist your touch. I telephoned her many times. I told her what sexual experiences I wanted her to have with you. I blackmailed her to submit to certain experiences. You recognized the differences at times, didn't you?" inquired Jennifer.

There was a huge sigh of relief in Jennifer. "I've told you the truth. Are you happy now?" she asked.

Something started to happen. The Jennifer standing in front of me began resembling the old Sondra more and more. Yes, I know she was a true twin sister. But she was more than that. She had the same posture, hairstyle, and make up... of...?

She had similar legs, feet, and facial expressions. The similarities were ridiculous. Sondra was here. She was here in this room. She was right in front of me! The more I stared at Jennifer... the more it brought back memories. Jennifer even had Sondra's smell. Jennifer may have entered my front door... but Sondra... walked back into my life. "Sondra wasn't dead!!!" I kept repeating over and over.

My heartbeats got even faster. I wanted Sondra in the worst way. I wished she were here in the flesh! Jennifer felt the same way. Actually, Jennifer had that certain look the moment she knocked on my front door. Jennifer took my hands. She led me to my trashy-lookin' bedroom. A clean, unsoiled sheet was the only clean thing left in my room. Good thing I'd slept in Jillian's chair all week long. Jennifer slowly undressed me. When she undid her own blouse, she was wearing a bra exactly like the one Sondra wore many times. It was similar to an old birthday gift I gave Sondra years ago. (Well, it was really a bra and panty set Sondra bought for me... to give back to her as her birthday gift. You've heard that before.)

I know our current actions are questionable. Yet, nothing mattered once she called for my love. We duplicated what Sondra and I had experienced. It was easy to do so. Everything felt exactly as it did back in the day. "What are the odds of this?" I wondered. "That similarities could exist between two identical but different women?"

As my mind drifted into our love, Jennifer abruptly cried, "I love you... My Goofy Detective Man!" Silence!

Silence filled the room! Sondra usually yelled out those same exact words. Only Sondra! Those words were very confidential.

How could Jennifer use those exact words? Did Sondra share them with Jennifer in past conversations? Did Jennifer scream those same words way back in Chicago… at the same exact time Sondra did in the big little town of Sircus Junction?

"This was truly amazing!" I thought. We held each other one last time. I buried my head into Jennifer's long brown hair. It was something I did to connect to Sondra's soul. I played with the scar above Jennifer's left ear. Only a few people knew it was there.

Only her true twin sister and I… and maybe her mother? The scar resembled half a figure eight. It healed well. I had to look hard to find it. It was a scar like that in front of my very eyes.

My Detective skills were coming alive. I've made love to twin sisters. Now I can't tell them apart! The truth was kicking me in the buttocks. I read in a women's magazine a while back no two women had the same body scent… sexually speaking.

I pushed Jennifer's love button one more time. I investigated every nook and canny of her personal self. The reality? This Jennifer wasn't Jennifer!

This Jennifer was the real Sondra! It surely had to be.

It was the real Sondra… in the flesh!!!!!! No matter what part of Jennifer's body I investigated, I found the Sondra I once knew. I was stimulated but questionably stunned. Needing more evidence, I made love to Jennifer… or Sondra… or whomever… one last time to strengthen my probable cause for arrest reasons only (of course)! I took no pride in doing what had to be done for the sake of justice. Jennifer… or Sondra, whomever, were exhausted. She… or they… were lying face down on the bed. I reached under my pillow. I grabbed a pair of sexy toy handcuffs. I slapped them on her… their wrists before my theories could react. I may appear to be somewhat baffled… but one (or both) of these chicks was (were) gonna' do some time.

I expected at least one "What the heck?" or some other verbal expression to escape the mouths of one or the other. None came.

Sondra or Jennifer looked up at me with those beautiful hazel eyes. Somebody gave me that smile I could never resist.

I sat on the edge of the bed. I was in total shock. I tried to call the Homicide Squad right then and there. I hesitated 'cause I had no idea how I was gonna' explain my up-close, first-hand proof of the physical evidence proving my arrest.

I could hear myself testifying at tomorrow's preliminary hearing. "Well Judge, it was like this. I touched here... tasted there... and pushed on this and that until I had enough probable cause to arrest one or the other... because of the motive for whomever to kill whoever... was not swimming upside down in that overflowing bathtub!"

"Yeah, Right!" I affirmed. Meanwhile, I pushed Sondra, or possibly Jennifer into the bedroom corner chair. I draped my bathrobe over their nakedness. I would no longer allow myself to be used by this woman, whoever she was.

"What the heck are you doing, Sondra?" I definitively asked. "Don't you know your sister's lying on a morgue table this very moment?"

"You sit there like nothing's happened. My finger is ready to dial 911. Talk to me and talk to me quick!" I urged. Sondra's (whoever's) response floored me. "I couldn't let my crazy twin sister share your love anymore!" one of the sisters shouted. "She came to Virginia to take what's left of you back to Chicago. All I had left were my memories of you. I could no longer love you for her. Or, for us as true twin sisters."

"I tried to deal with it but she... she wanted you all to herself. Bishop, you're still the man of my dreams... my dreams, only! Not hers? Right?" asked one of the Sondras of old. "Okay, I drowned Jennifer in the tub. I did it with my own two hands. Put my jewelry on her and everything. I tried to make her look as much like me as possible. I told my mother to quickly identify the body as me. No further questions like fingerprints had to be done. And, of course, Mama agreed," Sondra added.

"Mama wanted at least one of her little girls to live a normal life. She chose me over Jennifer 'cause Jennifer was absolutely uncontrollable!"

As Sircus Junction's best investigator, I could only put my hands over my face. I shook my head from side to side. I, Virginia's finest, was involved in a messy love jones situation gone haywire. I thought about this turn of events. Evidence I needed to clear my name was Jennifer's... or Sondra's... or I mean Jennifer's testimony that her true twin sister Sondra or Jennifer, whichever one it was... had a history of trying to kill herself... or her sister... or whomever was the supposedly "good sister" was trying to kill the bad sister... or whomever... with Mama assisting whichever daughter with a corroborating story against the other daughter—both of whom were sexually molested as little girls by momma's third and fourth husbands!

"Wow! That's it!"

As additional evidence to support the truth, I asked whomever to tell me what happened to those massive people-cats that used to live in that house. "They upped and became victims of some stupid burglary gone bad," she responded. "Still don't know the whereabouts of my babies... or even why several broomsticks were taken," she added.

This was verbal evidence only the real Sondra would know. I'm referring to the missing broomsticks: not those big ole' people cats. I recited that explanation another sixty-two times. It finally made sense. Once the real truth is discovered, I'll be an innocent cop lover involved in a twin-sister murder plot. A complex criminal situation is the kind of stuff Homicide knucklehead's love to justify. Something simple has to be made complicated to get a "Case Closed" rubber stamp.

I said nothing else to Sondra. I took the handcuffs off. I told her to get dressed. She smiled. I buttoned her blouse. I watched as she squirmed into a very tight min-shirt… way above the knee. I shoved her out the back door of my house. "Why are you doing this for me?" she asked. I took a while to answer.

"Get your mother to contact the Homicide Squad. Tell them I had nothing to do with the drowning, please?" I asked before her silhouette disappeared in the dark. Her distant frown agreed. She stopped about ten feet out the back door. She lovingly peeked back. Her expression asked about the possibility of a relationship. As much as I wanted her, I bit my lip, shook my head negatively, and closed the back door.

She vanished into the night. The following afternoon I received a call from Rob… my Homicide Squad softball buddy. "Got some good news, old buddy!" he yelled, "The drowned woman's momma' changed her story. She sent us to a Psychiatrist who verified Sondra was talkin' suicide over the years. Your name was in her confidential file. She mentioned in the file your breakup with her made her want to live no longer. The file indicated you were no longer an attraction in her life," Rob added.

"So, Big Daddy… with all this new info… you're a free man again!" he laughed. "I've already told the Watch Commander. He'll be calling you, shortly. You owe me a tall beer!" he screamed. "And, not the cheap stuff!"

"Thanks, Rob. I owe you." I hung up the phone. I called Jillian to give her the good news. She didn't answer. I wouldn't call again. What's the use? Jillian doesn't care about me anymore. All she wants is that monthly check. Somebody else is fulfilling her other needs.

The Law should be changed. As long as she gets my check, I should have the option of making love to her whenever so desired. That's only fair. Stupid court system, huh? I crawled back into Jillian's chair. I sipped the last of a watered-down Fuzzy Navel.

I drifted into a heart-warming drunken stupor. "Jillian, will you take me back?" I asked for the thousandth time. And, no… she didn't!

Even in my dreams… Jillian told me to "Loose Her Number!"

CHAPTER 16

And, then there was Phyllis. She was very pretty but had a few personal issues. The biggest issue was she couldn't wait to fall in love. She felt her time had arrived. She would, therefore, take complete control of her marriage destiny... Right Now!

I became her prime target. I had earned a couple of academic degrees. I wasn't scared to work for a living. I wasn't too hard on the eyes. This made me the object of her affections. I would not escape her heart.

Phyllis was locked in to love. I gave her no reason to be so connected. I hadn't become her soul mate nor sought that unwanted distinction. I purposely didn't do so. Okay. I have a minor confession to make. I might have, maybe just a teeny-weeny bit, ever-so-slightly misrepresented certain feelings I had for her! Talking long hours on the telephone meant more to her than to me. I was a lonely fella' at the time. She, I now recognized, sought to complete her desperate soul. It's my fault she believes in me as she does. I'll be more considerate of her feelings next time.

Phyllis's ears believed every word I said. She remembers every syllable I've ever spoken. Each comment I made was a statement to future love she expected to receive from me. I knew she was misinterpreting many things I said. Didn't matter. I kept shouting undeliverable promises anyway and received the glorious womanly spoils that accompanied them. It was totally my fault. Her feelings were worth more than that. I'll attempt to be more honest about her future. I keep repeating myself, huh?

I loved the fact I had the ears of an insecure, sensitive woman. A man feels more in control when all a woman wants to do is follow his directions. He can talk with no interruptions. He doesn't have to deal with facial expressions of disgust. No dogging out on issues that are none of her business. I often wondered if men discovered a value in this kind of relationship. Then again... why would men want to? It would be too boring. Think abut it. What would a relationship be like if there were no fights about in-law visits? No financial arguments? No sexual strife? If there were no financial or sexual woes... why even get up in the morning? It would be just another great day.

Honey-baby sweetie-pie would clean the entire house without being asked. Dirty underwear would be washed, bleached a couple of times, and neatly stacked. Dinner would be cooked to perfection. It would still be hot whenever you came home after work... if you came home at all. A "June Cleaver" smile would always greet you at the front door. A robe, cigar, and hot bath always awaited the perfect man... she, the almost perfect woman.

The man's interpretations on social issues were always the accepted norms. His political selection for President of the United States would be hers also. She'd stay home on election nights. He'd go to the election polls and pull the lever for both. Yes indeed!

She would allow him to control her every thought. She'd get mad at him only when he allowed her to get mad at him. They'd have two kids. A son would be the first born, of course. Her second pregnancy would occur when he had agreed she was ready to have daddy's little girl. Splendid!

Her parents would still adore the hubby even if he lost his job. "Here's a little somethin'-somethin' to keep you'all going 'til you get on your feet!" her parents would happily say. "Just keep my sweet little girl and those uncontrollable kids from coming back home to Indiana… back to where they started from. If there's anything you need, just ask!"

"Need a down payment on a house too big fer' yer britches? Here's a blank check. Feel like taking a vacation against the Euro? Whatever? Just don't send our third daughter back home as an ex-wife. She's officially your… for better or for worse problem, now! Right?"

Getting back to Phyllis, I told her during that forgettable or regrettable first telephone conversation I'd tell my mother about her. Again, it's my fault. Everybody knows only the right gals get introduced to momma. Never bring that connection into a dating equation. It's like proposing marriage without actually doing so. Either way, a fella's in trouble. Thus, am I? And, yes again, it's my fault.

Phyllis felt so at home with me. I wanted to talk only about her on the first date. I didn't need to. She spent an eternity talking about her. What she wanted outta' life. What she wanted in a man. Ahem, which, of course, was the perfect man.

The problem? She thought I was that man! She thought I was that person… the perfect man. After four hours of listening to her, she told herself all she needed to know. I would indeed be her destiny. I tried to disagree. I knew not how to disappoint that stupid destiny. I knew disappointing her would be inevitable.

By the second date, I decided to move in with her. My fault. She took very little time adopting the ways of a loving couple already in a lengthy marriage. Women usually wait a few months before they allow you to see them on the toilet. Not my Phyllis. She took one heck of a dump that first night. She was proud of it! She finished and gracefully stood tall. She glanced down into the bowl. She spread her hands far apart indicating the length of her prize-winning female turd. "Betcha' can't beat that one!" she hollered into the next room. "Geez" I uttered to myself. And this was after only one night of living together. Somebody… shoot me now… please! Making matters worst, Phyllis could fart louder than any trucker fella' I knew. I didn't have to pull her finger or nothin'! I took her to my Friday night poker games just to show her off. I couldn't hold a good poker face but won lot of bets on her farting abilities. I was sooooo proud of my honey-boo.

Our dating wasn't all fun and games. Did I mention I'm not a wig man? You can take all the wigs in the world and throw 'em into the ocean. Phyllis had a good half-head of hair but still wore wigs all the time. Socially, I couldn't take her too many places because her wig selections were downright horrendous. Have you ever had dinner with George Washington at the Outback Steakhouse? That's what it felt like. Her wigs were so bad even store mannequins were embarrassed when she walked by. That's just a bit of my humor. Even a cop's gotta' laugh, sometime. But, I'm as serious as can be.

Phyllis didn't care about the truth. She didn't care how quickly I'd snatch that thing off her head once in the driveway. A fella' can't have everything, I guess. Right now, though, I'd trade Phyllis straight-up for that gal President Clinton never had sex with! Her name was Monica Woziniackskinskijones… or something like that. It's all my fault. I should've done my homework before moving in with this chick. (I love using the word "chick", huh? It's the 1970s… grow up!)

I traveled a lot. I returned home one weekend to my wedding… a wedding I knew nothing about. It was the normal so-called surprise wedding party… for me! I was in shock. I was speechless. Invitations had been mailed out, rsvp'd, and everything. Everybody in town knew about it but me. I was speechless. Did I already say that?

I confronted Phyllis. She thought a surprise wedding was a great thing to do. We were getting married some time in the next four or five years anyway… what's the problem, Mister? I stared into her hazel contacts (I know). I wanted to strangle this chick in the worst way. There were too many witnesses. Too many of my so-called friends were dressed up like penguins awaiting the most ridiculous wedding ceremony to ever be witnessed.

Phyllis took a huge gamble. Duuuhhhhh? She figured... she figured... this chick figured if enough pressures were placed on my responsibilities, I would acquiesce to a wedding ceremony after the longest thirteen-day relationship in history. She was mistaken. I'd dealt with her kind before. Why women resort to such stupid tactics is beyond me. If I approved of this gathering I would never be viewed as the man in this relationship. I would have lost everything a man could lose. Dignity. Self Respect. Machismo. Money. Old Friends. Dignity. Self Respect.... and so on... everything my father and my father's father died for.

So, as I uttered those binding words... *I, Bishop Calloway, do hereby take...* my heart sank into the depths of no return. I had given in to the pressure. I had indeed, again, become a sissy of a man... a good police investigator, though.

In only two short weeks, I had been captured and slain by the wicked witch of the North. I tried my best to make it last. I tried my best to make it work. It didn't. I filed for a divorce before consummating the marriage. That, too, was totally my fault. I should have been honest from the start. I miss Phyllis tremendously. I want her back.... NOT!

I've learned two things for sure. The first thing I learned was that our breakup was totally my fault. I should've been more considerate about her feelings. Second, and even more important, my Friday night poker games would never be the same without that chick. And, yes... everything's entirely my fault! That's why I can't keep a decent relationship! That's why my kids never call me like they used to do! And, that's why I'm snorting little bags of white powder and swallowin' yellow and blue demons at the same time! Don't worry. I'll wash 'em down with 22 ounces of Fuzzy Navel mix and dream 'bout whatever. It's getting out-of-hand.

Ohhhh... Yaaahh!!!

My overuse of unknown prescriptions has turned me into a psychologically stressed-out toad. I'll still have to play this new world scenario out until its' end. My world's civilization prepared for its final hour.

At precisely midnight new world time, each citizen will have to make a free-will decision. The rains had pushed the ocean water levels to the mountaintops. The only options left for new world residents were to either drown or survive as one of several subterranean life forms.

"Whoooaaaaa! This ain't nothin' but a crazy dream!" I thought as I sought to recover from another splendid batch of amphetamines. It was too late. The magical medicine was doing what it was supposed to do. My migraine had disappeared... my life and my new world, however, were in shambles! The survival of new mankind hinged on hallucinogenic leadership. With little time to decide, each of my followers had to choose between two subterranean life forms... the Drepped Aouugaks or the Warbusted Piiiitshanks! Both reside on my newly developing ocean floor of darkness. The only edible food source, unfortunately, was each other... and us! It's gonna' be the survival of the fittest - literally!

The Drepped Aouugak scampers through the water with the assistance of oily, snake-like scales. It travels faster than ten times the old speed of light. You do the math. It hunts and defends with long rows of razor sharp teeth hidden under its outer skin. It eats every third day and hunts in groups of seven. The Drepped Aouugak protects its territory by squirting a belly-grease known as "nonsense oil" into the cold salt water. This mixture confuses the prey's brain... rendering it helpless! The Drepped Aouugak's weakness? Grinding its teeth creates a high-pitched rippling effect that gives intended victims a half-lite trickle second to escape.

The other subterranean menace is the Warbusted Piiiitshank! The Piiitshank is a bold predictor. The name on its back brags about its deadly force. Each additional small letter i following the capital P represents its level of killing intelligence! The highest known kill levels are three iii's. If you ever see the fourth letter i on a Warbusted Piiitshank's back... you're already dead!

The Warbusted Piiiitshank, while almost invisible, electrically Zaaapppps!!!! anything in its path. Three lizard-like tongues hunt the dark with sonar, and it has an appetite that must be satisfied every hour... on the hour.

This subterranean beast is the more vicious of the two but doesn't know it. Its' weaknesses?

Simply put... Warbusted Piiiitshanks are stupid. They have very little mobility. They tend to hide in the brightest dark places on the ocean's bottom (go figure) hoping to be preyed upon by the more intelligent, but home-schooled Drepped Aouugak species. The Warbusted Piiiitshanks, unfortunately, are their own worst enemies. They're basically 50/50 when it comes to who or what they consume on the hour.

At times, both of these species worked in tandem. You'll need a good Timex watch and pretty solid math skills when that happens.

I can't figure out why I've sent my valuable new world followers to an ocean full of Drepped Aouugaks and Warbusted Piiiitshanks.

Before I do, I'm waiting for Jillian to awaken me from this hallucination. I'm waiting so I can apologize for the grief I've caused in her life over the years.

I wanted to close my eyes for a second to escape my subterranean world. However, I had some unfinished business with the Drepped Aouugaks and Warbusted Piiiitshanks on the deep ocean floor. My allotted timetable for individual decisions between the two subterranean choices had passed. As slow as I am, I officially took the life form of the Warbusted Piiiitshank! Once everyone's selection had been officially recorded, no one was privy to choices by any other individual... not those of family and not those of friends. As previously mentioned, this new world was about survival—not love and friendships. At that moment, my natural senses detected an urgency to quickly maneuver to the left. As I did, a Drepped Aouugak's attack missed my neck by several inches. I could tell it was a Drepped Aouugak based on its noisy, grinding teeth. I had only a half-lite trickle second to escape its viscous killing intelligence. Thank Goodness!!! The Drepped Aouugak's waves were still circling my current location. Instead of being the hunter, it easily became the hunted as I quickly shocked, slashed, and gobbled up the slow invader. Egad! I just satisfied my first every hunger pain. The Drepped Aouugak's taste was truly unbearable. The ocean's cruel darkness wasn't enough. I now have to adjust to a foul combination of guts.I followed the Drepped Aouugak meal with remains of a fellow Warbusted Piiiitshank. My hunger had been satisfied. My taste buds demolished. My thirst as predator ceased... at least for the next couple of hours. But then came... the "LIGHT!" As my subterranean life went on as described, a discovery of Light was introduced to the other side of my universe. Light was described as an ability to understand the darkness. An ability to visualize more of the new world! An ability to effectively hunt and defend the short life span present species faced every moment. It is definitely something worth causing a war over. Yes. The devastation of a Light War! Something stranger occurred. A drop of moisture just fell onto my forehead! The drop of moisture awakened me at that very moment. But, that's impossible! How could that happen? I was currently swimming in an ocean of water. I'm awakening. I'm somewhat puzzled by the flapping of my arms across the bed. Then again, does it really matter? Isn't it okay for a man to have his own personal fantasies? I do. So... get a life!

My dream had become a reflection of my life as a human being. The connection... Personal Commitment! In real life, my psychologist discovered I subconsciously never wanted to commit to any one special woman. I apparently denied a lack of total commitment to Jillian by continuing to create new worlds... and that police job!

The subterranean world and its deadly inhabitants afforded an opportunity to not commit to any relationship other that of Child Abuse and Neglect Detective—something I loved.

The telephone started ringing. It had to be Jillian. I said hello to a voice I so badly needed to hear. The voice was Jillian's... and with her voice came the Light! The Light represented brightness in my future. But, was it a brightness of longevity?

Within seconds... gone were historical persecutions that consumed me for such a long time. Gone forever were religion, introducing new worlds, and thoughts of forty/forty rains. Gone forever were deadly dreams of Drepped Agouugaks and Warbusted Piiitshanks!

Jillian's Light challenged all my imaginations. This welcomed mindset had significant meanings. I was still in love with Jillian. She wanted me to return to her and the kids. She wanted us to commit to a nuclear family lifestyle. Yes! Jillian's Light created an expectation that "all is right in the world." She and I decided to give it another go, Thank God!

I knew when I awakened I would no longer be depressed. Whatever reality I faced when these eyes opened, would not be as negative as when I closed them.

Newly formed world's, from this point forward, shall no longer affect my existence. Nuff said.

CHAPTER 17

Time flies. A couple of years had passed. I, a more humbled and experienced Bishop Calloway, witnessed my Child Abuse and Neglect Caseload increased at a minimum 300 percent. I closely observed this unsought escalation of questionable social values. The Department had barely scratched the surface prevention-wise. Today's a new day. It comes with challenges. My reputation as an excellent Child Abuse Investigator spread throughout the Police Department and Family Court System. I gave speeches at hospitals, schools, and civic organizations. I even traveled to other jurisdictions as an expert on child abuse issues. Allowing Police Officers to investigate child abuse complaints had blossomed into a national issue. It was originally the responsibility of local Social Services entities.

The jurisdiction of Sircus Junction spearheaded a national change in this ideology.

Virginia lawmakers wanted to prove Police Officers were and could be sensitive enough to properly evaluate abusive versus non-abusive family situations. Such a theory was challenged daily by a barrage of unique neglect complaints.

I'm investigating another right now. There's a child at the Woodside Memorial Clinic suffering from fractures and considerable trauma to the skull. I was assigned this complaint because the parents submitted a Virginia address and said the accident occurred at that location.

The Woodside Memorial Clinic is located in the State of Maryland. Therefore, inter-state legalities must be considered. Maryland Child Neglect Laws are different than those of other jurisdictions. A legal writ on Virginia stationary would be questionably scrutinized in other localities.

Medical personnel in Virginia were compelled to complete exhaustive information forms for its Court System. This mandate didn't apply to medical personnel located in other jurisdictions. Because of policy differences, fulfilling the required court forms affected the private sector much more than the public sector. As an example, privately licensed practitioners would be as non-specific as possible when describing injuries to a child–a growing problem when court testimony was needed.

In this instance, the abused youngster, Sir Robert Kingsley, was a six-month old white male. It should also be noted that his family was politically influential. I've seen this political scenario many times. Influential parents would contact a loyal, long-time family physician and ask for an off the record visit to the medical facility. If the doctor remedied the medical issue, so be it. Nothing was legally documented for public scrutiny, and a documented visit never took place. Fortunately, most reliable doctors recognized the importance of proper treatment and the importance of notifying proper authorities. There have been situations where the parents removed the child from Virginia's jurisdiction. The child would be re-admitted to another state's medical facility and, hopefully, fewer questions were asked.

This scenario works until the introduction of proper insurance compensation. Thankfully, there tends to be a direct relationship between notifying proper medical authorities and receiving payment for services. Hospitals are more concerned about being properly compensated for medical services than keeping the family doctor's loyalty discreet.

Acknowledging these legalities as medical precursors, I conversed with Dr. Kenard Schultz, the admitting physician. While the child was being fitted into a body cast, the doctor and I closely scanned his x-rays. Dr. Schultz identified fractures to the arms and ribs. They were clear and evident. The child's skull injuries differed. They were of the concussion-type due to the softness of the youngster's head.

"Well Doc, I've two questions for you," I said.

"What excuse did the parents give?" And… "Do you think… within the scope of your professional medical opinion, the injuries could occur in that manner?" I gave the doctor an opportunity to think about his answers. I sought the men's room in a different hospital section. Although this poor defenseless child almost died, I knew the wrong answer from the doctor's conscience would negatively affect any future investigation.

I've found when a doctor isn't going to be cooperative, that decision was reached prior my arrival. I've since realized the longer I interact with doctors… the easier it is for them to expand their interpretation of the medical truth.

Even in outer jurisdictions, the law mandates such instances must be reported. It doesn't mandate a definite written opinion of fact–which is the kind of medical description I always seek. That's why I make it a point to visit the men's room after I've met the physician for the first time. The rest room visit allows time for a doctor to think about his/her professional responsibilities. I'd return and seek the best and most complete medical opinion they could give. "Well, Detective Bishop," he hesitantly said. "Jason Kingsley, the child's father, told me the child fell down the steps from the second floor at the house. These particular steps were described as uncarpeted, hard wood," he added.

"Dr. Schultz, is that explanation consistent with the injuries you observed?" I asked while making eye contact.

After moments of silence, the response I sought came. "No!" the doctor responded. "If the child fell down a hardwood stairway, there would be more evidence of that fact. If the child did fall down the stairs, each time he hit the next lower stair would create another dark bruise of some kind."

"His visual appearance would represent a multitude of superficially bruised areas."

"I will admit that maybe some injuries he now has could have come from that scenario, but other physical symptoms would be visible," said Dr. Schultz. I confidently smiled at Dr. Schultz for his genuine concern.

I traveled to the child's home. As indicated earlier, my attitude adjustment is needed whenever I interviewed influential parents. But, as always, I'll get through it. I knocked on the big French door. Mr. Kingsley answered. I identified myself and asked if I could observe the steps mentioned in the hospital report.

Without hesitation, Mr. Kingsley shouted, "My child is receiving his medical treatment in the State of Maryland! I don't need to discuss anything with you! So, kiss off!" He tried to shut the door in my face–an action totally unwarranted. I quickly blocked the door with my foot and countered, "You're very misinformed, Mr. Kingsley! You may be eluding interstate legalities pertaining to child abuse issues, but I will introduce felony assault charges against both you and your wife right now!"

"As a member of the lawyer community, you know what that means, don't you!" I asked while alluding to a probable hearing before the American Bar Association's Ethics Committee. "With what I've learned so far, I could obtain an arrest warrant in one short hour! Is that what you wish?" I cited.

The father called me every name in the book. He was a longtime pillar of this community, and "Who was I to question his responsibility as a father?"

But, you know what? What's my name? My name is Detective Sergeant Bishop Calloway and you just pissed me off! Sometimes you gotta' do what you gotta' do! This was definitely one of those times!

I advised him to be quiet. "You, Mr. Kingsley, should call a lawyer pronto. I'll return very shortly with all types of warrants!" said I with a wry smirk on my face.

I opened my police cruiser door. A trembling woman's voice called out to me. The voice pleaded for me not to leave. Not to drive away. It was the child's mother. I reluctantly honored her request. It was obvious both parents had different perspectives about the questionable injuries. I sorta' stalled a bit to allow them to come to a sensible next course of action.

The father kept yelling at his wife to keep quiet. She refused to do so. Katie slapped her husband across the face two or three times, pushed him aside, and while facing me in a sincere manner, reiterated her previous request. Legally, I couldn't enter their home. They eventually indicated their willingness to proceed with the investigation. I could now legally enter their home.

Mr. Kingsley finally calmed down. I reminded myself anything said could possibly be construed as a confession. If that occurred, I would cease with the interview and read their Miranda Rights.

Mrs. Kingsley sat next to her husband in an honorable way. While sobbing and holding his hands she stated, "The child just wouldn't stop crying! No matter what I did, he just wouldn't stop!"

Knowing a confession was forthcoming; I advised her of her Rights. I suggested this situation could be better handled at my office. Once there, I could take an official statement (with a lawyer present) and schedule a Court Hearing on this matter. All parties agreed.

Katie Kingsley struck the child three times with a large wooden hairbrush because he wouldn't stop crying. It happened while she was in a state of drunkenness. She didn't realize what she was doing until it was too late.

Mr. Kingsley came home and witnessed the bruises. He called for an ambulance and instructed it to take the child to the Maryland Clinic. The Maryland Clinic In-take Section recognized the possibility of the unquestioned cover-up. They wanted no part of it!

Criminal assault charges were administered and the mother was found guilty of assaulting the innocent child.

The Criminal Court Judge acknowledged the mother's alcohol abuse. She received three years as a result of her actions.

In Family Court, both mother and father were found guilty under the Child Abuse and Neglect Statute. The child was not returned to the custody of either parent—a decision that caused a problem with the father.

Mr. Kingsley didn't personally assault the child. He definitely attempted to hide this criminal action from the proper authorities. The Court did not trust his character enough to return the child to his personal supervision.

Mr. Kingsley chose to simply berate the Judge and the Family Court System for not recognizing his stature in the Virginia community. After verbally assaulting the Judge for several moments, the Judge gave the ole' Contempt of Court hand signal to the bailiff. Presto! Mr. Kingsley was escorted to the holding cell along with his personal opinion and his standing in the community.

The little Mr. Kingsley was placed under the custody of the Family Court.

To reacquire custody, Mrs. Kingsley had to prove she no longer depended on alcohol. Mr. Kingsley, Sr. had to prove he respected the Court's authority. This was hard for both of them. It took several years before the Court released the child to his father custody.

As I look back at this case, I find myself asking, "Do people who attempt to circumvent the Court System deserve the same opportunity to eliminate possible abusive behaviors?

The answer is… Absolutely. Yet, the saga continues.

I received a call several months later from Mr. Kingsley. He wanted to have a beer. He wanted to talk about his child. We met at Winston's–a yuppie spot over on the west side. Mr. Kingsley, or Jason as he wants to be called, started his conversation by apologizing for his son's injuries and his behavior. "I was just freaked out! I thought my wife was going to jail. I guess I kinda' lost it." "It happens to all parents," I responded. "I'm just glad everything worked out okay at the end," I added.

Jason spent the next hour buying beers. He told me about his job, family, and stuff like that. I was just a listener. I didn't talk too much about me. Never do. Especially to a stranger.

I waited for his real reason for wanting this meeting. To be asked out by a parent is unusual.

"Detective Calloway. May I call you Bishop?" he asked.

"Okay by me," I responded.

"Bishop, I'm having a big party at my weekend home. It's only about 25 miles from here. I want you to come. I want you to meet my friends. You know… people in high places. People who could help you do a lot of great things in Sircus Junction."

"It's scheduled for the 14th–a Saturday night. Your office already gave me your weekly schedule so I know you're available on that day. Please say you'll come?" he asked in a demanding sort of way.

I looked at him and listened–trying to be cordial but not letting down my guard. This was not the man who yelled at me the first time I saw him. His demeanor was strong that day. I didn't believe he could change that fast. He must've noticed the skepticism in my body language.

"Please show up," Jason pleaded. "I want the special people in my life to know how dedicated you are to saving the lives of children. How can you say no to such an invitation?" he asked.

The man was right. As much as I wanted to punch this maniac in the nose, I looked for the silver lining in situations. Not many parents admit to their parenting guilt. Of all people, here sat one.

"Okay. I'll be there," I said. "I don't know exactly what time I'll get there, but I'll show up." Once that special date arrived, I tried to get another woman to accompany me but couldn't find one. Instead, I decided to document this day. I'd save it in case something weird occurred.

Hello, Black Book!

The directions were very good. No tricky turns. No hidden stop signs. The mountain roads were paved and there was decent highway lighting. I drove up to the front door. Valet parking was available, of course. The value of cars and number of private limousines parked everywhere was impressive.

I navigated the manicured grass walkway. I entered what appeared to be a mansion. It had all the things attached to royalty—paintings, statues, and historical ornaments… you name it. There was a piece of each in every nook and cranny. I recognized no friendly faces. I knew not one 'cause these personalities were of the wealthy class. Jason spotted me. He quickly pushed a drink into my hand. The drink, according to him, contained very little alcohol. He said it was a screwdriver.

I sipped, cautiously. I then tried to fit in with this crazy crowd. My off-duty detective eyes noticed many guests entering and exiting certain rooms down the hallway. I wasn't inquisitive about it. "A normal reality of the times," I thought. An hour or so passed. I'd seen enough. I tired of the mingling and small talk with a crowd not my style. I searched for Jason and Katie to say my goodbyes. I would thank them for their hospitality. Somehow, I knew I wasn't going to be honored for my unique work this evening.

I moved through the spacious rooms just watching, looking, and smoozing while hoping to locate the elusive parents. Fifteen minutes later, still no sign of them. A butler-type fellow came to my rescue. He, reluctantly, pointed to the white door on the left. "If you're looking for Jason go through that white door," said the gentlemen. "If its Katie you seek, take the stairway to the upper level. Turn right and go through the red door," he added.

The white door was closer so I looked for Jason first. I entered the white door without knocking. Inside were several men and women enjoying a white substance freely available on a glass coffee table. I recognized one man. His head was bobbing up and down an awful lot. It was Jason. He didn't seem to have a care in the world.

My police intuition told me it was an illegal drug. It mattered not. I wasn't interested in the least. I was in another jurisdiction. Performing a drug raid would not a responsibility of mine... although, it would be kinda' hard to explain why I was in this place.

Enough was enough. "Jason, I'm outta' here!" I shouted in his drugged-out direction.

"Before you go, Bishop, can I do one more favor for you?" he asked. "Okay, but make it quick," I responded. Jason grabbed my hand. He led me through a sheer curtain-like fabric into a small, dark, adjoining room. The room had a red light flashing on the ceiling. "Have you ever made love to a man?" he asked as he looked at me with those hazel eyes. This is your opportunity to do so... to address your fantasies... but only if you want to, that is. No one will ever know and I'll not call you again... ever!" he said.

I stared down at him. I had a negative scowl on my face. I slowly shook my head in disgust. I shook my head in disgust not because of Jason's homosexuality; I did so because he mistakenly thought I, the macho Bishop Calloway, would accept an invitation to join his secret party games. He had the wrong impression.

Jason was amazed to feel no energy from me. By now, my eyes had adjusted to the darkness. I could see more clearly. I grabbed Jason by the chin, waved bye-bye, and delivered the punch he deserved throughout this child abuse investigation. Jason spun around several times. He fell into the far corner occupied by other gents doin' their own thing.

This Jason fella' was a real jerk. "I should have known," I thought to myself.

I walked from the small dark room. As I did, curse words frequently escaped Jason's bleeding mouth. He screamed, "You've ruined my life by embarrassing me in front of my son and my peers. I'm not finished with you yet, Calloway!"

Jason had crossed the line. I still owed a sincere goodbye to Katie. I quickly walked to the upper level. I entered the red door into another dimly lit room. It took a while for my eyes to adjust to the light. As reality unfolded, I realized I had entered a room filled with naked people... all entangled with each other like they were playing that polka dot on the floor game... whatever its called. I've seen a lot of things in my life; never a large group of naked men and women... at least fifteen stacked in a pile taking in anything within reach. Apparently, the rule was if you could reach it you could have it. I tried not to stare but my feet wouldn't take me away from this scene. From what I could observe, the more legs, mouths, and fingers involved; well... you get the message. I'd never witnessed a community orgy before. Now that I have... It will never make my bucket list.

I turned to escape this unwanted destiny. An unknown arm stretched from the pile of human flesh. It grabbed my ankle. I visually followed the arm's elbow into the pile of flesh. The arm belonged to Katie. She beckoned me to join her somewhere within this slippery crowd. It was a culturally diverse crowd of pleasure seekers. A collection of black, white, and brown toes squirmed inclusively. Verbal moans in all languages bounced from the walls. It was a growing revolving door of patrons. When one satisfied torso squeezed from the pile, two eager ones slithered into it. It resembled a wrestling tag-team match with no losers. No identities were sought. None were given. I waved goodbye to Katie… wherever she was. I took a step, became dizzy, and collapsed to the floor. I blacked out. I had no idea why I lost control. I was out for at least an hour but wasn't sure. When I regained consciousness, someone's little toe was in my mouth. Wasn't a nice toe? Wasn't a man's toe? It was a tiny woman's toe possessing the nastiest corn ever seen.

Egad!

A woman's foot was in my mouth! A woman's foot can be a pleasurable experience. This adventure, however, was no pleasurable experience. I followed the ankle and leg until the thigh disappeared into a pile of cocained humanity. I did not wish to know the identity of that toe.

I remained somewhat dazed. I couldn't tell which of the many legs within this pile were mine. Or, more importantly, which of the naked torsos just fired off one of the biggest farts imaginable.

No one in the pile cared… 'cept me. I twisted my nose and lips to eliminate that up-close introduction. I couldn't believe it. An unknown section of pubic hair just uncorked a big one. Nobody in the pile cared 'cept me. Someone deep within this cesspool should at least moan a dissatisfaction of sorts. No Oooops! No 'cuse me! No I'm Sorries! Nothin'! Obviously, these were veteran orgy goers. I made a mental note. I would never, ever invite these soon-to-be-forgotten faces to my house. Ever! My clothes had been stripped off. Only my purple and gold-checkered Laker socks remained. I was the only person wearing socks. I could feel a set of lips nibbling on my right ankle. I wondered who that could be. I did give some thought to movin' a hefty foot sore more in that direction. I thought better and pulled my right foot from the crowd. That foot over there must be my left foot. It had a sock on it that resembled my other sock. "This group is simply unreal!" I thought to my embarrassed self.

Someone poked their big head from the pile seeking anything with some life… or for a breath of fresh air. "How did I get here I asked?"

She gave no answer and disappeared back into the crowd. I kept asking every time an opening presented itself. Meanwhile, I slithered inch by inch from the mountain of slippery buttocks. I thought I was totally free when an unknown hand wearing a ten-carat diamond ring grabbed my ankle. I took the hand, validated the diamond, and pulled Katie's body out of the pile.

Jason approached me from the rear. He was mad and I wanted no part of him. He was upset because I welcomed neither his nor Katie's advances.

"I knew you'd be a jerk about tonight. That's why I gave you that special drink earlier!" he pointed out. "You took longer than most fella's. I knew it would knock you out sooner or later!"

Jason returned to whatever body parts he could find. He had gotten his revenge. "How stupid can I be?" I thought. I knew this Jason fella' was up to no good. Now, here I am… butt-naked in a cornfield of fingertips. I finally eased myself outta' that room. Never did locate my clothes. I put on whatever would fit.

That was the one thing I didn't mind. Clothes I choose from the corner pile were more expensive than anything I left behind. I don't think anyone really gave a darn. Drugs and booze were plentiful, as the party nowhere neared its end. At least my car was still there. I jumped in. I drove my silly self back to the city limits of Sircus Junction. I told not a soul about this strange escapade… No one.

I checked the mailbox two days later. I had received a large manila envelope. I opened it. I found another headache. The manila envelope contained pictures taken at Jason's party. The pictures were close-ups of yours truly participating in that pile of flesh. A hand-written note was attached to the pictures. The note read, "I told you I would destroy your life, didn't I?"

The note had the initials… J. K.

All right, Jason. It ain't over 'til it's over!

CHAPTER 18

"Cruiseeeeer... 507!" said the voice on the radio. "Respond to City Hospital. Investigate a medical situation. Pronto!"

"Here we go again!" I thought to myself. I was referring to an extended work shift nothing new to child abuse detectives. Our investigations were citywide. I passed City Hospital minutes ago on my way to Joey & Jay's for a burger and coffee. A twenty-minute turn-around is needed. *"Cruiser 507... is 10-99!"* I replied (indicating I was a one-man crew).

Unscheduled overtime hours are always a possibility. There's no need to gripe about it. Those unwanted hours were creating problems with my on-again off-again relationship with Jillian. I pleaded with her a long time to give me another chance to prove my love for her, the kids, and a normal family life. It's hard to keep those promises. The constant uncertainty of daily working hours prevented me from planning spousal interactions. For example, it's impossible to request a special home cooked meal from Jillian. She used to prepare one every evening at six o'clock sharp. Now, her "Don't waste my time!" scowls scare me each time my overtime creates a cold dinner. It's impractical to plan an intimate evening with her before I've actually checked off. That throws spontaneity out the window.

I'd call her hours in advance. I'd express such desires. Canceling because of a new investigation simply meant I loved the job more than I loved her. You know how Jillian feels about that.

I'd find nothing other than the phrases, "I'm too tired!" or that "headache" thing. That's why I value a woman's spontaneity so highly. The worst scenario is canceling a pre-planned vacation because of newly rescheduled court appearances. When that occurs, I take a dictionary to bed. I scrutinize the meaning of celibacy–with attention given to the word divorce in the next alphabetical section.

I was trying to not repeat my earlier marriage dilemmas. It took every apology in my arsenal to get my family relationship back to where it is right now. I never wanted to violate their love again. I cut back many of my overtime hours for the sake of a nuclear family. Lesser hours means a smaller paycheck. I quickly grew into an economic doghouse. And, that's enough of my personal problems. Some child abusers are known as "Ladies of the night." While doing what they do best, their children are left alone without adult supervision. Something tells me abandonment isn't the issue of that call from Vice Squad Detective Trey Owens.

Det. Owens requested a meeting at the home of a known streetwalker. A famous prostitute was going to be charged with robbery while performing a paid sexual act. She had two young daughters living with her.

Temporary placement would be needed for the daughters. I accepted the challenge. I took part in the apprehension. A forced entry was made and the Vice Squad stormed the apartment. The mother named in the warrant was entertaining a male patron at the time. That was expected. "Guess what wasn't expected?" No one expected to find both daughters nakedly entertaining adult males, also! We entered this apartment seeking one arrest. We ended up charging several males with rape, adding neglect charges against the mother, and placing her young daughters under the immediate supervision of the Family Court.

Both girls made it clear they were not being raped. They were simply performing sexual acts for money... business as usual.

"We're thirteen and fourteen years old. We know the difference between rape and prostitution," they declared. This was only a technicality as I saw it. Family Court papers was processed. A preliminary investigation revealed neither of these young ladies had previous criminal records. They were well-spoken, mature, possessed excellent school attendance records and, guess what? They were straight A students!

The daughters took care of themselves health-wise. They visited their mother's doctor on a bi-weekly basis and kept receipts to prove it. They provided favors for a fee only to obtain the necessities of life. They could eliminate that environment at will (so they said). No criminal charges were filed against the young ladies. They were obviously influenced by their mother's occupational environment.

The Court sent them to reside with their father in another state. Their mother was found guilty on a multitude of criminal and neglect charges. She was incarcerated.

Children receive few guarantees when they come into this world. As we've witnessed many times, they can adapt to many unwanted situations of survival. It was a tragedy such intelligent young ladies were placed in that position. The case remained in the Court system for many, many years. Six years later, both ladies had mastered a High School education and received Scholarships to highly rated Universities. I'm proud they retained self-esteem, strength, and character. I'm glad their identities were never known.One day, if we're lucky, they just might be our new future neighbors, close friends, or even wives. I admired their ability to change. I'm happy with what they've accomplished with their lives. In fact, I wish I was as accomplished. My life moved on. I needed my chosen profession to "Love me more." It never did and its importance quickly dwindled. I'd give anything to have my old life back. Its importance to others dwindled. I, the proud Det. Bishop Calloway, had to learn the hard way. And, Thanks! I needed someone to simply listen as a friend.

CHAPTER 19

Mr. Diary...

You're the only one who can hear me. My demeanor over the last few years has alienated me from family, friends, and even my ex-poker partners. Respect for who I am is no longer automatic. I received nothing but false smiles wherever I go no matter whom the acquaintance may be. What is happening to my life?

My zest for the job is dwindling. Depression on a daily basis is wearing me out. Not only me. Others, too! I will blame no one. I will blame no one because there's no one else to blame.

My love life has gone to waste. Everyone I meet either cannot live up to my Jillian's old standards, or she turns out to be a total nightmare.

My current nightmare? Her name is Gwendolyn Blakeley. I met her at a New Year's Eve party. She had the look I liked. She was about ten years too young.

I normally stayed away from the younger generation. I needed a woman who grew up with Motown ... not Michael Jackson and the Jackson Five. There's nothing wrong with the Jackson Five. I need someone closer to me. I need a woman within 2 years of my age. I know it's a silly prerequisite. I'm that way. Gwen saw me first. This devil disguised as an angel walked right into my sight. A perfect 10— she was an easy decision to make. I walked her to her car after the final dance of the evening. I opened the door. I made a discreet attempt to kiss her goodbye.

She offered a peck on the cheek. "That's about as far as I go tonight," she offered. "Give me your number. I know how you slick fellas' work. I'll call you one of these days." She was gone.

I knew little about her. I asked around. I could not uncover much about this Cinderella story. One thing was for sure? This woman was absolutely gorgeous! Three weeks later my telephone rang. It was 2 a.m. in the morning. A voice on the other end was the voice I had been waiting for. The voice was Gwendolyn's... she was crying. I asked what was wrong. "Please come over here right now! I have to talk to you as soon as possible," she screamed. I wrote down her address. It took thirty minutes to travel door to door. I didn't mind the late hour. If I could solve her problem, it might give me an opportunity to stay the night.

Gwen opened the door. She leaned into my grasp. My cop's attitude told me she was having trouble with an old friend or something similar. I caressed her for a minute. I asked her to explain what was going on.

"Bishop. Oh, Bishop," she started. "I hated calling you at this hour. You were the only one I could trust," she added. "Just tell me what you want me to do. Whatever it is... I'm here," I responded. Gwendolyn took me to the couch. She sat me down. She held my hands.

"Oh, Bishop. My ex-husband and I just had a fight. He's upset I've decided to have a life. It's been three years since our break-up. I told him I met a man I liked. I was going to pursue a relationship with him. That man is you, Bishop," she whispered as her hazel eyes met mine.

"My problem starts right there," she added. "He refuses to pay alimony until I promise never to see you again."

"His check for last month's alimony was never received because he learned about you. I have to pay my rent by tomorrow morning. The landlord will evict me and my child."

"Can you help me, Bishop? Please. Can you help me out of this mess?" she pleaded. *Did I forget to say Gwendolyn was wearing nothing but a skimpy peach-colored nightshirt? She pressed her body against mine. She stared at me again with those hazel eyes. The little princess patiently waited for the positive response she, you, and I knew was coming.*

"How much do you need," quickly found my tongue? The amount was staggering. I didn't even know this woman. How dare she seek such a favor? How dare the first call she makes to me be attached to a request for money? How stupid did she think I was? So, when I agreed to empty my wallet a few minutes later, I thought this might be the beginning of a pretty decent relationship. The amount she needed killed my eagerness to make love to her on that particular night. Trying to be only so stupid, I realized loving her would cost me even more in days to come.

I gave her a check for the amount she requested. I raced back to my own bed. Before leaving, she tried to repay my generosity by allowing me to sleep in her bed. "Excuse me, young lady. That is not the kind of relationship I want from you," I mumbled. My response was a bold-faced lie. I said it anyway. Stupid me. I thought there was a small opportunity for her to fill my love tanks in the future. Two days later, there was a knock at my door. It was 7 in the morning. It was Gwen. She had not been invited.

She was in the neighborhood. She dropped by to say hello. I wondered how she knew my address. It was printed on my check. I peeked out the door's shade. She was dressed for work so I opened the door for a short conversation.

"Gwendolyn, this is not a good time," I said. "I'm aware of the time young man. I wanted to thank you for helping me out of a tough situation," she said smilingly.

"No problem. I was glad I could help," I replied.

Gwendolyn then insisted, "Get dressed. Take me to breakfast. I promise to leave for work after a cup of coffee."

I jumped into the shower. Seconds later. I mean seconds later...
I had company in the shower. Gwendolyn had stripped and entered
the shower without my invitation. I tried to curse her out. That
led to nothing but a meaningless love making session. Ah, nothing
fantastic. Nothing to write home about. Just satisfaction between two
consenting adults.

Afterwards, I had to practically forced Gwendolyn to put her
clothes back on. She was in no hurry to leave. I promised to see her
sometime soon. It was the only way I could get her to leave.

"This woman's kinda' aggressive," I noted. Ten minutes later
the phone rang. It was Gwendolyn. "Baby," she excitedly whispered,
"I've... fallen' in luv' wit' you!" There was nothing but silence on my
end. I didn't even know Gwendolyn's last name. She was already
using the L word? I know I'm not that good. To slow this lady down,
I told her I'd call her... possibly, next year. I was trying to stay away
from her until several months of her rent were paid.

The following day, an annoyed dispatcher called with a message.
I was ordered back to the office to handle a citizen's complaint. When
I arrived, the Desk Sergeant pointed to the interview room on the far
right. I entered. It was none other than that Gwendolyn chick.

"I was in the neighborhood. I thought you might be hungry," she
said. She opened up a brown bag. In it were two Muk Don Nald's fish
sammiches, tartar sauce, and some cold fries. "I know how you like to
fish," she said.

"Gwen. You can't interfere with my job," I stated. Oh, by the way,
Gwendolyn was wearing the shortest mini-skirt she could find. It
was so short it exposed her fire-red underwear. I think she did this
because of the attention red demands. Gwen had this need to be the
center of attraction ... to be the best lookin' woman in the room... any
room... no matter what it took and at whatever cost. Her wonderful
legs caught every Detective's eye. I was flattered but embarrassed by
the attention. "I won't leave this building unless you see me tonight,"
she demanded.

"That's fine. Let's meet at IBEIRO's at 8 PM. I need to talk to you anyway. And, don't be late," I added.

I got to IBEIRO's early. Gwendolyn came fashionably late, of course. I was very uneasy yet kinda' proud a tad. My proudness was short lived.

I jumped right into a talk with my questionable lover. "This relationship is moving too fast, Gwendolyn. We have to slow it down. Maybe not see each other for a while," I muttered.

"Darling Bishop, how could that be?" she asked.

"We're truly in love, aren't we?"

"Didn't you make love to me a short time ago?"

"Didn't you tell me how you loved the way I made you feel in bed?" she added. "I've given you my most precious gift. Are you now trying to get rid of me?" She turned her head to the left. She put her hands on her hips. She started tappin' on her knee. I remained quiet. This woman was beginnin' to scare me. "Do I have to make personal visits to your commanding officer?"

"Do I need to talk to your neighbors?"

"Do I have to document a complaint against you for sexually abusing me with your police powers? Tell me what you want me to do,.. darlin'," she whispered.

I was speechless. I decided to be a man. I would not respond to her threats. Seconds later, I matched her threats by saying, "No need to do anything like that, dear. Let's talk about it later, my love."

I wimped out! I surely did. After my response, Gwendolyn agreed not to make a scene at the restaurant. She did, however, order the most expensive entrée she could find. She then asked for an expensive bottle of wine. "Don't bring me any of that Restaurante Chianti stuff," she said for all patrons to hear. "It makes my bows move." Yes. This was my high priced dinner guest. I should have known.

The dinner check was enormous. Getting rid of her was satisfying. I recognized I was in a mess with someone I hardly knew.

The next few days I received lots of hang-up calls. I could hear breathing on the other end. The number had an ID block so I did not know where the calls had originated.

When another person was on my other end, that person was an ex-girlfriend of mine, or an ex-wife of one of my few remaining pals. They, too, were complaining 'bout some unknown woman calling them to talk about my current relationship with some gal named Gwen. These calls were made in a stalking manner. My friends did not appreciate it.

The unknown woman's voice wanted to know the nature of my prior relationship with them as women. The voice made sure they knew Gwen was the new love of my life and they should leave me alone. Our planned marriage was in the near future?

I had no idea how this unknown voice got her hands on these personal numbers. I had my local numbers changed. It mattered not. The calls still came.

One of my neighbors told me they witnessed my new lover placing my trash bags into her trunk and driving away. My old mail was in those trash bags. Even old bills from the telephone company. Twelve months of them.

If my hunch was correct, Gwendolyn now possessed these telephone records. She was calling every name on the list to see who answered. Her uncontrolled jealously had become a major factor.

I'd seen enough of my new female partner. I rushed to her front door to set things straight. Gwendolyn was ready for me. She denied making the calls. She blasted me for alleging any association with my trash bags.

I had no proof so I apologized.

Gwendolyn asked me to help her get on her feet. "Please loan me the money to start anew. Maybe I can move in with you for a month, or two?" she suggested.

The look on my face reflected my immediate answer. I wanted no part of her as a roommate. I agreed to help her. She applauded *my decision. She offered love as her appreciation. Her love was fully accepted.*

Gwendolyn was a good lover. No, she was a great lover. Afterwards, I fell into a deep sleep. An hour later I felt the sheet covers move. I discreetly opened my eyes to observe Gwen's actions.

Her female silhouette stood at the base of the bed. The silhouette was going through the pockets of my trousers.

My wallet was removed and I watched as she counted the cash I had in my wallet. If I correctly recalled, I had about 300.00 dollars in cash. After checking my credit cards, she replaced the wallet.

My new lover returned to my side under the sheets. The next morning I acted like I was not aware of her trespassing. I dressed and headed for the door. Gwendolyn asked if I had any loose change I could give to her. The amount she requested? 300.00 dollars.

I replied I had nothing. She gave me this funny look. "Let me take a look?" she asked. She stuck her hand in my back pocket and grabbed my wallet. "I know a man like you always keep at least three hundred bucks at all times," she said. "Maybe so, but I do not," I replied.

Gwendolyn was out of control. I've had enough of this woman. This relationship was way over my head. She was more than I could handle.

I didn't call her for several days. I didn't answer the telephone. I did, however, answer a call from my favorite momma'—Ardie Calloway.

"How's my favorite son?" she always asked. Before I could answer, she shouted, "I've been getting a lot of calls from your new girlfriend. She called me at least ten times this week. She is already calling me "Mom!"

"I hear you and she may be getting married in the next month or two. I forgot her name. Is it Gwen or something like that? Why did I have to hear from her and not you?" she wondered?

I had nothing to say.

I told Mom I was busy. I would return her call in a coupla' years.

Congratulations started coming in from everywhere. Cards flooded my mailbox. Messages, good and bad, overflowed my telephone recorder.

People were asking for the exact wedding date... people related to her as well as those related to me.

I received calls from former female acquaintances. They politely cursed me based on what Gwendolyn falsely told them about our so-called lengthy relationship.

She told them we made love. She inquired about things she wanted to do with me. Her lies made my life a mess. I tried to remain friends with dates I've had in the past. Those days are gone.

When I returned home, Gwendolyn was sitting on my front steps. She had several large bags of luggage.

"Since we're in love and getting married in the near future, I might as well stay at your place for a few days," she muttered.

I stepped in front of her and stared directly into her eyes. She was talking up a storm. I could see her lips in motion. I heard not a single word she was saying.

I stepped over her. I unlocked my door. She prepared to follow me into the house. I shut the door in her face and shouted, "Not tonight Ms. Gwendolyn. Not tonight!"

Ten minutes later, flashing lights were in the front of my house. There was a hearty knock on my door. No problem. It was some of Sircus Junction's finest.

"The fine young lady at the curb reported you sexually attacked her and kicked her out of your house," voiced a Sergeant I've known for several years.

"She said you were a cop. I did not know it was you of all people."

The Sergeant pulled me over to the side. "Bishop. This pretty little thing said she'd drop her complaints if you let her stay here a few days. That way, I can keep this from becoming a major complaint. I'll report this as a domestic dispute. The decision is up to you, however.

If you reject this request, I'll have to take you downtown," stressed the Sergeant.

"Honey, please listen to the Sergeant," Gwendolyn said. "I know you didn't mean to sexually attack me. You were drinking. I was drinking, too. Let these cops go back to more important complaints. I'm sorry I called them," whispered my so-called love.

I nodded in the affirmative. I had been bested again. What kind of man am I? The entire department witnessed this event. A beautiful monster had bested me. The Sergeant merely saw the fantasy of having sex with this Goddess. Police gossip would focus on the sexiness of Gwendolyn... not the false allegations she made. I'd let it go at that.

I called the police the following morning. I reported an unwanted visitor refused to leave my house. Regardless of how she was allowed to enter, she had to leave once asked to leave. When she refused in a threatening manner, the police were called.

The police verified whose name was on the lease. They forced Gwendolyn and her bags to the curb.

Gwendolyn made a scene in front of the entire neighborhood. She kept shouting I had not seen the last of her. That I would be sorry I did this to her.

She finally left. I proceeded downtown to make a formal complaint. This would not be the last time I saw this woman. A week later, l traveled to my hometown to attend my mother's birthday. One hundred relatives and friends were there and they were having a great time.

My mother announced she had a surprise for me later. She wouldn't tell me what it was but assured me I would love it.

An hour later, we finished singing happy birthday to her. The surprise she had for me then walked through the door. Yes. The surprise was none other than Gwendolyn Blakeley.

She saw me and yelled, "Hi Honey. I love you and my new Mom!" and ran into my arms.

Relatives started pattin' me on the back. They congratulated an upcoming marriage I knew nothing about. I was mad as all get out!

Gwen began kissing and hugging all of my relatives. She called everyone either Mom, Brother-in law, cousin or whatever relationship she could acknowledge. When her back turned, I slipped out the side screen door. I started my engine. I headed back to Virginia.

Fifteen minutes and 10 miles down the road, the reflection in my rear mirror was Gwen's car. The faster I drove had no effect on her. A maniac on wheels was in her driver's seat. Every escape-related police trick I knew could not create a distance between our two vehicles.

I had one choice. I took the nearest exit. I drove right to a state trooper's office. I entered their facility. Gwen... right behind me.

"Please get this woman off me," I respectfully asked the trooper. He looked at her. He then looked at me... at her... and back again at me and said. "You're a police officer aren't you? Why do you need a different police department to handle your own personal business?"

"We don't want to get involved in your love life. Take this mess back to your own area," he yelled.

A smile came over Gwen's face. Surprisingly, she uttered as she exited the front door, "This is not the last you will see of me! See you back in old Virginia!"

"Bye, bye Baby! You are the love of my life!" she yelled as she drove away.

I sat on the curb. I was puzzled, wondering what mischief was in store for me in the near future.

All I could say was ... Stupid Me!

Two days later I went back to work. The expected interference from Gwendolyn never occurred. Oh, well. Another weird child neglect case waits.

I had to attend a funeral. I acknowledged the death of one of my best friends assigned to the Child Abuse Unit.

His name was Bobby Cooper. He was a six-year veteran and a pretty good investigator. His death was not from a criminal act, but *from human nature. Bobby Cooper was originally from Australia. He went to school in New York City. He decided to stay in this country.*

Bobby's only regret? His lovely wife and three kids were still in Australia. Perth, Australia to be exact.

He confided in me many times about how depressing it was to be here without them. They were in a world so far away. He missed the laughter from his children. He received no love from his wife. His apartment was empty. He promised to bring them to the new world in the next six months as soon as he saved enough for the house they would need.

Several weeks ago he reached that financial point. I took him to the airport for his journey home. He was so excited. His smile was one to remember. The smile was one of personal satisfaction and one of final accomplishment.

His journey home was an 18-hour flight. There was no one at the airport to welcome him when his airplane landed. He rented a car and drove to where his wife and kids lived. I used the former word because a different family now resided at that address.

Bobby looked all over. He could not locate the family he left behind. He returned back to all he had left.... his job in America.

I noticed Bobby was depressed. We had a couple of beers at Rusty's–a noted cop's joint. What I didn't know was once he returned from Australia there was a letter from his wife waiting for him. The letter stated she and the kids moved on with their lives and, in no way, wanted to relocate to America.

The life Bobby badly wanted meant nothing to those he loved so much. Six long years of loneliness had killed Bobby's insides. Losing his wife and never seeing his kids again was a huge setback.

I had nothing to say. I gave him a big manly hug. I told him I'd be there for him no matter what.

He had a wild look in his eyes? The look in his eyes was telling his future story. Life as he knew it. A new world for his children. All Gone.

Bobby wanted no part of being part of a group. He stayed to himself. He rarely spoke to those close to him. His demeanor changed right in front of me.

I was called to the Captain's office three weeks later. I entered and found Bobby's wife Jane and his three kids awaiting me.

"Bishop. You've been Bobby's best friend these last couple of weeks. Put his family in your police cruiser. Take them to Bobby's apartment. Kind of a surprise, you know what I mean?" he ordered.

I smiled. I was happy to be a part of this reunion.

Bobby was right. His wife was cute as a button. His kids looked just like him. I took a camera. This would be a great day.

His wife explained the pressures of a 15,000-mile marriage. She decided her place was next to her husband—no matter where that home was.

She cried. The children cried. I cried. We cried from the happiness sure to come. Bobby's car was parked outside. We knew he was home. I stepped out of sight and allowed his family to ring the doorbell. I stood there with the camera ready for the most exciting picture this family would ever have.

There was something different going on. There was something wrong with this total scenario. Tell me it isn't what I thought it was. Please, tell me I'm mistaken.

The doorbell was never answered. I put the family back into my cruiser. I went back to Bobby's door. I yelled Bobby's name as I banged on his door. "Bobby! Bobby! Please, Open the Door!" I kept shouting. As a veteran cop, I could recognize odor that accompanied death. Body odors from deceased bodies are unique smells.

Unfortunately, as the family and I stood outside Bobby's door, that possibility became a reality.

I told the Captain what I thought was possible. I decided I would, on my own authority, kick open Bobby's front door.

I did. I found what I hoped I would not. There laid Bobby on the kitchen floor. Gun in hand. I grabbed him. It was too late. No life was left in Bobby… and his family sat outside in the parking lot. I didn't have the heart to tell his family. I left that job for the Captain. He arrived several minutes later.

I hugged Bobby until the EMS ambulance pulled him from my grasp. I was all Bobby had in America. His family had come to their senses a little bit too late. They could take him back to his homeland. They could seek the life they wanted without him. They were just in time to collect his insurance money.

She showed no remorse when the truth lay before her. We told the children their daddy was not at home. He left and moved to another part of the country. We left it up to his wife to share the truth when most appropriate. I don't know if she ever did. That's none of my business.

Part of me died when Bobby died. I know loneliness can kill your spirits. I know missing your family causes depression so deep suicide is always a possibility.

I know because I have been there. I know because of Jillian and the kids.

Yes. I've been there.

Bobby left a note before he took his life. He blamed no one but himself for attempting to move his family so far away without their consent. He thanked me for being his friend when he had no one else had an ear. And, he thanked the Police Department for giving him an opportunity to become one of Virginia's finest.

The department allowed me to travel with Bobby to Perth, Australia. I read aloud at his funeral. I was honored to speak on his behalf.

I thanked him for helping me heal through him. The personal pain Bobby felt was similar to that I felt in the past. It was the kind of pain I had to learn to deal with every minute of my miserable life since the loss of Jillian. Yes Jillian. I'm 15,000 miles away I think only of her.

Can my life go on this way? Is it really worth it?

I wondered if it truly was.

Who am I kidding? I'm terribly depressed. My life feels like a large bowl of crap. Everything I had that was good blossomed into chaos. Don't pity me. It happened under my stupid direction. I, the leader of my depressed personality, can only blame myself.

I thought an extra thick fuzzy navel drink would ease my pain. Not so. It would take more tonight. Tonight, of all nights, I needed to visit the "Pill Doctor."

Remember him? He's that fantastic man who peddled whatever to whomever had the ready cash. I hadn't visited him in a long time. His illegal activities circulated through departmental hallways. He must still be in business. My fellow officers and half of the ADA's office used his services one time or another. If not, the mighty Mr. Pill Doctor would've been in felony lock-up by now.

My twenty-minute drive to his magical corner was a quick one. No hassles, whatsoever. I arrived at his fabled location and somberly described my mindset. The Pill Doctor, without hesitation, flipped several black capsules onto my passenger's seat. I didn't ask and he volunteered no information for fear of a secret recording device.

Black meant barbiturate for sure… a downer that should take me out for 24 hours. It was the new preferred pill suicidal users. Too many brought a deathwatch to those walking life's delicate line. Not I. Not tonight. This would not be the night I walk that line. Only rest. I only needed to rest for a while. I could forget what depresses me.

I tried to sleep but couldn't. The pills were not working or they were the wrong pills. Did the Pill Doctor give me amphetamine uppers instead of what I asked? I hoped not. I'm awake but tired as ever.

I noticed a flashing light on my laptop. It was a pop-up message I deleted every time I checked my messages. I stared at the light ten more minutes before I remembered I was looking at it. I recognized the blinking message as a dating service advertisement. While I waited for the pills to kick-in even more, I decided to see what this on-line dating stuff was all about. I pushed the button for more information. Before I moved an inch, up popped photos of five ladies… each in the forties or fifties (I'm being nice about their approximate ages). They had bunches of sugarplums dancing around their heads. Love was definitely in the air... at least for this bright-eyed group. Their facial expressions revealed a "here I am" aggression. Their hairdo's were tight and make-up just short of perfection. They smiled a smile that invited the onlooker into a welcomed warm heart.

There was Daisy from Southern California, Betty from New York State, Carol from Michigan, Lorraine from Florida, and Gertrude from Texas. Each had the prettiest little smile. Each had the same problem... they were seeking their soul mate. They were seeking the man of their dreams. They were seeking the right man to make them complete. "This was a bunch of bull," I thought. What they really sought was someone who would take a lot of stuff from them. They were seeking another man to replace the best man ever lost in a previous relationship. They were seeking someone who would overlook their personality quirks, handle their momma', and bring discipline to three of the worst teenager rug rats ever born.

These women sought the even greater man. They sought he who could love them like no other had, forever and ever, even though each woman dared not reciprocate that emotion. Yes, I figured out this computerized dating madness in one simple minute.

Why all the fuss? Can the research on this dating service stuff really be effective? I know there's a shortage of men in this country. I know men are incarcerated, and have not returned from wars, etc. I know the number of men in college has dropped to an all-time low. Even if you throw in other elements that reduced the availability of men, are these new computerized dating services the answer? Why are women desperate to find the perfect mate? If women possessed the attributes and personalities desired by the average man, would they be single? Are men that complicated? Are men that hard to figure out? I think not.

The thought of dating someone from this arena made me curious. The service offered the ability to have anonymous conversations at a small cost. Pushing the little red square on the blue screen would be the first step. You would learn something about an unknown person. I wasn't seeking someone new. I was seeking to understand the mentality of those willing to take such a risk to find that perfect love. I pushed the red square. Carol's name popped up a second later. Nothing fantastic. Basic information only.

Divorced and lookin' for a man not like the one she married. There was one thing… Carol was very lonely.

We acknowledged several messages about nothing. She asked for more information. She liked my written conversation.

My words were non-threatening. I used the right words at the right times… knowing every syllable was being scrutinized on the other end.

When I decided to share a little, I shared more than the truth. I was an average man with a PhD, had a second home in South Beach, Florida, and money in the bank. Oh, I was also an average looking guy seeking an average looking woman who wanted to only love one man. Sounds good, huh?

I probably stretched the truth a tad. I'm talking to an anonymous person through a laptop computer. I'm conversing with a completely faceless person. Why not be the best I can be? I'm sure the women's bios were enhanced.

The more conversation I had with Carol the more she wanted to know about my life. It did not matter what the topic was. It was of interest to her. I slanted my answers to be the best they could be. It didn't matter. The thought of a possible dream come true worked wonders. Was it a dream come true for the both of us?

I became more interested in the person on the other end of the conversation. Not as a possible lover but as a person. I had problems but not as prominent as hers. I thought loneliness was owned only by me. It wasn't. I thought hurt and pain from losing someone special was an individual feeling. It happened to everyone and pain was greater for me than for others.

The hole in my stomach was much larger. I could no longer camouflage my loneliness. It was not fair. I should be a man about it.

I confessed to trying to learn the truth about the mentality of on-line dating. The truth I sought became an online obsession. It quickly took on the quiet innocence of hurting those who sought nothing more than a happiness felt deserved. Who was I to challenge their wants and needs?

It's hard to look in a mirror. I'm ashamed of myself. I, of all people, understand what loneliness does to a person.

Wait 'til I get my hands on that Pill Doctor!

CHAPTER 20

Life takes its toll. Stresses associated with this everyday child abuse dogfight forced me to reconsider my future. Along comes a series of uncontrollable events... events propelling me deeper into the twilight zone. A minor complaint investigated properly: Yet, because of politics, I could never win. It was a wake-up call of sorts. It was an internal evaluation that questions all I've done in the past... and all that needs to be done in the future!

Ten years and hundreds of challenging child abuse and neglect cases have come and gone. "Are there any acceptable answers to those frequently asked questions?" I asked myself. Questions like, "What have I accomplished in my life?"

"Is there a report card somewhere in heaven?"

"Is somebody up there keeping a score on how well we treat our fellow man? And, if so, where do I stand?"

A familiar dispatcher calling a different investigator's name interrupted my thoughts. I was glad my name wasn't on the end of his tongue. I was mentally tired of life's depressions. Life's ups and downs. Do we all have to go though it? Is there an equality of life spread around the universe? Regardless of who you are and what you are, is dealing with life a universal norm?

I wish I knew. The familiar dispatcher's voice was heard, again, while I was taking a break. I was trying to read the Washington Post's sports page. Reading the sports page under a nice shade tree was one of few pleasantries I welcomed. The Post had the best sports writers in the United States. The Post also had close ties to that Washington Football Team!

Veteran tailback Larry Brown was running on one knee to keep Mike Norris–a prized rookie–off the painted grass at R.F.K. Stadium. Sonny Jurgenson and Billy Kilmer were fighting over who'd throw the "down and out" pass to Charlie Taylor. Of course, I never saw many games because of a backlog of newly reported child abuse or neglect investigations. Therefore, the only way I could see the game was by recapturing it through the eyes of several sports writers.

"With ten seconds on the clock, No. 87–Redskins' Tight-End Jerry Smith–dove for the game tying touchdown just when the irritating dispatcher shouted… *"Cruiseeeeeeer 507 for a message!"* I was instructed to respond to City Hospital immediately. *"See Dr. Focher in the Pediatric Section."*

I was observing superficial bruises on a child about 12 months old in a matter of minutes.

Dr. Focher told the following story. The child's mother and father recently separated. The mother agreed to let the father see his child this weekend. When she left the child with him two days ago, the child had no bruises. When momma' picked the child up today, she noticed bruises and brought the child here. The father said the child simply fell down a short flight of steps. The child wasn't hurt. It did leave several visible bruises.

"Based on my medical evaluation, these bruises were not serious. They could have occurred as the father reported. The child is light complexioned. Superficial bruises show very easily!" the doctor added.

I spoke with the mother–a mature twenty-one year old. Betty Simpkins was her name. Ms. Simpkins recited the explanation given earlier. She relinquished the name and address of the child's father. She agreed this appeared to be a misfortunate accident. I would talk to the father just the same.

Mr. Simpkins was home where the bruises occurred. He would cooperate with the investigation. He showed me the stairs where the child fell. Remorse was in his voice. Honesty was in his heart. The child's mother had previously begged me not to lock her separated husband up. "He's a good man. A good father, too! Please don't lock him up! Nothin' but an accident!" she vouched.

In cases of no criminal intent, I warn and counsel the parent of criminal circumstances. This was done. The case was closed. No Biggie!

I returned to the office. I checked for records of prior documentation. Nothing was noted under the child's name. The final paperwork was typed and placed in the out box for a supervisor's signature.

Meanwhile, strange things were happening around me. During a very short time-span, three close friends died of heart attacks. These detectives were ages 30 or so, suffered from heart failure, and "Guess what they did for a living?" They were assigned to the department's Child Abuse and Neglect Unit.

"Was there a message there?" I wondered. I thought only about the future from that point on. I, too, had entered my 30's! I didn't want to become a medical statistic. I did some research on my own. I found that police officers lucky enough to retire after 20 years lived an average of three to five years afterwards! Insurance actuaries validated that claim. I always wondered how police agencies could offer such tremendous retirement opportunities. Now, I know. Few retirees lived to collect on those pension plans. Ironically, a year later, I was present at an officer's retirement party. I received a telephone call from my Lieutenant.

The Homicide Squad was investigating a murder case. They requested my immediate presence at the city morgue. "Have you ever tried to tell Jillian Esther Carson-Calloway she has to leave the only social event she's attended in over a year? I did. It wasn't nice." Jillian gave me that look I never wanted to see again. She grabbed her coat, took the car, and basically threw me out of her life... a life she and our children would no longer tolerate.

"Darn! Darn! Darn!" I kept saying to myself as a buddy gave me a ride downtown. I entered the Medical Examiner's Office. I met Tommy Shamsky of Homicide. He escorted me to a small body–one that had recently been through a rigorous autopsy. He pulled back the sheet. He uncovered a very young child. The child had several organs removed for advanced medical research.

"Do you know who this child is?" he asked? The child was a Black male about two years old. He had no other recognized features. I assumed this was now my newest child abuse case. After all, I now had been labeled as the greatest child abuse and neglect detective in America!

I looked Det. Shamsky in the eyes. "No! Give me the particulars. I'll get started right away," I proudly answered.

Shamsky said, "Okay! Follow me back to my office. I'll give you the latest update." He was very quiet as we rode the elevator to the parking lot. This silence was... an unusual silence.

We entered his office doors.

I turned...

I slowly turned......... and looked directly into the swollen red eyes of Ms. Betty Simpkins! Mrs. Simpkins immediately recognized me. She then screamed... "That's the cop!"

"That's the cop who could've saved my baby's life! Yes, I'd recognize that pig anywhere!"

"I told him this would happen!"

"I begged him to lock the father up."

"He's another lazy cop, that's all!"

"My baby's gone! His lack of effort's the real reason," she added.

Within a few life-long seconds, the baby Simpkins Case became a recent memory. The abused and dissected tiny body before me a minute ago was... that little Baby Simpkins!

The identity of the autopsied child became apparent. A shocking chill captured my mind, body, and spirit. I was physically present–yet in another world psychologically. I leaned to the left. My limp body had no feeling.

Shamsky and I went into another room to discuss the old child abuse complaint. He already had the paperwork from my office. Based on his theory, my paperwork wasn't complete.

"Bishop. Put past hero accomplishments aside. They are of no concern to me! The facts, as you have listed them, do not agree with what the mother says she told you," he dared. "The child's mother is claiming she officially begged you to arrest that very abusive father last year. You never did. Now, a little child has been murdered," he defensively added.

"Excuse my language, Shamsky. Get outta' my face!" I replied.

"My official report was as complete as it had to be. If I said it was an unfounded abuse complaint, legally that's what it was," I chanted in his direction. "Tell me the facts this time," I asked?

"Well, the mother was tired of not having her weekends free! So, she started allowing the child to visit the father on weekends!"

"On this particular weekend, the little child was found dead! CASE CLOSED!!!!!!" Shamsky shouted. "The father said the child died from a fall down the stairs.... Sounds familiar???? "But, we already know that's not true, huh? The father's been arrested. He is charged with First Degree Manslaughter!"

The Homicide Detective then got very personal. He had handled many homicide cases but none when the victim was this young. He didn't appreciate my attitude of non-concern. Therefore, he was going to personally pursue "Negligence of Duty" charges against me for failing to arrest the father after last year's child abuse incident. "You could have saved this child's life with just a little more work last year!" he added.

Those charges are the most damaging of all police regulations. I sat down in total shock. I had spent my entire career helping children. This jerk of a cop had the audacity to utter those words. "That I didn't care! That the child's death was on my hands?" Who was this rookie Homicide investigator? Obviously, he hadn't heard of my reputation as Sircus Junction's... Mr. Child Abuse? Hadn't he heard Watch Commanders in each Police District say that once Bishop Calloway was on the scene, everything would be done right?

If I weren't mentally shocked at that time, I would've punched him. I would've welcomed more charges.

I stood to my feet. I walked away. As I exited, I looked into Betty Simpkins eyes. I nonverbally thanked her for that great acting performance. She again trusted the child's father. He violated that trust. Sometimes that happens.

Several weeks later, I was summoned to appear for a deposition at the D.A.'s office. I thought it was a normal question and answer session. I was mistaken. Once a microphone was placed in front of me and I was advised of my rights, the true seriousness of this event became clearer. The locality I pledged my life to protect and serve for ten tough years was going to send me to prison. I had nothing to hide. The facts were the facts. What else could I do? The question and answer session lasted for about thirty minutes. I answered each question as honestly as possible. I kept wondering why this was happening to me... Sircus Junction's finest?

At the hearing's conclusion, the Attorney said he'd call once a decision was made.

The call came. I would not to be charged with "Negligence of Duty!" A guilty verdict meant a jail term–definitely!

I was advised, however, the Department's Internal Affairs Division would present this case to a Police Trial Board.

"No way! No one has ever walked out of a Trial Board hearing with an innocent verdict. It was strictly the most recognized Child Abuse Detective's word against the mother's so.... Why was this even an issue?"

At the hearing, Ms. Betty Simpkins (still suffering from the loss of her child) told a panel of higher ups' how she begged me to arrest the father. That, if the father was in jail, he never could have killed her child.

"Again! That's a powerful accusation," I thought while sitting there. Acknowledging the politics of the Police Department, I knew they'd take the safe way out. I had no chance of receiving a favorable ruling. To be found innocent would catch the front page of the Washington Post. A guilty finding, while satisfying the mother and the integrity of the Police Department, would bury my police future and me for the remainder of my life!

I walked to my car. Each step took me further away from my proudest accomplishments. While awaiting a green crossing light, I broke down mentally. I did so right there on the corner. I lost control of my psychological self in the middle of pedestrian traffic.

Honestly! A higher power took control of my life at that exact intersection! The power told me to suffer no longer. The hundreds of abused and neglected children I've served over the years would not be for naught. A new direction in life awaited. That window of opportunity was right before me.

I regained consciousness a few minutes later. I had fallen against the traffic signal pole. Curious pedestrians asked if I needed medical attention... 911?

I declined. I stood tall. I continued the journey to my vehicle.

Several of life's negatives were about to become positives. This job was the only thing I had left in the world. I'm psychologically damaged over my bungled family life! The negative outcome expected from the Trial Board will travel with me forever! And, ten years and nine hundred child abuse and neglect investigations would take on questionable scrutiny! A major decision was necessary. I would never investigate another child abuse and neglect complaint again! I would not do so because of this department's lack of integrity!

There were thousands of innocent children out there waiting for an abusive parent to become abusive once again! There was no way I could sleep at night awaiting another dreaded reoccurrence. The history of the Simpkins baby would always set the precedent for a future prison cell for yours truly.

If my calculations were correct, approximately fifteen more years of non-recidivist luck were needed before my conscience would be totally cleared.

Yet, how could I ever clear my conscience of that infamous "dog vs. child" complaint?

What about the shooting death and injuries in that nudity situation?

I could never forget that suicide note.

Therefore, a very short Letter of Resignation wasn't as complicated to write as I thought. It relieved so many pressures I'd dealt with on a daily basis.

I'd carried a weapon of death for a decade. I could have taken human life on many occasions! It was time to mentally undo the hero in me. No longer was I proud to live or die on a moment's notice for the sake of Sircus Junction!

Lo and Behold! You mean there's life after law enforcement?

Amen! Yes. There's certainly life after being a cop. A good one... but still just a cop! And... there's life with Jillian! I'll confess to her I've changed my entire life! I tell her for the first time I have realized how important life with her and the kids really is! More importantly, that I've resigned from the Sircus Junction Police Department!

I imagined the tears of joy in Jillian's eyes as I dreamed of telling her.

There is a God!

Truths!!!

Truths shall be shared with my best listener... My Little Black Book! To my best of pals and my special pair of ears... My life is going downhill fast. As my law enforcement career took a special turn, my personal life took one, also. I've been attempting to locate Jillian for many a night. I've not been the least bit successful. She won't return my calls. Her parents won't tell me her whereabouts. The children no longer attend their old schools... no forwarding addresses. Jillian and my family had disappeared! Not for long, I hope. I do have a pretty good set of investigative skills. And, I've yet to secretly utilize some of my old police powers. With this in mind, I had a Robbery Squad buddy approach the local Post Office manager with his badge. He officially requested the latest forwarding address for Jillian. He said it was for an emergency family notification of some kind. Post Office supervisors' acquiesced. They surrendered the information. No big deal in terms of honesty. I met him in the alley behind Joey & Jay's. "Here's the information you wanted," he said. "Be careful how you use it!"

I had other things to do that evening. I would check out the address another time. I was working late that night on another new complaint. The complaints just keep coming and coming... and coming. Parents are going crazy these days.

The sky opened up. Rain fell in buckets. The weather report predicted no let up and traffic was now bumper to bumper. I pulled into Joey & Jay's Diner for coffee and fries. A vanilla malt, maybe? Time alone... I did not need. I tried to control feelings of loneliness since my family disappeared. The thought was hard to deal with. This was not the first time I tried to get them back into my life. This is the first time I wanted them to return based on my soon to be retirement from the police department. I officially submitted my resignation. I had only two more weeks before I'd become history... a good history, though.

I wanted to share this news with them. I needed to share this news with them. I wished to show how committed I would be to them, and family, this time. I know there were a few other commitments I didn't keep. None were as promising as this one.

I know I've said these things before. Things… deep in my heart… are different. I ordered coffee and fries. Dolly, the waitress with the double D cup, asked if something was bothering me.

"Nothing I can't fix!" I sorta' whispered as I smiled.

"It must be somethin' 'bout true love," she sorta' responded, but didn't.

"How right you are," I sorta' mumbled, and really did.

"I'm so in love wit' my new upcoming life… it's simply… unbelievable!" I said to Dolly.

It's true. I believed my life would finally be the best it could be. Jillian would finally be able to love me as much as she's always wanted. And the kids, now growing up faster and faster, would get the chance to find out more about their true father figure. I know they will like me even more.

Dolly brought the fries and coffee. She wanted to make me feel better so she added some extra fries and big cup of that special gravy I like. Dolly's a great lady. I helped her outta' some messy spots over the years. She's always trying to repay me with kindness… and fries. Or by adding more ice cream to the milk shakes I sometimes order. She's great to many cops. We kind of unofficially look after her. She appreciates it. It makes us feel good.

The food was good. The coffee was swell (Remember that word from the 1970's?). The rain was easing and the traffic not as bad. I reached in my pocket. I pulled out Jillian's new address. It was 14097 Williamson Lane. It was located in the high rent district of the Maryland suburb of Chevy Chase.

Great property resale value there, I recalled. Great schools. Very little crime. I should have known. Jillian expressed interest in that small suburb long ago. We could not afford property there at that time. Too bad. Property prices soared sky high every year since then.

A small problem? The address was located in the State of Maryland. Not far from the DC Line. Maybe a mile or two across the Virginia border. I advised that same irritating dispatcher I had to travel into Maryland. I needed to interview a doctor about an old child abuse case. "Place me out of service for about 45 minutes," I asked. "I'll call you as soon as I re-enter Virginia." The last thing I wanted was to show up at Jillian's uninvited. I called the telephone operator. She did not have a listing for that address or name. "Why would Jillian make it so easy for me to find her again?" I stupidly asked myself. "Naturally, her name and address would not be so readily available. It made sense." I knew the general whereabouts of Williamson Lane. It was not too hard to find.

I started to have feelings of a questionable nature. I would not know how to approach Jillian this one last time. I tried many of my approaches in the past. I wanted this speech to be the best I ever shared. It had to be a good one. It just had to be the very best for this was the most serious attempt I had in me.

I parked about a half of block from Jillian's front door. I practiced and practiced what I'd say when she answered that front door.

There was no guarantee she would even answer the door once she saw who was knocking. There was no guarantee she would allow my children to go through another depressing scene of "love me or love me not!"

I had to face reality. There was no guarantee either she or the children wanted me anymore. I had to face this fact... A fact that easily could be true.

Time was no longer and issue. Sixty minutes had gone by, yet there I sat in the unmarked police cruiser... thirty yards from the front entrance to my new life!

It had to be a step I could take. A step I must take. It was a question I had to ask. I will deal with the repercussions. The reality of *my life was in that front door. Nothing would ever be the same if this approach was denied. I loved Jillian.*

I exited the car. I approached my soon to be new home. Twenty feet from the door I noticed an adult silhouette walking inside. The children must not be home. If Jillian wished, we'd have the conversation of our lives! And, if she allowed, we would love each other like that first time we met. I tried to knock on the door but my knuckles wouldn't knock. I had talked myself out of this. "Why would Jillian consider my love again?" I kept wondering.

I turned.

I turned... and headed back to the police cruise. My male ego kicked in. It brought my feet to a halt.

"Be a man! Knock on that door!" my ego demanded. "It's the only way to move forward with your life, stupid!"

I returned to the door. I knocked softly... hoping Jillian would not hear it. That way, I could satisfied my ego and my heart and quickly leave this place!

Seconds later, somebody peeked out the window. It was Jillian. She had a puzzled look on her face.

"Is that you, Bishop?" she asked as she shaded her eyes from the porch light.

"Yes, Jillian. Can I talk to you for a second?" I asked.

"Only for a minute, please," she begged. "I've got stuff I've gotta' do, okay?"

Jillian slowly opened the door. She allowed me to enter. She stood back, crossed her arms, and waited for my speech.

Suddenly, something came over me. I had, somehow, discovered the ability to talk. I had discovered the ability to converse about my feelings. To admit I was wrong on so many things. To allow tears to flow with no regard to my manhood. To say I loved her in a more convincing manner. And, finally, to mention I was giving up my police officer world for the sake of our future! For the sake of our marriage! For the love of the kids! All were things I could not do before.

Jillian just stood there. She never moved from the same spot. Never unfolded her arms or stopped me from speaking. A long stream of tears flowed from her hazel eyes.

I moved a tad closer to her. I needed a great big welcome home hug. I thought she needed a great big hug, too! Maybe a kiss, or two, or three.

As I stepped forward, Jillian did not take a step backwards. That could only mean my invitation for a hug or kiss was accepted. I reached out to her and she accepted my hand. We embraced. We held each other without speaking. The embrace had to be five minutes or so.

I turned her chin. I kissed her. She kissed me in return. She exhaled… and squeezed me closer to her heart. Her returned kiss did not live up to her normal kisses. Jillian was more cautious this time.

She believed me before. She believed me before when I stood in this same space and time. She believed me before when I said I would change if she brought her love back to me. She did her part in those instances. I did not do mine.

"Will you take me back?" I asked my sweet Jillian. "Please take me back. I will never let you out of my life again. Never!" I pleaded.

Jillian didn't respond. Jillian never moved an inch during this whole interaction.

She let go of my hand. I heard steps in the next room. The sound of footsteps got closer and closer. The door opened. Out stepped a silhouette of a man. It was the silhouette of a man I'd seen before. He was about 6 foot 4 and weighed around 220 pounds.

Yes. I recognized this fella'. Say it ain't so. This was not a man I respected. It was none other than that Billy Credit fella'! Love 'em and leave 'em was still the word around town. This fella' wanted to make sure I knew he was there. His stance suggested he wanted to become a constant in Jillian's and the kids' life. My Jillian. My Kids. His sincere, powerful stance indicated he never intended to let Jillian out of his sight ever again! His stance said so much… and Jillian made no effort to deny anything he was supposing.

He never said a word. Not one word. Maybe he knew I was a cop! I surely didn't want to hear his unspoken message.

This was Bishop's world he was playing with. A highly volatile world at this moment. And, of course, the use of guns and volatile tempers were realistic issues!

The male silhouette gently stepped back into the room from whence he came. He quietly closed the door. He would allow Jillian to finish her business. Her business with me! Her final business with me!

Jillian, spoke.

"Bishop Calloway, I owe you so much. You're a fantastic father to our children. You loved them as best you could. They adore and respect you. The kids and I have tried to live in your police world. We could not," she whispered.

"I needed more from you than you could give. I'm sorry for asking that much of you. You were honest with me from the start. I knew how much you loved being a Child Abuse Detective. I know how much you loved being a hard working father. It was not fair to force you to decide between the two," she added.

"Life, however, is not fair. Ten years as your wife diminished the kind of love I needed to give and receive from you. I don't love you any less. I just can't love you any more! And, that ain't good enough," she demanded.

"That man in the back room is not someone important to me. He will not be the one I choose for my future. He is, however, an old friend who can give me what I need on a short-term basis," Jillian said. "He doesn't ask for more than I can give him. I don't want what he has to offer commitment-wise. We use each other to please ourselves… not the other way around," she added.

Jillian was sharing more information than I needed to hear. Jillian then stated, "You know I've truly tried, Bishop. You know I've given you many chances to be the man I needed over the years. I have reached my limit. I will not let you hurt the kids and me, anymore! I will not let you hurt us any longer. I will love you no longer. I will

not, however, hate you." "Goodbye! I love you Sir Bishop Calloway."
Jillian silently walked me the short walk to the door. She opened it
gently, placed a sweet little peck on my chin, and politely pushed me
out of her life!

I stepped out the door but stood on the front steps. I was looking
over my shoulder… hoping what I just experienced was not the final
option. I would give Jillian a couple of minutes to change her mind. I
would allow her to save face and beg for my ultimate return. She had
begged in the past. One more time won't hurt!

Jillian peered out the front door. She stared at me a mere ten feet
away. That silhouette of a man came to her side. He stood behind her…
supporting her decision. No words were spoken. The way he tightly
held her waist and tenderly positioned behind her spoke well enough.

In a last effort to keep my past, I reached out to the still-opened
door one last time. Jillian reached out. But… not to me. She reached
for the doorknob… and slowly shut the door.

As it closed, so did all the love she had for me. She might as well
have used my gun and shot me dead. When that door lock clicked, so
went the rest of my life.

Gone were the days of our first meeting. The thoughts of her initial
sighting at that Black Tie function. The first time she let me hold her
hand. The dance like Fred Astaire and Ginger Rodgers.

Gone was that special tap on my shoulder at Margo's Bookstore.
The first time she took my love from me at that mountain retreat. The
look she had on her face at the birth of each child. The smiles that came
with all of that…. Life!

Gone are feelings attached to those sweet little faces of child abuse
victims. The constant solicitation from mothers to ease the judicial
process surrounding their now special child. The sexual exploits
of others.

Gone are the Fuzzy Navels.

Gone are the dreams I had of the washed away world of Planet
Renaissance. The forty-day and forty-night wetness that rinsed

many souls and mindsets. The cleansing of new worlds. The choices each citizen had to make about the subterranean life forms… the lite-trickle seconds on the violent ocean floor.

Gone are the Drepped Aouugaks and Warbusted Piiiitshanks! Gone is the reality of Light!

Remembered will be the slow speed of which Jillian's door shut out my life.

The killing of me!

The killing of my love!

The killing of that which gave me so many fulfillments.

Most of all… gone are the unspoken "Thank Yous" from so many little innocent fans of my Donald, Daisy, and Goofy cartoon impersonations! Abused children's love and smiles will forever fill my heart!

Where will I go from here? Suicide is not an option. Never was. Never will. Will the Police Department ever take me back? Whatever.

I faked a medical problem and signed off on sick leave. I went straight to my home from Jillian's new Chevy Chase address. Along the way, several things baffled me to the max. I had lost everything. My wife. My Children. My dignity. My identity. The only thing I did have? …That special chair. I'll rename it the "J-Chair" for the record. Still a non-drinker, I whipped up a heavy fuzzy navel. I held it to the sky for three reasons.

I Thanked God for constantly smiling down on me—for it was through Him that I was in a capacity to help so many little others!

I praised the abused and neglected child who eventually became a responsible adult. I offered a special thanks to parents who never again mistreated their valuable children!

I sat in my special chair with Mr. Smith and Wesson in hand… took a giant swig of fuzzy navel… swallowed a bunch of yellow and blue pills… and cried for ME this one time! Other than feeling sorry for myself, there was only one thing left to do. As long as Sircus Junction's humidity was a major factor, I, Bishop Calloway, would always have work to do... That work was to fulfill a legal promise made to little Kevin... and Ms. Woodson!

And, Thanks for Joining My Literary Crew!

ABOUT THE AUTHOR

Sir Wolfdogg Moses-French is a Culturist at heart. He became a corporate culture change professional for Fortune 500 Organizations after a twenty-year career as expert in law enforcement and corporate security. He has recognized globally for his 21st century introspections on workplace change strategies. His global diversity resume includes Brazil, France, Australia, Italy, Mexico, the Czech Republic, and the Virgin Islands. Sir Moses-French has an educational background in Criminal Law (American University), BS & MS Degrees in Organizational Change Strategies (The University of Cincinnati), and MBA coursework at Fairleigh Dickinson University. His completed Doctoral Dissertation is due August 2013. He has published books and articles on the corporate leadership, workplace cultures, corporate diversity issues, and personal relationships. He seeks the title, "Father of 21st Century Culture Change" based on the level of workplace culture change he's witnessed since the 1970's. Sir Wolfdogg Moses-French is available for book signings, lectures, and personal appearances worldwide.

Part two of this trilogy!
The Iconic Solution!
Coming Soon: